CANDACE BUSHNELL

Summer and the City

A CARRIE DIARIES NOVEL

BALZER + BRAY

An Imprint of HarperCollins*Publishers*

Balzer + Bray is an imprint of HarperCollins Publishers.

Summer and the City: A Carrie Diaries Novel
Copyright © 2011 by Candace Bushnell All rights reserved. Printed in the United States
of America. No part of this book may be used or reproduced in any manner whatsoever
without written permission except in the case of brief quotations embodied in critical
articles and reviews. For information address HarperCollins Children's Books,
a division of HarperCollins Publishers, 10 East 53rd Street, New York, NY 10022.

ISBN 978-0-06-172893-8

Typography by Sarah Hoy

For Alyssa and Deirdre

PART ONE

Beginner's Luck

CHAPTER ONE

First Samantha asks me to find her shoe. When I locate it in the sink, she asks me to a party.

"You might as well come, seeing as you don't have any-place else to go and I don't feel like babysitting."

"I'm hardly a baby."

"Okay. You're a sparrow. Either way," she says, adjusting her silk bra as she wriggles into a green Lycra shift, "you've already been mugged. If you're kidnapped by a pimp, I don't want it on my hands."

She spins around and eyes my outfit—a navy blue gabardine jacket with matching culottes that I'd actually considered chic a few hours ago. "Is that all you've got?"

"I have a black cocktail dress from the 1960s."

"Wear that. And put these on." She tosses me a pair of gold aviator sunglasses. "They'll make you look normal."

I don't ask what normal is as I follow behind her,

clattering down the five flights of stairs to the street.

"Rule number one," she declares, stepping into traffic. "Always look like you know where you're going, even if you don't."

She holds up her hand, causing a car to screech to a halt. "Move fast." She bangs on the hood of the car and gives the driver the finger. "And always wear shoes you can run in."

I skittle behind her through the obstacle course of Seventh Avenue and arrive on the other side like a castaway discovering land.

"And for God's sake, those wedge sandals. Out," Samantha decries, giving my feet a disparaging glance.

"Did you know that the first wedge sandal was invented by Ferragamo for the young Judy Garland?"

"How on earth do you know that?"

"I'm a font of useless information."

"Then you should do just fine at this party."

"Whose party is it again?" I shout, trying to be heard over the traffic.

"David Ross. The Broadway director."

"Why is he having a party at four o'clock on a Sunday afternoon?" I dodge a hot dog cart, a supermarket basket filled with blankets, and a child attached to a leash.

"It's a tea dance."

"Will they be serving tea?" I can't tell if she's serious.

She laughs. "What do *you* think?"

The party is in a dusky pink house at the end of a cobblestoned street. I can see the river through a crack between the buildings, turgid and brown under glints of sunlight.

"David's very eccentric," Samantha warns, as if eccentricity might be an unwelcome trait to a new arrival from the provinces. "Someone brought a miniature horse to his last party and it crapped all over the Aubusson carpet."

I pretend to know what an Aubusson carpet is in favor of learning more about the horse. "How'd they get it there?"

"Taxi," Samantha says. "It was a very small horse."

I hesitate. "Will your friend David mind? Your bringing me?"

"If he doesn't mind a miniature horse, I can't imagine he'll mind you. Unless you're a drag or a bore."

"I might be a bore but I'm never a drag."

"And the stuff about coming from a small town? Nix it," she says. "In New York, you need a shtick."

"A shtick?"

"Who you are, but better. Embellish," she says with a flourish as we pause in front of the house. It's four stories high and the blue door is flung open in welcome, revealing a colorful throng, twirling and weaving like a chorus in a musical show. My insides throb with excitement. That door is my entrance to another world.

We're about to cross the threshold when a shiny black marble of a man comes rolling out, a bottle of champagne in one hand and a lit cigarette in the other. "Samantha!" he screams.

"Davide," Samantha shouts, giving the name a French twist.

"And who are you?" he asks, peering at me with friendly curiosity.

"Carrie Bradshaw, sir." I hold out my hand.

"How divine," he squeals. "I haven't been called 'sir' since I was in short pants. Not that I ever was in short pants. Where have you been hiding this delightful young person?"

"I found her on my doorstep."

"Did you arrive in a basket like Moses?" he asks.

"Train," I reply.

"And what brings you to the Emerald City?"

"Oh." I smile. And taking Samantha's advice to heart, I quickly blurt out, "I'm going to become a famous writer."

"Like Kenton!" he exclaims.

"Kenton James?" I ask breathlessly.

"Is there any other? He should be here somewhere. If you trip across a very small man with a voice like a miniature poodle, you'll know you've found him."

In the next second, David Ross is halfway across the room and Samantha is sitting on a strange man's lap.

"Over here." She waves from the couch.

I push past a woman in a white jumpsuit. "I think I just saw my first Halston!"

"Is Halston here?" Samantha asks.

If I'm at the same party with Halston and Kenton James, I'm going to die. "I meant the jumpsuit."

"Oh, the jumpsuit," she says with exaggerated interest to the man beneath her. From what I can see of him, he's tan and sporty, sleeves rolled up over his forearms.

"You're killing me," he says.

"This is Carrie Bradshaw. She's going to be a famous

writer," Samantha says, taking up my moniker as if it's suddenly fact.

"Hello, famous writer." He holds out his hand, the fingers narrow and burnished like bronze.

"This is Bernard. The idiot I didn't sleep with last year," she jokes.

"Didn't want to be another notch in your belt," Bernard drawls.

"I'm not notching anymore. Don't you know?" She holds out her left hand for inspection. An enormous diamond glitters from her ring finger. "I'm engaged."

She kisses the top of Bernard's dark head and looks around the room. "Who do I have to spank to get a drink around here?"

"I'll go," Bernard volunteers. He stands up and for one inexplicable moment, it's like watching my future unfold.

"C'mon, famous writer. Better come with me. I'm the only sane person here." He puts his hands on my shoulders and steers me through the crowd.

I look back at Samantha, but she only smiles and waves, that giant sparkler catching the last rays of sunlight. How did I not notice that ring before?

Guess I was too busy noticing everything else.

Like Bernard. He's tall and has straight dark hair. A large, crooked nose. Hazel-green eyes and a face that changes from mournful to delighted every other second, as if he has two personalities pulling him in opposite directions.

I can't fathom why he's paying me so much attention,

but I'm mesmerized. People keep coming up and congratulating him, while snippets of conversation waft around my head like dandelion fluff.

"You never give up, do you—"

"Crispin knows him and he's terrified—"

"I said, 'Why don't you try diagramming a sentence—'"

"Dreadful. Even her diamonds looked dirty—"

Bernard gives me a wink. And suddenly his full name comes back to me from some old copy of *Time* magazine or *Newsweek*. Bernard Singer? *The playwright?*

He can't be, I panic, knowing instinctively he is.

How the hell did this happen? I've been in New York for exactly two hours, and already I'm with the beautiful people?

"What's your name again?" he asks.

"Carrie Bradshaw." The name of his play, the one that won the Pulitzer Prize, enters my brain like a shard of glass: *Cutting Water.*

"I'd better get you back to Samantha before I take you home myself," he purrs.

"I wouldn't go," I say tartly. Blood pounds in my ears. My glass of champagne is sweating.

"Where do you live?" He squeezes my shoulder.

"I don't know."

This makes him roar with laughter. "You're an orphan. Are you Annie?"

"I'd rather be Candide." We're edged up against a wall near French doors that lead to a garden. He slides down so we're eye-level.

"Where did you come from?"

I remind myself of what Samantha told me. "Does it matter? I'm here."

"Cheeky devil," he declares. And suddenly, I'm glad I was robbed. The thief took my bag and my money, but he also took my identity. Which means for the next few hours, I can be anyone I want.

Bernard grabs my hand and leads me to the garden. A variety of people—men, women, old, young, beautiful, ugly—are seated around a marble table, shrieking with laughter and indignation as if heated conversation is the fuel that keeps them going. He wriggles us in between a tiny woman with short hair and a distinguished man in a seersucker jacket.

"Bernard," the woman says in a feathery voice. "We're coming to see your play in September." Bernard's response is drowned out, however, by a sudden yelp of recognition from the man seated across the table.

He's enveloped in black, a voluminous coat that resembles a nun's habit. Brown-shaded sunglasses hide his eyes and a felt hat is pressed over his forehead. The skin on his face is gently folded, as if wrapped in soft white fabric.

"Bernard!" he exclaims. "Bernardo. Darling. Love of my life. Do get me a drink?" He spots me, and points a trembling finger. "You've brought a child!"

His voice is shrill, eerily pitched, almost inhuman. Every cell in my body contracts.

Kenton James.

My throat closes. I grab for my glass of champagne, and drain the last drop, feeling a nudge from the man in the seersucker jacket. He nods at Kenton James. "Pay no attention to the man behind the curtain," he says, in a voice that's pure patrician New England, low and assured. "It's the grain alcohol. Years of it. Destroys the brain. In other words, he's a hopeless drunk."

I giggle in appreciation, like I know exactly what he's talking about. "Isn't everyone?"

"Now that you mention it, yes."

"Bernardo, *please*," Kenton pleads. "It's only practical. You're the one who's closest to the bar. You can't expect me to enter that filthy sweating mass of humanity—"

"Guilty!" shouts the man in the seersucker.

"And what are you wearing under that dishabille?" booms Bernard.

"I've been waiting to hear those words from your lips for ten years," Kenton yips.

"I'll go," I say, standing up.

Kenton James breaks into applause. "Wonderful. Please take note, everyone—this is exactly what children should do. Fetch and carry. You must bring children to parties more often, Bernie."

I tear myself away, wanting to hear more, wanting to know more, not wanting to leave Bernard. Or Kenton James. The most famous writer in the world. His name chugs in my head, picking up speed like The Little Engine That Could.

A hand reaches out and grabs my arm. Samantha. Her eyes are as glittery as her diamond. There's a fine sheen of moisture on her upper lip. "Are you okay? You disappeared. I was worried about you."

"I just met Kenton James. He wants me to bring him alcohol."

"Don't leave without letting me know first, okay?"

"I won't. I never want to leave."

"Good." She beams, and goes back to her conversation.

The atmosphere is revved up to maximum wattage. The music blares. Bodies writhe, a couple is making out on the couch. A woman crawls through the room with a saddle on her back. Two bartenders are being sprayed with champagne by a gigantic woman wearing a corset. I grab a bottle of vodka and dance my way through the crowd.

Like I always go to parties like this. Like I belong.

When I get back to the table, a young woman dressed entirely in Chanel has taken my place. The man in the seersucker jacket is pantomiming an elephant attack, and Kenton James has pulled his hat down over his ears. He greets my appearance with delight. "Make way for alcohol," he cries, clearing a tiny space next to him. And addressing the table, declares, "Someday, this child will rule the city!"

I squeeze in next to him.

"No fair," Bernard shouts. "Keep your hands off my date!"

"I'm not anyone's date," I say.

"But you will be, my dear," Kenton says, blinking one bleary eye in warning. "And then you'll *see*." He pats my hand with his own small, soft paw.

CHAPTER TWO

Help!

I'm suffocating, drowning in taffeta. I'm trapped in a coffin. I'm . . . dead?

I sit up and wrench free, staring at the pile of black silk in my lap.

It's my dress. I must have taken it off sometime during the night and put it over my head. Or did someone take it off for me? I look around the half darkness of Samantha's living room, crisscrossed by eerie yellow beams of light that highlight the ordinary objects of her existence: a grouping of photographs on the side table, a pile of magazines on the floor, a row of candles on the sill.

My head throbs as I vaguely recall a taxi ride packed with people. Peeling blue vinyl and a sticky mat. I was hiding on the floor of the taxi against the protests of the driver, who kept saying, "No more than four." We were actually six but Samantha kept insisting we weren't. There was hysterical laughter. Then a crawl up the five flights of steps and more music and phone calls and a guy wearing Samantha's makeup, and sometime after that I must have collapsed on the futon couch and fallen asleep.

I tiptoe to Samantha's room, avoiding the open boxes. Samantha is moving out, and the apartment is a mess. The door to the tiny bedroom is open, the bed unmade but empty, the floor littered with shoes and articles of clothing as if someone tried on everything in her closet and cast each piece away in a rush. I make my way to the bathroom, and weaving through a forest of bras and panties, step over the edge of the ancient tub and turn on the shower.

Plan for the day: find out where I'm supposed to live, without calling my father.

My father. The rancid aftertaste of guilt fills my throat.

I didn't call him yesterday. I didn't have a chance. He's probably worried to death by now. What if he called George? What if he called my landlady? Maybe the police are looking for me, another girl who mysteriously disappears into the maw of New York City.

I shampoo my hair. I can't do anything about it now.

Or maybe I don't want to.

I get out of the tub and lean across the sink, staring at my reflection as the mist from the shower slowly evaporates and my face is revealed.

I don't look any different. But I sure as hell feel different.

It's my first morning in New York!

I rush to the open window, taking in the cool, damp breeze. The sound of traffic is like the whoosh of waves gently lapping the shore. I kneel on the sill, looking down at the street with my palms on the glass—a child peering into an enormous snow globe.

I crouch there forever, watching the day come to life. First come the trucks, lumbering down the avenue like dinosaurs, creaky and hollow, raising their flaps to receive garbage or sweeping the street with their whiskery bristles. Then the traffic begins: a lone taxi, followed by a silvery Cadillac, and then the smaller trucks, bearing the logos of fish and bread and flowers, and the rusty vans, and a parade of pushcarts. A boy in a white coat pumps the pedals of a bicycle with two crates of oranges attached to the fender. The sky turns from gray to a lazy white. A jogger trips by, then another; a man wearing blue scrubs frantically hails a taxi. Three small dogs attached to a single leash drag an elderly lady down the sidewalk, while merchants heave open the groaning metal gates on the storefronts. The streaky sunlight illuminates the corners of buildings, and then a mass of humanity swarms from the steps beneath the sidewalk. The streets swell with the noise of people, cars, music, drilling; dogs bark, sirens scream; it's eight a.m.

Time to get moving.

I search the area around the futon for my belongings. Tucked behind the cushion is a heavy piece of drafting paper, the edge slightly greasy and crumpled, as if I'd lain clutching it to my chest. I study Bernard's phone number, the numerals neat and workmanlike. At the party, he made

15

a great show of writing out his number and handing it to me with the statement, "Just in case." He pointedly didn't ask for my number, as if we both knew that seeing each other again would have to be my decision.

I carefully place the paper in my suitcase, and that's when I find the note, anchored under an empty bottle of champagne. It reads:

Dear Carrie,
Your friend George called. Tried to wake you but couldn't.
Left you a twenty. Pay me back when you can.
Samantha

And underneath that, an address. For the apartment I was supposed to go to yesterday but didn't. Apparently I called George last night after all.

I hold up the note, looking for clues. Samantha's writing is strangely girlish, as if the penmanship part of her brain never progressed beyond seventh grade. I reluctantly put on my gabardine suit, pick up the phone, and call George.

Ten minutes later, I'm bumping my suitcase down the stairs. I push open the door and step outside.

My stomach growls as if ravenously hungry. Not just for food, but for everything: the noise, the excitement, the crazy buzz of energy that throbs beneath my feet.

I hail a taxi, yank open the door and heave my suitcase onto the backseat.

"Where to?" the driver asks.

"East Forty-seventh Street," I shout.

"You got it!" the driver says, steering his taxi into the melee of traffic.

We hit a pothole and I'm momentarily launched from my seat.

"It's those damn New Jersey drivers." The cabbie shakes his fist out the window while I follow suit. And that's when it hits me: It's like I've always been here. Sprung from the head of Zeus—a person with no family, no background, no *history*.

A person who is completely new.

As the taxi weaves dangerously through traffic, I study the faces of the passersby. Here is humanity in every size, shape, and hue, and yet I'm convinced that on each face I divine a kinship that transcends all boundaries, as if linked by the secret knowledge that this is the center of the universe.

Then I clutch my suitcase in fear.

What I said to Samantha was true: I don't ever want to leave. And now I have only sixty days to figure out how to stay.

The sight of George Carter brings me back to earth with a thump. He's sitting dutifully at the counter of the coffee shop on Forty-seventh Street and Second Avenue, where we agreed to meet before he trots off to his summer job at *The New York Times*. I can tell by the set of his mouth that he's exasperated—I've been in New York for less than twenty-four hours and already I'm off course. I haven't even managed to make it to the apartment where I'm supposed to be staying. I tap him on the shoulder, and he turns around, his expression both relieved and irritated.

"What happened to you?" he demands.

I set down my suitcase and take the stool next to him. "My purse got stolen. I didn't have any money. So I called this girl, the cousin of someone I know from Castlebury. She took me to a party and—"

George sighs. "You shouldn't be hanging around people like that."

"Why not?"

"You don't know them."

"So what?" Now I'm annoyed. This is the problem with George. He always acts like he thinks he's my father or something.

"I need you to promise you'll be more careful in the future."

I make a face.

"Carrie, I'm serious. If you get into another jam, I'm not going to be around to help you out."

"Are you abandoning me?" I ask jokingly. George has had a crush on me for nearly a year. And he's one of my dearest friends. If it weren't for George, I might not be in New York at all.

"Actually, I am," he says, sliding three crisp twenty-dollar bills in my direction. "This should tide you over. You can pay me back when you get to Brown."

I look from the bills to his face. He's not kidding.

"The *Times* is sending me to DC for the summer. I'll get to do some actual reporting, so I agreed."

I'm stunned. I don't know whether to congratulate him or chastise him for deserting me.

The impact of his defection hits me, and the floor drops out from below my feet. George is the only person I really know in New York. I was counting on him to show me the ropes. How am I going to get by without him?

As if reading my thoughts, he says, "You'll be fine. Just stick to the basics. Go to class and do your work. And try not to get mixed up with any crazy people, okay?"

"Sure," I say. This wouldn't be a problem but for the fact I'm a little crazy myself.

George picks up my suitcase and we stroll around the corner to a white brick apartment building. A tattered green awning with the words WINDSOR ARMS shields the entrance. "This isn't so bad," George remarks. "Perfectly respectable."

Inside the glass door is a row of buttons. I press the one marked 15E.

"Yes?" a shrill voice shrieks from the intercom.

"It's Carrie Bradshaw."

"Well," says the voice, in a tone that could curdle cream. "It's about time."

George kisses me on the cheek as a buzzer sounds and the second door clicks open. "Good luck," he says, and pauses to give me one last piece of advice: "Will you *please* call your father? I'm sure he's worried about you."

CHAPTER THREE

"Is this Carrie Bradshaw?" The voice is girlish but demanding, as if the caller is slightly annoyed.

"Y-e-e-e-e-s," I say cautiously, wondering who it could be. It's my second morning in New York and we haven't had our first class yet.

"I have your bag," the girl announces.

"What!" I nearly drop the phone.

"Well, don't get too excited. I found it in the garbage. Someone dumped nail polish all over it. I was thinking about leaving it in the garbage, but then I thought: What would I want someone to do if I lost my purse? So I called."

"How'd you find me?"

"Your address book. It was still in the bag. I'll be in front of Saks from ten o'clock on if you want to pick it up," she says. "You can't miss me. I have red hair. I dyed it the same color red as the Campbell's soup can. In honor of Valerie Solanas." She pauses. "The *SCUM Manifesto?* Andy Warhol?"

"Oh, sure." I have absolutely no idea what's she talking about. But I'm not about to admit my ignorance. Plus, this girl sounds kind of . . . bizarre.

"Good. I'll see you in front of Saks." She hangs up before I can get her name.

Yippee! *I knew it.* The whole time my Carrie bag was gone, I had a strange premonition I'd get it back. Like something out of one of those books on mind control: visualize what you want and it will come to you.

"A-hem!"

I look up from my cot and into the scrubbed pink face of my landlady, Peggy Meyers. She's squeezed into a gray rubber suit that fits like sausage casing. The suit, combined with her shining round face, gives her an uncanny resemblance to the Michelin Man.

"Was that an outgoing call?"

"No," I say, slightly offended. "*They* called *me.*"

Her sigh is a precise combination of annoyance and disappointment. "Didn't we go over the rules?"

I nod, eyes wide, pantomiming fear.

"All phone calls are to take place in the living room. And no calls are to last more than five minutes. No one needs longer than five minutes to communicate. And all outgoing calls must be duly listed in the notebook."

Duly, I think. That's a good word.

"Do you have any questions?" she asks.

"Nope." I shake my head.

"I'm going for a run. Then I have auditions. If you decide to go out, make sure you have your keys."

"I will. I promise."

She stops, takes in my cotton pajamas, and frowns. "I hope you're not planning to go back to sleep."

"I'm going to Saks."

Peggy purses her lips in disapproval, as if only the indolent go to Saks. "By the way, your father called."

"Thanks."

"And remember, all long-distance calls are collect." She lumbers out like a mummy. If she can barely walk in that rubber suit, how can she possibly run in it?

I've only known Peggy for twenty-four hours, but already, we don't get along. You could call it hate at first sight.

When I arrived yesterday morning, disheveled and slightly disoriented, her first comment was: "Glad you decided to show up. I was about to give your room to someone else."

I looked at Peggy, whom I suspected had once been attractive but was now like a flower gone to seed, and half wished she *had* given the room away.

"I've got a waiting list a mile long," she continued. "You kids from out of town have no idea—*no idea*—how impossible it is to find a decent place in New York."

Then she sat me down on the green love seat and apprised me of "the rules":

No visitors, especially males.

No overnight guests, especially males, even if she is

away for the weekend.

No consumption of her food.

No telephone calls over five minutes—she needs the phone line free in case she gets a call about an audition.

No coming home past midnight—we might wake her up and she needs every minute of sleep.

And most of all, no cooking. She doesn't want to have to clean up our mess.

Jeez. Even a gerbil has more freedom than I do.

I wait until I hear the front door bang behind her, then knock hard on the plywood wall next to my bed. "Ding-dong, the witch is dead," I call out.

L'il Waters, a tiny butterfly of a girl, slips through the plywood door that connects our cells. "Someone found my bag!" I exclaim.

"Oh, honey, that's wonderful. Like one of those magical New York coincidences." She hops onto the end of the cot, nearly tipping it over. Nothing in this apartment is real, including the partitions, doors, and beds. Our "rooms" are built into part of the living room, forming two tiny six-by-ten spaces with just enough room for a camp bed, a small folding table and chair, a tiny dresser with two drawers, and a reading light. The apartment is located right off Second Avenue, so I've taken to calling L'il and me *The Prisoners of Second Avenue* after the Neil Simon movie.

"But what about Peggy? I heard her yelling at you. I told you not to use the phone in your room." L'il sighs.

"I thought she was asleep."

L'il shakes her head. She's in my program at The New School, but arrived a week earlier to get acclimated, which also means she got the slightly better room. She has to walk through my space to get to hers, so I have even less privacy than she does. "Peggy always gets up early to go jogging. She says she has to lose twenty pounds—"

"In that rubber suit?" I ask, astounded.

"She says it sweats the fat out."

I look at L'il in appreciation. She's two years older than I am, but looks about five years younger. With her birdlike stature, she's one of those girls who will probably look like she's twelve for most of her life. But L'il is not to be underestimated.

When we first met yesterday, I joked about how "L'il" would look on the cover of a book, but she only shrugged and said, "My writing name is E. R. Waters. For Elizabeth Reynolds Waters. It helps to get published if people don't know you're a girl." Then she showed me two poems she'd had published in *The New Yorker*.

I nearly fell over.

Then I told her how I'd met Kenton James and Bernard Singer. I knew meeting famous writers wasn't the same as being published yourself, but I figured it was better than nothing. I even showed her the paper where Bernard Singer had written his phone number.

"You have to call him," she said.

"I don't know." I didn't want to make too big a deal of it.

Thinking of Bernard made me all jellyish until Peggy came in and told us to be quiet.

Now I give L'il a wicked smile. "Peggy," I say. "She really goes to auditions in that rubber suit? Can you imagine the smell?"

L'il grins. "She belongs to a gym. Lucille Roberts. She says she takes a shower there before. That's why she's always so crazy. She's sweating and showering all over town."

This cracks us up, and we fall onto my bed in giggles.

The red-haired girl is right: I have no problem finding her.

Indeed, she's impossible to miss, planted on the sidewalk in front of Saks, holding a huge sign that reads, DOWN WITH PORNOGRAPHY on one side, and PORNOGRAPHY EXPLOITS WOMEN on the other. Behind her is a small table covered with graphic images from porno magazines. "Women, wake up! Say no to pornography!" she shouts.

She waves me over with her placard. "Do you want to sign a petition against pornography?"

I'm about to explain who I am, when a stranger cuts me off.

"Oh, puhleeze," the woman mutters, stepping around us. "You'd think some people would have better things to do than worrying about other people's sex lives."

"Hey," the red-haired girl shouts. "I heard that, you know? And I don't exactly appreciate it."

The woman spins around. "And?"

"What do you know about my sex life?" she demands. Her hair is cut short like a boy's and, as promised, dyed a bright tomato red. She's wearing construction boots and overalls, and underneath, a ragged purple T-shirt.

"Honey, it's pretty clear you don't have one," the woman responds with a smirk.

"Is that so? Maybe I don't have as much sex as you do, but you're a victim of the system. You've been brainwashed by the patriarchy."

"Sex sells," the woman says.

"At the expense of women."

"That's ridiculous. Have you ever considered the fact that some women actually *like* sex?"

"And?" The girl glares as I take advantage of the momentary lull to quickly introduce myself.

"I'm Carrie Bradshaw. You called me. You have my bag?"

"*You're* Carrie Bradshaw?" She seems disappointed. "What are you doing with her?" She jerks her thumb in the woman's direction.

"I don't even know her. If I could just get my bag—"

"Take it," the redheaded girl says, as if she's had enough. She picks up her knapsack, removes my Carrie bag, and hands it to me.

"Thank you," I say gratefully. "If there's anything I can ever do—"

"Don't worry about it," she replies proudly. She picks up her placard and accosts an elderly woman in pearls. "Do you want to sign a petition against pornography?"

The old woman smiles. "No thank you, dear. After all, what's the point?"

The red-haired girl looks momentarily crestfallen.

"Hey," I say. "I'll sign your petition."

"Thanks," she says, handing me a pen.

I scribble my name and skip off down Fifth Avenue. I dodge through the crowds, wondering what my mother would have thought about me being in New York. Maybe she's watching over me, making sure the funny red-haired girl found my bag. My mother was a feminist, too. At the very least, she'd be proud I signed the petition.

"There you are!" L'il calls out. "I was afraid you were going to be late."

"Nope," I say, panting, as I join her on the sidewalk in front of The New School. The trek downtown was a lot farther than I expected, and my feet are killing me. But I saw all kinds of interesting things along the way: the skating rink at Rockefeller Center. The New York Public Library. Lord & Taylor. Something called the Toy Building. "I got my bag," I say, holding it up.

"Carrie was robbed her very first hour in New York," L'il crows to a cute guy with bright blue eyes and wavy black hair.

He shrugs. "That's nothing. My car was broken into the second night I was here. They smashed the window and stole the radio."

"You have a car?" I ask in surprise. Peggy told us no one had cars in New York. Everyone is supposed to walk or take the bus or ride the subway.

"Ryan's from Massachusetts," L'il says as if this explains it. "He's in our class too."

I hold out my hand. "Carrie Bradshaw."

"Ryan McCann." He's got a goofy, sweet smile, but his eyes bore into me as if summing up the competition. "What do you think about our professor, Viktor Greene?"

"I think he's extraordinary," L'il jumps in. "He's what I consider a serious artist."

"He may be an artist, but he's definitely a creep," Ryan replies, goading her.

"You hardly know him," L'il says, incensed.

"Wait a minute. You guys have *met* him?" I ask.

"Last week," Ryan says casually. "We had our conferences. Didn't you?"

"I didn't know we were supposed to have a conference," I falter. How did this happen? Am I already behind?

L'il gives Ryan a look. "Not everyone had a conference. It was only if you were going to be in New York early. It doesn't matter."

"Hey, you kids want to go to a party?"

We turn around. A guy with a Cheshire cat grin holds up some postcards. "It's at The Puck Building. Wednesday night. Free admission if you get there before ten o'clock."

"Thanks," Ryan says eagerly as the guy hands us each a postcard and strolls away.

"Do you know him?" L'il asks.

"Never seen him before in my life. But that's cool, isn't it?" Ryan says. "Where else would some stranger walk up to you and invite you to a party?"

"Along with a thousand other strangers," L'il adds.

"Only in New York, kids," Ryan says.

We head inside as I examine the postcard. On the front is an image of a smiling stone cupid. Underneath are the words, LOVE. SEX. FASHION. I fold the postcard and stick it into my bag.

CHAPTER FOUR

Ryan wasn't kidding. Viktor Greene *is* strange.

For one thing, he droops. It's like someone dropped him out of the sky and he never quite got his sea legs here on earth. Then there's his mustache. It's thick and glossy across his upper lip, but curls forlornly around each side of his mouth like two sad smiles. He keeps stroking that mustache like it's some kind of pet.

"Carrie Bradshaw?" he asks, consulting a list.

I raise my hand. "That's me."

"It is *I*," he corrects. "One of the things you'll learn in this seminar is proper grammar. You'll find it improves your manner of speaking as well."

I redden. Five minutes into my first real writing class and I've made a bad impression.

Ryan catches my eye and winks as if to say, "I told you so."

"Ah, and here's L'il." Viktor Greene nods as he gives his mustache a few more comforting pats. "Does everyone know Ms. Elizabeth Waters? She's one of our most promising writers. I'm sure we'll be hearing a lot from her."

If Viktor Greene had said something like that about me, I'd be worried everyone in the class was going to hate me. But not L'il. She takes Viktor's praise in stride, as if she's used to being regaled for her talent.

For a moment, I'm jealous. I try to reassure myself that everyone in the class is talented. Otherwise they wouldn't be here, right? Including myself. Maybe Viktor Greene just doesn't know how talented I am—yet?

"Here's how this seminar works." Viktor Greene shuffles around as if he's lost something and can't remember what it is. "The theme for the summer is home and family. In the next eight weeks, you'll write four short stories or a novella or six poems exploring these themes. Each week, I'll choose three or four works to be read aloud. Then we'll discuss them. Any questions?"

A hand shoots up belonging to a slim guy with glasses and a mane of blond hair. Despite his resemblance to a pelican, he nevertheless manages to give off the impression that he thinks he's better than everyone else. "How long are the short stories supposed to be?"

Viktor Greene taps his mustache. "As long as it takes to tell the story."

"So that could mean two pages?" demands a girl with an angular face and tawny eyes. A baseball cap is perched backward over her luxurious crop of dark hair and she's wearing a pile of beaded necklaces slung around her neck.

"If you can tell a whole story in five hundred words, be my guest," Viktor Greene says mournfully.

The girl nods, a triumphant expression on her beautiful face. "It's just that my father is an artist. And he says—"

Viktor sighs. "We all know who your father is, Rainbow."

Wait a minute. *Rainbow?* What kind of name is that? And who is this artist father of hers?

I sit back and fold my arms. The guy with the long nose and blond hair catches Rainbow's eye and nods, edging his chair a little closer to hers, as if they're already friends.

"I have a question." Ryan raises his hand. "Can you guarantee that after taking this course, we'll all become writers?"

This causes Viktor Greene to droop even more. I actually wonder if he's going to disappear into the floor.

He frantically pats down his mustache with both hands. "Good question. And the answer is no. Chances are ninety-nine point nine percent of you won't make it as writers at all."

The class groans.

"If I'm not going to make it as a writer, I'll have to demand my money back," Ryan says jokingly.

Everyone laughs, except Viktor Greene. "If that's the way you feel, you should contact the bursar's office."

He twirls the ends of his mustache between his fingers.

That mustache is going to drive me insane. I wonder if Viktor Greene is married and what his wife thinks of all his mustache stroking. Living with that mustache must be like having an extra person in the house. Does it have its own name and eat its own food as well?

And suddenly, I'm burning with passion. I don't care what Viktor Greene says: I'm going to make it. I'm going to become a real writer if it kills me.

I look around the room at my fellow students. Now I'm the one judging the competition.

"All right," I say, plopping onto L'il's bed. "Who is Rainbow's father?"

"Barry Jessen," she says with a sigh.

"Who the hell is Barry Jessen? I know he's an artist and all, but—"

"He's not just any artist. He's one of the most important artists in New York right now. He's the leader of some new art movement. They live in abandoned buildings in SoHo—"

"Rainbow lives in an abandoned building?" I ask, perplexed. "Do they have running water? Heat? She doesn't look like she's homeless."

"She's not," L'il says in exasperation. "They only *used* to be abandoned buildings. Garment and print factories. But then all these artists moved in and started fixing them up. And now they have parties in their lofts and take drugs and people buy their art and write about them in *The New York Times* and *New York Magazine*."

"And Rainbow?"

"Well, her father is Barry Jessen. And her mother is Pican—"

"The *model*?"

"That's why she's so beautiful and will get anything she wants. Which includes becoming a writer. Does that answer your question?"

"So she's a million times cooler than us."

"Than 'we are,'" L'il corrects. "And, yes, she is. Her parents know a ton of people, and if Rainbow wants to get a book published, all she has to do is snap her fingers and her father will find someone to publish it for her. And then he'll get a bunch of journalists to write about it and critics to give her good reviews."

"Damn," I say, impressed.

"Meanwhile, if the rest of us want to be successful, we have to do it the old-fashioned way. We have to write something great."

"What a bore," I say sarcastically.

L'il laughs while I pick at an imaginary thread. "And what about that guy with the blond hair and the attitude? He acts like he knows her."

"Capote Duncan?" she says in surprise. "I'm sure he does. Capote's the type who knows everyone."

"Why?"

"Oh, he just is. He's from the South," she says, as if this explains it. "He's kind of dreamy, isn't he?"

"No. But he is kind of an asshole."

"He's older. He and Ryan are seniors in college. They're friends. Apparently the two of them are quite the ladies' men."

"You're kidding."

"I'm not." She pauses, and in a slightly formal tone of voice, adds, "If you don't mind—"

"I know, I know," I say, jumping off the bed. "We're supposed to be writing."

L'il doesn't seem to share my overweening interest in other people. Perhaps she's so confident in her own talents, she feels like she doesn't need to. I, on the other hand, could easily spend the entire day engaged in gossip, which I prefer to call "character analysis." Unfortunately, you can't engage in character analysis by yourself. I go back into my cubbyhole, sit down at my desk, roll a piece of paper into my typewriter, and sit there.

Ten minutes later, I'm still sitting there, staring at the wall. There's only one window in our area, and it's in L'il's room. Feeling like I'm suffocating, I get up, go into the living room, and look out the window there.

Peggy's apartment is in the back of the building, facing the back of another nearly identical building on the next street. Maybe I could get a telescope and spy on the apartments across the way. I could write a story about the residents. Unfortunately, the denizens of that building appear to be as dull as we are. I spot the flickering blue screen of a television set, a woman washing the dishes, and a sleeping cat.

I sigh, feeling thwarted. There's a whole world out there and I'm stuck in Peggy's apartment. I'm missing everything. And now I only have fifty-nine days left.

I've got to make something happen.

I race to my cubby, grab Bernard's number, and pick up the phone.

I hesitate, considering what I'm about to do, and put it down.

"L'il?" I call out.

"Yes?"

"Should I call Bernard Singer?"

L'il comes to the door. "What do you think?"

"What if he doesn't remember me?"

"He gave you his number, didn't he?"

"But what if he didn't mean it? What if he was only being polite? What if—"

"Do you want to call him?" she asks.

"Yes."

"Then do." L'il is very decisive. It's a quality I hope to develop in myself someday.

And before I can change my mind, I dial.

"Y-ello," he says, after the third ring.

"Bernard?" I say, in a voice that's way too high. "It's Carrie Bradshaw."

"Aha. Had a feeling it might be you."

"You did?" I curl the phone cord around my finger.

"I'm a bit psychic."

"Do you have visions?" I ask, not knowing what else to say.

"Feelings," he murmurs sexily. "I'm very in touch with my feelings. What about you?"

"I guess I am too. I mean, I never seem to be able to get rid of them. My feelings."

He laughs. "What are you doing right now?"

"Me?" I squeak. "Well, I'm just kind of sitting here trying to write—"

"Want to come over?" he asks suddenly.

I'm not sure what I was expecting, but it isn't this. I suppose I had a vague yet hopeful idea that he would invite me to dinner. Take me out on a proper date. But asking me to come to his apartment? Yikes. He probably thinks I'm going to have sex with him.

I pause.

"Where are you?" he asks.

"On Forty-seventh Street?"

"You're less than ten blocks away."

"Okay," I cautiously agree. As usual, my curiosity trumps my better judgment. A very bad trait, and one I hope to amend. Someday.

But maybe dating is different in New York. For all I know, inviting a strange girl to your apartment is just the way they do things around here. And if Bernard tries anything funny, I can always kick him.

On my way out, I run into Peggy coming in. She's got her hands full trying to maneuver three old shopping bags onto the love seat. She looks me up and down and sighs. "Going out?"

I deliberate, wondering how much I need to tell her. But my excitement gets the better of me. "I'm going to see my friend. Bernard Singer?"

The name has its desired effect. Peggy inhales, nostrils flaring. The fact that I know Bernard Singer has to be killing her. He's the most famous playwright in all of New York and she's still a struggling actress. She's probably dreamed of meeting him for years, and yet here I am, only three days in the city, and already I know him.

"Some people have quite the life, don't they?" She grumbles as she goes to the refrigerator and extracts one of her many cans of Tab—which are also off-limits for L'il and me.

For a moment, I feel victorious, until I take in Peggy's despondent expression. She jerks the ring from the top of the can and drinks thirstily, like the solutions to all her problems lie in that can of Tab. She drains it, absentmindedly rubbing the metal ring against her thumb.

"Peggy, I—"

"Damn!" She drops the can and sticks her thumb in her mouth, sucking the blood from the cut where the ring has sliced the skin. She closes her eyes as if holding back tears.

"Are you all right?" I ask quickly.

"Of course." She looks up, furious that I've witnessed this moment of weakness. "You're still here?"

She brushes past me on her way to her room. "Tonight's my night off and I intend to make it an early one. So don't be home late."

She closes the door. For a second, I stand there, wondering what just happened. Maybe it's not me Peggy hates. Maybe it's her *life*.

"Okay," I say to no one in particular.

CHAPTER FIVE

Bernard lives in Sutton Place. It's only a few blocks away, but it might as well be in another city. Gone are the noise, the grime, and the vagrant types that populate the rest of Manhattan. Instead, there are buildings constructed of soft-colored stone with turrets and green copper mansards. Uniformed doormen wearing white gloves stand under quiet awnings; a limousine idles at the curb. I pause, breathing in the atmosphere of luxury as a nanny passes me wheeling a baby carriage, behind which prances a small fluffy dog.

Bernard must be rich.

Rich, famous, and attractive. What am I getting myself into?

I scan the street, looking for number 52. It's on the east side facing the river. Swanky, I think, hurrying toward the building. I step inside, where I'm immediately halted by a low growl from a stern-faced doorman. "Can I help you?"

"Going to see a friend," I mutter, attempting to snake my way around him. And that's when I make my first mistake: never, ever try to get around a doorman in a white-glove building.

"You can't just walk in here." He holds up one gloved mitt, as if the mere sight of his hand is enough to ward off the unwashed.

Unfortunately, something about that glove sets me off. There's nothing I hate more than some old guy telling me what to do. "How did you expect me to enter? By horse-back?"

"Miss!" he exclaims, taking a step back in displeasure. "Please state your business. And if you cannot state your business, I suggest you take your business elsewhere."

Aha. He thinks I'm some kind of hooker. He must be half blind. I'm hardly even wearing makeup. "I'm here to see Bernard," I say tightly.

"Bernard who?" he demands, refusing to budge.

"Bernard Singer?"

"*Mr.* Singer?"

How much longer can this go on? We stare at each other in a stalemate. He must know he's beat. After all, he can't actually deny that Bernard lives here—or can he?

"I'll ring Mr. Singer," he finally concedes.

He makes a great show of strolling across the marble lobby to a desk containing a huge spray of flowers, a note-book, and a telephone. He presses a few buttons and, while he waits for Bernard to answer, rubs his jaw in aggravation.

"Mr. Singer?" he says, into the receiver. "There's a"—he glares at me—"young, er, *person* downstairs asking to see you." His expression changes to one of disappointment as he glances my way. "Yes, thank you, sir. I'll send her right up."

And just when I think I've made it past that guard dog of a doorman, I'm confronted by yet another man in a uniform, who operates the elevator. Being the twentieth century and all, you'd think most people would have figured out how to press the button themselves, but apparently the occupants of Sutton Place are slightly feeble when it comes to technology.

"Can I help you?" he asks.

Not again. "Bernard Singer," I say. As he presses the button for the ninth floor, he clears his throat in disapproval. But at least he's not peppering me with questions.

The elevator doors fold open to reveal a small hallway, another desk, another spray of flowers, and patterned wallpaper. There are two doors at either end of the corridor, and mercifully, Bernard is standing in one of them.

So this is the lair of a wunderkind, I think, taking a look around the apartment. It's surprising, all right. Not because of what's in it, but because of what isn't.

The living room, with its mullioned windows, cozy fireplace, and stately bookshelves, calls out for well-loved, well-worn furniture, but contains a single beanbag chair. Ditto for the dining room, which is populated by a Ping-Pong table and a couple of folding chairs. Then there's the bedroom: a king-size bed, a king-size television. On the bed itself, a lone sleeping bag.

"I love to watch TV in bed," Bernard says. "I think it's sexy, don't you?"

I'm about to give him a don't-even-try-it look, when I notice his expression. He seems sad.

"Did you just move in?" I ask brightly, searching for an explanation.

"Someone just moved out," he replies.

"Who?"

"My wife."

"You're married?" I shriek. Of all the possibilities, I never considered the one in which he might be hitched. What kind of married man invites a girl he just met to his apartment?

"My *ex*-wife," he corrects. "I keep forgetting we're not married. We got divorced a month ago and I'm still not used to it."

"So you *were* married?"

"For six years. But we were together for two before that."

Eight years? My eyes narrow as I do a quick calculation. If Bernard was in a relationship for that long, it means he has to be at least thirty. Or thirty-one. Or even . . . thirty-five?

When was his first play released? I remember reading about it, so I had to be at least ten. To cover up my ruminations, I quickly ask, "How was it?"

"How was what?"

"Your marriage."

42

"Well," he laughs. "Not so good. Considering we're divorced now."

It takes me a second to emotionally recalibrate. During the walk over, the far-off reaches of my imagination were constructing visions of Bernard and me together, but nowhere in that picture was there an ex-wife. I always figured my one true love would have only one true love, too—me. The fact of Bernard's previous marriage throws a real monkey wrench into my fantasy.

"And my wife took all the furniture. What about you?" he asks. "Have you ever been married?"

I look at him in astonishment. I'm barely old enough to drink, I nearly say. Instead, I shake my head as if I, too, have been disappointed in love.

"I guess we're both a couple of sad sacks," he says. I go along with his mood. I'm finding him particularly attractive at the moment and I'm hoping he'll put his arms around me and kiss me. I'm longing to be pressed up against that lean chest. I sit in the beanbag chair, instead.

"Why'd she take the furniture?" I ask.

"My wife?"

"I thought you were divorced," I say, trying to keep him on point.

"She's mad at me."

"Can't you make her give it back?"

"I don't think so. No."

"Why not?"

"She stubborn. Oh Lord. She's as stubborn as a mule on race day. Always has been. That's how she got so far."

"Hmmm." I roll around seductively on the beanbag.

My actions have their desired effect, that being why should he think about his ex-wife when he has a lovely young woman—me—to concentrate on instead? Sure enough, in the next second, he asks, "How about you? Are you hungry?"

"I'm always hungry."

"There's a little French place around the corner. We could go there."

"Terrific," I say, leaping to my feet, despite the fact that the word "French" reminds me of the restaurant I used to go to in Hartford with my old boyfriend, Sebastian, who dumped me for my best friend, Lali.

"You like French food?" he asks.

"Love it," I reply. Sebastian and Lali were a long time ago. And besides, I'm with Bernard Singer now, not some mixed-up high school boy.

The "little French place around the corner" turns out to be several blocks away. And it's not exactly "little." It's La Grenouille. Which is so famous, even I've heard of it.

Bernard ducks his head in embarrassment as the maître d' greets him by name. "Bonsoir, Monsieur Singer. We have your usual table."

I look at Bernard curiously. If he comes here all the time, why didn't he say he was a regular?

The maître d' picks up two menus and with an elegant tip of his head, leads us to a charming table by the window.

Then Mr. Monkey-suit pulls out my chair, unfolds my

napkin, and places it on my lap. He rearranges my wine glasses, picks up a fork, inspects it, and, the fork having passed muster, replaces it next to my plate. Honestly, all the attention is disorienting. When the maître d' finally retreats, I look to Bernard for help.

He's studying the menu. "I don't speak French. Do you?" he asks.

"*Un peu.*"

"Really?"

"*Vraiment.*"

"You must have gone to a very fancy school. The only foreign language I learned was fisticuffs."

"Ha."

"I was pretty good at it too," he says, making jabbing motions in the air. "Had to be. I was this runt of a kid and everyone's favorite punching bag."

"But you're so tall," I point out.

"I didn't grow until I was eighteen. What about you?"

"I stopped growing when I was six."

"Hahaha. You're funny."

And just as the conversation is about to take off, the maître d' returns with a bottle of white wine. "Your Pouilly-Fuissé, Monsieur Singer."

"Oh, thanks," Bernard says, looking sheepish again. This is very odd. The apartment, the restaurant, the wine—surely Bernard is wealthy. Why, then, does he insist on acting like he's not? Or rather, that it's all a burden which he must somehow endure?

The wine pouring is yet another ritual. When it's over,

I breathe a sigh of relief.

"It's annoying, isn't it?" Bernard says, echoing my thoughts.

"Why do you let them do it, then?"

"It makes them happy. If I didn't sniff the cork, they'd be very disappointed."

"You might even lose your special table."

"I've been trying to sit at that table"—he points to an empty table in the back of the room—"for years. But they won't let me. It's Siberia," he adds, in a dramatic whisper.

"Is it colder there?"

"Freezing."

"And what about this table?"

"Right on the equator." He pauses. "And you—you're on the equator too." He reaches out and takes my hand. "I like your gumption," he says.

The chef pulls out all the stops for Bernard. After a stomach-numbing meal of seven courses—including soup, a soufflé, two desserts, and some delicious after-dinner wine that tastes like ambrosia—I look at my watch and discover it's just after midnight. "I ought to go."

"Why? Will you turn into a pumpkin?"

"Something like that," I say, thinking about Peggy.

His next move hangs in the air, spinning like a lazy disco ball. "I suppose I should walk you home," he says finally.

"And ruin all this?" I laugh.

"I haven't done 'this' for a while. What about you?"

"Oh, I'm an expert," I tease.

We walk back to my building, swinging our hands between us.

"Good night, pussycat," he says, stopping in front of my door. We stand awkwardly, until he makes his move. He tilts up my chin and leans in for a kiss. It's gentle and civilized at first, then more and more urgent, ending just before some imaginary line of lust is crossed.

The kiss leaves me swooning. Bernard looks at me longingly, but settles for a gentlemanly peck on the cheek and a squeeze of my hand. "I'll call you tomorrow, okay?"

"Okay." I can barely breathe.

I watch him stroll off into the night. At the corner, he turns and waves. When he's disappeared completely, I slip inside.

I creep down the hallway to the apartment, brushing my fingers against the pea-green wall for support, wondering why anyone would paint a hallway such an ugly color. At the door, I carefully insert my key into the first lock. The bolt drops with an alarming ping.

I hold my breath, wondering if Peggy has heard the sound, and if so, what she'll do. But when I don't hear anything for several seconds, I try the next lock.

It, too, turns easily, which means I should now be able to enter the apartment. I twist the knob and try to ease open the door, but it won't move.

Huh? Maybe Peggy didn't lock the door after all and I've ended up locking it instead. It doesn't seem like something Peggy would do, but I try turning the locks in the opposite direction just to make sure.

No luck. The door moves precisely one-sixteenth of an inch, and then refuses to budge, as if someone has shoved a heavy piece of furniture in front of it.

The dead bolt, I think, with rising panic. It's a metal bar that runs across the door and can only be opened and closed from inside the apartment. We're supposed to use it strictly in an emergency, like a nuclear war or a blackout or a zombie attack. But apparently Peggy has decided to break her own stupid rule and has locked it to teach me a lesson.

Crap. I have to either wake her up or sleep in the hall-way.

I scratch on the door. "L'il?" I hiss, hoping L'il is awake and will hear me. "L'il?"

Nothing.

I slump to the floor, resting my back against the wall. Does Peggy really hate me that much? And why? What have I ever done to her?

Another half hour passes, and I give up. I curl into a ball with my Carrie bag nestled between my arms, and try to get some sleep.

And then I guess I do fall asleep, because the next thing I hear is L'il whispering, "Carrie? Are you okay?"

I open my eyes, wondering where the hell I am, and what the hell I'm doing in the hallway.

And then I remember: Peggy and her damn dead bolt.

L'il puts her finger to her lips and motions for me to come inside.

"Thanks," I mouth. She nods as we quietly shut the door. I pause, listening for sounds of Peggy, but there's only silence.

I turn the knob on the bolt and lock us inside.

CHAPTER SIX

The next morning, triumphant, perhaps, in her perceived victory, Peggy sleeps until nine. This allows the Prisoners of Second Avenue a much-needed extra hour of shut-eye.

But once Peggy's up, she's up. And while early-morning silence has never been her forte, this morning she appears to be in an especially good mood.

She's singing show tunes.

I turn over on my cot, and rap quietly on the plywood. L'il raps back, indicating she's awake and has heard the singing as well.

I slide under the sheet and pull the covers up to my nose. Maybe if I lie flat on my bed and put the pillow over my head, Peggy won't notice me. It was a trick my sisters and I perfected when we were kids. But I'm quite a bit bigger now, and Peggy, with her beady crow eyes, is sure to notice the lumps. Perhaps I could hide under my cot?

This, I decide, is beyond ridiculous.

I won't have it. I'm going to confront Peggy. And full of brio, I hop out of bed and put my ear to the door.

The shower is running, and above that, I can hear Peggy's particularly grating rendition of "I Feel Pretty" from *West Side Story*.

I wait, my hand on the doorknob.

Finally, the water stops. I imagine Peggy toweling herself off and applying creams to her body. She carries her toiletries to and from the bathroom in a plastic shower basket she keeps in her room. It's yet another deliberate reminder that no one is to use her precious possessions on the sly.

When I hear the bathroom door open, I step out into the living room. "Good morning, Peggy."

Her hair is wrapped in a pink towel, and she's wearing a worn chenille robe and fluffy slippers in the shape of bears. At the sound of my voice, she throws up her arms, nearly dropping her basket of toiletries. "You almost scared me to death."

"Sorry," I say. "If you're finished in the bathroom—"

Perhaps Peggy's not such a bad actress after all, because she immediately recovers. "I need it back in a minute. I have to dry my hair."

"No problem." We stand there, wondering who's going to bring up the locking-out issue first. I say nothing and neither does Peggy. Then she gives me a shrewd, vicious smile and goes into her room.

She's not going to mention it.

On the other hand, she doesn't have to. She made her point.

I trip into the bathroom. If she isn't going to say anything to me, I'm certainly not going to say anything to her.

When I exit, Peggy is standing there with a blow-dryer in her hand. "Excuse me," I say as I wriggle past her.

She goes back into the bathroom and shuts the door.

While the apartment is filled with the buzz of the dryer, I take the opportunity to check in on L'il. She's so tiny, she looks like a doll someone laid under the comforter, her round face as pale as porcelain.

"She's drying her hair," I report.

"You should sneak in there and drop her blow-dryer into the sink."

I tilt my head. The whirring has suddenly ceased, and I skittle back to my cell. I quickly plop myself in the chair in front of my mother's old Royal typewriter.

A few seconds later, Peggy's behind me. I just love the way she insists we respect her privacy, yet doesn't believe we deserve the same, barging into our rooms whenever she feels like it.

She's slurping down her ubiquitous can of Tab. It must be like mother's milk to her—good for any occasion, including breakfast.

"I've got an audition this afternoon, so I'll need quiet in the apartment while I'm practicing." She eyes my typewriter doubtfully. "I hope you're not planning on using that noisy thing. You need to get an electric typewriter. Like everyone else."

"I'd love to, but I can't exactly afford one right now," I reply, trying to keep the sarcasm out of my tone.

"That's not my problem, is it?" she says with more saccharine than an entire six-pack of diet soda.

"It's that *little* itch." Pause. "No. It's *that* little itch.

"Damn. It's that little *itch*."

Yes, it's true. Peggy is auditioning for a hemorrhoid commercial.

"What did you expect?" L'il mouths. "Breck?" She checks her appearance in a hand mirror, carefully dabbing her cheeks with a pot of blush.

"Where are you going?" I hiss in outrage, as if I can't believe she's going to abandon me to Peggy and her little itch.

"Out," she says, mysteriously.

"But where?" And then, feeling like Oliver Twist asking for more grub, I say, "Can I come?"

L'il is suddenly flustered. "You can't. I have to—"

"What?"

"See someone," she says firmly.

"Who?"

"A friend of my mother's. She's very old. She's in the hospital. She can't have visitors."

"How come she can see you?"

L'il blushes, holding up the mirror as if to block my inquiries. "I'm like family," she says, fiddling with her lashes. "What are you doing today?"

"Haven't decided," I grumble, eyeing her suspiciously. "Don't you want to hear about my evening with Bernard?"

"Of course. How was it?"

"Incredibly interesting. His ex-wife took all his furniture. Then we went to La Grenouille."

"That's nice." L'il is annoyingly distracted this morning. I wonder if it's due to Peggy locking me out—or something else entirely. I'm sure she's lying about her mother's sick friend, though. Who puts on blush and mascara to go to a hospital?

But then I don't care, because I get an idea.

I dash into my cubbyhole and come back with my Carrie bag. I rifle through it and pull out a piece of paper. "I'm going to see Samantha Jones."

"Who's that?" L'il murmurs.

"The woman who let me stay at her apartment?" I ask, trying to jog her memory. "Donna LaDonna's cousin? She lent me twenty dollars. I'm going to pay her back." This, of course, is merely an excuse. Both to get out of the apartment and to talk to Samantha about Bernard.

"Good idea." L'il puts down the mirror and smiles, as if she hasn't heard a word I've said.

I open my bag to replace the paper, and find the folded-up invitation to the party at The Puck Building, which I wave in L'il's face. "That party is tonight. We should go." And maybe, if Bernard calls, he could come with us.

L'il looks skeptical. "I'm sure there's a party every night in New York."

"I'm sure there is," I counter. "And I plan to go to every one."

Samantha's steel and glass office building is a forbidding bastion of serious business. The lobby is sharply air-conditioned, with all manner of people rushing about, harassed and irritated. I find the name of Samantha's company—Slovey, Dinall Advertising—and board an elevator for the twenty-sixth floor.

The elevator ride actually makes me a little queasy. I've never ridden an elevator so high up. What if something happens and we crash to the ground?

But no one else seems the least concerned. Everyone has their eyes turned to the numbers that tick off the floors, their faces intentionally blank, deliberately ignoring the fact that there are at least half a dozen people in the space of a large closet. This must be elevator protocol, and I attempt to copy their demeanor.

But I don't quite get it right, because I actually manage to catch the eye of a middle-aged woman holding a sheaf of folders in front of her chest. I smile, and she quickly looks away.

Then it occurs to me that popping in unexpectedly on Samantha in her place of work might not be the best idea. Nevertheless, when the elevator opens on her floor, I get out and bump around in the softly carpeted hallway until I find two enormous doors with SLOVEY, DINALL ADVERTISING INCORPORATED etched into the glass. On the other side is a large desk behind which sits a small woman with black hair that rises in sharp spikes. She takes in my appearance, and after a beat, says, "Can I help you," in a doubtful, grating tone that sounds like her nose is speaking instead of her mouth.

This is very disconcerting, and in a hesitant voice intended to convey the fact that I hope I'm not bothering her, I say, "Samantha Jones? I just want to—"

I'm about to say I want to leave the twenty dollars for her in an envelope, but the woman waves me to a seat and picks up the phone. "Someone's here for Samantha," she whines into the receiver. Then she asks for my name and nods. "Her assistant will be out to get you," she says wearily. She picks up a paperback book and starts reading.

The reception area is decorated with posters of advertisements, some of which appear to go back to the 1950s. I'm kind of surprised that Samantha Jones has her own assistant. She doesn't look old enough to be anyone's boss, but I guess Donna LaDonna was right when she said her cousin was a "big deal in advertising."

In a few minutes, a young woman appears, wearing a navy suit, a light blue shirt with two straps tied around her neck in a loose bow, and blue running shoes.

"Follow me," she commands. I jump up and trot behind her, through a maze of cubicles, ringing telephones, and the sound of a man shouting.

"Seems like everyone around here is pretty cranky," I wisecrack.

"That's because we are," she snaps, coming to a halt by the open door of a small office. "Except for Samantha," she adds. "She's *always* in a good mood."

Samantha looks up and waves at the chair in front of her. She's seated behind a white Formica table, wearing an outfit that's nearly identical to her assistant's, with the exception of her shoulder pads, which are much wider. Perhaps the wider your shoulder pads, the more important you are. Her head is cocked against an enormous phone cradle. "Yes, of course, Glenn," she says, making a yakking motion with her hand. "The Century Club is perfect. But I don't see why we have to have flower arrangements in the shape of baseballs. . . . Well, I know it's what Charlie wants, but I've always thought the wedding was supposed to be the bride's day. . . . Yes, of course. . . . I'm sorry, Glenn, but I have a meeting. I really have to go," she continues, with mounting frustration. "I'll call you later. I promise." And with a roll of her eyes, she firmly replaces the receiver, looks up, and tosses her head.

"Charlie's mother," she explains. "We've been engaged for about two minutes and already she's driving me crazy. If I ever get married again, I'm going to skip the engagement completely and go right to City Hall. The minute you get engaged, you become public property."

"But then you wouldn't have the ring," I say awkwardly, suddenly intimidated by Samantha, her office, and her glamorous life.

"I suppose that's true," she concedes. "Now if I could only find someone to sublet my apartment—"

"Aren't you moving in with Charlie?"

"My God. You really are a sparrow. When you have an

apartment like mine, rent-controlled and only two hundred and twenty-five dollars a month, you don't ever give it up."

"Why not?"

"Because real estate is impossible in this town. And I might need it back someday. If things don't work out with Charlie. I'm not saying they *won't*, but you never know with men in New York. They're spoiled. They're like kids in a candy store. If you have a good deal—well, naturally, you want to hang on to it."

"Like Charlie?" I ask, wondering if he's a good deal as well.

She smiles. "You catch on quick, Sparrow. As a matter of fact, Charlie is a good deal. Even if he is a baseball freak. He wanted to be a player himself, but of course, his father wouldn't let him."

I nod encouragingly. Samantha seems to be in a mood to talk, and I'm like a sponge, ready to absorb anything she says. "His father?"

"Alan Tier."

When I look at her blankly, she adds, "The Tiers? The mega real estate family?" She shakes her head as if I'm hopeless. "Charlie is the oldest son. His father expects him to take over the business."

"I see."

"And it's about time. *You* know how it is with men," she says, as if I, too, am some kind of guy expert. "If a man doesn't ask you to marry him—or at least live with him—after two years, he never will. It means he's only interested in having a good time." She folds her arms and puts her feet on the desk. "I'm as interested in having a good time as any man, but the difference between me and Charlie is that my clock is ticking. And his isn't."

Clocks? Ticking? I have no idea what she's talking about, but I keep mum, nodding my head as if I understand.

"He may not have a timetable, but I do." She holds up her hand and ticks off the moments on her fingers. "Married by twenty-five. Corner office by thirty. And somewhere in there—*children*. So when that bachelor story came out, I decided it was time to do something about Charlie. Speed things along."

She pushes aside some papers on her desk to retrieve a battered copy of *New York Magazine*.

"Here." She holds it out. The headline reads, NEW YORK'S MOST ELIGIBLE BACHELORS, above a photograph of several men standing on bleachers like a sports team in a high school yearbook. "That's Charlie," she says, pointing to a man whose face is partially hidden by a baseball cap. "I told him not to wear that stupid cap, but he wouldn't listen."

"Do people still care about this stuff?" I ask. "I mean, aren't debutantes and eligible bachelors sort of over?"

Samantha laughs. "You really are a rube, kiddo. If only it *didn't* matter. But it does."

"All right—"

"So I broke up with him."

I smile knowingly. "But if you wanted to be with him—"

"It's all about getting the guy to realize he wants to

be with *you*." She swings her feet off the desk and comes around to the side. I sit up, aware that I'm about to receive a valuable lesson in man management.

"When it comes to men," she begins, "it's all about their egos. So when I broke up with Charlie, he was furious. Couldn't believe I'd leave him. Giving him no choice but to come crawling after me. Naturally, I resisted. 'Charlie,' I said. 'You know how crazy I am about you, but if I don't respect myself, who will? If you really care about me—I mean me as a person and not just as a lover—then you're going to have to prove it. You're going to have to *make a commitment.*'"

"And did he?" I ask, on the edge of my seat.

"Well, obviously," she says, waving her ringed finger. "And it didn't hurt that the Yankees are on strike."

"The Yankees?"

"Like I said, he's obsessed. You don't know how many baseball games I've had to sit through in the last two years. I'm more of a football girl, but I kept telling myself that someday, it'd be worth it. And it was. With no baseball, Charlie didn't have anything to distract him. And voilà," she says, indicating her hand.

I take the opportunity to mention Bernard. "Did you know Bernard Singer was married?"

"Of course. He was married to Margie Shephard. The actress. Why? Did you see him?"

"Last night," I say, blushing.

"And?"

"We kissed."

"That's it?" She sounds disappointed.

I squirm in my chair. "I only just met him."

"Bernard's a bit of a mess right now. Which is not surprising. Margie walked all over him. Cheated on him with one of the actors in his play."

"You're kidding," I say, aghast.

Samantha shrugs. "It was in all the papers so it's hardly a secret. Not very nice for Bernard, but I always say there's no such thing as bad publicity. Besides, New York is a small town. Smaller than small, if you really think about it."

I nod carefully. Our interview seems to be over. "I wanted to return the twenty dollars you gave me," I say quickly, digging around in my pocket. I pull out a twenty-dollar bill and hand it to her.

She takes the bill and smiles. And then she laughs. I suddenly wish I could laugh like that—knowing and tinkling at the same time.

"I'm surprised," she says. "I wasn't expecting to see you, or my twenty dollars, ever again."

"And I wanted to thank you. For lending me the money. And for taking me to the party. And for introducing me to Bernard. If there's anything I can do—"

"Not a thing," she says, rising to her feet.

She walks me to the door and holds out her hand. "Good luck. And if you need to borrow another twenty sometime—well, you know where to find me."

"Are you sure nobody called?" I ask L'il for the twentieth time.

"I've been here since two. The phone didn't ring once."

"He might have called. While you were visiting your mother's friend. In the hospital."

"Peggy was home then," L'il points out.

"But maybe he did call and Peggy didn't tell me. On purpose."

L'il gives her hair a firm brush. "Why would Peggy do that?"

"Because she hates me?" I ask, rubbing my lips with gloss.

"You only saw him last night," L'il says. "Guys never call the next day. They like to keep you guessing."

"I don't like to be kept guessing. And he said he would call—" I break off as the phone rings. "It's him!" I yelp. "Can you get it?"

"Why?" L'il grumbles.

"Because I don't want to seem too eager. I don't want him to think I've been sitting by the phone all day."

"Even though you have?" But she picks up the phone anyway. I wait in anticipation as she nods and holds out the receiver. "It's your father."

Of course. His timing couldn't be worse. I called him yesterday and left a message with Missy, but he didn't call back. What if Bernard tries to call while I'm talking to my father and it's busy? "Hi, Dad," I sigh.

"Hi, Dad? Is that how you greet your father? Whom you haven't called once since you got to New York?"

"I did call you, Dad." My father, I note, sounds slightly strange. Not only is he in a really good mood, he doesn't seem to remember that I tried to reach him. Which is fine by me. So many things have happened since I've arrived in New York—not all of which my father would consider good—that I've been dreading this conversation. Unnecessarily, it seems.

"I've been really busy," I say.

"I'm sure you have."

"But everything's great."

"Glad to hear it," he says. "Now that I know you're still alive, I can rest easy." And with a quick good-bye, he hangs up.

This really is odd. My father has always been distracted, but he's never been this enthusiastic *and* removed. I tell myself it's only because my father, like most men, hates talking on the phone.

"Are you ready?" L'il demands. "You're the one who wanted to go to this party. And we can't get home too late. I don't want Peggy locking both of us out this time."

"I'm ready," I sigh. I grab my Carrie bag, and with one last, longing look at the phone, follow her out.

A few minutes later, we're strolling down Second Avenue in a flurry of giggles as we do our best Peggy imitations.

"I'm so glad I got you as a roommate," L'il says, taking my arm.

There's a line in front of the entrance to the Puck Building, but by now we've realized that in New York, there's a line for everything. We've already passed three lines on Second Avenue: two in front of movie theaters, and one for a cheese shop. Neither L'il nor I could understand why so many people felt they needed cheese at nine p.m., but chalked it up to yet another fascinating mystery about Manhattan.

We get through the line pretty quick, though, and find ourselves in an enormous room filled with what appears to be every variety of young person. There are rocker types in leather and punk kids with piercings and crazy-colored hair. Tracksuits and heavy gold chains and shiny gold watches. A glittering disco ball spins from the ceiling, but the music is something I've never heard, discordant and haunting and insistent, the kind of music that demands you dance. "Let's get a drink," I shout to L'il. We make our way to the side, where I've spotted a makeshift bar set up on a long plywood table.

"Hey!" a voice exclaims. It's the arrogant blond guy from our class. Capote Duncan. He has his arm around a tall, painfully thin girl with cheekbones like icebergs. Who must be a model, I think, in annoyance, realizing that maybe L'il was right about Capote's ability to get girls.

"I was just saying to Sandy here," he says, in a slight Southern accent, indicating the startled girl next to him, "that this party is like something out of *Swann's Way*."

"Actually, I was thinking Henry James," L'il shouts back.

"Who's Henry James?" the girl named Sandy asks. "Is he here?"

Capote smiles as if the girl has said something charming and tightens his grip around her shoulders. "No, but he could be if you wanted."

Now I know I was right. Capote is an asshole. And since no one is paying attention to me anyway, I figure I'll get a drink on my own and catch up with L'il later.

I turn away, and that's when I spot her. The red-haired girl from Saks. The girl who found my Carrie bag.

"Hi!" I say, frantically waving my arm as if I've discovered an old friend.

"Hi what?" she asks, put out, taking a sip of beer.

"It's me, remember? Carrie Bradshaw. You found my bag." I hold the bag up to her face to remind her.

"Oh, right," she says, unimpressed.

She doesn't seem inclined to continue the conversation, but for some reason, I do. I suddenly have a desire to placate her. To make her like me.

"Why do you do that, anyway?" I ask. "That protesting thing?"

She looks at me arrogantly, as if she can hardly be bothered to answer the question. "Because it's important?"

"Oh."

"And I work at the battered women's center. You should volunteer sometime. It'll shake you out of your secure little world," she says loudly over the music.

"But . . . doesn't it make you think all men are bad?"

"No. Because I *know* all men are bad."

I have no idea why I'm even having this conversation. But I can't seem to let it—or her—go. "What about being in love? I mean, how can you have a boyfriend or husband knowing this stuff?"

"Good question." She takes another sip of her beer and looks around the room, glaring.

"I meant what I said," I shout, trying to regain her attention. "About thanking you. Could I buy you a cup of coffee or something? I want to hear more about . . . what you do."

"Really?" she asks, dubious.

I nod enthusiastically.

"Okay," she says, giving in. "I guess you could call me."

"What's your name?"

She hesitates. "Miranda Hobbes. H–o–b–b–e–s. You can get my number from information."

And as she walks away, I nod, making a dialing motion with my finger.

CHAPTER SEVEN

"It's Chinese silk. From the 1930s."

I finger the blue material lovingly and turn it over. There's a gold dragon stitched on the back. The robe is probably way more than I can afford, but I try it on anyway. The sleeves hang at my sides like folded wings. I could really fly in this.

"That looks good on you," the salesman adds. Although "salesman" is probably not the right word for a guy in a porkpie hat, plaid pants, and a black Ramones T-shirt. "Purveyor" might be more appropriate. Or "dealer."

I'm in a vintage clothing store called My Old Lady. The name of which turns out to be startlingly appropriate.

"Where do you get this stuff?" I ask, reluctant to remove the robe but too scared to ask the price.

The owner shrugs. "People bring things in. Mostly from their old relatives who have died. One man's trash is another one's treasure."

"Or one woman's," I correct him. I screw up my courage. "How much is this, anyway?"

"For you? Five dollars."

"Oh." I slide my arms out of the sleeves.

He wags his head back and forth, considering. "What can you pay?"

"Three dollars?"

"Three fifty," he says. "That old thing's been sitting around for months. I need to get rid of it."

"Done!" I exclaim.

I exit the store still wearing the robe, and head back up to Peggy's.

This morning, when I tried to face the typewriter, I once again drew a blank. *Family.* I thought I could write about my own, but they suddenly felt as foreign to me as French people. French people made me think of La Grenouille, and that made me think about Bernard. And how he still hasn't called. I considered calling him, but told myself not to be weak. Another hour passed, in which I clipped my toenails, braided and unbraided my hair, and scanned my face for blackheads.

"What are you doing?" L'il demanded.

"I've got writer's block."

"There's no such thing as writer's block," she proclaimed. "If you can't write it's because you don't have anything to say. Or you're avoiding something."

"Hmph," I said, squeezing my skin, wondering if maybe I just wasn't a writer after all.

"Don't do that," L'il yelped. "You'll only make it worse. Why don't you go for a walk or something?"

So I did. And I knew exactly where to go. Down to Samantha's neighborhood, where I'd spotted the vintage store on Seventh Avenue.

I catch my reflection in a plate-glass window and stop to admire the robe. I hope it will bring me good luck and I'll be able to write. I'm getting nervous. I don't want to end up in Viktor's 99.9 percent of failed students.

"My Lord!" L'il exclaims. "You look like something the cat dragged in."

"I feel like something the cat dragged in. But look what I got." I spin around to show off my new purchase.

L'il appears doubtful, and I realize how flaky I must seem, shopping instead of writing. Why do I keep evading my work? Is it because I'm afraid of being confronted by my lack of abilities?

I collapse onto the love seat and gently ease off my sandals. "It was about fifty blocks away and my feet are killing me. But it was worth it," I add, trying to convince myself.

"I finished my poem," L'il says casually.

I smile, biting back envy. Am I the only one who has to struggle? L'il doesn't seem to labor at all. But that's probably because she's way more talented.

"And I got some Chinese food, too," she says. "Moo shu pork. There's plenty left over if you want some."

"Oh, L'il. I don't want to eat your food."

"No need to stand on ceremony." She shrugs. "Besides,

you've got to eat. How can you work if you're hungry?"

She's right. And it will give me a few more minutes to put off writing.

L'il sits on my bed as I polish off the moo shu pork straight from the carton.

"Don't you ever get scared?" I ask.

"Of what?" she says.

"Of not being good enough."

"You mean at writing?" L'il asks.

I nod. "What if I'm the only one who thinks I can do it and no one else does? What if I'm completely fooling myself—"

"Oh, Carrie." She smiles. "Don't you know that every writer feels that way? Fear is part of the job."

She picks up her towel to take a long bath, and while she's in the bathroom, I manage to eke out one page, and then two. I type in a title, "Home." I cross it out and write, "My New Home." This somehow reminds me of Samantha Jones. I picture her in her four-poster bed, wearing fancy lingerie and eating chocolates, which, for some strange reason, is how I imagine she spends her weekends.

I push these thoughts out of my head and try to focus, but now the throbbing in my feet is overwhelming and I can't concentrate for the pain.

"L'il?" I knock on the bathroom door. "Do you have any aspirin?"

"I don't think so," she calls out.

"Damn." Peggy must have aspirin somewhere. "Can I come in?" I ask. L'il is in the shallow tub, under a soft pile of bubbles. I check the medicine cabinet. Nothing. I look around, my gaze resting on the closed door to Peggy's bedroom.

Don't do it, I think, remembering Peggy's one final rule. We're not allowed into her room. Ever. Under any circumstances. Her bedroom is strictly verboten.

I carefully open the door.

"What are you doing?" L'il shrieks, jumping out of the tub and grabbing her towel. Remnants of bubbles cling to her shoulders.

I put my finger to my lips to shush her. "I'm only looking for aspirin. Peggy's so cheap, she probably keeps the aspirin hidden in her room."

"What if she realizes some of her aspirin is missing?"

"Even Peggy can't be that crazy." I push the door wider. "You'd have to be really wacky to count your aspirin. Besides," I hiss, "aren't you dying to know what her room's like?"

The blinds are drawn, so it takes a second for my eyes to adjust. When they do, I squeal in horror.

Peggy's bed is covered with bears. Not real bears, of course, but what appears to be every variation on the stuffed animal kind. There are big bears and small bears, bears holding tennis rackets and bears wearing aprons. Bears with pink fur and bears with earmuffs. There's even a bear that appears to be constructed entirely of clothespins.

"That's her big secret?" L'il asks, disappointed. "Bears?"

"She's a middle-aged woman. What kind of middle-aged woman has stuffed animals all over her room?"

"Maybe she collects them," L'il says. "People do, you know."

"Not normal people." I pick up the pink bear and hold it in front of L'il's face. "Hello," I say, in a funny voice. "My name is Peggy and I'd like to explain a few of my rules. But first I need to put on my rubber suit—"

"Carrie, stop," L'il pleads, but it's too late. We're already in stitches.

"Aspirin," I remind her. "If you were Peggy, where would you keep it?" My eye goes to the top drawer in Peggy's bedside table. Like everything else in the apartment, it's cheap, and when I tug on the knob, the whole drawer flies out, spilling the contents onto the floor.

"Now she's going to kill us for sure," L'il moans.

"We won't tell her," I say, scrambling to pick up the pieces. "Besides, it's only a bunch of pictures." I begin gathering the snapshots when I'm startled by what seems to be an image of a naked breast.

I take a closer look.

Then I scream and drop the picture like it's on fire.

"What is it?" L'il shouts.

I sit down on the floor, shaking my head in disbelief. I pick up the photograph and examine it more closely, still not convinced. But it's exactly what I thought it was. I shuffle through the other photographs, trying to suppress my laughter. They're of Peggy, all right, but in each and every one of them she's buck naked.

And not just any old naked. She's arranged herself like a model in a porn magazine.

Unfortunately, she doesn't exactly look like one. "L'il?" I ask, wanting to delve into this mystery of why Peggy would have posed for these photographs and who might have taken them, but L'il is gone. I hear a faint thud as the door to her room closes, followed by the louder bang of the front door. And before I have a chance to move, Peggy is standing over me.

We both freeze. Peggy's eyes get bigger and bigger as her face turns from red to purple and I wonder if her head is going to explode. She opens her mouth and raises her arm.

The photograph falls from my fingers as I shrink back in fear.

"Get out! Get out!" she screams, swatting at my head. I drop to my hands and knees, and before she can figure out what's happening, crawl between her legs to the hall. I stand up, run to my room, and shut the door.

She immediately yanks it open. "Listen, Peggy—" I begin, but really, what can I say? Besides, she's shouting too much for me to get a word in.

"The minute I laid eyes on you, I knew you were trouble. Who do you think you are, coming into my home and going through my things? Where did you grow up? In a barn? What kind of animal are you?"

"A bear?" I want to say. But she's right. I did violate her privacy. I knew it was wrong and I did it anyway. It was worth it to see those naked photos, though.

"I want you, and your stuff, out of here now!"

"But—"

"You should have thought about your 'buts' before you went into my room," she snaps, which doesn't help much, because after seeing those photographs, all I *can* think about is her butt. Indeed, I'm so absorbed by the image, I hardly notice her segue into how good it will be for me to spend a night or two on the streets.

The next thing I know, she's pulling my suitcase out from under the bed and heaving it onto the mattress. "Start packing," she orders. "I'm going out for twenty minutes and when I get back, you'd better be gone. If you're not, I'm calling the police."

She grabs her purse and storms out.

I stand there in shock. The plywood door opens and L'il comes in, white as a sheet.

"Oh, Lord, Carrie," she whispers. "What are you going to do?"

"Leave," I say, picking up a pile of my clothes and dumping them into the suitcase.

"But where will you go? This is New York City. It's night and it's dangerous. You can't be out there on your own. What if you're attacked or end up dead? Maybe you could go to the YMCA—"

I'm suddenly angry. At Peggy and her irrationality. "I have plenty of places to go."

"Like where?"

Good question.

I slip on the Chinese robe for good luck and snap my suitcase shut. L'il looks dazed, as if she can't believe I'm going to carry through with my plan. I give her a wan smile and a brief hug. My stomach is clenched in fear, but I'm determined not to back down.

L'il follows me to the street, begging me to stay. "You can't just leave with no place to go."

"Honestly, L'il. I'll be fine," I insist, with way more confidence than I actually feel.

I hold out my arm and hail a cab.

"Carrie! Don't," L'il pleads as I shove my suitcase and typewriter into the backseat.

The cab driver turns around. "Where to?"

I close my eyes and grimace.

Thirty minutes later, stuck outside in the torrential rain of a thunderstorm, I wonder what I was thinking.

Samantha's not home. In the back of my mind, I guess I was figuring if Samantha wasn't there, I could always go to Bernard's and throw myself on his mercy. But now, having splurged on one cab, I don't have enough money for another.

A rivulet of water runs down the back of my neck. My robe is soaked and I'm scared and miserable but I attempt to convince myself that everything is going to be all right. I imagine the rain washing the city clean, and washing Peggy away with it.

But another rumble of thunder changes my mind, and suddenly I'm being attacked by pinpricks of ice. The rain has turned to hail and I need to find shelter.

I drag my suitcase around the corner, where I spot a small, glass-fronted shop at the bottom of a short flight of steps. At first, I'm not sure it even is a store, but then I see a big sign that reads, NO CHANGE—DO NOT EVEN ASK. I peer through the glass and spot a shelf dotted with candy bars. I pull open the door and go inside.

A strange, hairless man who looks quite a bit like a boiled beet is sitting on a stool behind a Plexiglas barrier. There's a small opening cut into the plastic where you can slide your money across the counter. I'm dripping all over the floor, but the man doesn't seem to mind. "What can I get for you, girlie?" he asks.

I look around in confusion. The store is even tinier on the inside than it looked from the outside. The walls are thin and there's a door in the back that's bolted shut.

I shiver. "How much for a Hershey's bar?"

"Twenty-five cents."

I reach into my pocket and extract a quarter, sliding it through the slot. I pick out a candy bar and start to unwrap it. It's pretty dusty, and I immediately feel sorry for the man. Apparently he doesn't have much business. I wonder how he's able to survive.

Then I wonder if *I'm* going to be able to survive. What if Samantha doesn't come home? What if she goes to Charlie's apartment instead?

No. She has to come home. She just *has to.* I close my eyes and picture her leaning against her desk. *You really are a sparrow,* she says.

And then, as if I've willed it to happen, a cab stops on the corner and Samantha gets out. She's clutching her briefcase across her chest, her head ducked against the rain, when suddenly, she stops, looking defeated. By the weather and, just possibly, by something else.

"Hey!" I yank open the door and race toward her, waving my arms. "It's me!"

"Huh?" She's startled, but quickly regains her composure. "You," she says, wiping the rain from her face. "What are you doing here?"

I muster up my last ounce of confidence. I shrug, as if I'm used to standing on corners in the rain. "I was wondering—"

"You got kicked out of your apartment," she says.

"How did you know?"

She laughs. "The suitcase and the fact that you're soaked to the skin. Besides, that's what always happens to sparrows. Jesus, Carrie. What am I going to do with you?"

CHAPTER EIGHT

"You're alive!" L'il throws her arms around my neck.

"Of course I am," I say, as if getting kicked out of an apartment happens to me all the time. We're standing in front of The New School, waiting to go in.

"I was worried." She steps back to give me a searching once-over. "You don't look so good."

"Hangover," I explain. "Couldn't be helped."

"Did you finish your story?"

I laugh. My voice sounds like it's been scraped over the sidewalk. "Hardly."

"You'll have to tell Viktor what happened."

"*Viktor?* Since when did you start calling him by his first name?"

"It's his name, isn't it?" She starts into the building ahead of me.

I was beyond relieved when Samantha showed up and

rescued me, explaining how she'd decided to give Charlie the night off to keep him guessing. And I was thrilled when I realized Charlie's night off meant Samantha's night out, and that she expected me to accompany her. It wasn't until I discovered that Samantha's night out literally meant *all* night that I began to get worried.

First we went to a place called One Fifth. The inside was a replica of a cruise ship, and even though it was technically a restaurant, no one was eating. Apparently, no one actually eats in trendy restaurants because you're only supposed to be *seen* in them. The bartender bought us drinks, and then two guys started buying us drinks, and then someone decided we should all go to this club, Xenon, where everyone was purple under the black lights. It was pretty funny because no one was acting like they were purple, and just when I was getting used to it, Samantha found some other people who were going to a club called The Saint, so we all piled into taxis and went there. The ceiling was painted like the sky, illuminated by tiny lights over a revolving dance floor that spun like a record, and people kept falling down. Then I got caught up dancing with a bunch of guys who were wearing wigs and lost Samantha but found her again in the bathroom, where you could hear people having sex. I danced on top of a speaker and one of my shoes fell off and I couldn't find it, and Samantha made me leave without it because she said she was hungry, and we were in a taxi again with more people, and Samantha made the driver stop at a twenty-four-hour drugstore in Chinatown to see if they had shoes. Mysteriously, they did but they were bamboo flip-flops. I tried them on along with a pointy hat, which was apparently so hilarious, everyone else had to have bamboo flip-flops and pointy hats as well. Finally, we managed to get back into the taxi, which took us to a metal diner where we ate scrambled eggs.

I think we got home around five a.m. I was too scared to look at my watch, but the birds were singing. Who knew there were so many damn birds in New York? I figured I'd never be able to sleep with the racket, so I got up and started typing. About fifteen minutes later Samantha came out of her room, pushing a velvet sleeping mask onto her forehead.

"Carrie," she said. "What are you *doing*?"

"Writing?"

"Can you please save it for morning?" She groaned in pain. "Plus, I've got terrible cramps. They don't call it 'the curse' for nothing."

"Sure," I said, flustered. The last thing I needed was to annoy her or her cramps.

Now, following L'il's neat head up the stairs to class, I'm racked with guilt. I need to start writing. I have to get serious.

I only have fifty-six days left.

I run after L'il and tap her on the shoulder. "Did Bernard call?"

She shakes her head and gives me a pitying look.

Today we're treated to the pleasure of Capote Duncan's work. It's the last thing I need, considering my condition.

I rest my head in my hand, wondering how I'm going to get through this class.

"'She held the razor between her fingers. A piece of glass. A piece of ice. A savior. The sun was a moon. The ice became snow as she slipped away, a pilgrim lost in a blizzard.'" Capote adjusts his glasses and smiles, pleased with himself.

"Thank you, Capote," Viktor Greene says. He's slumped in a chair in the back of the room.

"You're welcome," Capote says, as if he's just done us an enormous favor. I study him closely in an attempt to discover what L'il and, supposedly, hundreds of other women in New York, including models, see in him. He does have surprisingly masculine hands, the kind of hands that look like they'd know how to sail a boat or hammer a nail or pull you up from the edge of a steep rock face. Too bad he doesn't have the personality to match.

"Any comments on Capote's story?" Viktor asks. I turn around to give Capote a dirty look. Yes, I want to say. I have a response. It sucked. I actually feel like I might puke. There's nothing I hate more than some cheesy romantic story about a perfect girl who every guy is in love with and then she kills herself. Because she's so tragic. When in reality, she's just crazy. But, of course, the guy can't see that. All he can see is her beauty. And her sadness.

Guys can be so stupid.

"Who is this girl again?" Ryan asks, with a touch of skepticism that tells me I'm not alone in my thinking.

Capote stiffens. "My sister. I thought that was pretty

apparent from the beginning."

"I guess I missed it," Ryan says. "I mean, the way you write about her—she doesn't sound like your sister. She sounds like some girl you're in love with." Ryan's being pretty hard on Capote, especially since they're supposed to be friends. But that's what it's like in this class. When you enter the room, you're a writer first.

"It does sound a little . . . incestuous," I add.

Capote looks at me. It's the first time he's acknowledged my presence, but only because he has to. "That's the point of the story. And if you didn't get the point, I can't help you."

I press on. "But is it really *you*?"

"It's fiction," he snaps. "Of course it's not really me."

"So if it's not really you or your sister, I guess we can criticize her after all," Ryan says as the rest of the class titters. "I wouldn't want to say something negative about a member of your family."

"A writer has to be able to look at everything in their life with a critical eye," L'il says. "Including their own family. They do say the artist must kill the father in order to succeed."

"But Capote hasn't killed anyone. Yet," I say. The class snickers.

"This discussion is totally stupid," Rainbow interjects. It's the second time she's deigned to speak in class, and her tone is world-weary, defiant and superior, designed to put us in our place. Which seems to be somewhere far below hers. "Anyway, the sister is dead. So what difference does it make what we say about her? I thought the story was great. I identified with the sister's pain. It seemed very real to me."

"Thank you," Capote says, as if he and Rainbow are two aristocrats stranded in a crowd of peasants.

Now I'm sure Rainbow is sleeping with him. I wonder if she knows about the model.

Capote takes his seat, and once again I find myself staring at him with open curiosity. Studied in profile, his nose has character—a distinctive bump of the type passed from one generation to another—"the Duncan nose"—likely the bane of every female family member. Combined with closely spaced eyes, the nose would give the face a rodent-like demeanor, but Capote's eyes are wide-set. And now that I'm really looking at him, a dark inky blue.

"Will L'il read her poem, please?" Viktor murmurs.

L'il's poem is about a flower and its effect on three generations of women. When she's finished, there's silence.

"That was wonderful." Viktor shuffles to the front of the room.

"Anyone can do it," L'il says with cheerful modesty. She might be the only genuine person in this class, probably because she really does have talent.

Viktor Greene stoops over and picks up his knapsack. I can't imagine what's in it besides papers, but the weight tilts him perilously to one side, like a boat listing in the waves. "We reconvene on Wednesday. In the meantime, for those of you who haven't handed in your first story, you need to do so by Monday." He scans the room. "And I need to see

Carrie Bradshaw in my office."

Huh? I look to L'il, wondering if she might know the reason for this unexpected meeting, but she only shrugs.

Maybe Viktor Greene is going to tell me I don't belong in this class.

Or *maybe* he's going to tell me I'm the most talented, brilliant student he's ever had.

Or maybe . . . I give up. Who knows what he wants. I smoke a cigarette and make my way to his office.

The door is closed. I knock.

It opens a crack, and the first thing I'm confronted by is Viktor's enormous mustache, followed by his soft sloping face, as if skin and muscle have abandoned any attempt to attach to the skull. He silently swings open the door and I enter a small room filled with a mess of papers and books and magazines. He removes a pile from the chair in front of his desk and looks around helplessly.

"Over there," I say, pointing to a relatively small mound of books perched on the sill.

"Right," he says, plopping the papers on top, where they balance precariously.

I sit down in the chair as he clumsily drops into his seat.

"Well." He touches his mustache.

It's still there, I want to scream, but don't.

"How do you feel about this class?" he asks.

"Good. Really good." I'm pretty sure I suck, but there's no reason to give him ammunition.

"How long have you wanted to become a writer?"

"Since I was a kid, I guess."

"You guess?"

"I *know*." Why do conversations with teachers always go around in circles?

"Why?"

I sit on my hands and stare. There's no good answer to this question. "I'm a genius and the world can't live without my words," is too pretentious and probably untrue. "I love books and want to write the great American novel" is true, but is also what every student wants, because why else would they be in this class? "It's my calling," sounds overly dramatic. On the other hand, why is he even asking me this question? Can't he tell that I *should* be a writer?

In consequence, I end up saying nothing. Instead, I open my eyes as wide as possible.

This has an interesting effect. Viktor Greene suddenly becomes uncomfortable, shifting in his chair and then opening and closing a drawer.

"Why do you have that mustache?" I ask.

"Mmph?" He covers his lips with his tapered, waxy fingers.

"Is it because you think that mustache is a part of you?" I've never talked to a teacher this way, but I'm not exactly in school. I'm in a seminar. And who says Viktor Greene has to be the authority?

"Don't you like the mustache?" he asks.

Hold on. Viktor Greene is *vain*?

"Sure," I say, thinking about how vanity is a weakness. It's a chink in the armor. If you're vain, you should do everything possible to conceal it.

I lean forward slightly to emphasize my admiration. "Your mustache is really, er, great."

"You think so?" he repeats.

Jeez. What a Pandora's box. If he only knew how Ryan and I make fun of that mustache. I've even given it a name: "Waldo." Waldo is not any ordinary mustache, however. He's able to go on adventures without Viktor. He goes to the zoo and Studio 54, and the other day, he even went to Benihana, where the chef mistook him for a piece of meat and accidently chopped him up.

Waldo recovered, though. He's immortal and cannot be destroyed.

"Your mustache," I continue. "It's kind of like me wanting to be a writer. It's a part of me. I don't know who I'd be if I didn't want to be a writer." I deliver this line with great conviction, and Viktor nods.

"That's fine, then," he says.

I smile.

"I was worried you'd come to New York to become famous."

What?

Now I'm confused. And kind of insulted. "What does my wanting to be a writer have to do with wanting to become famous?"

He wets his lips. "Some people think writing is glamorous. They make the mistake of thinking it's a good vehicle for becoming famous. But it isn't. It's only hard work. Years and years and years of it, and even then, most people don't get what they want out of it."

Like you, I wonder? "I'm not worried, Mr. Greene."

He sadly fingers his mustache.

"Is that it?" I stand up.

"Yes," he says. "That's it."

"Thanks, Mr. Greene." I glare at him, wondering what Waldo would say.

But when I get outside, I'm shaking.

Why shouldn't I? I demand silently. Why shouldn't I become a famous writer? Like Norman Mailer. Or Philip Roth. And F. Scott Fitzgerald and Hemingway and all those other men. Why can't I be like them? I mean, what is the point of becoming a writer if no one reads what you've written?

Damn Viktor Greene and The New School. Why do I have to keep proving myself all the time? Why can't I be like L'il, with everyone praising and encouraging me? Or Rainbow, with her sense of entitlement. I bet Viktor Greene never asked Rainbow why she wanted to be a writer.

Or what if—I wince—Viktor Greene is right? I'm *not* a writer after all.

I light a cigarette and start walking.

Why did I come to New York? Why did I think I could make it here?

I walk as fast as I can, pausing only to light yet another cigarette. By the time I get to Sixteenth Street, I figure I've probably smoked nearly half a pack.

I feel sick.

It's one thing to write for the school newspaper. But New York is on a whole different level. It's a mountain, with a few successful people like Bernard at the top, and a mass of dreamers and strivers like me at the bottom.

And then there are people like Viktor, who aren't afraid to tell you that you're never going to reach that peak.

I flick my cigarette butt onto the sidewalk and grind it out in a fury. A fire truck roars down the avenue, horns blaring. "I am pissed off," I scream, my frustration mingling with the wail of the siren.

A couple of people glance my way but don't pause. I'm only another crazy person on the street in New York.

I stomp down the sidewalk to Samantha's building, take the stairs two at a time, unlock the three bolts, and fling myself onto her bed. Which makes me feel, once again, like an interloper. It's a four-poster with a black coverlet and what Samantha calls silk sheets, which, she claims, prevent wrinkles. Except they're really made of some kind of super slippery polyester and I have to push my foot against one of the posts to keep from sliding onto the floor.

I grab a pillow and put it over my head. I think about Viktor Greene and Bernard. I think about how I'm all alone. How I'm constantly having to pull myself up from the depths of despair, trying to convince myself to try one more time. I bury my face deeper into the pillow.

Maybe I should give up. Go back home. And in two months, I'll go to Brown.

My throat closes at the thought of leaving New York.

Am I going to allow what Viktor Greene said to cause me to quit? I have to talk to someone. But who?

That girl. The one with the red hair. The one who found my Carrie bag. She seems like the kind of person who would have something to say about my situation. She hates life, and right now, I do too.

What was her name, again? Miranda. Miranda Hobbes. "H-o-b-b-e-s." I hear her voice in my head.

I pick up the phone and dial information.

CHAPTER NINE

"All men are a disappointment. No matter what anyone says." Miranda Hobbes glares at the cover of *Cosmopolitan*. "'How to Get Him and Keep Him,'" she says, reading the cover line aloud in disgust.

She places the magazine back in the rack. "Even if you could get Him—and why do they always capitalize His name like He's God—I can personally guarantee He wouldn't be worth keeping."

"What about Paul Newman?" I count out four dollars and hand the money to the cashier. "I'm sure he's worth keeping. Joanne Woodward thinks so."

"First of all, no one knows what goes on between two people in a marriage. And secondly, he's an actor. Which means by definition he's a narcissist." She looks at the package of chicken thighs doubtfully. "Are you sure you know what you're doing?"

I put the chicken thighs, rice, and the tomato into a bag, feigning ignorance about her concerns. Truth is, I'm a little worried about the chicken myself. Besides being minuscule, the supermarket is none too clean. Maybe that's why no one cooks in New York. "Don't you think everyone's a narcissist?" I ask. "I have this theory that all anyone ever really thinks about is themself. It's human nature."

"Is this human nature?" Miranda demands, still absorbed by the rack of magazines. "'How to De-dimple Your Thighs in Thirty Days.' 'Kissable Lips.' 'How to Tell What He's Really Thinking.' I can tell you what he's really thinking. *Nothing.*"

I laugh, partly because she's probably right, and partly because I'm in the giddy throes of a new friendship.

It's my second Saturday in New York, and what no one tells you is how the city empties out on the weekends. Samantha goes to the Hamptons with Charlie, and even L'il said she was going to the Adirondacks. I told myself I didn't mind. I'd had enough excitement for the week, and besides, I had to write.

And I did work, for a few hours, anyway. Then I started to feel lonely. I decided there must be a particular kind of lonely in New York, because once you start thinking about all the millions of people out there eating or shopping or going to movies or museums with friends, it's pretty depressing not to be one of them.

I tried calling Maggie, who's spending the summer in South Carolina, but her sister said she was at the beach.

Then I tried Walt. He was in Provincetown. I even called my father. But all he said was how much I must be looking forward to Brown in the fall and he'd talk more but he had an appointment.

I wished I could tell him what a hard time I was having with my writing class, but it would have been pointless. He's never been interested in my writing anyway, convinced it's a phase I'll get over when I go to Brown.

Then I looked through Samantha's closet. I found a pair of neon-blue Fiorucci boots that I particularly coveted, and even tried them on, but they were too big. I also discovered an old leather biker jacket that appeared to be from her former life—whatever that was.

I tried Miranda Hobbes again. I'd actually tried her three times since Thursday, but there was no answer.

But apparently she doesn't protest on Saturdays, because she picked up the phone on the first ring.

"Hello?" she asked suspiciously.

"Miranda? It's Carrie Bradshaw."

"Oh."

"I was wondering . . . what are you doing right now? Do you want to get a cup of coffee or something?"

"I don't know."

"Oh," I said again, disappointed.

I guess she felt sorry for me, because she asked, "Where do you live?"

"Chelsea?"

"I'm on Bank Street. There's a coffee shop around

the corner. As long as I don't have to take the subway, I guess I could meet you."

We spent two hours at the coffee shop, discovering all kinds of things we had in common. Like we both went to our local high schools. And we both loved the book *The Consensus* as kids. When I told her I knew the author, Mary Gordon Howard, she laughed. "Somehow, I knew you were the type who would." And over yet another cup of coffee, we began to have that magical, unspoken realization that we were going to be friends.

Then we decided we were hungry, but also admitted we didn't have any money. Hence my plan to cook us dinner.

"Why do magazines do this to women?" Miranda complains now, glaring at *Vogue*. "It's all about creating insecurity. Trying to make women feel like they're not good enough. And when women don't feel like they're good enough, guess what?"

"What?" I ask, picking up the grocery bag.

"Men win. That's how they keep us down," she concludes.

"Except the problem with women's magazines is that they're written by women," I point out.

"That only shows you how deep this thing goes. Men have made women coconspirators in their own oppression. I mean, if you spend all your time worrying about leg hair, how can you possibly have time to take over the world?"

I want to point out that shaving your legs takes about five minutes, leaving plenty of time for world-taking-over, but I know she only means it as a rhetorical question.

"Are you sure your roommate won't mind my coming over?" she asks.

"She's not really my roommate. She's engaged. She lives with her boyfriend. She's in the Hamptons anyway."

"Lucky you," Miranda says as we start up the five flights of stairs to the apartment. By the third flight, she's panting. "How do you do this every day?"

"It's better than living with Peggy."

"That Peggy sounds like a nightmare. People like that should be in therapy."

"She probably is, and it's not working."

"Then she needs to find a new shrink," Miranda says, puffing. "I could recommend mine."

"You see a shrink?" I ask, startled, fitting my key into the lock.

"Of course. Don't you?"

"No. Why would I?"

"Because everyone needs to see a shrink. Otherwise you keep repeating the same unhealthy patterns."

"But what if you don't have unhealthy patterns?" I throw open the door and Miranda stumbles in. She flops onto the futon.

"Thinking you don't have unhealthy patterns is an unhealthy pattern in itself. And everyone has something unhealthy from their childhood. If you don't deal with it, it can ruin your life."

I open the cantilevered doors to reveal the small kitchen and place the grocery bag onto the few inches of counter space next to the tiny sink. "What's yours?" I ask.

"My mother."

I find a bent skillet in the oven, pour in some oil, and light one of the two burners with a match. "How do you know all this stuff?"

"My father's a shrink. And my mother is a perfectionist. She used to spend an hour every morning styling my hair before I went to school. Which is why I cut it and dyed it as soon as I could get away from her. My father says she suffers from guilt. But I say she's a classic narcissist. Everything is about her. Including me."

"But she's your mother," I say, placing the chicken thighs in the hot oil.

"And I hate her. Which is okay, because she hates me, too. I don't fit into her narrow idea of what a daughter should be. What about your mother?"

I pause, but she doesn't seem all that interested in the answer. She's examining the collection of photographs Samantha keeps on the side table, with the zeal of an anthropologist who has suddenly discovered an old piece of pottery. "Is this the woman who lives here? Christ, is she an egomaniac or what? She's in every photograph."

"It *is* her apartment."

"Don't you think it's weird when someone has photographs of themselves all over the place? It's like they're trying to prove they exist."

"I don't know her that well."

"What is she?" Miranda sneers. "An actress? A model? Who has five photographs of themselves in a bikini?"

"She's in advertising."

"Another business designed to make women feel inse-cure."

She gets up and comes into the kitchen. "Where'd you learn to cook?"

"I sort of had to."

"My mother tried to teach me, but I refused. I rejected anything that could turn me into a housewife." She leans over the skillet. "That smells pretty good though."

"It will be," I say, adding two inches of water to the pan. When it boils, I pour in the rice, add the tomato, then turn down the heat and cover the skillet. "And it's cheap. We get a whole meal for four dollars."

"Which reminds me." She reaches into her pocket and pulls out two one-dollar bills. "My share. I hate owing anyone anything. Don't you?"

We go back into the living room and curl up on either end of the couch. We light cigarettes, and I inhale contem-platively. "What if I can't become a writer and I have to get married, instead. What if I have to ask my husband for money? I couldn't do it. I'd hate myself."

"Marriage turns women into whores," Miranda declares. "The whole thing is a sham."

"That's what I think too!" I can hardly believe I've found someone who shares my secret suspicions. "But if you let people know, they want to kill you. They hate the truth."

"That's what happens to women when they go against the system." Miranda fumbles awkwardly with her cig-arette. I can tell she's not really a smoker, but maybe, because everyone else in New York smokes, she's trying it out. "And I, for one, plan to do something about it," she continues, coughing.

"What?"

"Haven't decided yet. But I will." She narrows her eyes. "You're lucky you're going to be a writer. You can change people's perceptions. You should write about marriage and what a lie it is. Or even sex."

"Sex?" I grind my cigarette out in the ashtray.

"Sex. It's the biggest sham of all. I mean, your whole life, all you ever hear is how you're supposed to save yourself for marriage. And how it's so special. And then you finally do it. And you're like, *that's it*? This is what everyone's been raving about?"

"You're kidding."

"Come on," she says. "You've done it."

I grimace. "Actually, I haven't."

"Really?" She's surprised. Then pragmatic. "Well, it doesn't make a bit of difference. You're not missing anything. In fact, if you haven't done it, I would recommend not doing it. Ever." She pauses. "And the worst thing about it? Once you do it, you have to *keep* doing it. Because the guy expects you to."

"Why'd you do it in the first place?" I ask, lighting another cigarette.

"Pressure. I had the same boyfriend all through high school. Although, I have to admit, I was curious."

"And?"

"Everything but 'it' is fine," she says matter-of-factly.

"'It' itself is boring as hell. That's what no one tells you. How boring it is. And it hurts."

"I have a friend who did it for the first time and loved it. She said she had an actual orgasm."

"From intercourse?" Miranda yelps. "She's lying. Everyone knows women cannot have an orgasm from intercourse only."

"Then why does everyone do it?"

"Because they have to," she practically screams. "And then you just lie there, waiting for it to be over. The only good thing about it is that it only lasts a minute or two."

"Maybe you have to do it a lot to like it."

"Nope. I've done it at least twenty times, and each time it was as bad as the first." She crosses her arms. "You'll see. And it doesn't matter who you do it with. I did it with another guy six months ago to make sure it wasn't me, and it was just as lousy."

"What about with an older guy?" I ask, thinking about Bernard. "A guy with experience—"

"How old?"

"Thirty?"

"That's even worse," she declares. "His thing could be all wrinkly. There's nothing more disgusting than a wrinkly thing."

"Have you ever seen one?" I ask.

"Nope. And I hope I never have to."

"Well," I say, laughing. "What if I do it and I like it? Then what?"

Miranda snickers, as if this is not a possibility. She jabs her finger at Samantha's photograph. "I bet even she thinks it's boring. She looks like she likes it, but I promise you, she's pretending. Just like every other goddamn woman on the planet."

PART TWO

Bite the Big Apple

CHAPTER TEN

Bernard!

"He called me," I sing to myself like a little bird, skipping down Forty-fifth Street into the Theater District. Apparently, he did call my old apartment and Peggy told him I no longer lived there and she didn't know where I was. And then Peggy had the gall to ask Bernard if she could audition for his new play. Bernard coldly suggested she call his casting director, and suddenly, Peggy's memory as to my whereabouts mysteriously returned. "She's staying with a friend of hers. Cindy? Samantha?"

Just as I'd given up hope of him calling me on his own, Bernard, bless his soul, managed to put two and two together and rang me first.

"Can you meet me at the theater around lunchtime tomorrow?" he asked.

Bernard sure has some odd ideas about what constitutes

a date. But he is a wunderkind, so perhaps he lives outside the rules.

The Theater District is so exciting, even during the day. There are the flashing lights of Broadway, the cute little restaurants, and the seedy theaters promising "LIVE GIRLS," which makes me scratch my head. Would anyone want dead ones?

And then on to Shubert Alley. It's only a narrow street, but I can't help imagining what it would be like to have my own play performed in this theater. If that happened, it would mean everything in my life was perfect.

As per Bernard's instructions, I enter through the stage door. It's nothing special—just a dingy lobby with gray cement walls and peeling linoleum on the floor and a man stationed behind a little window that slides open. "Bernard Singer?" I ask.

The guard looks up from his *Post*, his face a map of veins. "Here to audition?" he asks, taking down a clip-board.

"No, I'm a friend."

"Ah. You're the young lady. Carrie Bradshaw."

"That's right."

"He said he was expecting you. He's out, but he'll be back soon. He said I should take you on a backstage tour."

"Yes, please," I exclaim. The Shubert Theatre. *A Chorus Line.* Backstage!

"Ever been here before?"

"No!" I can't keep the squeal of excitement out of my voice.

"Mr. Shubert founded the theater in 1913." The guard pulls apart a heavy black curtain to reveal the stage. "Katharine Hepburn performed here in 1939. *The Philadelphia Story*."

"On this very stage?"

"Used to stand right where you are now, every evening, before her first entrance. 'Jimmy,' she'd say, 'how's the house tonight?' And I'd say, 'All the better for you being here, Miss Hepburn.'"

"Jimmy," I plead. "Could I—"

He smiles, catching my enthusiasm. "Only for a second. No one's allowed on that stage who ain't union—"

And before he can change his mind, I'm crossing the boards, looking out at the house. I stride to the footlights and take in row after row of velvet chairs, the balconies, the luxurious boxes on the side. And for a moment, I imagine the theater filled with people, all there to see little ol' me.

I fling out my arms. "Hello, New York!"

"Oh my." I hear a deep, throaty laugh, followed by the sound of one person clapping. I turn around in horror, and there, in the wings, is Bernard, wearing sunglasses, an open white shirt, and Gucci loafers. Next to him is the clapper, whom I immediately recognize as the actress Margie Shephard. His ex-wife. What the hell is she doing here? And what must she think of me, after witnessing my little performance?

It doesn't take long to find out, because the next thing she says is, "I see a star is born," in a flinty voice.

"Take it easy, Margie," Bernard says, having the sense to at least sound slightly annoyed by her.

"Hello. I'm Carrie." I hold out my hand.

She does me the honor of shaking it, but doesn't provide her own name, confident that I already know who she is. I think I'll always remember what her hand feels like—the long, smooth fingers, the palm, warm and firm. Someday I'll probably even say, "I met Margie Shephard. I shook her hand and she was amazing."

Margie opens her mouth prettily, and emits a sly laugh. "Well, well," she says.

Nobody can say, "Well, well," and get away with it, except Margie Shephard. I can't stop gaping at her. She isn't technically beautiful, but has some kind of inner light that makes you think she's one of the most attractive women you've ever seen.

I totally understand why Bernard married her. What I can't understand is why he isn't *still* married to her.

I don't stand a chance.

"Nice to meet you," Margie says, with a whisper of a wink at Bernard.

"Me too." I stumble over the words. Margie probably thinks I'm an idiot.

She twinkles at Bernard. "We'll continue this discussion later."

"I suggest we don't continue it at all," Bernard mutters. Apparently he isn't as starstruck by her as I am.

"I'll call you." Again, there's the pretty smile, and the eyes that seem to know everything. "Good-bye, Carrie."

"Good-bye." I'm suddenly disappointed to see her go.

Bernard and I watch as she strides through the hallway,

one hand caressing the back of her neck—a poignant reminder to Bernard of what he's missing.

I swallow, prepared to apologize for my little show, but instead of being embarrassed, Bernard grabs me under my arms and presses me to him, spinning me around like a child. He kisses me all over my face. "Am I glad to see you, kiddo. You've got great timing. Did anyone ever tell you that?"

"No—"

"You do. If you hadn't been here, I wouldn't have been able to get rid of her. C'mon." He grabs my hand and briskly leads me out the other end of the alley like a madman on a mission. "It's you, baby," he says. "When I saw you, it suddenly made sense."

"Sense?" I ask breathlessly, trying to keep up, confused about his sudden adoration. It's what I'd been hoping for, but now that he actually seems smitten, I'm a bit wary.

"Margie is over. Finished. I'm moving on." We come out on Forty-fourth Street and head to Fifth Avenue. "You're a woman. Where can I buy some furniture?"

"Furniture?" I laugh. "I have no idea."

"Someone's got to know. Excuse me." He accosts a nicely dressed lady in pearls. "Where's the best place to buy furniture around here?"

"What kind of furniture?" she asks, as if this kind of encounter with a stranger is perfectly normal.

"A table. And some sheets. And maybe a couch."

"Bloomingdale's," she says, and moves on.

Bernard looks down at me. "You busy this afternoon?

Got time to do some furniture shopping?"

"Sure." It wasn't exactly the romantic lunch I had in mind, but so what?

We jump into a cab. "Bloomingdale's," Bernard directs the driver. "And make it fast. We need to buy sheets."

The cabbie smiles. "You two lovebirds getting married?"

"The opposite. I'm officially getting unmarried," Bernard says, and squeezes my leg.

When we get to Bloomingdale's, Bernard and I run around the fifth floor like two little kids, trying out the beds, bouncing on the sofas, pretending to drink tea from the china display. One of the salesmen recognizes Bernard ("Oh, Mr. Singer. It's an honor. Will you sign this sales slip for my mother?") and follows us around like a puppy.

Bernard buys a dining room set, a brown leather couch and ottoman, an armoire, and a pile of pillows, sheets, and towels. "Can I have it delivered right away?"

"Normally, no," the salesman simpers. "But for you, Mr. Singer, I'll try."

"Now what?" I ask Bernard.

"We go to my apartment and wait."

"I still don't understand why Margie took the furniture," I say as we stroll up Fifty-ninth Street.

"To punish me, I suppose."

"But I thought she was the one who left," I venture, carefully avoiding the word "cheated."

"Chickadee, don't you know anything about women? Fair play doesn't enter into their vocabulary."

"Not all women. I would never be like that. I'd be reasonable."

"That's what's so great about you. You're unspoiled." Still holding hands, we breeze into his building, right past the nasty doorman. Take that, buddy, I think. In the apartment, Bernard puts on a record. Frank Sinatra. "Let's dance," he says. "I want to celebrate."

"I can't dance to this."

"Sure you can." He opens his arms. I rest one hand on his shoulder the way we learned to do in ballroom dancing classes, a million years ago when I was thirteen. He pulls me tighter, his breath scorching my neck. "I like you, Carrie Bradshaw. I really do. Do you think you can like me back?"

"Of course," I giggle. "If I didn't like you, I wouldn't dance with you."

"I don't believe that's true. I think you'd dance with a man and when you got tired of him, you'd dance with another."

"Never." I twist my head to look at his face. His eyes are closed, his expression beatific. I still can't fathom his new attitude. If I didn't know better, I'd think he was falling in love with me.

Or maybe he's falling in love with the idea of falling in love with me. Maybe he wants to be in love with someone and I've ended up in the right place at the right time.

And suddenly, I'm nervous. If Bernard were to fall in love with me, I'd never be able to live up to his expectations.

I'd end up being a disappointment. And what am I going to do if he tries to have sex with me?

"I want to know what happened," I say, trying to change the subject. "Between you and Margie."

"I told you what happened," he murmurs.

"I meant this afternoon. What were you arguing about?"

"Does it matter?"

"I guess not."

"The apartment," he says. "We were arguing about the apartment. She wants it back and I said no."

"She wants the apartment, too?" I ask, astounded.

"She might have convinced me if it weren't for you." He takes my hand and twirls me around and around. "When I saw you on that stage, I thought, That's a sign."

"What kind of sign?"

"A sign that I should put my life back together. Buy furniture. Make this place my home again."

He lets go of my hand but I keep spinning and spinning until I collapse to the floor. I lie still as the bare room revolves around me and for a moment I picture myself in an insane asylum, in a white space with no furniture. I close my eyes, and when I open them again, Bernard's face is hovering above mine. He has pretty eyelashes and a crease on either side of his mouth. A small mole is buried in the hair of his right eyebrow. "Crazy, crazy girl," he whispers, before he leans in to kiss me.

I allow myself to be carried away by the kiss. Bernard's mouth envelops mine, absorbing all reality until life seems to consist only of these lips and tongues engaged in a funny dance of their own.

I freeze.

And suddenly, I'm suffocating. I put my hands on Bernard's shoulders. "I can't."

"Something I said?" His lips close back over mine. My heart races. An artery throbs in my neck. I wriggle away.

He sits back on his haunches. "Too intense?"

I fan my face and laugh a little. "Maybe."

"You're not used to guys like me."

"I guess not!" I stand up and brush myself off.

There's a clap of thunder outside. Bernard comes up behind me, pushing my hair aside to mouth my neck. "Have you ever made love in a thunderstorm?"

"Not yet." I giggle, trying to put him off.

"Maybe it's time you did."

Oh no. Right now? Is this the moment? My body trembles. I don't think I can do it. I'm not prepared.

Bernard massages my shoulders. "Relax." He leans in and nibbles my earlobe.

If I do it with him now, he's going to compare me to Margie. I imagine them having sex all the time, in this apartment. I picture Margie kissing Bernard with an intensity that matches his, like in the movies. Then I see myself lying naked on that bare mattress, my arms and legs splayed out stiffly to the side.

Why didn't I do it with Sebastian when I had the chance? At least I'd know how to do it. I never guessed someone like Bernard would come along. A grown man who obviously assumes his girlfriend has sex regularly and wants to do it all the time.

"C'mon," he says gently, pulling at my hand.

I balk and he squints at me. "Don't you want to make love?"

"I do," I say quickly, not wanting to hurt his feelings. "It's just that—"

"Yes?"

"I forgot my birth control."

"Oh." He drops my hand and laughs. "What do you use? A diaphragm?"

I blush. "Yeah. Sure. Uh-huh." I nod.

"A diaphragm's a pain. And it's messy. With the cream. You use a cream with it, right?"

"Yes." I mentally pedal backward to the health classes we had in high school. I picture the diaphragm, a funny little object that looks like a rubber cap. But I don't recall any mention of cream.

"Why don't you go on the pill? It's so much easier."

"I will. Yes indeedy." I agree vigorously. "I keep meaning to get a prescription but—"

"I know. You don't want to take the pill until you know the relationship is serious."

My throat goes dry. Is this relationship serious? Am I ready for it? But in the next second, Bernard is lying on the bed, and has turned on the TV. Is it my imagination, or does he look slightly relieved?

"C'mere, puddy tat," he says, patting the spot next to

him. He holds out his hands. "Do you think my nails are too long?"

"Too long for what?" I frown.

"Seriously," he says.

I take his hand in mine, running my fingers over the palm. His hands are lovely and lean, and I can't help thinking about those hands on my body. The sexiest part of a man is his hands. If a man has girlish hands, it doesn't matter what the rest of him is like. "They are, a little."

"Could you cut them and file them for me?" he asks.

What?

"Margie used to do it for me," he explains. My heart softens. He's so sweet. I had no idea a man could be so cozy. But it's not surprising, given my limited experience with romance.

Bernard goes into the bathroom to get clippers and a nail file. I look around the spare bedroom. Poor Bernard, I think, for the hundredth time.

"Primate grooming," he says when he returns. He sits across from me, and I begin carefully clipping his nails. I can hear the rain drumming on the awning below while I file rhythmically, the motion and the rain putting me into a soothing trance. Bernard strokes my arm and then my face as I lean over his hand.

"This is nice, isn't it?" he asks.

"Yes," I reply simply.

"This is what it should be like. No fighting. Or arguing about whose turn it is to walk the dog."

"Did you have a dog?"

"A long-haired dachshund. He was Margie's dog first, but she could never be bothered to pay attention to him."

"Is that what happened to you?"

"Yeah. She stopped paying attention to me, too. It was all about her career."

"That's terrible," I say, filing contentedly. I can't imagine any woman ever losing interest in Bernard.

CHAPTER ELEVEN

I wake up the next morning with an idea.

Maybe it's because of all the time I spent with Bernard, but I'm finally inspired. I know what I have to do: write a play.

This brilliant notion lasts for about three seconds before it's crushed under a million and one reasons why it's impossible. Like Bernard will think I'm copying him. Like I won't be able to do it anyway. Like Viktor Greene won't let me.

I sit on Samantha's bed with my legs crossed, making faces. The fact is, I need to prove I can make it in New York. But how? Maybe I'll get lucky and be discovered. Or maybe it will turn out I have hidden talents even I don't know about. I clutch the silk bedcovers like a survivor clinging to a lifeboat. Despite my fears, it seems my life is starting to take off here—and Brown is less than seven weeks away.

I pluck at a thread. Not that there's anything wrong with Brown, but I've already gotten in there. On the other hand, if New York were a college, I'd still be applying. And if all these other people can make it in New York, why can't I?

I jump out of bed and run around the apartment just for the hell of it, throwing on my clothes while typing the following three sentences: "I will succeed. I must succeed. Damn everyone," and then I grab my Carrie bag and practically slide down all five flights to the lobby.

I beetle up Fourteenth Street, expertly weaving through the crowd, picturing my feet flying a few inches off the ground. I turn right on Broadway and hurl myself into the Strand.

The Strand is a legendary secondhand bookstore where you can find any book for cheap. It's musty and all the salespeople have a very big attitude, like they're the keepers of the flame of high literature. Which wouldn't matter, except the salespeople cannot be avoided. If you're looking for a specific book, you can't find it without help.

I buttonhole a weedy fellow wearing a sweater with elbow patches.

"Do you have *Death of a Salesman*?"

"I should hope so," he says, crossing his arms.

"And *The Importance of Being Earnest*? And maybe *The Little Foxes*? *The Women*? *Our Town*?"

"Slow down. Do I look like a shoe salesman?"

"No," I murmur, as I follow him into the stacks.

After fifteen minutes of searching, he finally finds *The Women*. At the end of the stacks I spot Ryan from class. He's got his nose in *Swann's Way*, scratching his head and jiggling his foot as if overcome by the text.

"Hey," I say.

"Hey." He closes the book. "What are you doing here?"

"Going to write a play." I indicate my small pile of books. "Thought I should read a few first."

He laughs. "Good idea. The best way to avoid writing is by reading. Then you can at least *pretend* you're working."

I like Ryan. He seems okay as a person, unlike his best friend, Capote Duncan.

I pay for my books, and when I turn around, Ryan is still there. He has the air of someone who doesn't quite know what to do with himself. "Want to get a coffee?" he asks.

"Sure."

"I've got a couple of hours to kill before I have to meet my fiancée," he says.

"You're engaged?" Ryan can't be more than twenty-one or two. He seems too young to get married.

"My fiancée's a model." He scratches his cheek, as if he's both proud and ashamed of her profession. "I always find if a woman really, really, really wants you to do something, you should do it. It's easier in the long run."

"So you don't *want* to marry her?"

He smiles awkwardly. "If I sleep with a woman ten times, I think I should marry her. I can't help myself. If she

117

weren't so busy, we'd already be married by now."

We walk down Broadway and go into a hamburger joint. "I wish I could find a guy like that," I say jokingly. "A guy who does everything I want."

"Can't you?" He peers at me in confusion.

"I don't think I'm the man-wrangler type."

"I'm surprised." He absentmindedly picks up his fork and tests the prongs on his thumb. "You're pretty hot."

I grin. Coming from another guy, I'd take this as a pickup line. But Ryan doesn't seem to have an agenda. I suspect he's one of those guys who says exactly what he's thinking and is then stupefied by the consequences.

We order coffee. "How'd you meet her? Your model fiancée?"

He jiggles his leg. "Capote introduced us."

"What is with that guy?" I ask.

"Don't tell me you're interested too."

I give him a dirty look. "Are you kidding? I can't stand him. He's supposedly got all these women after him—"

"I know." Ryan nods in appreciative agreement. "I mean, the guy's not even that good-looking."

"He's like the guy every girl has a crush on in sixth grade. And no one can figure out why."

Ryan laughs. "I always thought *I* was that guy."

"Were you?"

"Kind of, yeah."

I can see it. Ryan at twelve—masses of dark hair, bright blue eyes—a real teen heartthrob. "No wonder you're engaged to a model."

"She wasn't a model when we met, though. She was studying to be a veterinary assistant."

I take a sip of my coffee. "That's like the default profession for girls who don't know what they want to do. But they 'love' animals."

"Harsh but true."

"How'd she become a model?"

"Discovered," Ryan says. "She came to visit me in New York and a guy came up to her in Bergdorf's and gave her his card."

"And she couldn't resist."

"Don't all women want to be models?" he asks.

"No. But all men want to date them."

He chuckles. "You should come to this party tonight. It's a fashion show for some downtown designer. Becky's modeling in it. And Capote's coming."

"Capote?" I scoff. "How can I resist?" But I write down the address on a napkin, anyway.

After Ryan, I pop by Viktor Greene's office to tell him about my exciting new plan to write a play. If I'm really jazzed about it, he'll have to say yes.

Viktor's door is wide open as if he's expecting someone, so I walk right in. He grunts, startled, and pets his mustache.

He doesn't offer me a seat, so I stand in front of his desk. "I've figured out what my project should be."

"Yes?" he asks cautiously, his eyes going past me to the hallway.

"I'm going to write a play!"

"That's fine."

"You don't mind? It's not a short story or a poem—"

"As long as it's about family," he says quickly.

"It will be." I nod. "I'm thinking it should be about this couple. They've been married for a few years and they hate each other—"

Viktor stares at me blankly. It appears he has nothing more to say. I stand awkwardly for a moment then add, "I'll get started right away."

"Good idea." It's now patently clear he wants me out of there. I give him a little wave as I exit.

I run right into L'il. "Carrie!" She flushes.

"I'm going to write a play," I inform her excitedly. "Viktor says it's okay."

"That's perfect for you. I can't wait to read it."

"I've got to write it first."

She steps to the side, trying to get around me.

"What are you doing tonight?" I ask quickly. "Want to have dinner with me and my friend Miranda?"

"I'd love to, but—"

Viktor Greene comes out of his office. L'il glances up at him. "You sure?" I ask, pressing her. "Miranda's really interesting. And we're going to go to one of those cheap Indian places on Sixth Street. Miranda says she knows the best ones—"

L'il blinks as she focuses her attention back on me. "All right. I guess I could—"

"Meet me on Fourteenth and Broadway at eight-thirty.

120

And afterward, we can go to this party," I say over my shoulder.

I leave L'il and Viktor standing there, staring at me like I'm a mugger who has suddenly decided to spare them.

CHAPTER TWELVE

I write three pages of my play. It's all about Peggy and her lover—the guy who took those naughty photos—whom I've named Moorehouse. Peggy and Moorehouse are having an argument about toilet paper. I think it's pretty funny and pretty real—I mean, what couple doesn't argue about toilet paper—and I actually feel satisfied with my work.

At eight o'clock, I pick up Miranda at her house. Miranda's lucky—she has an old aunt who lives in a small, run-down townhouse, consisting of four floors and a basement, where Miranda lives. The basement has its own entrance and two windows just below the sidewalk. It would be perfect but for the fact that it's damp and perpetually dark.

I ring the bell, thinking about how I love the way I can walk to my friends' apartments and how my life has this frenetic, unstructured pace where I never know exactly what's going to happen. Miranda opens the door, her hair still wet from the shower. "I'm not ready."

"That's okay." I stroll past her and plop onto an ancient sofa covered in worn damask. Miranda's aunt used to be rich, about thirty years ago. Then her husband took off with another woman and left her flat broke, except for the house. The aunt worked as a waitress and put herself through school and now she's a professor of Women's Studies at NYU. The apartment is filled with books like *Woman, Culture, and Society* and *Women: A Feminist Perspective*. I always think the best part about Miranda's apartment is the books. The only books Samantha has are astrology, self-help, and *The Kama Sutra*. Other than those, she mostly reads magazines.

Miranda goes into her room to change. I light a cigarette and idly survey the bookshelves, picking out a book by Andrea Dworkin. It falls open and I read the following: "just some wet, ratty, bedraggled thing, semen caked on you, his piss running down your legs . . ."

"What's that?" Miranda asks, peering over my shoulder. "Oh. I love that book."

"Really? I just read this part about semen caked on you—"

"And what about the part when it oozes out and runs down your leg?"

"Says here, it's pee."

"Semen, pee, what's the difference?" Miranda shrugs. "It's all gross." She slings a brown saddlebag over her shoulder. "Did you see that guy after all?"

"'That guy' happens to have a name. Bernard. And yes, I did see him. I'm pretty crazy about him. We went furniture shopping."

"So he's already turned you into his slave."

"We're having fun," I say pointedly.

"Has he tried to get you into bed?"

"No," I say, somewhat defensively. "I need to go on the pill, first. And I've decided I'm not going to sleep with him until my eighteenth birthday."

"I'll be sure to mark it on my calendar. 'Carrie's birthday and lose-her-virginity day.'"

"Maybe you'd like to be there. For moral support."

"Does Bernie have any idea you're planning to use him as a stud service?"

"I believe the word 'stud' only applies if you're planning on reproducing. Which I'm not."

"In that case, 'dud' might be more appropriate."

"Bernard is no dud," I say threateningly. "He's a famous playwright—"

"Yada yada yada."

"And I'm sure his 'sword' is mightier than his word."

"You'd better hope so," Miranda says. She raises her index finger and slowly lowers it into a crook as we burst out laughing.

"I just love these prices," L'il says, scanning the menu.

"I know." Miranda nods, pleased. "You can get a whole meal for three dollars."

"And a whole beer for fifty cents," I add.

We're seated at a table in the Indian restaurant Miranda kept telling us about, although it wasn't so easy to find. We walked up and down the block three times past nearly identical restaurants until Miranda insisted this was the place, recognizable by the three peacock feathers in a vase in the window. The tablecloths are red-and-white-checkered plastic; the knives and forks tinny. The air is musty and sweet.

"This reminds me of home," L'il says.

"You live in India?" Miranda asks, astonished.

"No, silly. North Carolina." She gestures around the restaurant. "This is exactly like one of those barbecue places tucked off the freeway."

"Freeway?" Miranda queries.

"Highway," I translate.

I hope the whole dinner isn't like this. Miranda and L'il are both intense in their own way, so I assumed they'd like each other. And I need them to get along. I miss having a group of friends. Sometimes it feels like every part of my life is so different, I'm constantly visiting another planet.

"You're a poet?" Miranda asks L'il.

"Indeed," she replies. "What about you?"

I jump in. "Miranda's majoring in Women's Studies."

L'il smiles. "No offense, but what can you do with that?"

"Anything." Miranda glares. She's probably wondering what you can do with a poetry degree.

"Miranda is doing very important work. Protesting

125

against pornography. And she volunteers at a women's shelter," I say.

"You're a feminist." L'il nods.

"I wouldn't consider being anything else."

"I'm a feminist," I volunteer. "I think every woman should be a feminist—"

"But it means you hate men." L'il takes a sip of her beer, and stares straight across the table at Miranda.

"What if I do?" Miranda says.

This is not going well. "I don't hate all men. Just some men," I say, trying to lighten the atmosphere. "Especially men whom I like and they don't like me back."

L'il gives me a sharp look, meaning she's determined to lock horns with Miranda. "If you hate men, how can you ever marry? Have babies?"

"I guess if you truly believe a woman's only purpose in life is to marry and have children—" Miranda breaks off and gives L'il a superior smile.

"I never said that," L'il replies calmly. "Just because you're married and have children doesn't mean it's the only point to your life. You can do all kinds of things and have children."

"Good answer," I say.

"I happen to think it's wrong to bring a child into this patriarchal society," Miranda replies swiftly. And just as the conversation is about to go completely haywire, our samosas arrive.

I quickly grab one of the pastries, dip it into a red sauce, and pop it into my mouth. "Fantastic," I exclaim, as my eyes begin to water and my tongue burns. I frantically wave my hand in front of my face, reaching for a glass of water, as Miranda and L'il laugh. "Why didn't you tell me that sauce was hot?"

"Why didn't you ask?" Miranda giggles. "You dove right in. I figured you knew what you were doing."

"I do!"

"Does that include sex?" Miranda asks wickedly.

"What is it with everyone and sex?"

"It's very exciting," L'il says.

"Ha," I say. "She hates it." I point to Miranda.

"Only the 'intercourse' part." Miranda makes quotation marks with her fingers. "Why do they call it intercourse anyway? It makes it sound like it's some kind of conversation. Which it isn't. It's penetration, pure and simple. There's no give-and-take involved."

Our curries arrive. One is white and creamy. The other two are brown and red, and look dangerous. I take a scoop of the white curry. L'il takes some of the brown and pushes it toward Miranda. "If you know how to do it properly, supposedly it *is* like a conversation," she says.

"How?" Miranda asks, thoroughly unconvinced.

"The penis and vagina communicate."

"No way," I say.

"My mother told me," L'il says. "It's an act of love."

"It's an act of war," Miranda objects, getting heated. "The penis is saying, 'Let me in,' and the vagina is saying, 'Get the hell away from me, creep.'"

"Or maybe the vagina is saying, 'Hurry up,'" I add.

L'il dabs at her mouth, and smiles. "That's the problem. If you think it's going to be terrible, it will be."

"Why?" I dip my fork into the red curry to test it for hotness.

"Tension. If you tense up, it makes it more difficult. And painful. That's why the woman should always have an orgasm first," L'il says nonchalantly.

Miranda finishes her beer and immediately orders another. "That's the dumbest thing I've ever heard. How can you tell if you've even had this supposed orgasm?"

L'il laughs.

"Yeah." I gulp. "How?"

L'il slides back in her chair and puts on a teacherly face. "You're kidding, right?"

"I'm not," I say, looking at Miranda. Her face is closed, as if she doesn't want to hear this.

"You have to know your own body," L'il says cryptically.

"Meaning?"

"Masturbation."

"Eeeeewwww." Miranda puts her hands over ears.

"Masturbation is not a dirty word," L'il scolds. "It's part of a healthy sexuality."

"And I suppose your mother told you this, too?" Miranda demands.

L'il shrugs. "My mother's a nurse. She doesn't believe in mincing words when it comes to health. She says healthy sex is simply a part of a healthy life."

"Well." I'm impressed.

"And she did all that consciousness-raising stuff," L'il continues. "In the early seventies. When the women sit around in a circle with mirrors—"

"Aha." This, I suppose, explains everything.

"She's a lesbian now," L'il says casually.

Miranda's mouth opens as if she's about to speak, but suddenly thinks better of it. For once, she has nothing to say.

After dinner, L'il begs off the party, claiming a headache. Miranda doesn't want to go either, but I point out if she goes home, she'll look like she's sulking.

The party is on Broadway and Seventeenth Street in a building that was once a bank. A security guard tells us to take the elevator to the fourth floor. I figure this must be a big party if the guard is letting people in so easily.

The elevator opens into a white space with crazy art on the walls. As we're taking it in, a small, rotund man with hair the color of butter bustles over, beaming.

"I'm Bobby," he says, extending his hand to me.

"Carrie Bradshaw. And Miranda Hobbes." Miranda gives Bobby a stiff smile while Bobby squints, summing us up.

"Carrie Bradshaw," he says, like he's delighted to meet me. "And what do you do?"

"Why is that always the first question out of everyone's mouth?" Miranda mutters.

I glance at her so she knows I agree, and say boldly, "I'm a playwright."

"A playwright!" Bobby exclaims. "That's good. I love writers. Everyone loves writers. I used to be a writer before I became an artist."

"You're an artist?" Miranda asks, as if this can't possibly be true.

Bobby ignores her. "You must tell me the names of your plays. Perhaps I've seen one—"

"I doubt it," I falter, never expecting he'd assume I'd actually written a play. But now that I've said it, I can't take it back.

"Because she hasn't written any," Miranda blurts out.

"Actually"—I give her a steely look—"I'm in the middle of writing one right now."

"Wonderful," Bobby cheers. "And when it's finished, we can stage it here."

"Really?" This Bobby must be some kind of crazy.

"Of course," he says with a swagger, leading us farther into the room. "I'm doing all kinds of experimental productions. This is a nexus—a nexus," he repeats, savoring the word, "of art, fashion, and photography. I haven't done a play yet, but it seems exactly the right sort of thing. And we can get all kinds of people to come."

Before I can begin to process the idea, Bobby is pawing his way through the crowd, with Miranda and me on his heels. "Do you know Jinx? The fashion designer? We're showing her new collection this evening. You'll love her," he insists, depositing us in front of a scary-looking woman with long, blue-black hair, about a hundred coats of eyeliner, and black lipstick. She's leaning over to light a joint when Bobby interrupts.

"Jinx, darling," he says, which is extremely ironic, as it's clear Jinx is nobody's darling. "This is"—he searches for my name—"Carrie. And her friend," he adds, indicating Miranda.

"Nice to meet you," I say. "I can't wait to see your fashion show."

"Me too," she responds, inhaling the smoke and holding it in her lungs. "If those friggin' models don't get here soon—I hate friggin' models, don't you?" Jinx holds up her left hand, displaying a contraption of metal through which each finger is inserted. "Brass knuckles," she says. "Don't even think about messing with me."

"I won't." I look around, desperate to escape, and spot Capote Duncan in the corner.

"We have to go," I say, nudging Miranda. "I just saw a friend of mine—"

"What friend?" Miranda asks. God, she really is bad at parties. No wonder she didn't want to come.

"Someone I'm very happy to see right now." Which is patently untrue. But as Capote Duncan is the only person I know at this party, I'll take him.

And as we push through the crowd, I wonder if living in New York makes people crazy, or if they're crazy to begin with and New York attracts them like flies.

Capote is leaning against an air conditioner talking to a medium-tall girl with one of those noses that turns up like a little snout. She has masses of blond hair and brown eyes, which gives her an interesting look, and since she's with Capote, I assume she's one of the errant models Jinx was referring to.

"I'll give you a reading list," Capote is saying. "Hemingway. Fitzgerald. And Balzac." I immediately want to puke. Capote is always talking about Balzac, which reminds me of why I can't stand him. He's so pretentious.

"Hel*lo*," I say in a singsong voice.

Capote's head jerks around as if he's anticipating someone special. When he sees me, his face falls. He appears to undergo a brief, internal struggle, as if he'd like to ignore me, but his Southern manners won't let him. Eventually, he manages to summon a smile.

"Carrie Bradshaw," he says, in a slow drawl. "I didn't know you were coming to this."

"Why would you? Ryan invited me."

At the name "Ryan," the modely girl pricks up her ears. Capote sighs. "This is Becky. Ryan's fiancée."

"Ryan's told me so much about you," I say, extending my hand. She takes it limply. Then her face screws up like she's about to cry, and she runs off.

Capote looks at me accusingly. "Nice job."

"What'd I do?"

"She just told me she's planning to dump Ryan."

"That so?" I snicker. "And here I thought you were trying to improve her brain. The reading list?" I point out.

Capote's face tightens. "That wasn't smart, Carrie," he says, pushing past us to follow Becky.

"It's all about being smart with you, isn't it?" I shout after him.

"Nice to meet you, too," Miranda calls out sarcastically.

Unfortunately, the Capote exchange has pushed Miranda over the edge, and she insists on going home. Given Capote's rudeness, I don't really want to stay at the party alone, either.

I'm bummed we didn't get to see the fashion show. On the other hand, I'm glad I met that Bobby character. During the walk home under the salty yellow lights, I keep talking about my play and how it would be so cool to have it performed in Bobby's space, until Miranda finally turns to me and says, "Will you just write the damn thing?"

"Will you come to the reading?"

"Why wouldn't I? Other than the fact that Bobby and all his friends are complete idiots. And what about Capote Duncan? Who the hell does he think he is?"

"He's a big jerk," I say, remembering the expression of fury on his face. I smile. I suddenly realize I enjoy making Capote Duncan angry.

Miranda and I part ways, with me promising to call her tomorrow. When I get inside my building, I swear I can hear Samantha's phone ringing all the way down the stairs. A ringing phone is like a call to arms for me, and I take the steps two at a time. After about the tenth ring, the phone stops, but then it starts again.

I burst through the door and grab it from where it's slid under the couch. "Hello?" I ask breathlessly.

"What are you doing on Thursday night?" It's Samantha herself.

"Thursday night?" I ask dumbly. When is Thursday night? Oh, right, the day after tomorrow. "I have no idea."

"I need you to help me with something. I'm throwing an intimate little dinner party with Charlie at his apartment—"

"I'd love to come," I gush, thinking she's inviting me. "Can I bring Bernard, too?"

"I don't think that's a good idea."

"Why not?"

"Don't take this the wrong way," she purrs. "But I actually need you to cook. You did say you could cook, right?"

I frown. "I might have. But—"

"I can't cook at all. And I don't want Charlie to find out."

"So I'll be in the kitchen all night."

"You'd be doing me an enormous favor," she coos. "And you did say you'd do me a favor someday, if I asked."

"That's true," I admit reluctantly, still not convinced.

"Look," she says, putting on the pressure. "If it's that big a deal, I'll trade you. One night of cooking for any pair of my shoes."

"But your feet are bigger than mine."

"You can put tissue in the toes."

"What about the Fiorucci boots?" I ask craftily.

She pauses, mulling it over. "Oh, why not?" she agrees. "I can always get Charlie to buy me another pair. Especially when he finds out what a wonderful cook I am."

"Right," I mutter as she says good-bye.

How did I get into this mess? Technically, I do know

134

how to cook. But I've only cooked for friends. How many people is she expecting at this intimate dinner? Six? Or sixteen?

The phone rings again. Probably Samantha calling back to discuss the menu. "Samantha?" I ask, cautiously.

"Who's Samantha?" demands the familiar voice on the other end.

"Maggie!" I yip.

"What's going on? I tried calling your number and this nasty woman said you didn't live there anymore. Then your sister said you moved—"

"It's a long story," I say, settling onto the couch for a chat.

"You can tell me tomorrow," she exclaims. "I'm coming to New York!"

"You *are*?"

"My sister and I are visiting our cousins in Pennsylvania. I'm taking the bus into the city tomorrow morning. I figured I'd stay with you for a couple of nights."

"Oh, Mags, that's fantastic. I can't wait to see you. I have so much to tell you. I'm dating this guy—"

"Maggie?" someone asks in the background.

"Got to go. I'll see you tomorrow. My bus gets in at nine a.m. Can you meet me at Port Authority?"

"Of course." I hang up the phone, thrilled. Then I remember I'm supposed to see Bernard tomorrow night. But maybe Maggie can come with us. I can't wait for her to meet him. She'll probably freak out when she sees how sexy he is.

Full of excitement, I sit down at the typewriter to write a few more pages of my play. I'm determined to take advantage of Bobby's offer to stage a reading in his space. And maybe, just maybe, if the reading is a success, I can stay in New York. I'll have officially become a writer and I won't have to go to Brown at all.

I work like a demon until three a.m., when I force myself to go to bed. I toss and turn with anticipation, thinking about my play and Bernard and all the interesting people I've met. What will Maggie think of my new life?

Surely she has to be impressed.

CHAPTER THIRTEEN

"You actually live here?" Maggie asks, aghast.

"Isn't it great?"

She drops her knapsack on the floor and surveys the apartment. "Where's the bathroom?"

"Right here," I say, pointing to the door behind her. "The bedroom is there. And this is the living room."

She exhales. "It's so small."

"It's big for New York. You should have seen where I was living before."

"But—" She walks to the window and looks out. "It's so dirty. And this building. I mean, it's kind of falling down. And those people in the hallway—"

"The old couple? They've lived here their whole lives. Samantha keeps hoping they'll die so she can get their apartment," I quip, without thinking. "It has two bedrooms and the rent is cheaper than this place."

Maggie's eyes widen. "That's awful. Wanting someone

to die so you can get their apartment. This Samantha sounds like a horrible person. But I'm not surprised, being Donna LaDonna's cousin."

"It's only a joke."

"Well," she says, patting the futon to make sure it's sturdy before she sits down, "I should hope so."

I look at her in surprise. When did Maggie become this prim and proper? She hasn't stopped complaining about New York since I met her at Port Authority. The smell. The noise. The people. The subway terrified her. When we got out on Fourteenth Street and Eighth Avenue, I had to coach her on when to cross the street.

And now she's insulting my apartment? And Samantha? But maybe it's not intentional. Of course she assumes Samantha must be like Donna LaDonna. I would, too, if I didn't know better.

I sit across from her, leaning forward. "I can't believe you're actually here."

"I can't either," she says, full of enthusiasm. We're both trying to recapture our old rapport.

"You look great!"

"Thanks," she says. "I think I lost five pounds. I started windsurfing. Have you ever windsurfed? It's amazing. And the beaches are so beautiful. And there are all these little fishing villages."

"Wow." The thought of fishing villages and long stretches of empty sand suddenly sounds as quaint as living two hundred years ago.

"What about guys?" I ask.

She wriggles her feet out of her tennis shoes, rubbing

one heel like she's already developed a blister. "They're gorgeous. Hank—that's this one guy—he's six two and he's on the varsity tennis team at Duke. I swear, Carrie, we should both transfer to Duke. They have the hottest guys."

I smile. "We have lots of hot guys in New York, too—"

"Not like these guys." She sighs dramatically. "Hank would be perfect, except for one thing."

"He has a girlfriend?"

"No." She gives me a pointed look. "I would never date someone who had a girlfriend. Not after Lali."

"Lali." I shrug. Each mention of the past causes my intestines to lurch. Next thing I know, we'll be talking about Sebastian. And I really don't want to. Since I arrived in New York, I've barely thought about Lali or Sebastian or what went on last spring. It feels like all that stuff happened to someone else, not me. "So Hank," I say, attempting to remain in the present.

"He's . . ." She shakes her head, picks up her sneaker, and puts it down. "He's not . . . good in bed. Have you ever had that?"

"I've certainly heard about it."

"You still haven't—"

I try to brush this away as well. "What does that mean, exactly? 'Bad in bed'?"

"He doesn't really do anything. Just sticks it in. And then it's over in like three seconds."

"Isn't it always like that?" I ask, remembering what Miranda's told me.

"No. Peter was really good in bed."

"He was?" I still can't believe that nerdly old Peter was such a big stud.

"Didn't you know? That was one of the reasons I was so angry when we broke up."

"What are you going to do, then?" I ask, twisting my hair into a bun. "About Hank?"

She gives me a secret smile. "I'm not married. I'm not even engaged. So—"

"You're sleeping with another guy?"

She nods.

"You're sleeping with two guys. At the same time?" Now I'm aghast.

She gives me a look.

"Well, I'm sure you don't sleep with both of them at once, but—" I waver.

"It's the eighties. Things have changed. Besides, I'm using birth control."

"You could get a disease."

"Well, I haven't." She glares at me and I drop it. Maggie's always been stubborn. She does what she wants when she wants, and there's no talking her out of it. I absentmindedly rub my arm. "Who's this other guy?"

"Tom. He works at a gas station."

I look at her in consternation.

"What?" she demands. "What is wrong with a guy who works at a gas station?"

"It's such a cliché."

"First of all, he's an incredible windsurfer. And secondly, he's trying to make something of his life. His father has a fishing boat. He could be a fisherman, but he doesn't want to end up like his father. He's going to community college."

"That's great," I say, chastised.

"I know," she agrees. "I kind of miss him." She looks at her watch. "Do you mind if I call him? He's probably back from the beach by now."

"Go ahead." I hand her the phone. "I'm going to take a shower."

I head to the bathroom while I inform her of our itinerary: "Tonight we're going to meet Bernard for a drink at Peartree's, which is this fancy bar near the United Nations. And maybe this afternoon we can go to the White Horse Tavern for lunch. It's where all these famous writers hang out. And in between, we can go to Saks. I'd love you to meet my friend Miranda."

"Sure," she says, as if she's barely heard a word. Her concentration is focused entirely on the phone as she dials her boyfriend's—or should I say "lover's"—number.

Ryan and Capote Duncan are at the White Horse Tavern, seated at a table on the sidewalk. There's a pot of coffee in front them, and they look rough, like they went to bed late and just got up. Ryan's eyes are puffy and Capote is unshaven, his hair still damp from a shower.

"Hey," I say. They're next to the entrance, making it impossible to avoid them.

"Oh. Hi," Capote says wearily.

"This is my friend Maggie."

Ryan immediately perks up at the sight of Maggie's fresh-faced, all-American prettiness. "What are you girls up to?" he asks flirtatiously, which seems to be his default mode with women. "Do you want to join us?"

Capote gives him a frustrated look, but Maggie sits down before either one of us can object. She probably thinks Ryan is cute.

"Where are you from, Maggie?" Ryan asks.

"Castlebury. Carrie and I are best friends."

"Really?" Ryan asks, as if this is supremely interesting.

"Ryan and Capote are in my writing class," I explain.

"I still can't believe Carrie got into that class. And actually came to New York and everything."

Capote raises his eyebrows.

"What do you mean?" I ask, slightly annoyed.

"Well, no one ever really thought you'd become a writer." Maggie laughs.

"That's crazy. I always said I wanted to be a writer."

"But you didn't really write. Until senior year. Carrie worked on the school newspaper," she says to Ryan. She turns back to me. "But even then you didn't actually *write* for the newspaper, did you?"

I roll my eyes. Maggie never figured out I was writing all those stories for the newspaper under a pen name. And I'm not about to tell her now. On the other hand, she's making me sound like a dilettante in front of Capote. Who already seems to believe I don't belong in the class.

Fantastic. Maggie's just added fuel to his fire.

"I've always written a lot. I just didn't show you."

"Sure," Maggie says, grinning as if it's a joke. I sigh. Can't she see how much I've changed? Perhaps it's because she hasn't changed at all. She's the same old Maggie, so she probably assumes I'm the same as well.

"How was the fashion show?" I ask, diverting the conversation away from my supposed lack of writing.

"Great," Capote says listlessly.

"As you can tell, Capote is a man who knows nothing about fashion. He does, on the other hand, know quite a bit about models," Ryan says.

"Aren't models really stupid?" Maggie asks.

Ryan laughs. "That's not really the point."

"Ryan's engaged to a model," I say, wondering if Becky broke up with Ryan after all. He certainly isn't acting like a man who's been dumped. I glance at Capote inquiringly. He shrugs.

"When are you getting married?" Maggie asks politely. She and Ryan seem to have developed a connection and I wonder if she's disappointed he's not available.

"Next year," Ryan says easily. "She went to Paris this morning." Aha. So no need for a formal breakup after all. And poor Ryan, sitting here without a clue. On the other hand, Capote is probably perfectly capable of lying about the situation. He might have told me Becky was going to dump Ryan because he wants Becky for himself.

"Interesting," I say, to no one in particular.

Capote puts five dollars on the table. "I'm taking off."

"But—" Ryan objects. Capote gives a small shake of his head. "I guess I am too," Ryan says reluctantly. "Nice to meet you." He smiles at Maggie. "What are you doing tonight?"

"Carrie's making us have drinks with some guy."

"Bernard Singer is not 'some guy,'" I point out.

Capote pauses. "Bernard Singer? The playwright?"

"He's Carrie's boyfriend," Maggie says dismissively.

Capote's eyes widen behind his glasses. "You're dating Bernard Singer?" he asks, as if it can't be possible someone as esteemed as Bernard Singer would be interested in me.

"Uh-huh," I say, like it's no big deal.

Capote rests his hand on the back of his chair, unsure if he should go after all. "Bernard Singer is a genius."

"I know."

"I'd love to meet Bernard Singer," Ryan says. "Why don't we meet up with you guys for a drink, later?"

"That would be great," Maggie says.

As soon as they're gone, I groan.

"What?" Maggie asks, slightly defensive, knowing she's done something wrong.

"I can't bring them to drinks with Bernard."

"Why not? Ryan is *nice*," she says, as if he's the only normal person she's met so far. "I think he likes me."

"He's engaged."

"And?" Maggie picks up the menu. "You heard him. She's not around."

"He's a big flirt. It doesn't mean anything."

"I'm a flirt too. So it's perfect."

I was wrong. Maggie has changed. She's become a sex addict. And how can I explain about Bernard? "Bernard won't want to meet them—"

"Why not?"

"Because he's older. He's thirty."

She looks at me in horror. "Oh my God, Carrie. *Thirty?* That's disgusting!"

144

CHAPTER FOURTEEN

Given Maggie's attitude, I decide not to introduce her to Miranda after all. They'd probably get into a big fight about sex and I'd be stuck in the middle. Instead, we walk around the Village, where Maggie has her tarot cards read by a psychic—"I see a man with dark hair and blue eyes." "Ryan!" Maggie exclaims—and then I take her to Washington Square Park. There's the usual assortment of freaks, musicians, drug dealers, Hare Krishnas, and even two men walking on stilts, but all she can talk about is how there isn't any grass. "How can they call it a park if it's all dirt?"

"There probably was grass, once. And there *are* trees," I point out.

"But look at the leaves. They're black. Even the squirrels are dirty."

"Nobody notices the squirrels."

"They should," she says. "Did I tell you I'm going to

become a marine biologist?"

"No—"

"Hank's a biology major. He says if you're a marine biologist, you can live in California or Florida."

"But you don't like science."

"What are you talking about?" Maggie asks. "I didn't like chemistry, but I loved biology."

This is news to me. When we had to take biology in junior year, Maggie refused to memorize the names of the species and phyla, saying it was the kind of stupid thing that no one would ever use in their real life, so why bother?

We walk around a bit more, with Maggie becoming increasingly distressed about the heat and the odd people and how she thinks she's getting another blister. When I take her back to the apartment, she complains about the lack of effective air-conditioning. By the time we're supposed to leave to meet Bernard, I'm nearly at the end of my rope. Once more, Maggie balks at taking the subway. "I'm not going down there again," she declares. "It stinks. I don't know how you do it."

"It's the best way to get around," I say, trying to urge her down the stairs.

"Why can't we take a taxi? My sister and brother-in-law told me to take taxis because they're safe."

"They're also expensive. And I don't have the money."

"I have fifty dollars."

What? I wish she'd told me she had money earlier. She could have paid for our hamburgers.

When we're safely in a cab, Maggie reveals her conclusion

about why New Yorkers wear black. "It's because it's so dirty here. And black doesn't show dirt. Could you imagine what their clothes would look like if they wore white? I mean, who wears black in the summer?"

"I do," I say, nonplussed, especially as I'm in black. I'm wearing a black T-shirt, black leather pants that are two sizes too big—which I bought for 90 percent off at one of those cheap stores on Eighth Street—and pointy-toed black high heels from the 1950s that I found at the vintage shop.

"Black is for funerals," Maggie says. "But maybe New Yorkers like black because they feel like they've died."

"Or maybe for the first time in their lives they feel like they're *living*."

We get stuck in traffic by Macy's, and Maggie rolls down her window, fanning herself with her hand. "Look at all those people. This isn't living. It's surviving."

I have to admit, she's right about that. New York is about survival.

"Who are we meeting again?" she asks.

I sigh. "Bernard. The guy I'm seeing. The playwright."

"Plays are boring."

"Bernard doesn't agree. So please don't say 'plays are boring' when you meet him."

"Does he smoke a pipe?"

I glare at her.

"You said he was over thirty. I picture him smoking a pipe and wearing slippers."

"Thirty is not *old*. And don't tell him my age, either. He thinks I'm nineteen or twenty. So you have to be nineteen or twenty too. We're sophomores in college. Okay?"

"It's not good when you have to lie to a guy," Maggie says.

I take a deep breath. I want to ask her if Hank knows about Tom, but I don't.

When we finally push through the revolving door at Peartree's, I'm relieved to see Bernard's dark head bent over a newspaper, a glass of scotch in front of him. I still get the jitters when I know I'm going to see him. I count down the hours, reliving the sensation of his soft mouth on mine. As our rendezvous approaches, I get nervous, worried he's going to call and cancel, or not show up at all. I wish I didn't care so much, but I'm glad to have a guy who makes me feel this way.

I'm not sure Bernard feels the same, though. This morning, when I told him I had a friend coming to town unexpectedly, he said, "See your friend, then. We'll get together another time."

I emitted a gasp of disappointment. "But I thought we were going to see each other. *Tonight*."

"I'm not going anywhere. We can see each other when she leaves."

"I told her all about you. I want her to meet you."
"Why?"

"Because she's my best friend. And—" I broke off. I didn't know how to tell him that I wanted to show him off,

148

wanted Maggie to be impressed by him and my astonishing new life. Wanted her to see how far I'd come in such a short time.

I thought he should be able to tell from my voice.

"I don't want to babysit, Carrie," he said.

"You're not! Maggie's nineteen, maybe twenty—" I must have sounded very insistent, because he relented and agreed to meet for a drink.

"But only one drink," he cautioned. "You should spend time with your friend. She came to see you, not me."

I hate it when Bernard acts all serious.

Then I decided his comment was vaguely insulting. Of course I wanted to spend time with Maggie. But I wanted to see him, too. I thought about calling him back and canceling, just to show him I didn't care, but the reality of not seeing him was too depressing. And I suspected I'd secretly resent Maggie if I couldn't see Bernard because of her.

Things are tense enough with Maggie as it is. Getting ready to go out tonight, she kept saying she couldn't understand why I was "dressing up" to go to a bar. I tried to explain it wasn't that kind of bar, but she only stared at me in incomprehension and said, "Sometimes I really do not get you."

That's when I had a moment of clarity: Maggie is never going to like New York. She's constitutionally unsuited for the city. And when I realized this, my simmering animosity disappeared.

It's okay. It's not Maggie's fault, or mine. It's simply the way we are.

"There's Bernard," I say now, nudging Maggie past the maître d' to the bar. The interior of Peartree's is slick—black walls with chrome sconces, black marble tables, and a mirror along the back wall. Samantha says it's the best pickup place in town: She met Charlie here, and she gets irritated when he comes here without her, thinking he might meet another girl.

"Why is it so dark in here?" Maggie asks.

"It's supposed to be mysterious."

"What's mysterious about not being able to see who you're talking to?"

"Oh, Mags," I say, and laugh.

I creep up behind Bernard and tap him on the shoulder. He starts, grins, and picks up his drink. "I was beginning to think you weren't coming. Thought maybe you'd had a better offer."

"We did, but Maggie insisted we had to meet you first." I briefly touch the back of his hair. It's like a talisman for me. The first time I touched it I was shocked by its delicate softness, so much like a girl's, and I was surprised by how tender it made me feel toward him, as if his hair was a harbinger of his soft, kind heart.

"You must be the friend," he says, crinkling his eyes at Maggie. "Hello, friend."

"Hello," Maggie says cautiously. With her sun-bleached hair and pink cheeks, she's as creamy as a wedding cake, in sharp contrast to Bernard's angles and crooked nose, and the bags under his eyes that make him appear to be a person who spends all of his time inside—in dark caves like

Peartree's. I'm hoping Maggie will see the romance of him, but at the moment her expression is one of pure wariness.

"Drink?" Bernard asks, seemingly unaware of the culture clash.

"Vodka tonic," I say.

"I'll have a beer."

"Have a cocktail," I urge.

"I don't want a cocktail. I want a beer," Maggie insists.

"Let her have a beer if she wants one," Bernard says jocularly, the implication being that I'm needlessly giving Maggie a hard time.

"Sorry." My voice sounds hollow. I can already tell this is a mistake. I don't have a clue how to reconcile my past—Maggie—with my present—Bernard.

Two men squeeze in next to Maggie, intent on establishing a place at the bar. "Should we get a table?" Bernard asks. "We could eat. I'd be happy to feed you girls dinner."

Maggie gives me a questioning look. "I thought we were going to meet Ryan."

"We could have dinner. The food's good here."

"It's lousy. But the atmosphere is entertaining." Bernard waves to the maître d' and motions to an empty table near the window.

"Come on." I nudge Maggie and give her a meaningful look. Her stare is slightly hostile, as if she still doesn't understand why we're here.

Nevertheless, she follows Bernard to the table. He even pulls out her chair for her.

I sit next to him, determined to make this work. "How was the rehearsal?" I ask brightly.

"Lousy," Bernard says. He smiles at Maggie to include her in the conversation. "There's always a point in the middle of rehearsals when all the actors seem to forget their lines."

Which is exactly how I feel right now.

"Why is that?" Maggie asks, playing with her water glass.

"I have no idea."

"But they've been saying their lines for at least two weeks, right?" I frown, as if knowing Bernard has given me an inside track on the theater.

"Actors are like children," Bernard says. "They sulk and get their feelings hurt."

Maggie gives him a vacant look.

Bernard smiles tolerantly and opens his menu. "What would you like, Maggie?"

"I don't know. Duck breast?"

"Good choice." Bernard nods. "I'm going to have the usual. Skirt steak."

Why does he sound so formal? Was Bernard always like this and I never noticed before? "Bernard is a creature of habit," I explain to Maggie.

"That's nice," Maggie says.

"What do you always say about being a writer?" I ask him. "You know—about how you have to live a life of habit."

Bernard nods indulgently. "Others have said it better than I can. But the basic idea is that if you're a writer, you need to live your life on the page."

"In other words, your real life should be as uncomplicated as possible," I clarify to Maggie. "When Bernard is working he eats practically the same thing every day for lunch. A pastrami sandwich."

Maggie attempts to look interested. "It sounds kind of boring. But I'm not a writer. I don't even like writing a letter."

Bernard laughs, playfully pointing a finger at me. "I think you need to take more of your own advice, young lady." He shakes his head at Maggie, as if the two of them are in cahoots. "Carrie's an expert at living large. I keep telling her to focus more on the page."

"You've never said that," I reply, indignant. I look down, as if I simply have to readjust my napkin. Bernard's comment brings all of my insecurities about being a writer to the surface.

"I've been meaning to say it." He squeezes my hand. "So there you go. I've said it. Do we want wine?"

"Sure," I say, stung.

"Beaujolais okay for you, Maggie?" he asks politely.

"I like red," Maggie says.

"Beaujolais is red," I comment, and immediately feel like a heel.

"Maggie knew that," Bernard says kindly. I look from one to the other. How did this happen? Why am I the bad guy? It's like Bernard and Maggie are ganging up on me.

I get up to go to the bathroom. "I'll come with you," Maggie says. She follows me down the stairs as I try to compose myself.

"I really want you to like him," I say, parking myself in front of the mirror while Maggie goes into the stall.

"I just met him. How can I know if I like him or not?"

"Don't you think he's sexy?" I ask.

"Sexy?" Maggie says. "I wouldn't call him that."

"But he is. Sexy," I insist.

"If you think he's sexy, that's all that counts."

"Well, I do. And I really, really like him."

The toilet flushes and Maggie comes out. "He doesn't seem very much like a boyfriend," she ventures.

"What do you mean?" I take a lipstick out of my bag, trying not to panic.

"He doesn't act like he's your boyfriend. He seems like he's more of an uncle or something."

I freeze. "He certainly isn't."

"It just seems like he's trying to help you. Like he likes you and, I don't know—" She shrugs.

"It's only because he's going through a divorce," I say.

"That's too bad," she remarks, washing her hands.

I apply the lipstick. "Why?"

"I wouldn't want to marry a divorced man. It kind of ruins it, doesn't it? The idea that a man has been married to someone else? I wouldn't be able to take it. I'd be jealous. I want a guy who's only ever been in love with me."

"But what if—" I pause, remembering that's what I've always thought I wanted as well. Until now. I narrow my eyes. Maybe it's simply a leftover sentiment from Castlebury.

We get through the rest of dinner, but it's awkward, with me saying things I know make me sound like a jerk, and Maggie being mostly silent, and Bernard pretending to enjoy the food and wine. When our plates are cleared, Maggie runs to the bathroom again, while I scoot my chair closer to Bernard's and apologize for the lousy evening.

"It's fine," he says. "It's what I expected." He pats my hand. "Come on, Carrie. You and Maggie are in college. We're from different generations. You can't expect Maggie to understand."

"I do, though."

"Then you're going to be disappointed."

Maggie comes back to the table beaming, her demeanor suddenly light and fizzy. "I called Ryan," she announces. "He said he's going over to Capote's and we should meet them there and then maybe we can go out."

I look at Bernard, pleadingly. "But we're already out."

"Go," he says, pushing back his chair. "Have fun with Maggie. Show her the town."

He takes out his wallet and hands me twenty dollars. "Promise me you'll take a cab. I don't want you riding the subway at night."

"No." I try to give back the twenty but he won't take it. Maggie is already at the exit as if she can't get out of there fast enough.

Bernard gives me a quick peck on the cheek. "We can see each other anytime. Your friend is only here for two nights."

"When?" I ask.

"When what?"

"When will I see you again?" I hate myself, sounding like a desperate schoolgirl.

"Soon. I'll call you."

I leave the restaurant in a huff. I'm so mad, I can barely look at Maggie.

A cab pulls up to the curb and a couple gets out. Maggie slides into the backseat. "Are you coming?"

"What choice do I have?" I grumble under my breath.

Maggie has written Capote's address on the back of a napkin. "Green-wich Street?" she asks, pronouncing each syllable.

"It's 'Grenich.'"

She looks at me. "Okay. *Grenich*," she says to the cabbie.

The taxi peels away, throwing me against Maggie. "Sorry," I murmur coldly.

"What's wrong?" she asks.

"Nothing."

"Is it because I didn't like Bernard?"

"How could you not like him." It's not a question.

She folds her arms. "Do you want me to lie to you?" And before I can protest, she continues, "He's too old. I know he's not as old as our parents, but he might as well be. And he's strange. He's not like anyone we grew up with. I just can't see you with him." To soften the blow, she adds kindly, "I'm only telling you this for your own good."

I hate when friends tell you something is "for your own good." How do they know it's for your own good? Do they know the future? Maybe in the future, I'll look back and see that Bernard has actually been "good for me."

"Okay, Mags." I sigh. The taxi is racing down Fifth Avenue, and I study each landmark: Lord & Taylor, the Toy Building, the Flatiron Building, committing each to memory. If I lived here forever, would I ever get tired of these sights?

"Anyway," Maggie says cheerfully, "I forgot to tell you the most important part. Lali's gone to France!"

"Really?" I ask dully.

"You know how the Kandesies have all that land? Well, some big developer came along and bought, like, fifty acres and now the Kandesies are millionaires."

"I bet Lali went to France to meet Sebastian," I say, trying to act like I care.

"That's what I think too," Maggie agrees. "And she'll probably get him back. I always thought Sebastian was one of those guys who used women. He'll probably be with Lali because of her money."

"He has his own money," I point out.

"Doesn't matter. He's a *user,*" Maggie says.

And while Maggie natters on, I spend the rest of the taxi ride thinking about relationships. There must be such a thing as "pure" love. But there also seems to be quite a bit of "impure" love as well. Look at Capote and Ryan with their models. And Samantha with her rich mogul boyfriend. And what about Maggie and her two boyfriends—one for show and one for sex? And then there's me. Maybe what Maggie was hinting at is true. If Bernard wasn't a famous playwright, would I even be interested?

The taxi pulls up in front of a pretty brownstone with chrysanthemums in the window boxes. I grit my teeth. I like to think of myself as a good person. A girl who doesn't cheat or lie or pretend to be something she's not in order to get a guy. But maybe I'm no better than anyone else. Maybe I'm worse.

"Come on," Maggie says gaily, leaping from the cab and hurrying up the steps. "Now we can finally have fun!"

CHAPTER FIFTEEN

Capote's apartment is not what I expected. The furniture consists of soft couches and armchairs, covered in chintz. There's a small dining room with decorative plates on the walls. In the bedroom is an antique armoire; the bedspread is yellow chenille. "It looks like an old lady lives here," I say.

"She does. Or did. The woman who lived here is an old family friend. She moved to Maine," Capote explains.

"Right," I say, dropping onto the couch. The springs are shot and I sink several inches below the cushions. Capote and his "old family friends," I think grumpily. He seems to have an inside track on everything, including apartments. He's one of those people who expect to get things with very little effort, and does.

"Drink?" he asks.

"What do you have?" Maggie says coquettishly.

Huh? I thought she was interested in Ryan. But maybe it's Capote she's after. On the other hand, maybe Maggie flirts with every guy she meets. Every guy except Bernard.

I shake my head. Either way, this situation can lead to no good. How did I get involved in the aiding and abetting of this?

"Anything you want, I have," Capote replies. He doesn't sound particularly flirtatious back. He actually sounds very matter-of-fact, as if he's not exactly thrilled we're here, but has decided to tolerate us nonetheless.

"Beer?" Maggie asks.

"Sure." Capote opens the refrigerator, takes out a Heineken, and hands it to her. "Carrie?"

I'm surprised he's being so polite. Maybe it's his Southern upbringing. Manners trump personal dislikes.

"Vodka?" I get up and follow him into the kitchen. It's a proper kitchen, with a counter that opens into the living room. I'm suddenly a bit envious. I wouldn't mind living here in this charming old apartment with a fireplace and working kitchen. Several pans hang from a rod in the ceiling. "Do you cook?" I ask, with a mixture of sarcasm and surprise.

"I love to cook," Capote says proudly. "Mostly fish. I'm famous for my fish."

"*I* cook," I say, somewhat defiantly, as if I know everything about it and far more than he can possibly comprehend.

"Like what?" He takes two tumblers out of the cabinet and sets them down, adding ice and vodka and a splash of cranberry juice.

"Everything," I say. "Mostly desserts though. I'm really good at Bûche de Noël. It takes two days to make it."

"I'd never want to dedicate that much time to cooking," he says dismissively, raising his glass. "Cheers."

"Cheers."

The buzzer rings and Capote strides to the door, no doubt relieved at the interruption.

Ryan comes in with Rainbow and another girl, who's the size of a twig. She has short dark hair, enormous brown eyes, acne, and is wearing a skirt that barely covers her bottom. For some reason, I'm immediately jealous. Despite the acne, she must be another one of Ryan's model friends. I feel horribly out of place.

Rainbow's eyes scour the room and land on me. She, too, looks as though she can't imagine what I'm doing here.

"Hi." I wave from the kitchen.

"Oh. Hi." She comes over, while Ryan greets Maggie and plops next to her on the couch. "Are you serving drinks?" she asks.

"I guess so. What do you want? Capote says he has everything."

"Tequila."

I find the bottle and pour some into a glass. Why am I serving *her*? I wonder in annoyance. "So are you and Capote seeing each other?"

"No." Her nose wrinkles. "What makes you say that?"

"You seem so close, is all."

"We're friends." She pauses, looks around again, and

seeing that Ryan is still engaged with Maggie and Capote is talking to the strange skinny girl, decides I'm her only option for conversation. "I would never go out with him. I think any girl who dates him is insane."

"Why?" I take a gulp of my drink.

"She'll have her heart broken."

Well. I take another gulp of my drink, and add a little more vodka and ice. I don't feel particularly drunk. In fact, I feel disturbingly sober. And resentful. Of everyone else's life.

I join Maggie and Ryan on the couch. "What are you guys talking about?"

"You," Ryan says. This is a person who cannot lie.

Maggie blushes. "Ryan!" she scolds.

"What?" he asks, looking from Maggie to me. "I thought you guys were best friends. Don't best friends tell each other everything?"

"You know nothing about women," Maggie giggles.

"At least I try. Unlike most men."

"What *about* me?" I ask.

"Maggie was telling me about you and Bernard." There's a note of admiration in Ryan's voice. Bernard Singer is obviously some kind of hero to both him and Capote. He's exactly what they'd like to be someday. And apparently my association with him elevates my status. But I knew that, didn't I?

"Maggie doesn't like him. She says he's too old."

"I didn't say that. I said he wasn't right for you."

"No man is ever too old," Ryan says, half jokingly. "If

Carrie can go out with a guy fifteen years older, it means there's hope for me when I'm in my thirties."

Maggie's face twists in distaste. "You really want to date someone who's seventeen when you're thirty?"

"Maybe not seventeen." Ryan winks. "I'd prefer it if she were legal."

Maggie titters. Ryan's looks and charm seem to have overcome his stupidity about women.

"Anyway, who's seventeen?" he asks.

"Carrie," Maggie says accusingly.

"I'll be eighteen in a month." I glare at her. Why is she doing this to me?

"Does Bernard know you're seventeen?" Ryan asks with too much interest.

"No," Maggie says. "She told me to lie and say she was nineteen."

"Aha. The old lying-up trick," Ryan teases.

The apartment buzzer goes off again. "Reinforcements," Ryan announces as Maggie laughs. Five more people arrive— three scruffy guys and two very serious young women.

"Let's go," I say to Maggie.

Ryan looks at me in surprise. "You can't go," he insists. "The party's just getting started."

"Yeah." Maggie agrees. "I'm having fun." She holds out her empty beer bottle. "Do you mind getting me another?"

"Fine." I get up, annoyed, and go into the kitchen. The new arrivals wander over and ask for drinks. I comply, because I don't have anything better to do and there's really no one I want to talk to at this party.

I spot the phone on the wall next to the refrigerator. Maggie is completely occupied with Ryan, who is now sitting cross-legged on the couch, entertaining her with what appears to be a long and animated story. I tell myself Maggie won't mind if I take off without her. I pick up the phone and dial Bernard's number.

It rings and rings. Where is he? A dozen scenarios run through my head. He went out to a club, but if he did, why didn't he invite Maggie and me? Or he met another girl at Peartree's and he's with her, having sex. Or worse, he's decided he doesn't want to see me anymore and isn't answering his phone.

The suspense is killing me. I call again.

Still no answer. I hang up, rattled. Now I'm really convinced I'm never going to see him again. I can't bear it. I don't care what Maggie says. What if I am in love with Bernard and Maggie just ruined it?

I search the room for her, but she and Ryan have disappeared. Before I can look for them, one of the shaggy guys strikes up a conversation.

"How do you know Capote?"

"I don't," I snap. Then I feel bad and add, "He's in my writing class."

"Ah yes. The fabled New School writing course. Is Viktor Greene still teaching?" he asks in a Boston accent.

"If you'll excuse me," I say, wanting to get away from him, "I have to find my friend."

"What's she look like?"

"Blond. Pretty. All-American?"

"She's with Ryan. In the bedroom."

I scowl at him like it's his fault. "I have to get her out."

"Why?" he asks. "They're two healthy young animals. What do you care?"

I feel even more lost than I did just a few minutes ago. Are all my values and ideals just plain wrong? "I need to use the phone."

"You've got somewhere better to go?" He laughs. "This is where it's all happening."

"I certainly hope not," I mutter, dialing Bernard's number. No answer. I slap down the phone and head to the bedroom.

The music is blaring while one of the serious girls bangs on the door of the bathroom. It finally opens and Capote comes out with Rainbow and the model girl. They're laughing loudly. Normally, I'd love to be at a party like this, but all I can think about is Bernard. And if I can't see him, I want to go home.

I want to crawl into Samantha's bed and pull her slippery sheets over my head and cry.

"Maggie?" I knock briskly on the door. "Maggie, are you in there?" Silence. "I know you're in there, Maggie." I try the handle, but it's locked. "Maggie, I want to go home," I wail.

Finally, the bedroom door opens. Maggie is flushed, twisting her hair. Behind her, Ryan stands grinning, tugging on his pants. "Jesus, Carrie," Maggie says.

"I need to go home. We have class tomorrow," I remind

Ryan, sounding like an old schoolmarm.

"Let's go to your house, then," Ryan suggests.

"No."

Maggie gives me a look. "That's a great idea."

I weigh my options and decide it's the better choice. At least I can get out of here.

We walk to Samantha's building. Upstairs, Ryan extracts a bottle of vodka he pinched from Capote and proceeds to pour us drinks. I shake my head. "I'm tired." While Ryan finds the stereo, I go into Samantha's room and call Bernard.

The phone rings and rings. He's still not there. It's over.

I go out into the living room, where Maggie and Ryan are dancing. "Come on, Carrie." Maggie holds out her arms. What the hell, I think, and join them. Within minutes, though, Maggie and Ryan are making out.

"Hey, guys. Cut it out," I scold.

"Cut what out?" Ryan laughs.

Maggie takes his hand, leading him to the bedroom. "Do you mind? We'll be right out."

"What am *I* supposed to do?"

"Have a drink," Ryan chortles.

They go into the bedroom and close the door. The Blondie album is still playing. "Heart of Glass." That's me, I think. I pick up my vodka and sit at the tiny table in the corner. I light up a cigarette. I try Bernard again.

I know it's wrong. But something alien has taken over my emotions. Having sunk this far, the only place to go is down.

The album stops playing, and from inside the bedroom,

I hear panting and the occasional comment, like, "Oh, that's good."

I light another cigarette. Do Maggie and Ryan have any idea how inconsiderate they are? Or do they simply not care?

I ring Bernard once more. Smoke another cigarette. An hour has passed and they're still going at it. Aren't they tired? Then I tell myself to get over it. I shouldn't be so judgmental. I know I'm not perfect. But I would never do what they're doing. I just wouldn't.

I may have suddenly learned something about myself after all. I have what Miranda would call "boundaries."

I should probably bunk down on the futon. Maggie and Ryan don't sound like they're going to be finished any-time soon. But anger and frustration and fear are keeping me wide awake. I smoke yet another cigarette and dial Bernard.

This time he answers on the second ring. "Hello?" he asks, confused as to who could be calling him at two in the morning.

"It's me," I whisper, suddenly realizing what a bad idea it was to call him.

"Carrie?" he asks sleepily. "What are you doing up?"

"Maggie is having sex," I hiss.

"And?"

"She's doing it with some guy from my class."

"Are they doing it in front of you?"

What a question! "They're in the bedroom."

"Ah," he says.

"Can I come over?" I don't want to sound like I'm begging, but I am.

"Poor thing. You're having a lousy night, aren't you?"

"The worst."

"Coming over here probably won't make it better," he cautions. "I'm tired. I need to sleep. And so do you."

"We could just sleep then. It'd be nice."

"I can't do it tonight, Carrie. I'm sorry. Some other time."

I swallow. "Okay," I say, sounding like a little mouse.

"Good night, kiddo," he says, and hangs up.

I gently replace the receiver. I go to the futon and sit with my knees to my chest, rocking back and forth. My face screws up, and tears trickle out of the corners of my eyes.

Miranda was right. Men do suck.

CHAPTER SIXTEEN

Ryan sneaks out at five in the morning. I keep my eyes squeezed shut, pretending to be asleep, not wanting to look at him or talk to him. I hear his footsteps cross the floor, followed by the squeak of the door. Get over it, I scold myself. It's not a big deal. They had sex. So what? It's not my business. But still. Doesn't Ryan care about his fiancée? And what about Maggie and her two boyfriends? Are there no limits when it comes to sex? Is sex really so powerful it can erase your history and common sense?

I fall into a fitful sleep and then a deeper one. I'm in the middle of a dream in which Viktor Greene is saying he loves me, except that Viktor looks just like Capote, when Maggie startles me awake.

"Hi," she says cheerfully, as if nothing untoward has happened. "Want some coffee?"

"Sure," I say, the whole rotten evening coming back to

me. I'm drained and slightly angry again. I light a cigarette.

"You're smoking a lot," Maggie says.

"Ha," I say, thinking about how much she smokes.

"Did you notice I quit?"

Actually, I hadn't. "When?" I defiantly blow a few smoke rings.

"After I met Hank. He said it was disgusting and I realized he was right."

I wonder what Hank would think about Maggie's behavior last night.

She goes into the kitchen, finds the instant coffee and a kettle, and waits for the water to boil. "That was so much fun, wasn't it?"

"Yeah. I had a great time." I can't keep the sarcasm out of my voice.

"What's wrong now?" Maggie says. As if I'm the one who's been constantly complaining.

It's too early for a contentious discussion. "Nothing. But Ryan's in my class—"

"Which reminds me. Ryan is taking me to a movie. By some Chinese director. *The Seven* something?"

"*The Seven Samurai*. By Kurosawa. He's Japanese."

"How do you know?"

"The guys are always talking about it. It's like six hours or something."

"I don't think we'll last six hours," she says slyly, handing me a mug of coffee.

One night I can excuse. But two? No way. "Listen, Mags. It's not a good idea if Ryan comes here tonight.

Samantha might find out—"

"Don't worry." She settles next to me on the futon. "Ryan said we can go to his apartment."

I pick a floating grain of coffee from my brew. "What about his fiancée?"

"He said he thinks she's cheating."

"So that makes it okay?"

"Jesus, Carrie. What's your problem? You're so uptight."

I take a sip of coffee, willing myself not to react. "Uptight" is the one thing I pride myself on not being. But perhaps I don't know myself so well after all.

Class is at one, but I leave the apartment early, claiming errands. Maggie and I were perfectly civil to each other on the surface, but I was walking on eggshells. It took a concerted effort not to bring up Ryan, and even more strength not to mention Bernard. I promised myself I wouldn't talk about him, because if I did, I was afraid I'd accuse Maggie of ruining my relationship. And even to my illogical brain, this seemed a bit extreme.

When Maggie turned on the TV and started doing leg lifts, I made my escape.

There's still an hour before class, so I head over to the White Horse Tavern, where I can load up on decent coffee for a mere fifty cents. To my happy surprise, L'il is there, writing in her journal.

"I'm exhausted," I sigh, sitting across from her.

"You look fine," she says.

"I think I slept about two hours."

She closes her journal and looks at me knowingly. "Bernard?"

"I wish. Bernard dumped me—"

"I'm sorry." She gives me a sympathetic smile.

"Not officially," I say quickly. "But after last night, I think he will." I stir three packets of sugar into my coffee. "And my friend Maggie had sex with Ryan last night."

"That's why you're so pissed off."

"I'm not pissed off. I'm disappointed." She looks unconvinced, so I add, "I'm not jealous, either. Why would I be attracted to Ryan when I have Bernard?"

"Then why are you angry?"

"I don't know." I pause. "Ryan's engaged. And she has two boyfriends. It's wrong."

"The heart wants what the heart wants," she says, somewhat cryptically.

I purse my lips in disapproval. "You'd think the heart would know better."

I keep to myself in class. Ryan tries to engage me with talk about Maggie and how great she is, but I only nod coldly. Rainbow actually says hi, but Capote ignores me, as usual. At least he's still behaving normally.

And then Viktor asks me to read the first ten pages of my play. I'm shocked. Viktor has never asked me to read anything before, and it takes me a minute to adjust. How am I going to read the play alone? There are two parts—a man and a woman. I can't read the man's part too. I'll sound like an idiot.

Viktor has managed to divine this as well. "You'll read the part of Harriet," he says. "And Capote can read Moorehouse."

Capote glances around the room, peeved at the request. "Harriet? *Moorehouse?* What kind of name is Moorehouse?"

"I suppose we'll find out," Viktor says, twirling his mustache.

This is the best thing that's happened to me in at least two days. It might even make up for all the bad.

Clutching my script, I make my way to the front of the room, followed by a red-faced Capote. "What am I playing?" he asks.

"You're a forty-year-old guy who's going through a midlife crisis. And I'm your bitchy wife."

"Figures," he grumbles.

I smile. Is this the reason for his continuing animosity? He thinks I'm a bitch? If he actually thinks I'm a bitch, I'm glad.

We begin reading. By the second page, I'm into the part, focusing on what it must be like to be Harriet, an unhappy woman who wanted to be a success but whose success has been eclipsed by her childish husband.

By the third page, the class gets the idea it's supposed to be funny, and begins snickering. By the fifth page, I hear spurts of actual laughter. When we finish, there's a smattering of applause.

Wow.

I look at Capote, foolishly expecting his approval. But his expression is firm as he studiously avoids my glance. "Good job," he murmurs out of obligation.

I don't care. I go back to my seat floating on air.

"Comments?" Viktor asks.

"It's like a junior version of *Who's Afraid of Virginia Woolf?*," Ryan ventures. I look at him gratefully. Ryan has a loyalty about him that I suddenly appreciate. It's too bad his loyalty ends when it comes to sex. If a guy is a jerk about infidelity, but decent about everything else, is it okay to like him as a person?

"What I found intriguing is the way Carrie was able to make the most banal domestic scene interesting," Viktor says. "I liked that it takes place while the couple is brushing their teeth. It's an everyday activity we all do, no matter who we are."

"Like taking a crap," Capote remarks.

I smile as though I'm far too superior to take offense at his comment. But now it's official, I decide. I hate him.

Viktor pats his mustache with one hand and the top of his head with the other—a gesture that suggests he's attempting to keep all of his hair from running away. "And now, perhaps L'il will grace us with her poem?"

"Sure." L'il stands and goes to the front of the class. "'The Glass Slipper,'" she begins.

"'My love broke me. As if my body were glass, smashed against the rocks, something used and disposed of. . . .'" The poem continues in this vein for several more lines, and when L'il is finished, she smiles uneasily.

"Thoughts?" Viktor says. There's an unusual edge to his voice.

"I liked it," I volunteer. "The broken glass is a great description of a broken heart." Which reminds me of how I'm going to feel if Bernard ends our relationship.

"It's pedantic and obvious," Viktor says. "Schoolgirlish and lazy. This is what happens when you take your talent for granted."

"Thank you," L'il says evenly, as if she doesn't care. She takes her seat, and when I glance over my shoulder, her head is down, her expression stricken. I know L'il is too strong to cry in class, but if she did, everyone would understand. Viktor can be unkind in his straightforward assessments, but he's never been deliberately mean.

He must be feeling guilty, though, because he's raking at poor Waldo like he's trying to rip him off his face. "To summarize, I'm looking forward to hearing more from Carrie's play. While L'il—" He breaks off and turns away.

This should make me ecstatic, but it doesn't. L'il doesn't deserve the criticism. Which could mean, conversely, that I don't deserve the excessive approval either. Being great isn't so fabulous when it comes at someone else's expense.

I gather my papers, wondering what just happened. Perhaps, when it comes right down to it, Viktor is just another fickle guy. Only instead of being fickle about women, he's fickle about his favorite students. He bestowed his honors on L'il at the beginning, but now he's bored, and I'm the one who's captured his attention.

L'il races out of class. I catch up with her at the elevator,

175

pressing the "close" button before anyone else can get on. "I'm sorry. I thought your poem was wonderful. I truly did," I say profusely, trying to make up for Viktor's critique.

L'il clutches her book bag to her chest. "He was right. The poem sucked. And I do need to work harder."

"You already work harder than anyone in the class, L'il. You work a hell of a lot harder than I do. I'm the one who's lazy."

She gives a little shake of her head. "You're not lazy, Carrie. You're unafraid."

Now I'm confused, given our discussion about my fears as a writer. "I wouldn't say *that*."

"It's true. You're not afraid of this city. Not afraid to try new things."

"You're not either," I say kindly.

We get out of the elevator and step outside. The sun is blazing and the heat is like a slap in the face. L'il squints and puts on a pair of cheap sunglasses, the kind the street vendors sell at every other corner. "Enjoy it, Carrie," she insists. "And don't worry about me. Are you going to tell Bernard?"

"About what?"

"Your play. You should show it to him. I'm sure he'll love it."

I peer at her closely, wondering if she's being cynical, but I can't see any trace of malice. Besides, L'il isn't like that. She's never been jealous of anyone. "Yeah," I say. "Maybe I will."

Bernard. I *should* show him my play. But after last night, is he even speaking to me anymore?

Nothing I can do about it, though. Because now I have to meet Samantha to help her with her crazy dinner party.

CHAPTER SEVENTEEN

"What do we do first?" Samantha asks, clapping her hands in an attempt at enthusiasm.

I look at her like she has to be kidding. "Well, first we buy the food," I say, as if I'm talking to a kindergartner.

"Where do we do that?"

My jaw drops in disbelief. "At a supermarket?" When Samantha said she knew nothing about cooking, I never assumed she meant absolutely nothing, including the fact that "food" is usually made from "ingredients" purchased at a "supermarket."

"And where's the supermarket?"

I want to scream. Instead, I stare at her blankly.

She's sitting behind her desk in her office, wearing a low-cut sweater with linebacker shoulders, pearls, and a short skirt. She looks sexy, cool, and collected. I, on the other hand, look ragged and out of place, especially as I'm wearing what is basically some old lady's slip that I've cinched with a cowboy belt. Another great find at the vintage store. "Have you considered takeout?" I ask smartly.

She emits her tinkling laugh. "Charlie thinks I can cook. I don't want to disabuse him of the fact."

"And why, pray tell, does he think that?"

"Because I told him, Sparrow," she says, becoming slightly irked. She stands up and puts her hands on her hips. "Haven't you heard the expression 'Fake it till you make it'? I'm the original fake-it girl."

"Okay." I throw up my hands in defeat. "I'll need to see Charlie's kitchen first. See what kind of pans he has."

"No problem. His apartment is spectacular. I'll take you there now." She picks up a giant Kelly bag, which I've never seen before.

"Is that new?" I ask, half in admiration and half in envy.

She strokes the soft leather before she slings it over her shoulder. "It's nice, isn't it? Charlie bought it for me."

"Some people have quite the life."

"Play your cards right, and you'll have quite the life too, Sparrow."

"How's this grand scheme of yours going to go down?" I ask. "What if Charlie finds out—"

She waves this away. "He won't. The only time Charlie's been in the kitchen is when we have sex on the counter."

I make a face. "And you honestly expect me to prepare food on it?"

"It's clean, Carrie. Haven't you ever heard of maids?"

"Not in my universe."

We're interrupted by the entry of a short man with sandy brown hair who looks exactly like a tiny Ken doll. "Are you leaving?" he says sharply to Samantha.

A flash of annoyance crosses her face before she quickly composes herself. "Family emergency," she says.

"What about the Smirnoff account?" he demands.

"Vodka has been around for over two hundred years, Harry. I daresay it will still be here tomorrow. My sister, on the other hand," she says, indicating me, "may not."

As if on cue, my entire body floods in embarrassment, rendering me bright red.

Harry, however, isn't buying it. He scrutinizes me closely—apparently, he needs glasses but is too vain to wear them. "Your sister?" he asks. "When did you get a sister?"

"Really, Harry." Samantha shakes her head.

Harry stands aside to let us pass, then follows us down the hall. "Will you be back later?"

Samantha stops and slowly turns around. Her lips curl into a smile. "My goodness, Harry. You sound just like my father."

This does the trick, all right. Harry turns about fifteen shades of green. He's not much older than Samantha, and I'm sure the last thing he expected was to be compared to someone's old man.

"What was that about?" I ask, when we're out on the street.

"Harry?" she says, unconcerned. "He's my new boss."

"You talk to your new boss like that?"

"Have to," she says. "Considering how he talks to me."

"Meaning?"

"Well, let's see," she says, pausing at the light. "On his first day of work, he comes into my office and says, 'I've heard you're highly competent at everything you put your mind to.' Sounds like a compliment, right? But then he adds, 'Both in and out of the office.'"

"Can he actually get away with that?"

"Of course." She shrugs. "You've never worked in an office, so you have no idea. But eventually, sex always comes up. When it does, I give it right back to them."

"But shouldn't you tell someone?"

"Who?" she says. "His boss? Human Resources? He'll either say he was joking or I came on to him. What if I'm fired? I don't plan to sit at home all day, popping out babies and baking cookies."

"I don't know about your mothering skills, but considering your cooking abilities, it's probably not a good idea."

"Thank you," she says, having made her point.

Samantha may have lied to Charlie about her culinary knowledge, but she wasn't kidding about the apartment. His building is on Park Avenue in Midtown, and it's gold. Not real gold, of course, but some kind of shiny gold metal. And if I thought the doormen in Bernard's building were sharp, the doormen in Charlie's building have them beat. Not only are they wearing white gloves, they're sporting caps with gold braid. Even their uniforms have loops of gold braid hanging from the shoulders. It's all pretty tacky. But impressive.

"You really live here?" I ask in a whisper as we cross the lobby. It's marble and it echoes.

"Of course," she says, greeting a doorman who is politely holding the elevator. "It's very me, don't you think? Glamorous yet classy."

"I guess that's one way to look at it," I murmur, taking in the smoky mirrored walls that line the interior of the lift.

Charlie's apartment is, not surprisingly, enormous. It's on the forty-fifth floor with floor-to-ceiling windows, a sunken living room, another wall of smoky mirrors, and a large Plexiglas case filled with baseball memorabilia. I'm sure it has several bedrooms and bathrooms, but I don't get to see them because Samantha immediately directs me to the kitchen. It, too, is enormous, with marble countertops and gleaming appliances. It's new all right. Too new.

"Has anyone ever cooked in here?" I ask, opening the cabinets to look for pots and pans.

"I don't think so." Samantha pats me on the shoulder. "You'll figure it out. I have faith in you. Now wait till you see what I'm going to wear."

"Great," I mutter. The kitchen is practically bare. I find a roll of aluminum foil, some muffin tins, three bowls, and a large frying pan.

"Ta-da!" She says, reappearing in the doorway in a French maid's outfit. "What do you think?"

"If you're planning to work on Forty-second Street, it's just peachy."

"Charlie loves it when I wear this."

"Look, sweetie," I say, between gritted teeth. "This is a dinner party. You can't wear that."

"I know," she says, exasperated. "God, Carrie, can't you take a joke?"

"Not when I have to prepare an entire meal with three bowls and a roll of aluminum foil. Who's coming to this shindig anyway?"

She holds up her hand. "Me, Charlie, some really boring couple who Charlie works with, another really boring couple, and Charlie's sister, Erica. And my friend Cholly, to liven things up."

"Cholly?"

"Cholly Hammond. You met him at the same party where you met Bernard."

"The seersucker guy."

"He runs a literary magazine. You'll like him."

I wave the aluminum foil in her face. "I won't get to see him, remember? I'll be in here, cooking."

"If cooking makes you this neurotic, you really shouldn't do it," Samantha says.

"Thanks, sweetie. But I believe this was your idea, remember?"

"Oh, I know," she says airily. "C'mon. I need you to help me pick out something to wear. Charlie's friends are very conservative."

I follow her down a carpeted hallway and into a large suite with a walk-in closet and his-and-her bathrooms. I gawk at the splendor of it all. Imagine having this much space in Manhattan. No wonder Samantha's so eager to get hitched.

When we enter the closet, I nearly fall over in a dead faint. The closet alone is the size of Samantha's entire apartment. On one side are racks and racks of Charlie's clothing, arranged by type and color. His jeans are ironed and folded over hangers. Stacks of cashmere sweaters in every color are piled neatly on the shelves.

At the other end is Samantha's section, made obvious not only by her work suits and high-heeled pumps and the slinky dresses she loves to wear, but by its relative meagerness. "Hey, sister, looks like you've got some catching up to do," I point out.

"I'm working on it," she laughs.

"What's this?" I ask, indicating a bouclé suit with white piping. "Chanel?" I look at the price tag, which is still on the sleeve, and gasp. "Twelve hundred dollars?"

"Thank you." She removes the hanger from my hands.

"Can you afford that?"

"I can't not afford it. If you want the life, you have to look the part." She frowns. "I would think you of all people would understand. Aren't you obsessed with fashion?"

"Not at these prices. This lovely garment I'm wearing cost two bucks."

"It looks it," she says, taking off the French maid's outfit and dropping it onto the floor.

She slides into the Chanel suit and considers her image in the full-length mirror. "What do you think?"

"Isn't that what all those ladies wear? The ones who lunch? I know it's Chanel, but it's not really you."

"Which makes it perfect for an up-and-coming Upper East Side lady."

"But you're not one," I object, thinking about all those crazy nights we've spent together.

She puts her finger to her lips. "I am now. And I will be, for as long as I need to be."

"And then what?"

"I'll be independently wealthy. Maybe I'll live in Paris."

"You're planning to divorce Charlie before you've even married him? What if you have kids?"

"What do you think, Sparrow?" She kicks the French maid's uniform into the closet and looks at me pointedly. "I believe someone has some cooking to do."

Four hours later, despite the fact that the oven is going and two burners are lit, I'm shivering with cold. Charlie keeps the apartment cooled to the temperature of a refrigerated truck. It's probably ninety degrees outside, but I sure could use one of his cashmere sweaters right now.

How can Samantha take it? I wonder, stirring the pan. But I suppose she's used to it. If you marry one of these mogul types, you kind of have to do what they want.

"Carrie?" Samantha asks, coming into the kitchen. "How's it going?"

"The main course is almost ready."

"Thank God," she says, taking a gulp of red wine from a large goblet. "I'm going insane out there."

"What do you think I'm doing in here?"

"At least you don't have to talk about window treatments."

"How do you 'treat' a window? Do you send it to a doctor?"

"Decorator," she sighs. "Twenty thousand dollars. For curtains. I don't think I can do it."

"You'd better do it. I'm freezing my butt off in here so you can look good. I still don't understand why you didn't hire a caterer."

"Because Superwoman doesn't hire a caterer. She does everything herself."

"Here," I say, handing her two finished plates. "And don't forget your cape."

"What are we having, anyway?" She looks at the plates in consternation.

"Lamp chops with a mushroom cream sauce. The green stuff is asparagus. And those brown things are potatoes," I say sardonically. "Has Charlie figured out I'm back here cooking?"

"Doesn't have a clue." She smiles.

"Good. Then just tell him it's French."

"Thanks, Sparrow." She wheels out. Through the open door, I hear her exclaim, "Voilà."

Unfortunately, I can't see the guests, because the dining room is around the corner. I caught a glimpse of it though. The table was also Plexiglas. Apparently Charlie has a love of plastic.

I get to work on the mini chocolate soufflés. I'm about to put them into the oven when a voice exclaims, "Aha! I knew it was too good to be true."

I jump a mile, nearly dropping the muffin pan. "Cholly?" I hiss.

"Carrie Bradshaw, I presume," he says, strolling purposefully into the kitchen and opening the freezer. "I was wondering what became of you. Now I know."

"Actually, you don't," I say, gently closing the oven door.

"Why is Samantha keeping you hidden back here?"

I open my mouth to explain, then catch myself. Cholly seems like the gossipy type—he'll probably run out and spill the beans that it's me doing the cooking. I'm just like Cyrano, except I don't think I'm going to get the guy at the end.

"Listen, Cholly—"

"I get it," he says with a wink. "I've known Samantha for years. I doubt she can boil an egg."

"Are you going to tell?"

"And spoil the fun? No, little one," he says, kindly. "Your secret's safe with me."

He goes out, and two minutes later, Samantha comes running back in. "What happened?" she asks in a panic. "Did Cholly see you? That meddling old man. I knew I shouldn't have invited him. And it was going so well. You could practically see the steam coming out of the other women's ears, they were so jealous." She grits her teeth in frustration and puts her hands over her face. It's the first time I've seen her genuinely distraught, and I wonder if her fabulous relationship with Charlie is everything she says it is.

"Hey," I say, touching her shoulder. "It's okay. Cholly promised he wouldn't tell."

"Really?"

"Yes. And I think he'll keep his word. He seems like a pretty nice old guy."

"He is," she says in relief. "And those women out there, they're like snakes. During cocktails, one of them kept asking me when we were planning to have children. When I said I didn't know, she got all superior and told me I'd better get on it right away before Charlie changed his mind about marrying me. And then she asked me when I was planning to quit my job."

"What'd you say?" I ask, in indignation.

"I said, 'Never. Because I don't consider my work a job. I consider it a career. And you don't quit a career.' That shut her up for a minute. Then she asked where I went to college."

"And?"

Samantha straightens. "I lied. Said I went to a little school in Boston."

"Oh, sweetie."

"What difference does it make? I'm not going to risk losing Charlie because some uptight society matron doesn't approve of where I went to school. I've gotten this far, and I don't plan to go back."

"Of course not," I say, touching her shoulder. I pause. "Maybe I should go. Before anyone else wanders in."

She nods. "That's a good idea."

"The soufflés are in the oven. All you have to do is take them out in twenty minutes, turn them over onto a plate, and put a scoop of ice cream on top."

She looks at me gratefully, and envelops me in a hug. "Thanks, Sparrow. I couldn't have pulled this off without you."

She takes a step back and smoothes her hair. "Oh, and Sparrow?" she adds carefully. "Would you mind going out the service entrance?"

CHAPTER EIGHTEEN

Where is everybody? I think in annoyance as I bang down the phone for the millionth time.

When I got home last night, I kept wondering about Samantha and Charlie. Was that the way to a happy relationship? Turning yourself into what the man wanted?

On the other hand, it seemed to be working. For Samantha, anyway. And in comparison, my own relationship with Bernard was sorely lacking. Not only in sex, but in the simple fact that I still wasn't sure I was ever going to see him again. I guess the best thing about living with a guy is that you know you're going to see him again. I mean, he has to come home at some point, right?

Unfortunately, the same can't be said of Bernard. And it's all Maggie's fault. If she hadn't been so rude, if she hadn't insisted on tracking down Ryan and seducing him . . . And she's still *with* Ryan, having a mini affair, while I've got nothing. I've become a handmaiden to other people's relationships. Aiding and abetting. And now *I'm* all alone.

Thank God for Miranda. I'll always have her. Miranda will never have a relationship. So where the hell is she?

I pick up the phone and try her again. No answer. Strange, as it's raining, which means she can't be marching around in front of Saks. I try Bernard again too. No answer there either. Feeling thoroughly pissed off, I call Ryan. Jeez. Even he's not picking up. Figures. He and Maggie are probably holed up having sex for the twentieth time.

I give up. I stare at the rain. Drip, drip, drip. It's depressing.

At last the buzzer goes off. Two short toots, followed by a long one, like someone's leaning on the button. *Maggie.* Great friend she is. She came to New York to see me, but spent all her time with stupid old Ryan. I go out into the hallway and lean over the stairs, prepared to give her a piece of my mind.

Instead I see the top of Miranda's head. The rain has flattened her bright red hair into a neat cap.

"Hey," I exclaim.

"It's pissing out there. Thought I'd stop off here till it lets up."

"C'mon in." I hand her a towel and she rubs her hair, the damp strands standing up from her head like the crest on a rooster. Unlike me, she appears to be full of good cheer. She goes into the kitchen, opens the refrigerator, and peers in. "Got anything to eat in this place?"

"Cheese."

"Yum. I'm starving." She grabs a small knife and attacks the brick of cheddar. "Hey. Have you noticed how you haven't heard from me for two days?"

Actually, I haven't. I've been too busy with Maggie and Samantha and Bernard. "Yeah," I say. "Where were you?"

"Guess." She grins.

"You went to a rally? In Washington?"

"Nope. Guess again."

"I give up." I wander to the futon and flop down, gazing out the window. I light a cigarette, thinking about how I'm not in the mood for games.

She balances on the arm of the futon, munching her cheese. "Having sex."

"Huh?" I stub out the cigarette.

"Having sex," she repeats. She slides onto the cushion. "I met a guy and we've been having nonstop sex for the last two days. And the worst thing about it? I couldn't poop. I honestly could not poop until he finally left this morning."

"Hold on. *You* met a guy?"

"Yes, Carrie. *I* did. Believe it or not, there are some men who find me attractive."

"I never said there weren't. But you always say—"

"I know." She nods. "Sex sucks. But this time, it didn't."

I stare at her wide-eyed and slightly jealous, not knowing where to begin.

"He's a law student at NYU," she says, settling into the couch. "I met him in front of Saks. At first, I didn't want to talk to him because he was wearing a bow tie—"

"*What?*"

"And it was yellow. With black polka dots. He kept walking by and I kept trying to ignore him, but he signed the petition, so I thought I'd try to be polite. Turns out he's been studying all these cases about free speech and pornography. He says the porn industry was the first to use the printing press. Did you know that? It wasn't because everyone wanted to read all this great literature. It was because men wanted to look at dirty pictures!"

"Wow," I bleat, trying to get into the spirit of things.

"We were talking and talking, and then he said why don't we continue this discussion over dinner? I wasn't really attracted to him, but he seemed like an interesting guy and I thought maybe we could be friends. So I said yes."

"Fantastic." I force a smile. "Where did you go?"

"Japonica. This Japanese restaurant on University. And it wasn't cheap, by the way. I tried to split it with him but he wouldn't."

"You let a man pay for you?" This isn't at all like Miranda.

She smiles awkwardly. "It goes against everything I believe in. But I told myself that maybe this once, I could let it go. I kept thinking about that night with you and your friend L'il. About how her mother was a lesbian. I kept wondering if maybe I was a lesbian, but if I am, how come I'm not attracted to women?"

"Maybe you haven't met the right one," I joke.

"Carrie!" she says, but she's in too good a mood to be offended. "I've always been attracted to guys. I just wish they were more like women. But with Marty—"

"That's his name? Marty?"

"He can't help his name. I mean, you don't exactly get to name yourself, do you? But I was kind of worried. Because I wasn't sure I could even kiss him." She lowers her voice. "He's not the best-looking guy. But I told myself that looks aren't everything. And he really *is* smart. Which can be a turn-on. I've always said I'd rather be with a smart, ugly guy than a good-looking dumb guy. Because what are you going to talk about with a dumb guy?"

"The weather?" I ask, wondering if Bernard thinks the same thing about me. Maybe I'm not smart enough for him and that's why he hasn't called.

"So then," Miranda continues, "we're walking through the Mews—that cute little cobblestoned street—and suddenly he pushes me up against the wall and starts making out with me!"

I shriek while Miranda bobs her head. "I couldn't believe it myself," she titters. "And the crazy thing about it was that it was totally sexy. We made out every five seconds on the street and when we got to my house, we ripped off our clothes and we did it!"

"Amazing," I say, lighting another cigarette. "Absolutely amazing."

"We did it three times that night. And the next morning, he took me to breakfast. I was worried it was a one-night stand, but he called in the afternoon and came over and we had sex again and he spent the night and we've seen each other practically every minute since then."

"Hold on," I say, waving my cigarette. "Every minute?" And another one bites the dust. Miranda is going to have some big romance with this guy she just met, and I'll never see her again either.

"I hardly know him," she giggles, "but so what? If it's right, it's right, don't you think?"

"I guess so," I say grudgingly.

"Can you believe it? Me? Having nonstop sex? Especially after all those things I told you. And now that I've finally had good sex, I'm thinking it might give me a new perspective on life. Like all men aren't necessarily horrible after all."

"That's great," I say weakly, feeling sorry for myself.

And then it happens. My eyes well up with tears.

I quickly brush them away, but Miranda catches me. "What's wrong?"

"Nothing."

"Why are you crying?" Her face screws up with worry. "You're not mad because I have a boyfriend now, are you?"

I shake my head.

"Carrie. I can't help you unless you tell me what's wrong," she says gently.

I spill the whole story, starting with the disastrous dinner with Bernard and how Maggie insisted we go to a party and how she ended up with Ryan and how Bernard hasn't called me and now it's probably over. "How did this happen to me?" I wail. "I should have slept with Bernard when I had the chance. Now it will never happen. I'll be a virgin for the rest of my life. Even L'il isn't a virgin. And my friend Maggie is sleeping with three guys. At once! What's wrong with me?"

Miranda puts her arms around my shoulders. "Poor baby," she says soothingly. "You're having a bad day."

"Bad day? More like bad week," I sniffle. But I'm grateful for her kindness. Miranda is usually so prickly. I can't help but wonder if maybe she's right and two days of great sex have awakened her maternal instinct.

"Not everyone is the same," she says firmly. "People develop at different times."

"But I don't want to be the last."

"Lots of famous people are late bloomers. My father says it's an advantage to be a late bloomer. Because when good things start happening, you're ready for it."

"Like you were finally ready for Marty?"

"I guess so." She nods. "I liked it, Carrie. Oh my God. I really liked it." She covers her mouth in horror. "If I like sex, do you think it means I can't be a feminist?"

"No." I shake my head. "Because being a feminist— I think it means being in charge of your sexuality. You decide who you want to have sex with. It means not trading your sexuality for . . . other things."

"Like marrying some gross guy who you're not in love with just so you can have a nice house with a picket fence."

"Or marrying a rich old geezer. Or a guy who expects

196

you to cook him dinner every night and take care of the children," I say, thinking of Samantha.

"Or a guy who makes you have sex with him whenever he wants, even if you don't," Miranda concludes.

We look at each other in triumph, as if we've finally solved one of the world's great problems.

CHAPTER NINETEEN

At about seven, when Miranda and I have taken a few swigs from the bottle of vodka and have proceeded to interpretive-dance our way through Blondie, the Ramones, The Police, and Elvis Costello, Maggie arrives.

"Magwitch!" I exclaim, throwing my arms around her, determined to forgive and forget.

She takes in Miranda, who has picked up a candle and is singing into it like it's a microphone. "Who *is* that?"

"Miranda!" I shout. "This is my friend Maggie. My best friend from high school."

"Hi." Miranda waves the candle at her.

Maggie spots the vodka, storms toward it, and proceeds to pour half the bottle down her throat. "Don't worry," she snaps, catching my expression. "I can buy more. I'm eighteen, remember?"

"So?" I say, wondering what this has to do with

anything. She glares at Miranda and drops onto the futon.

"Ryan stood me up," she snarls.

"Huh?" I'm puzzled. "Haven't you been with him for the last twenty-four hours?"

"Yes. But the minute I let him out of my sight, he disappeared."

I can't help it. I start laughing.

"It isn't funny. We were at some coffee shop getting breakfast at six in the evening. I went into the bathroom, and when I came out, he was gone."

"He ran away?"

"Sure sounds like it, doesn't it?"

"Oh, Mags." I'm trying to be sympathetic. But I can't quite get there. It's all too ridiculous. And not terribly surprising.

"Could you turn that thing off?" Maggie shouts at Miranda. "It's hurting my ears."

"Sorry," I say, to both Maggie and Miranda, as I scurry across the room to lower the volume on the stereo.

"What's her problem?" Miranda asks. She sounds put out, which I know she doesn't intend. She's just a bit soused.

"Ryan ran out of the coffee shop while she was in the bathroom."

"Ah," Miranda says with a smile.

"Mags?" I ask, making a cautious approach. "There's nothing Miranda likes more than guy troubles. Mostly because she hates all men." I hope this introduction will make Maggie and Miranda appreciate each other. After all, guy troubles, along with clothing and body parts, are a major source of bonding among women.

But Maggie isn't having it. "Why didn't you tell me he was a dick?" she demands.

This isn't fair. "I thought I did. You knew he was engaged."

"You're dating a guy who's engaged?" Miranda asks, not liking the sound of this.

"He isn't really engaged. He *says* he's engaged. She made him get engaged so she could string him along." Maggie takes another swig of vodka. "That's what I think, anyway."

"It's a good thing he left," I say. "Now at least you know his true nature."

"Here, here," Miranda adds.

"Hey. Miranda just got a new boyfriend," I tell Maggie.

"Lucky you." Maggie scowls, unimpressed.

"Maggie has two boyfriends," I say to Miranda, as if this is something to be admired.

"That's something I've never understood. How do you handle it? I mean, they're always saying you should date two or three guys at once, but I've never seen the point," Miranda says.

"It's fun," Maggie retorts.

"But it goes both ways, right?" Miranda counters. "We hate guys who date more than one woman at a time. I've always believed that what's unacceptable in one sex should, by definition, be unacceptable in the other."

"Excuse me." Maggie sounds a warning note. "I hope you're not calling me a slut."

"Of course not!" I jump in. "Miranda's only talking about feminism."

"Then you shouldn't have any problem with women having sex with as many men as they want," Maggie says pointedly. "To me, that's feminism."

"You can do anything you want, sweetie," I reassure her. "No one's judging you."

"All I'm saying is that men and women are the same. They should be held to the same standards," Miranda insists.

"I totally disagree. Men and women are completely different," Maggie replies obstinately.

"I kind of hate when people say men and women are different," I interject. "It sounds like an excuse. Like when people say, 'Boys will be boys.' It makes me want to scream."

"It makes me want to sock someone," Miranda agrees.

Maggie stands up. "All I can say is that you two deserve each other." And while Miranda and I look at her in bewilderment, Maggie runs into the bathroom and slams the door.

"Was it something I said?" Miranda asks.

"It's not you. It's me. She's mad at me. About something. Even though I should be mad at her."

I knock on the bathroom door. "Mags? Are you okay? We were just having a conversation. We weren't saying anything bad about you."

"I'm taking a shower," she shouts.

Miranda gathers her things. "I'd better go."

"Okay," I demur, dreading being left alone with Maggie. Once she gets angry, she can carry a grudge for days.

"Marty's coming over anyway. After he finishes studying." She waves and hurries down the stairs.

Lucky her.

The shower is still going full blast. I straighten up my desk, hoping the worst is not to come.

Eventually Maggie comes out of the bathroom toweling her hair. She begins picking up her things, stuffing clothing into her duffel bag.

"You're not leaving, are you?"

"I think I should," she grumbles.

"C'mon, sweetie. I'm sorry. Miranda is just very adamant about her views. She doesn't have anything against you. She doesn't even know you."

"You can say that again."

"Since you're not seeing Ryan, maybe we could go to a movie?" I ask hopefully.

"There's nothing I want to see." She looks around. "Where's the phone?"

It's under the chair. I grab it and hand it over reluctantly. "Listen, Mags," I say, trying not to be confrontational. "If you don't mind, could you not call South Carolina? I have to pay for the long distance calls, and I don't have that much money."

"Is that all you're about now? Money?"

"No—"

"As a matter of fact, I'm calling the bus."

"You don't have to go," I say, desperate to make up. I don't want her visit to end in a fight.

Maggie ignores me, looking at her watch as she nods into the receiver. "Thanks." She hangs up. "There's a bus that leaves for Philadelphia in forty-five minutes. Do you think I can make it?"

"Yes. But, Maggie—" I break off. I really don't know what to say.

"You've changed, Carrie," she says, zipping up her bag with a snap.

"I still don't know why you're so angry. Whatever I've done, I'm sorry."

"You're a different person. I don't know who you are anymore." She punctuates this with a shake of her head.

I sigh. This confrontation has likely been brewing since the moment Maggie turned up at the apartment and declared it a slum. "The only thing that's different about me is that I'm in New York."

"I know. You haven't stopped reminding me of the fact for two days."

"I do live here—"

"You know what?" She picks up her bag. "Everyone here is crazy. Your roommate Samantha is crazy. Bernard is a creep, and your friend Miranda is a freak. And Ryan is an asshole." She pauses while I cringe, imagining what's coming next. "And now you're just like them. You're crazy too."

I'm stunned. "Thanks a lot."

"You're welcome." She starts for the door. "And don't

worry about taking me to the bus station. I can get there myself."

"Fine." I shrug.

She exits the apartment, banging the door behind her. For a moment, I'm too shaken to move. How dare she attack me? And why is it always about her? The whole time she was here, she barely had the decency to ask me how I was doing. She could have tried to understand my situation instead of criticizing everything about it.

I take a deep breath. I yank open the door and run after her. "Maggie!"

She's already outside, standing on the curb, her arm raised to hail a taxi. I hurry toward her as a taxi pulls up and she opens the door.

"Maggie!"

She spins around, her hand on the handle. "What?"

"Come on. Don't leave this way. *I'm sorry.*"

Her face has turned to stone. "Good." She crawls into the backseat and shuts the door.

My body sags as I watch the taxi weave into traffic. I tilt my head back, letting the rain's drizzle soothe my hurt feelings. "Why?" I ask aloud.

I stomp back into the building. Damn Ryan. He *is* an asshole. If he hadn't stood Maggie up, we wouldn't have had this fight. We'd still be friends. Sure, I'd be a little pissed off with her for sleeping with Ryan, but I would have ignored it. For the sake of our friendship.

Why can't she extend the same courtesy to me?

I bang around in the apartment a while, all churned up

about Maggie's disastrous visit. I hesitate, then pick up the phone and call Walt.

While it rings, I remember how I've neglected Walt all summer and how he's probably pissed at me too. I shudder, thinking about what a bad friend I've been. I'm not even sure Walt is still living at home. When his mother picks up, I say, "It's Carrie," in the sweetest voice possible. "Is Walt there?"

"Hello, Carrie," Walt's mother says. "Are you still in New York?"

"Yes, I am."

"I'm sure Walt will be very happy to hear from you," she adds, sticking another knife into the wound. "Walt!" she calls out. "It's Carrie."

I hear Walt coming into the kitchen. I picture the red Formica table crowded with chairs. The dog's bowl slopped over with water. The toaster oven where Walt's mother keeps the sugar so ants won't get it. And, no doubt, the look of confusion on Walt's face. Wondering why I've decided to call him now, when I've forgotten him for weeks.

"Hello?" he asks.

"Walt!" I exclaim.

"Is this *the* Carrie Bradshaw?"

"I guess so."

"What a surprise. I thought you were dead."

"Oh, Walt." I giggle nervously, knowing I deserve a hard time.

Walt seems ready to forgive, because the next thing he asks is, "Well, *qué pasa*? How's Nuevo?"

"*Bueno. Muy bueno*," I reply. "How are you?" I lower my voice. "Are you still seeing Randy?"

"*Mais oui!*" he exclaims. "In fact, my father has decided to look the other way. Thanks to Randy's interest in football."

"That's great. You're having a real relationship."

"It appears so, yes. Much to my surprise."

"You're lucky, Walt."

"What about you? Anyone special?" he asks, putting a sarcastic spin on "special."

"I don't know. I've been seeing this guy. But he's older. Maggie met him," I say, getting to my underlying reason for the call. "She hated him."

Walt laughs. "I'm not surprised. Maggie hates everyone these days."

"Why?"

"Because she has no idea what to do with her life. And she can't stand anyone who does."

Thirty minutes later, I've told Walt the whole story about Maggie's visit, which he finds immensely entertaining. "Why don't you come to visit me?" I ask, feeling better. "You and Randy. You could sleep in the bed."

"A bed's too good for Randy," Walt says jokingly. "He can sleep on the floor. In fact, he can sleep anywhere. If you take him to a store, he'll fall asleep standing up."

I smile. "Seriously, though."

"When are you coming home?" he asks.

"I don't know."

"You know about your father, of course," he says smoothly.

"No."

"Oops."

"Why?" I ask. "What's going on?"

"Hasn't anyone told you? Your father has a girlfriend."

I clutch the phone in disbelief. But it makes sense. No wonder he's been acting so strange lately.

"I'm sorry. I figured you knew," Walt continues. "I only know because my mother told me. She's going to be the new librarian at the high school. She's like twenty-five or something."

"My father is dating a twenty-five-year-old?" I shriek.

"I thought you'd want to know."

"Damn right," I say, furious. "I guess I'll be coming home this weekend after all."

"Great," Walt says. "We could use some excitement around here."

CHAPTER TWENTY

"This will never do," Samantha says, shaking her head.

"It's luggage." I, too, glare at the offending suitcase. It's ugly, but still, the sight of that suitcase makes me insanely jealous. I'm going back to boring old Castlebury while Samantha is headed for Los Angeles.

Los Angeles! It's a very big deal and she only found out yesterday. She's going to shoot a commercial and stay at the Beverly Hills Hotel, which is where all the movie stars hang out. She bought enormous sunglasses and a big straw hat and a Norma Kamali bathing suit that you wear with a white T-shirt underneath. In honor of the occasion, I tried to find a palm tree at the party store, but all they had were some green paper leafy things that I've wrapped around my head.

There are clothes and shoes everywhere. Samantha's enormous green plastic Samsonite suitcase lies open on the living room floor.

"It's not luggage, it's baggage," she complains.

"Who's going to notice?"

"Everyone. We're flying first-class. There'll be porters. And bellhops. What are the bellhops going to think when they discover Samantha Jones travels with Samsonite?"

I love it when Samantha does that funny thing and talks about herself in the third person. I tried it once myself, but there was no way I could pull it off. "Do you honestly think the bellhops are going to be more interested in Samsonite than Samantha Jones?"

"That's just it. They'll expect my luggage to be glamorous as well."

"I bet that jerky Harry Mills carries American Tourister. Hey," I say, swinging my legs off the back of the couch. "Did you ever think that someday you'd be traveling with a man you hardly knew? It's kind of weird, isn't it? What if your suitcase opens by accident and he sees your Skivvies?"

"I'm not worried about my lingerie. I'm worried about my image. I never thought I'd have this life when I bought that." She frowns at the suitcase.

"What *did* you think?" I hardly know anything about Samantha's past, besides the fact that she comes from New Jersey and seems to hate her mother. She never mentions her father, so these tidbits about her early life are always fascinating.

"Only about getting away. Far, far away."

"But New Jersey's just across the river."

"Physically, yes. Metaphorically, no. And New York wasn't my first stop."

"It wasn't?" Now I'm really intrigued. I can't imagine Samantha living anywhere but New York.

"I traveled all around the world when I was eighteen."

I nearly fall off the couch. "How?"

She smiles. "I was a groupie. To a very famous rock 'n' roll guy. I was at a concert and he picked me out of the crowd. He asked me to travel with him and I was stupid enough to think I was his girlfriend. Then I found out he had a wife stashed away in the English countryside. That suitcase has been all around the world."

I wonder if Samantha's hatred of her luggage is actually due to a bad association with the past. "And then what happened?"

She shrugs, picking out lingerie from the pile and folding the pieces into little squares. "He dumped me. In Moscow. His wife suddenly decided to join him. He woke up that afternoon and said, 'Darling, I'm afraid it's over. You're binned.'"

"Just like that?"

"He was English," she says, laying the squares into the bottom of the suitcase. "That's what Englishmen do. When it's over, it's over. No phone calls, no letters, and especially no crying."

"Did you? Cry?" I can't picture it.

"What do you think? I was all alone in Moscow with nothing but this stupid suitcase. And a plane ticket to New York. I was jumping up and down for joy."

I can't tell if she's kidding or not.

"In other words, it's your runaway suitcase," I point out.

"And now that you don't need to run anymore, you need something better. Something permanent."

"Hmmm," she says cryptically.

"What's it like?" I ask. "When you pass a record store and see the rock 'n' roll guy's face on a poster? Does it make you feel weird to think you spent all that time with him?"

"I'm grateful." She grabs a shoe and looks around for its partner. "Sometimes I think if it weren't for him, I wouldn't have made it to New York at all."

"Didn't you always want to come here?"

She shrugs. "I was a wild child. I didn't know what I wanted. I only knew I didn't want to end up a waitress and pregnant at nineteen. Like Shirley."

"Oh."

"My mother," she clarifies.

I'm not surprised. There's an underlying pulse of determination in Samantha that has to come from somewhere.

"You're lucky." She finds the matching shoe and pushes it into the corner of the suitcase. "At least you have parents who will pay for college."

"Yeah," I say vaguely. Despite her confessions about her past, I'm not ready to tell her about my own. "But I thought you went to college."

"Oh, Sparrow." She sighs. "I took a couple of night courses when I arrived in New York. I got a job through a temp agency. The first place they sent me was Slovey, Dinall. I was a secretary. They didn't even call them 'assistants' back then. Anyway, it's boring."

Not to me. But the fact that she's come so far from

nothing puts my own struggles to shame. "It must have been hard."

"It was." She presses down on the top of the suitcase. There's practically her whole closet in there, so naturally, it won't shut. I kneel on the cover as she clicks the locks into place.

The phone rings as we're dragging the suitcase to the door. Samantha ignores the insistent ringing, so I make a move to grab it. "Don't answer," she warns. But I've already picked it up.

"Hello?"

"Is Samantha still there?"

Samantha frantically shakes her head. "Charlie?" I ask.

"Yeah." He doesn't sound terribly friendly. I wonder if he found out it was me doing the cooking after all.

I hold out the receiver. Samantha rolls her eyes as she takes it. "Hello, darling. I'm about to walk out the door." There's an edge of annoyance in her tone.

"Yes, I know," she continues. "But I can't make it." She pauses and lowers her voice. "I told you. I have to go. I don't have a choice," she adds, sounding resigned. "Well, life's inconvenient, Charlie." And she hangs up the phone.

She briefly closes her eyes, inhales, and forces a smile. "Men."

"Charlie?" I ask, perplexed. "I thought you guys were so happy."

"Too happy. When I told him I suddenly had to go to LA, he freaked out. Said he'd made plans for us to have dinner with his mother tonight. Which he somehow neglected to tell me. As if I don't have a life of my own."

"Maybe you can't have it both ways. His life *and* your life. How do you put two lives together, anyway?"

She gives me a look as she picks up her suitcase. "Wish me luck in Hollywood, Sparrow. Maybe I'll be discovered."

"What about Charlie?" I hold open the door as she bangs the suitcase down the stairs. It's a good thing it is a Samsonite. Most suitcases probably couldn't take the abuse.

"What about him?" she calls out.

Boy. She must really be angry.

I run to the window and lean out over the parapet to catch a glimpse of the street below. An enormous limousine is idling at the curb. A uniformed driver stands next to the passenger door. Samantha emerges from the building as the driver hurries forward to take her suitcase.

The passenger door opens, and Harry Mills gets out. He and Samantha have a brief exchange as he lights up a cigar. Samantha slides past him and gets into the car. Harry takes a big puff on the cigar, looks up and down the street, and follows. The door closes and the limo pulls away, a puff of cigar smoke drifting from the open window.

Behind me, the phone rings. I approach it cautiously, but curiosity gets the better of me and I pick it up. "Is Samantha there?" It's Charlie. Again.

"She just left," I say politely.

"Damn," he shouts, and hangs up.

Damn you, too, I think, quietly replacing the receiver.

213

I retrieve my own Hartmann suitcase from under Samantha's bed. The phone rings some more, but I know better than to answer it.

After a while, the caller gives up. Then the buzzer goes off. "Yes?" I ask brusquely, into the intercom.

"It's Ryan," comes back the garbled reply.

I click open the door. Ryan. I'm working myself up to give him what-for about Maggie, when he appears at the top of the stairs holding a lone rose. The stem is limp and I briefly wonder if he picked it up off the street.

"You're too late," I say accusingly. "Maggie left last night."

"Rats. I knew I fucked up."

I should probably tell him to go away, but I'm not finished. "Who runs out of a diner while their date is in the bathroom?"

"I was tired," he says helplessly, as if this is a legitimate excuse.

"You're kidding. Right?"

He gives me a hangdog look. "I couldn't figure out how to say good-bye. I was exhausted. And I'm not Superman. I try to be, but somewhere along the line I seem to have encountered kryptonite."

I smile in spite of myself. Ryan is one of those guys who can always joke himself out of the bad books. I know he knows it, and I know it's disloyal, but I can't stay mad at him. After all, he didn't stand me up.

"Maggie was really, really hurt," I scold.

"I figured she would be. That's why I came by.

To make it up to her."

"With that rose?"

"It is pretty sad, isn't it?"

"It's pathetic. Especially since she took her anger out on me."

"On you?" He's surprised. "Why would she take it out on you? It wasn't your fault."

"No. But somehow I got lumped in with your bad behavior. We got into a fight."

"Was there hair pulling?"

"No, there was not," I say, indignant. "Jesus, Ryan."

"I'm sorry." He grins. "Guys love girl fights. What can I say?"

"Why don't you just admit you're an asshole?"

"Because that would be too easy. Capote's an asshole. I'm just a jerk."

"Nice way to talk about your best friend."

"Just because we're friends doesn't mean I have to lie about his personality," he says.

"I suppose that's true," I unwillingly agree, wondering why women are so judgmental of each other. Why can't we say, "Hey, she's kind of messed up, but I love her anyway?"

"I came by to ask Maggie to Rainbow's father's art opening. It's tonight. There's a dinner afterward. It's going to be really cool."

"I'll go," I volunteer, wondering why no one invites me to these glamorous parties.

"You?" Ryan asks, unsure.

"Why not? Am I chopped liver or something?"

"Not at all," he says, backpedaling. "But Maggie said you were obsessed with Bernard Singer."

"I don't have to see Bernard every night." I fudge, unwilling to admit that Bernard and I are probably over.

"Okay, then," he gives in. "I'll meet you at the gallery at eight."

Yippee, I think, when he's gone. I've been hearing about this art opening for weeks, wondering if Rainbow would ask me, and if not, how I could wrangle an invitation. I kept telling myself it was only a stupid party, while secretly knowing it was an event I didn't want to miss.

And since Bernard hasn't called, why not? I'm certainly not going to put my life on hold for him.

CHAPTER TWENTY-ONE

The gallery is in SoHo, a deserted patch of run-down blocks with cobblestoned streets and enormous buildings that were once factories. It's hard to imagine Manhattan as a center of industrialism, but apparently they used to make everything here, from clothing to lightbulbs to tools. A metal ramp leads to the gallery's entrance, the railing decorated with all manner of chic, downtown types, smoking cigarettes and discussing what they did the night before.

I push my way through the crowd. It's packed inside, a mass of patrons forming a bottleneck by the entrance as everyone seems to have run into someone they know. The air is filled with smoke and the damp smell of sweat, but there's the familiar buzz of excitement that indicates this is the place to be.

I take refuge along a wall, avoiding the circle of

well-wishers gathered around a portly man with a goatee and hooded eyes. He's dressed in a black smock and embroidered slippers, so I assume this is the great Barry Jessen himself, the most important artist in New York and Rainbow's father. Indeed, Rainbow is standing behind him, looking, for the first time, lost and rather insignificant, despite the fact that she's wearing a bright green fringed dress. Next to Barry, and towering over him by at least a head, is the model Pican.

She has the deliberately unself-conscious look of a woman who's aware she's exceptionally beautiful and knows you know it too, but is determined not to make her beauty the main attraction. She holds her head cocked slightly to the side and leaning toward her husband, as if to say, "Yes, I know I'm beautiful, but this night is all about him." It is, I suppose, the ultimate indication of true love.

Either that, or it's very good acting.

I don't see Ryan or Capote yet, so I pretend to be extremely interested in the art. You'd think other people would be curious as well, but the spaces in front of the paintings are mostly empty, as if socializing is what an opening is really about.

And maybe for good reason. I can't decide what I think about the paintings. They're black and gray, with stick figures that appear to be victims of terrible violence or purveyors of injury. Hellish drops of blood drip from every angle. The stick figures are pierced with knives and needles while claws rip their ankles. It's all very disturbing and quite unforgettable, which may be the point.

"What do you think?" asks Rainbow, coming up

behind me. I'm surprised she's lowered herself to solicit my opinion, but so far I'm the only person here who's remotely close to her age.

"Powerful," I say.

"I think they're creepy."

"You do?" I'm surprised she's so honest.

"Don't tell my father."

"I won't."

"Ryan said he's bringing you to the dinner," she says, twirling a piece of fringe. "I'm glad. I would have invited you myself, but I didn't have your number."

"That's okay. I'm happy to be here."

She smiles and drifts away. I go back to staring at the paintings. Maybe New York isn't so complicated after all. Perhaps belonging is simply a matter of showing up. If people see you enough, they assume you're part of their group.

Eventually, Ryan and Capote appear, already in their cups. Ryan is weaving slightly and Capote is jovial, greeting everyone he sees like they're an old friend.

"Carrie!" he says, kissing me on both cheeks as if he couldn't be more pleased to see me.

A secret signal pulses through the crowd, and several people glide to the exit. These, apparently, are the chosen ones—chosen to attend the dinner, anyway.

"C'mon," Ryan says, jerking his head toward the door. We follow the select group onto the street as Ryan runs his hands through his hair.

"Man, that was terrible," he exclaims. "You've got to

wonder what the world is coming to when we call that 'art.'"

"You're a philistine," Capote says.

"You can't tell me you actually liked that shit."

"I did," I say. "I thought it was disturbing."

"Disturbing, but not in a good way," Ryan says.

Capote laughs. "You can take the boy out of the suburbs but you can't take the suburbs out of the boy."

"I take serious offense to that comment," Ryan cracks.

"*I'm* from the suburbs," I say.

"Of course you are," Capote says, with a certain amount of disdain.

"And you're from someplace better?" I challenge him.

"Capote's from an old Southern family, darlin'," Ryan says, imitating Capote's accent. "His grandmother fought off the Yankees. Which would make her about a hundred and fifty years old."

"I never said my grandmother fought the Yankees. I said she told me never to *marry* one."

"I guess that lets me out," I comment, while Ryan snickers in appreciation.

The dinner is being held at the Jessens' loft. It seems like ten years ago when L'il laughed at me for thinking the Jessens lived in a building without running water, but my early assessment isn't far off. The building is a little scary. The freight elevator has a door that slides open manually, followed by one of those clanging wire gates. Inside is a crank to move the elevator up and down.

The operation of said elevator is a source of consternation.

When we get in, five people are discussing the alternate possibility of finding the stairs.

"It's terrible when people live in these places," says a man with yellow hair.

"It's cheap," Ryan points out.

"Cheap shouldn't mean dangerous."

"What's a little danger when you're the most important artist in New York?" Capote says, with his usual arrogance.

"Oh my. You're so macho," the man replies. The lighting in the elevator is dim and when I turn around to take a closer look, I discover the speaker is none other than Bobby. The Bobby from the fashion show. Who promised me a reading in his space.

"Bobby," I nearly shout.

He doesn't recognize me at first. "Hello, yes, great to see you again," he replies automatically.

"It's me," I insist. "Carrie Bradshaw?"

He suddenly remembers. "Of course! Carrie Bradshaw. The playwright."

Capote snorts and, since no one else seems either capable or interested, takes over the operation of the crank. The elevator lurches upward with a sickening jolt that throws several of the occupants against the wall.

"I'm so happy I didn't eat anything today," remarks a woman in a long silver coat.

Capote manages to get the elevator reasonably close to the third story, meaning the doors open a couple of feet above the floor. Ever the gentleman, he hops out and extends his hand to the lady in the silver coat. Ryan gets out on his own, followed by Bobby, who jumps and falls to his knees. When it's my turn, Capote hesitates, his arm poised midair.

"I'm fine," I say, rejecting his offer.

"Come on, Carrie. Don't be a jerk."

"In other words, try being a lady," I murmur, taking his hand.

"For once in your life."

I'm about to continue this argument, when Bobby inserts himself and links his arm through mine. "Let's get a drink and you can tell me all about your new play," he gushes.

The huge open space has been hastily remodeled into something resembling an apartment by the addition of Sheetrock walls. The area near the windows is as big as a skating rink; along one side is a table, covered with a white cloth, that probably seats sixty. In front of the ceiling-high windows is a grouping of couches and arm-chairs draped with sailcloth. The wooden floor is worn, scuffed by the feet of hundreds of factory workers. In a few places, it's actually black, as if someone set a small fire, thought better of it, and extinguished the flames.

"Here you go," Bobby says, handing me a plastic cup filled with what turns out to be cheap champagne. He takes my hand. "Who do you want to meet? I know everyone."

I want to extract my hand, but it seems rude. And besides, I'm sure Bobby is only being friendly. "Barry Jessen?" I ask boldly.

"Don't you know him?" Bobby asks, with such genuine surprise it makes me laugh. I can't imagine why Bobby would think I knew the great Barry Jessen, but apparently he assumes I get around quite a bit. Which only reinforces my theory: if people see you enough, they think you're one of them.

Bobby marches me straight up to Barry Jessen himself, who is engaged in conversation with several people at once, and pulls me into the circle. My sense of belonging dissipates like a mist but Bobby seems immune to the hostile glances. "This is Carrie Bradshaw," he announces to Barry. "She's dying to meet you. You're her favorite artist."

Not one word of this is true, but I don't dare contradict him. Especially as Barry Jessen's expression changes from irritation to mild interest. He isn't immune to flattery— just the opposite. He expects it.

"Is that so?" His black eyes lock on mine and I suddenly have the eerie sensation of staring into the face of the devil.

"I loved your show," I say awkwardly.

"Do you think others will love it as well?" he demands.

His intensity unnerves me. "It's so powerful, how can anyone not love it?" I blurt out, hoping he won't question me further.

He doesn't. Having received his kudos, he abruptly turns away, addressing himself to the lady in the silver coat.

Unfortunately, Bobby doesn't get the message. "Now, Barry," he begins insistently. "We have to talk about Basil," at which point I seize the opportunity to escape. The thing about famous people, I realize, is that just because you can meet them doesn't make you a famous person yourself.

I skitter down a little hallway and past a closed door, from which I hear laughter and hushed whisperings, then past another door that's probably the bathroom because several people are lined up beside it, and right on through to an open door at the end of the corridor.

I pull up short, startled by the decor. The room is completely different from the rest of the loft. Oriental rugs are strewn across the floor and an ornate antique Indian bed covered with silk pillows sits in the center.

I figure I've wandered in the Jessens' bedroom by accident, but it's Rainbow who's resting on the bed, talking to a guy wearing a knit Jamaican cap perched over dreadlocks.

"Sorry," I murmur quickly, as the guy looks up in surprise. He's shockingly handsome, with chiseled features and beautiful black eyes.

Rainbow whips around, startled, worried she's been caught out, but when she sees me, she relaxes. "It's only Carrie," she says. "She's cool."

"Only Carrie" ventures a step closer. "What are you guys doing?"

"This is my brother, Colin," Rainbow says, indicating the guy with the dreadlocks.

"You get high?" Colin asks, holding up a small marijuana pipe.

"Sure." Somehow, I don't think being a little stoned at this party is going to be a problem. Half the people here already seem like they're on something.

Rainbow makes space for me on the bed. "I love your

room," I say, admiring the luxurious furnishings.

"You do?" She takes the pipe from Colin, leaning forward as he flicks the bowl with a gold lighter.

"It's very anti-Barry," Colin says, in a clipped accent. "That's what's so great about it."

I take a hit from the pipe and pass it to Colin. "Are you English?" I ask, wondering how he can be English while Rainbow seems so American.

Rainbow giggles. "He's Amhara. Like my mother."

"So Barry isn't your father?"

"Lord, no!" Colin exclaims. He and Rainbow exchange a secretive look.

"Does anyone actually like their father?" Rainbow asks.

"I do," I murmur. Maybe it's the dope, but I'm suddenly feeling sentimental about my old man. "He's a really good guy."

"You're lucky," Colin says. "I haven't seen my real father since I was ten."

I nod as though I understand, but honestly, I don't. My father might not be perfect, but I know he loves me. If something bad happened, he'd be there for me—or would try to be, anyway.

"Which reminds me," Colin says, reaching into his pocket and extracting a small aspirin bottle that he shakes in Rainbow's face. "I found these in Barry's stash."

"Oh, Colin. You didn't," Rainbow squeals.

Colin pops open the top and shakes out three large round pills. "I did."

"What if he notices they're gone?"

"He won't. By the end of the night, he'll be too high to notice anything."

Rainbow plucks one of the pills out of Colin's hand and washes it down with a gulp of champagne.

"You want one, Carrie?" Colin offers me a pill.

I don't ask what it is. I don't want to know. I already feel like I've found out more than I should. I shake my head.

"They're really fun," Colin urges, popping the pill into his mouth.

"I'm good," I say.

"If you change your mind, you know where to find me. Just ask for an aspirin," he says as he and Rainbow fall onto the cushions, laughing.

Back in the main room, there's the usual frenetic energy of people jabbering and shouting into one another's faces to be heard above the din. Cigarette and marijuana smoke waft through the air, while Pican and some of her model friends lounge indolently on the couches with half-closed eyes. I walk past them to the open window for some fresh air.

I remind myself that I'm having a good time.

Bobby spots me and begins waving frantically. He's talking to a middle-aged woman in a skin-tight white dress that looks like it's made of bandages. I wave back and hold up my cup, indicating I'm on my way to the bar, but he won't be deterred. "Carrie," he shouts. "Come meet Teensie Dyer."

I put on my best game face and saunter over.

Teensie looks like someone who eats small children for

breakfast. "This is Carrie Bradshaw," Bobby crows. "You should be her agent. Did you know she's written a play?"

"Hello," she says, giving me a narrow smile.

Bobby puts his arm around my shoulder, trying to press me closer as I stiffly resist. "We're going to perform Carrie's new play in my space. You must come."

Teensie flicks her cigarette ash on the floor. "What's it about?"

Damn Bobby, I think, as I wriggle out of his grasp. I'm not about to talk about my play to a complete stranger. Especially as I hardly know what it's about myself.

"Carrie won't say." Bobby pats my arm. And leaning into my ear, adds in a stage whisper, "Teensie's the biggest agent in town. She represents everyone. Including Bernard Singer."

The smile freezes on my face. "That's nice."

There must be something in my expression that sets off a warning bell because Teensie deigns to finally look me in the eye.

I glance away, hoping to steer the conversation in another direction. Something tells me this Teensie person will be none too pleased to discover her biggest client is dating little ol' me. Or was dating little ol' me, anyway.

The music stops.

"Dinner is served!" shouts Barry Jessen from the top of a ladder.

CHAPTER TWENTY-TWO

As if the night couldn't get any weirder, I find myself seated next to Capote.

"You again?" I ask, squeezing past him onto my folding chair.

"What's your problem?" he says.

I roll my eyes. Where to begin? With the fact that I miss Bernard and wish he were here? Or that I'd prefer to be sitting next to someone else? I settle on: "I just met Teensie Dyer."

He looks impressed. "She's a big agent."

Figures he'd say that. "She seemed like a bitch to me."

"That's stupid, Carrie."

"Why? It's the truth."

"Or your perspective."

"Which is?"

"This is a hard city, Carrie. You know that."

228

"So?" I say.

"You want to end up hard too? Like most of these people?"

I look at him in disbelief. Doesn't he realize he's one of them? "I'm not worried," I retort.

A bowl of pasta comes our way. Capote grabs it and politely serves me, then himself. "Tell me you're not really going to do your play at Bobby's."

"Why not?"

"Because Bobby is a joke."

I give him a nasty smile. "Or is it because he hasn't asked you to perform your great work?"

"I wouldn't do it even if he did. It's not the way to do things, Carrie. You'll see."

I shrug. "I guess that's the difference between you and me. I don't mind taking chances."

"Do you want me to lie to you? Like everyone else in your life?"

I shake my head, mystified. "How do you know people lie to me? More likely they lie to you. But the biggest liar in your life? *Yourself.*" I take a gulp of wine, hardly believing what I just said.

"Fine," he says, as if I'm hopeless.

He turns to the woman on his other side. I follow his cue and smile at the man on my left.

I breathe a sigh of relief. It's Cholly. "Hello," I say brightly, determined to forget about my encounter with Teensie and my hatred of Capote.

"Little one!" he exclaims. "My goodness. You certainly

do get around. Is New York turning out to be everything you hoped?"

I glance around the table. Rainbow is slumped in her chair, eyes half closed, while Capote is pontificating about his favorite topic again—Proust. I spot Ryan, who has had the good luck to be seated next to Teensie. He's making eyes at her, no doubt hoping she'll take him on as a client. Meanwhile, Bobby is standing behind Barry Jessen, desperately trying to engage him while Barry, now sweating profusely, angrily wipes his face with a napkin.

I experience one of those bizarre moments where the universe telescopes and everything is magnified: the movement of Pican's lipsticked mouth, the stream of red wine Bobby pours into his glass, the gold signet ring on Teensie's right finger as she raises her hand to her temple.

I wonder if Maggie was right. Maybe we are all crazy.

And suddenly, everything goes back to normal. Teensie gets up. Barry makes room for Bobby next to him. Ryan leans over to Rainbow and whispers something in her ear.

I turn back to Cholly. "I think it's fantastic."

He seems interested, so I start telling him about my adventures. How I got kicked out of Peggy's. And how I named Viktor Greene's mustache Waldo. And how Bobby wants me to do a reading of my play when I haven't even finished it yet. When I'm done, I have Cholly in stitches. There's nothing better than a man who's a good audience.

"You should come to a soiree at my house sometime," he says. "I have this wonderful little publication called *The*

New Review. We like to pretend it's literary, but every so often it requires a party."

I'm writing my phone number on a napkin for him when Teensie approaches. At first I think I'm her target, but it's Cholly she's after.

"Darling," she says, aggressively inserting a chair between Cholly and me, therefore effectively cutting me off. "I've just met the most charming young writer. Ryan somebody. You ought to meet him."

"Love to," Cholly says. And with a wink, he leans around Teensie. "Have you met Carrie Bradshaw? She's a writer too. She was just telling me—"

Teensie abruptly changes the subject. "Have you seen Bernard, lately?"

"Last week," Cholly says dismissively, indicating he has no interest in talking about Bernard.

"I'm worried about him," Teensie says.

"Why?" Cholly asks. Men are never concerned about each other the way women are.

"I heard he's dating some young girl."

My stomach clenches.

"Margie says Bernard's a mess," Teensie continues, with a sidelong glance my way. I try to keep my face disinterested, as if I hardly know who she's talking about. "Margie said she met her. And frankly, she's concerned. She thinks it's a very bad sign that Bernard is seeing someone so young."

I pour myself more wine while pretending to be fascinated by something at the other end of the table. But my hand is shaking.

"Why would Margie Shephard care? She's the one who left him," Cholly says.

"Is that what he told you?" Teensie asks slyly.

Cholly shrugs. "Everyone knows she cheated on him. With an actor in his play."

Teensie snickers. "Sadly, the reverse is true. Bernard cheated on her."

A wire wraps around my heart and squeezes tight.

"In fact, Bernard cheated on Margie several times. He's a wonderful playwright, but a lousy husband."

"Really, Teensie. What does it matter?" Cholly remarks.

Teensie puts a hand on his arm. "This party is giving me an awful headache. Could you ask Barry for some aspirin?"

I glare at her. Why can't she ask Barry herself? Damn her and what she said about Bernard and me. "Colin has aspirin," I interject helpfully. "Pican's son?"

Teensie's eyebrows rise in suspicion, but I give her an innocent smile.

"Well, thank you." She gives me a sharp look and goes off to find Colin.

I hold my napkin to my face and laugh.

Cholly laughs along with me. "Teensie's a very silly woman, isn't she?"

I nod, speechless. The thought of the evil Teensie on one of Colin's pills is just too funny.

Of course, I don't really expect Teensie to take the pill. Even I, who know nothing about drugs, was smart enough to realize Colin's big white pill wasn't an aspirin. I don't give it much thought until an hour later, when I'm dancing with Ryan.

Swaying precariously on bended knees, Teensie appears in the middle of the floor, clutching Bobby's shoulder for support. She's giggling madly while attempting to remain upright. Her legs are like rubber. "Bobby!" she screams. "Did I ever tell you how much I love you?"

"What the hell?" Ryan asks.

I'm overcome by hysteria. Apparently, Teensie took the pill after all, because she's lying on her back on the floor, laughing. This goes on for several seconds until Cholly swoops in, pulls Teensie to her feet, and leads her away.

I keep on dancing.

Indeed, everyone keeps dancing until we're interrupted by a loud scream followed by several shouts for help.

A crowd gathers by the elevator. The door is open, but the shaft appears to be empty.

Cries of "What happened?" "Someone fell!" "Call 911," echo through the loft. I rush forward, fearing it's Rainbow and that she's dead. But out of the corner of my eye I see Rainbow hurrying to her room, followed by Colin. I push in closer. Two men have jumped into the shaft, so the elevator must be a mere foot or two below. A limp woman's hand reaches out and Barry Jessen grabs it, hauling a disheveled and dazed Teensie out of the hole.

Before I can react, Capote elbows me. "Let's go."

"Huh?" I'm too startled to move.

He jerks my arm. "We need to get out of here. *Now.*"

"What about Teensie?"

"She's fine. And Ryan can take care of himself."

"I don't understand," I protest as Capote propels me to the exit.

"Don't ask questions." He flings open the door and starts down the stairs. I pause on the landing, baffled. "Carrie!" He turns around to make sure I'm following him. When he sees I'm not, he hops up the stairs and practically pushes me down in front of him. "Move!"

I do as he says, hearing the urgent thump of his feet after me. When we get to the lobby, he bangs through the door and yanks me out after him. "Run!" he shouts.

He races to the corner as I struggle to keep up in the Fiorucci boots Samantha gave me. Seconds later, two police cars, lights flashing and sirens wailing, pull up to the Jessens' building. Capote slings his arm around my shoulders. "Act normal. Like we're on a date or something."

We cross the street, my heart exploding in my chest. We walk like this for another block until we get to West Broadway and Prince Street. "I think there's a cool bar around here," Capote says.

"A 'cool' bar? Teensie just fell down the elevator shaft, and all you can think about is a 'cool' bar?"

He releases me from his grasp. "It's not my fault, is it?"

No, but it is mine. "We should go back. Aren't you worried about Teensie?"

"Look, Carrie," he says, exasperated. "I just saved your life. You should be grateful."

"I'm not sure what I'm supposed to be grateful for."

"You want to end up in the papers? Because that's what

234

would have happened. Half the people there were on drugs. You think the police aren't going to notice? And the next day it's all over Page Six. Maybe you don't care about your reputation. But I happen to care about mine."

"Why?" I ask, unimpressed by his self-importance.

"Because."

"Because why?" I taunt.

"I have a lot of people counting on me."

"Like who?"

"Like my family. They're very upright, good people. I would never want them to be embarrassed. On account of my actions."

"You mean like if you married a Yankee."

"Exactly."

"What do all these Yankee girls you date think? Or do you just not tell them?"

"I figure most women know what they're getting into when they date me. I never lie about my intentions."

I look down at the sidewalk, wondering what I'm doing standing on a corner in the middle of nowhere, arguing with Capote Duncan. "I guess I should tell you the truth too. I'm the one who's responsible for Teensie's accident."

"You?"

"I knew Colin had pills. He said they were aspirin. So I told Teensie to get an aspirin from him."

It takes a moment for Capote to process this information. He rubs his eyes while I worry he's going to turn me in. But then he tips back his head and laughs, his long curls falling over his shoulders.

"Pretty funny, huh?" I boast, preening in his approval. "I never thought she'd actually take the damn thing—"

Without warning, he cuts me off with a kiss.

I'm so surprised, I don't respond at first as his mouth presses on mine, pushing eagerly at my lips. Then my brain catches up. I'm confounded by how nice and natural it feels, like we've been kissing forever. Then I get it: this is how he gets all those women. He's a pouncer. He kisses a woman when she least expects it and once he's got her off-balance, he maneuvers her into bed.

Not going to happen this time, though. Although a terrible part of me wishes it would.

"No." I push him away.

"Carrie," he says.

"I can't." Have I just cheated on Bernard?

Am I even with Bernard?

A lone taxi snakes down the street, light on. It's available. I'm not. I flag it down.

Capote opens the door for me.

"Thanks," I say.

"See ya," he replies, as if nothing at all just happened.

I sag into the backseat, shaking my head.

What a night. Maybe it's a good time to get out of Dodge after all.

CHAPTER TWENTY-THREE

"Oh," my youngest sister, Dorrit, says, looking up from a magazine. "You're home."

"Yes, I am," I say, stating the obvious. I drop my bag and open the refrigerator, more out of habit than hunger. There's an almost-empty container of milk and a package of moldy cheese. I take out the bottle of milk and hold it up. "Doesn't anyone bother to shop around here?"

"No," Dorrit says sullenly. Her eyes go to my father, but he seems oblivious to her displeasure.

"I've got all my girls home!" he exclaims, overcome with emotion.

That's one thing that hasn't changed about my father: his excessive sentimentality. I'm glad there's still a remnant of my old father left. Because otherwise, he appears to have been taken over by an alien.

First off, he's wearing jeans. My father has never worn

jeans in his life. My mother wouldn't allow it. And he's sporting Ray-Ban sunglasses. But most bewildering of all is his jacket. It's by Members Only and it's orange. When I stepped off the train, I barely recognized him.

He must be going through a midlife crisis.

"Where's Missy?" I ask now, trying to ignore his strange getup.

"She's at the conservatory. She learned to play the violin," my father says proudly. "She's composing a symphony for an entire orchestra."

"She learned to play the violin in one month?" I ask, astounded.

"She's very talented," my father says.

What about me?

"Yeah, right, Dad," Dorrit says.

"You're okay too," my father replies.

"C'mon, Dorrit," I say, picking up my suitcase. "You can help me unpack."

"I'm busy."

"Dorrit!" I insist meaningfully, with a glance at my father.

She sighs, closes her magazine, and follows me upstairs.

My room is exactly how I left it. For a moment, I'm filled with memories, going to the shelves and touching the old books my mom gave me as a kid. I open my closet door and peek inside. I could be mistaken, but it looks like half my clothes are missing. I spin around and glare at Dorrit accusingly. "Where are my clothes?"

She shrugs. "I took some. And Missy. We figured that

since you were in New York, you wouldn't be needing them."

"What if I do?"

She shrugs again.

I let it go. It's too early in my visit to get into a fight with Dorrit—although given her sulky attitude, there's sure to be an altercation by the time I leave on Monday. In the meantime, I need to probe her for information about my father and this supposed girlfriend of his.

"What's up with Dad?" I ask, sitting cross-legged on the bed. It's only a single and suddenly feels tiny. I can't believe I slept in it for so many years.

"He's gone crazy. Obviously," Dorrit says.

"Why is he wearing jeans? And a Members Only jacket? It's hideous. Mom would never let him dress like that."

"Wendy gave it to him."

"Wendy?"

"His girlfriend."

"So this girlfriend thing is true?"

"I guess so."

I sigh. Dorrit is so blasé. There's no getting through to her. I only hope she's given up the shoplifting. "Have you met her?"

"Yeah," Dorrit says, noncommittally.

"And?" I nearly scream.

"Eh."

"Do you hate her?" This is a stupid question. Dorrit hates everyone.

"I try to pretend she doesn't exist."

239

"What does Dad think?"

"He doesn't notice," she says. "It's disgusting. When she's around, he only pays attention to her."

"Is she pretty?"

"*I* don't think so," Dorrit replies. "Anyway, you can see for yourself. Dad's making us go to dinner with her tonight."

"Ugh."

"And he has a motorcycle."

"What?" This time I really do scream.

"Didn't he tell you? He bought a motorcycle."

"He hasn't told me anything. He hasn't even told me about this Wendy person."

"He's probably afraid," Dorrit says. "Ever since he met her, he's become totally whipped."

Great, I think, unpacking my suitcase. This is going to be a terrific weekend.

A little bit later, I find my father in the garage, rearranging his tools. I immediately suspect that Dorrit is right—my father is avoiding me. I've been home for less than an hour, but already I'm wondering why I came back at all. No one seems the least bit interested in me or my life. Dorrit ran off to a girlfriend's house, my father has a motorcycle, and Missy is all caught up with her composing. I should have stayed in New York.

I spent the entire train ride mulling over last night. The kiss with Capote was a terrible mistake and I'm horrified I went along with it, if only for a few seconds. But what does it mean? Is it possible I secretly like Capote? No. He's probably one of those "love the one you're with" guys—meaning he automatically goes after whatever woman happens to be around when he's feeling horny. But there were plenty of other women at the party, including Rainbow. So why'd he pick me?

Feeling lousy and hungover, I bought some aspirin and drank a Coke. I kept torturing myself with all the unfinished business I was leaving behind, including Bernard. I even considered getting off the train in New Haven and taking the next train back to New York, but when I thought about how disappointed my family would be, I couldn't do it.

Now I wish I had.

"Dad!" I intone in annoyance.

He turns, startled, a wrench in his hand. "I was just cleaning out my workbench."

"I can see that." I peer around for this notorious motorcycle and spot it next to the wall, partly hidden behind my father's car. "Dorrit said you bought a motorcycle," I say craftily.

"Yes, Carrie, I did."

"Why?"

"I wanted to."

"But why?" I sound like a woeful girl who's just been dumped. And my father's acting like a jerky boy who doesn't have any answers.

"Do you want to see it?" he asks finally, unable to keep his obvious enthusiasm in check.

He wheels it out from behind the car. It's a motorcycle, all right. And not just any old motorcycle. It's a Harley. With enormous handlebars and a black body decaled with flames. The kind of motorcycle favored by members of the Hells Angels.

My father rides a Harley?

On the other hand, I'm impressed. It's no wussie motorcycle, that's for sure.

"What do you think?" he asks proudly.

"I like it."

He seems pleased. "I bought it off this kid in town. He was desperate for money. I only paid a thousand dollars."

"Wow." I shake my head. Everything about this is so unlike my father—from his sentence construction to the motorcycle itself—that for a moment I don't know what to say. "How'd you find this kid?" I ask.

"He's Wendy's cousin's son."

My eyes bug out of my head. I can't believe how casually he's mentioned her. I go along with the game. "Who's Wendy?"

He brushes the seat of the motorcycle with his hand. "She's my new friend."

So that's how he's going to play it. "What kind of friend?"

"She's very nice," he says, refusing to catch my eye.

"How come you didn't tell me about her?"

"Oh, Carrie." He sighs.

"Everyone says she's your girlfriend. Dorrit and Missy and even Walt."

"Walt knows?" he asks, surprised.

"Everyone knows, Dad," I say sharply. "Why didn't you tell *me*?"

He slides onto the seat of the motorcycle, playing with the levers. "Do you think you could cut me some slack?"

"Dad!"

"This is all very new for me."

I bite my lip. For a moment, my heart goes out to him. In the past five years, he hasn't shown an ounce of interest in any woman. Now he's apparently met someone he likes, which is a sign that he's moving forward. I should be happy for him. Unfortunately, all I can think about is my mother. And how he's betraying her. I wonder if my mother is up in heaven, looking down at what he's become. If she is, she'd be horrified.

"Did Mom know her? This Wendy friend of yours?"

He shakes his head, pretending to study the instrument panel. "No." He pauses. "I don't think so, anyway. She's a little bit younger."

"How young?" I demand.

I've suddenly pushed too hard, because he looks at me defiantly. "I don't know, Carrie. She's in her late twenties. I've been told it's rude to ask a woman her age."

I nod knowingly. "And how old does she think you are?"

"She knows I have a daughter who's going to Brown in the fall."

There's a sharpness in his tone I haven't heard since I was a kid. It means, *I'm in charge. Back off.*

"Fine." I turn to go.

"And Carrie?" he adds. "We're having dinner with her tonight. I'm going to be very disappointed if you're rude to her."

"We'll see," I mutter under my breath. I head back to the house, convinced my worst fears have been confirmed. I already hate this Wendy woman. She has a relative who's a Hells Angel. And she lies about her age. I figure if a woman is willing to lie about her own birth date, she's willing to lie about pretty much anything.

I start to clean out the refrigerator, tossing out one scientific experiment after another. That's when I remember that I've lied about my age as well. To Bernard. I pour the last of the sour milk down the drain, wondering what my family is coming to.

"Don't you look special?" Walt quips. "Though a mite overdressed for Castlebury."

"What does one wear to a restaurant in Castlebury?"

"Surely not an evening gown."

"Walt," I scold. "It's not an evening gown. It's a hostess gown. From the sixties." I found it at my vintage store and I've been wearing it practically nonstop for days. It's perfect for sweaty weather, leaving my arms and legs unencumbered, and so far, no one has commented on my unusual garb except to say they liked it. Odd clothing is expected in New York. Here, not so much.

"I'm not going to change my style for Wendy. Did you know she has a cousin who's a Hells Angel?"

Walt and I are sitting on the porch, sipping cocktails while we wait for the notorious Wendy to arrive. I begged Walt to join us for dinner, but he declined, claiming a previous engagement with Randy. He did, however, agree to come by for a drink, so he could see the Wendy person in the flesh.

"Maybe that's the point," he says now. "She's completely different."

"But if he's interested in someone like Wendy, it calls into question his whole marriage to my mother."

"I think you're taking the analogy too far," Walt responds, acting as the voice of reason. "Maybe the guy's just having fun."

"He's my father." I scowl. "He shouldn't be allowed to have fun."

"That's mean, Carrie."

"I know." I stare out the screen at the neglected garden. "Did you talk to Maggie?"

"Yup," Walt says, enigmatically.

"What did she say? About New York?"

"She had a great time."

"What did she say about *me*?"

"Nothing. All she talked about was some guy you introduced her to."

"Ryan. Whom she immediately bonked."

"That's our Maggie," Walt says with a shrug.

"She's turned into a sex fiend."

"Oh, let her," he says. "She's young. She'll grow out of it. Anyway, why do you care?"

"I *care* about my *friends*." I swing my Fiorucci boots off the table for emphasis. "I just wish my friends cared about me."

Walt stares at me blankly.

"I mean, even my family hasn't asked me about my life in New York. And frankly, my life is so much more interesting than anything that's happening to them. I'm going to have a play produced. And I went to a party last night at Barry Jessen's loft in SoHo—"

"Who's Barry Jessen?"

"Come on, Walt. He's like the most important artist in America right now."

"As I said, 'Aren't you special?'" Walt teases.

I fold my arms, knowing I sound like a jerk. "Doesn't anyone care?"

"With your big head?" Walts jokes. "Careful, it might explode."

"Walt!" I give him a hurt look. Then my frustration gets the better of me. "I'm going to be a famous writer someday. I'm going to live in a big, two-bedroom apartment on Sutton Place. And I'm going to write Broadway plays. And then everyone will have to come and visit *me*."

"Ha-ha-ha," Walt says.

I stare down at the ice cubes in my glass.

"Look, Carrie," Walt says. "You're spending one summer in New York. Which is great. But it's hardly your life. And in September, you're going to Brown."

"Maybe I'm not," I say suddenly.

Walt smiles, sure I can't be serious. "Does your father

know? About this change of plans?"

"I just decided. This minute." Which is true. The thought has been fluttering around the edges of my consciousness for weeks now, but the reality of being back in Castlebury has made it clear that being at Brown will only be more of the same. The same kinds of people with exactly the same attitudes, just in a different location.

Walt smiles. "Don't forget I'll be there too. At RISD."

"I know." I sigh. I sound as arrogant as Capote. "It'll be fun," I add, hopefully.

"Walt!" my father says, joining us on the porch.

"Mr. Bradshaw." Walt stands up, and my father embraces him in a hug, which makes me feel left out again.

"How you doin', kid?" my father asks. "Your hair's longer. I barely recognized you."

"Walt's always changing his hair, Dad." I turn to Walt. "What my father means is that you probably didn't recognize him. He's trying to look *younger*," I add, with enough bantering in my voice to prevent this statement from coming across as nasty.

"What's wrong with looking younger?" my father declares in high spirits.

He goes into the kitchen to make cocktails, but takes his time about it, going to the window every second or so like a sixteen-year-old girl waiting for her crush to arrive. It's ridiculous. When Wendy does turn up, a mere five minutes later, he runs out of the house to greet her.

"Can you believe this?" I ask Walt, horrified by my father's silly behavior.

247

"He's a man. What can I say?"

"He's my *father*," I protest.

"He's still a man."

I'm about to say, "Yeah, but my father isn't supposed to act like other men," when he and Wendy come strolling up the walk, holding hands.

I want to gack. This relationship is obviously more serious than I'd thought.

Wendy is kind of pretty, if you like women with dyed blond mall hair and blue eye shadow rimmed around their eyes like a raccoon.

"Be nice," Walt says warningly.

"Oh, I'll be perfectly nice. I'll be nice if it kills me." I smile.

"Shall I call the ambulance now or later?"

My father opens the screen door and urges Wendy onto the porch. Her smile is wide and patently fake. "You must be Carrie!" she says, enveloping me in a hug as if we're already best friends.

"How could you tell?" I ask, gently extracting myself.

She glances at my father, her face full of delight. "Your dad has told me all about you. He talks about you constantly. He's so proud of you."

There's something about this assumed intimacy that immediately rubs me the wrong way. "This is Walt," I say, trying to get her off the topic of myself. What can she possibly know about me anyway?

"Hello, Walt," Wendy says too eagerly. "Are you and Carrie—"

"Dating?" Walt interjects. "Hardly." We both laugh.

She tilts her head to the side, as if unsure how to proceed. "It's wonderful the way men and women can be friends these days. Don't you think?"

"I guess it depends on what you call 'friends,'" I murmur, reminding myself to be pleasant.

"Are we ready?" my father asks.

"We're going to this great new restaurant. Boyles. Have you heard of it?" Wendy asks.

"No." And unable to stop myself, I grumble, "I didn't even know there were restaurants in Castlebury. The only place we ever went was the Hamburger Shack."

"Oh, your father and I go out at least twice a week," Wendy chirps on, unperturbed.

My father nods in agreement. "We went to a Japanese restaurant. In Hartford."

"That so," I say, unimpressed. "There are tons of Japanese restaurants in New York."

"Bet they're not as good as the one in Hartford, though," Walt jokes.

My father gives him a grateful look. "This restaurant really is very special."

"Well," I say, just for the hell of it.

We troop down the driveway. Walt gets into his car with a wave of his hand. "Ta-ta, folks. Have fun."

I watch him go, envious of his freedom.

"So!" Wendy says brightly when we're in the car. "When do you start at Brown?"

I shrug.

"I'll bet you can't wait to get away from New York," she enthuses. "It's so dirty. And loud." She puts her hand on my father's arm and smiles.

Boyles is a tiny restaurant located in a damp patch off Main Street where our renowned Roaring Brook runs under the road. It's highfalutin for Castlebury: the main courses are called pasta instead of spaghetti, and there are cloth napkins and a bud vase on each table containing a single rose.

"Very romantic," my father says approvingly as he escorts Wendy to her chair.

"Your father is such a gentleman," Wendy says.

"He is?" I can't help it. He and Wendy are totally creeping me out. I wonder if they have sex. I certainly hope not. My father's too old for all that groping around.

My father ignores my comment and picks up the menu. "They have the fish again," he says to Wendy. And to me: "Wendy loves fish."

"I lived in Los Angeles for five years. They're much more health-conscious there," Wendy explains.

"My roommate is in Los Angeles right now," I say, partly to get the conversation away from Wendy. "She's staying at the Beverly Hills Hotel."

"I had lunch there once," Wendy says, with her unflappable cheeriness. "It was so exciting. We sat next to Tom Selleck."

"You don't say," my father replies, as if Wendy's momentary proximity to a television actor raises her even further in his eyes.

"I met Margie Shephard," I interject.

"Who's Margie Shephard?" My father frowns.

Wendy winks at me, as if she and I possess a secret intimacy regarding my father's lack of knowledge regarding popular culture. "She's an actress. Up-and-coming. Everyone says she's beautiful, but I don't see it. I think she's very plain."

"She's beautiful in person," I counter. "She sparkles. From within."

"Like you, Carrie," Wendy says suddenly.

I'm so surprised by her compliment, I'm temporarily disabled in my subtle attack. "Well," I say, picking up the menu. "What were you doing in Los Angeles?"

"Wendy was a member of an—" My father looks to Wendy for help.

"Improv group. We did improvisational theater."

"Wendy's very creative." My father beams.

"Isn't that one of those things where you do mime, like Marcel Marceau?" I ask innocently, even though I know better. "Did you wear white greasepaint and gloves?"

Wendy chuckles, amused by my ignorance. "I studied mime. But mostly we did comedy."

Now I'm completely baffled. Wendy was an actress— and a comedic one at that? She doesn't seem the least bit funny.

"Wendy was in a potato chip commercial," my father says.

"You shouldn't tell people that," Wendy gently scolds. "It was only a local commercial. For State Line potato chips. And it was seven years ago. My big break." She rolls her eyes with appropriate irony.

Apparently Wendy doesn't take herself too seriously after all. It's another check in her "pluses" column. On the other hand, it might only be a show for my benefit. "It must be a drag to be in Castlebury. After Los Angeles."

She shakes her head. "I'm a small-town girl. I grew up in Scarborough," she says, naming the town next door. "And I love my new job."

"But that's not all." My father nudges her. "Wendy's going to be teaching drama, too."

I wince as Wendy's life story becomes clear to me: local girl tries to make it big, fails, and crawls home to teach. It's my worst fear.

"Your father says you want to be a writer," Wendy continues blithely. "Maybe you should write for the *Castlebury Citizen*."

I freeze. The *Castlebury Citizen* is our small-town newspaper, consisting mostly of the minutes from zoning board meetings and photographs of Pee Wee baseball teams. Steam rises from behind my eyes. "You think I'm not good enough to make it in New York?"

Wendy frowns in confusion. "It's just so difficult in New York, isn't it? I mean, don't you have to do your laundry in the basement? A friend of mine lived in New York and she said—"

"My building doesn't have a laundry." I look away, trying to contain my frustration. How dare Wendy or her friend presume anything about New York? "I take my dirty clothes to a Laundromat." Which isn't exactly true. Mostly I let them pile up in a corner of the bedroom.

"Now, Carrie. No one is making any assumptions about your abilities—" my father begins, but I've had enough.

"No, they're not," I say spitefully. "Because no one seems to be interested in me at all." And with that, I get up, my face burning, and zigzag around the restaurant in search of the restroom.

I'm furious. At my father and Wendy for putting me in this position, but mostly at myself, for losing my temper. Now Wendy will come across as kind and reasonable, while I'll appear jealous and immature. This only inflames my anger, causing me to recall everything I've always hated about my life and my family but refused to admit.

I go into the stall and sit on the toilet to think. What really galls me is the way my father has never taken my writing seriously. He's never given me a word of encouragement, never said I was talented, has never even given me a compliment, for Christ's sake. I might have lived my entire life without noticing, if it weren't for the other kids at The New School. It's pretty obvious that Ryan and Capote and L'il and even Rainbow have grown up praised and encouraged and applauded. Not that I want to be like them, but it wouldn't hurt to have some belief from my own parent that I had something special.

I dab at my eyes with a piece of toilet paper, reminding myself that I have to go back out there and sit with them. I need to come up with a strategy, pronto, to explain my pathetic behavior.

There's only one choice: I'm going to have to pretend my outburst never happened. It's what Samantha would do.

I raise my chin and stride out.

Back at the table, Missy and Dorrit have arrived, along with a bottle of Chianti set in a woven straw basket. It's the kind of wine I'd be embarrassed to drink in New York.

And with an ugly pang, I realize how average it all is. My father, the middle-aged widower, inappropriately dressed and going through a midlife crisis by taking up with a somewhat desperate younger woman, who, against the plain backdrop of Castlebury, probably appears interesting and different and exciting. And my two sisters, a punk and a nerd. It's like some lousy sitcom.

If they're so ordinary, does it mean I am too? Can I ever escape my past?

I wish I could change the channel.

"Carrie!" Missy cries out. "Are you okay?"

"Me?" I ask with feigned surprise. "Of course." I take my place next to Wendy. "My father says you helped him find his Harley. I think it's so interesting that you like motorcycles."

"My father is a state trooper," she responds, no doubt relieved that I've managed to get ahold of myself.

I turn to Dorrit. "You hear that, Dorrit? Wendy's father is a state trooper. You'd better be careful—"

"Carrie." My father looks momentarily distraught. "We don't need to air our dirty laundry."

"No, but we do need to wash it."

No one gets my little joke. I pick up my wine glass and sigh. I'd planned to go back to New York on Monday, but there's no way I can possibly last that long. Come tomorrow, I'm taking the first train out of here.

CHAPTER TWENTY-FOUR

"I do love you, Carrie. Just because I'm with Wendy—"

"I know, Dad. I *like* Wendy. I'm only leaving because I have this play to write. And if I can get it done, it's going to be performed."

"Where?" my father asks. He's clutching the wheel of the car, absorbed in changing lanes on our little highway. I'm convinced he doesn't really care, but I try to explain anyway.

"At this space. That's what they call it—'a space.' It's really a kind of loft thing at this guy's apartment. It used to be a bank—"

I can tell by his glance into the rearview mirror that I've lost him.

"I admire your tenacity," he says. "You don't give up. That's good."

Now he's lost *me*. "Tenacity" isn't the word I was hoping

for. It makes me sound like someone clinging to a rock face.

I slump down in the seat. Why can't he ever say something along the lines of "You're really talented, Carrie, of course you're going to succeed." Am I going to spend the rest of my life trying to get some kind of approval from him that he's never going to give?

"I wanted to tell you about Wendy before," he says, swerving into the exit lane that leads to the train station. Now's my opportunity to tell him about my struggles in New York, but he keeps changing the subject back to Wendy.

"Why didn't you?" I ask hopelessly.

"I wasn't sure about her feelings."

"And you are now?"

He pulls into a parking spot and kills the engine. With great seriousness, he says, "She loves me, Carrie."

A cynical puff of air escapes my lips.

"I mean it. She really loves me."

"Everyone loves you, Dad."

"You know what I mean." He nervously rubs the corner of his eye.

"Oh, Dad." I pat his arm, trying to understand. The last few years must have been terrible for him. On the other hand, they've been terrible for me, too. And Missy. And Dorrit.

"I'm happy for you, Dad, I really am," I say, although the thought of my father in a serious relationship with another woman makes me shaky. What if he marries her?

"She's a lovely person. She——" He hesitates. "She reminds me of Mom."

This is the cherry on the crap sundae. "She's not anything like Mom," I say softly, my anger building.

"She is. When Mom was younger. You wouldn't remember because you were just a baby."

"Dad." I pause deliberately, hoping the obvious falseness of his statement will sink in. "Wendy likes motorcycles."

"Your mother was very adventurous when she was young too. Before she had you girls——"

"Just another reason why I'll never get married," I say, getting out of the car.

"Oh, Carrie." He sighs. "I feel sorry for you, then. I worry that you'll never find true love."

His comment stops me. I stand rigid on the sidewalk, about to explode, but something prevents me. I think of Miranda and how she'd interpret this situation. She'd say it was my father who was worried about never finding true love again, but because he's too scared to admit it, he pins his fears on me.

I grab my suitcase from the backseat.

"Let me help you," he says.

I watch as my father lugs my suitcase through the wooden door that leads into the ancient terminal. I remind myself that my father isn't a bad guy. Compared to most men, he's pretty great.

He sets down my suitcase and opens his arms. "Can I have a hug?"

"Sure, Dad." I hug him tightly, inhaling a whiff of lime. Must be a new cologne Wendy gave him.

A yawning emptiness opens up inside me.

"I want the best for you, Carrie. I really do."

"I know, Dad." Feeling like I'm a million years old, I pick up my suitcase and head to the platform. "Don't worry, Dad," I say, as if to convince myself as well. "Everything is going to be *fine*."

The moment the train pulls out of the station, I start to feel better. Nearly two hours later, when we're passing the projects in the Bronx, I'm positively giddy. There's the brief, magical view of the skyline—the Emerald City!—before we plunge into the tunnel. No matter where I might travel—Paris, London, Rome—I'll always be thrilled to get back to New York.

Riding the elevator in Penn Station, I make an impromptu decision. I won't go straight to Samantha's apartment. Instead, I'll surprise Bernard.

I have to find out what's going on with him before I can proceed with my life.

It takes two separate subway trains to get near his place. With each stop, I become more and more excited about the prospect of seeing him. I arrive at the Fifty-ninth Street station under Bloomingdale's, the heat coursing through my blood threatening to scald me from the inside.

He has to be home.

"Mr. Singer's out, miss," the doorman says, with, I suspect, a certain amount of relish. None of the doormen in this building particularly like me. I always catch them looking at me sideways as if they don't approve.

"Do you know when he'll be back?"

"I'm not his secretary, miss."

"Fine."

I scan the lobby. Two leather-clad armchairs are stationed in front of a faux fireplace, but I don't want to sit there with the doorman's eyes on me. I spin out the door and park myself on a pretty bench across the street. I rest my feet on my suitcase, as if I have all the time in the world.

I wait.

I tell myself I'll only wait for half an hour, and then I'll go. Half an hour becomes forty-five minutes, then an hour. After nearly two hours, I begin to wonder if I've fallen into a love trap. Have I become the girl who waits by the phone, hoping it will ring, who asks a friend to dial her number to make sure the phone is working? Who eventually picks up a man's dry cleaning, scrubs his bathroom, and shops for furniture she'll never own?

Yup. And I don't care. I can be that girl, and someday, when I've got it all figured out, I won't be.

Finally, at two hours and twenty-two minutes, Bernard comes strolling up Sutton Place.

"Bernard!" I say, rushing toward him with unbridled enthusiasm. Maybe my father was right: I am tenacious. I don't give up that easily on anything.

Bernard squints. "Carrie?"

"I just got back," I say, as if I haven't been waiting for nearly three hours.

"From where?"

"Castlebury. Where I grew up."

"And here you are." He slings his arm comfortably around my shoulders.

It's like the dinner with Maggie never happened. Nor my series of desperate phone calls. Nor his not calling me the way he promised. But maybe, because he's a writer, he lives in a slightly different reality, where the things that seem earth-shattering to me are nothing to him.

"My suitcase," I murmur, glancing back.

"You moving in?" he laughs.

"Maybe."

"Just in time, too," he teases. "My furniture finally arrived."

I spend the night at Bernard's. We sleep in the crisp new sheets on the enormous king-size bed. It's so very, very comfortable.

I sleep like a baby and when I wake up, darling Bernard is next to me, his face buried in his pillow. I lie back and close my eyes, enjoying the luxurious quiet while I mentally review the events of the evening.

We started by fooling around on the new couch. Then we moved into the bedroom and fooled around while we watched TV. Then we ordered Chinese food (why does sex always seem to make people hungry?) and fooled around some more. We finished off with a bubble bath. Bernard was very gentle and sweet, and he didn't even try to put in the old weenie. Or at least I'm pretty sure he didn't. Miranda says the guy really has to jam it in there, so I doubt I could have missed it.

I wonder if Bernard secretly knows I'm a virgin. If there's something about me that flashes "undefiled."

"Hiya, butterfly," he says now, stretching his arms toward the ceiling. He rolls over and smiles, and moves in for a kiss, morning breath and all.

"Have you gotten the pill yet?" Bernard asks, making coffee in the spiffy new machine that gurgles like a baby's belly.

I casually light a cigarette and hand him one. "Not yet."

"Why not?"

Good question. "I forgot?"

"Pumpkin, you can't neglect these kinds of things," he chastises gently.

"I know. But it's just that—with my father and his new girlfriend—I'll take care of it this week, I promise."

"If you did, you could spend the night more often." Bernard sets two cups of coffee on the sleek dining room table. "And you could get a small valise for your things."

"Like my toothbrush?" I giggle.

"Like whatever you need," he says.

A valise, huh? The word makes spending the night sound planned and glamorous, as opposed to last-minute and smutty. I laugh. A valise sounds very expensive. "I don't think I can afford a *valise*."

"Oh well then." He shrugs. "Something nice. So the doormen won't be suspicious."

"They'll be suspicious if I'm carrying a plastic grocery

bag but not if I'm carrying a valise?"

"You know what I mean."

I nod. With a valise, I wouldn't look so much like a troubled teenager he'd picked up at Penn Station. Which reminds me of Teensie.

"I met your agent. At a party," I say easily, not wanting to ruin the mood.

"Did you?" He smiles, clearly unconcerned about the incident. "Was she a dragon lady?"

"She practically ripped me to shreds with her claws," I say jokingly. "Is she always like that?"

"Pretty much." He rubs the top of my head. "Maybe we should have dinner with her. So the two of you can get to know each other."

"Whatever you want, Mr. Singer," I purr, climbing into his lap. If he wants me to have dinner with his agent, it means our relationship is not only back on track, but speeding forward like a European train. I kiss him on the mouth, imagining I'm a Katharine Hepburn character in a romantic black-and-white movie.

CHAPTER TWENTY-FIVE

Later, on my way downtown, I pass a store for medical supplies. In the window are three mannequins. Not the pretty kind you see in Saks or Bergdorf's, where they make the mannequins from molds of actual women, but the scary cheap ones that look like oversized dolls from the 1950s. The dolls are wearing surgical scrubs, and it suddenly hits me that scrubs would make the perfect New York uniform. They're cheap, washable, and totally cool.

And they come neatly packaged in cellophane. I buy three pairs in different colors, and remember what Bernard said about a valise.

The only good thing about going to my father's this weekend was that I found an old binoculars case that belonged to my mother, which I purloined to use as a handbag. Perhaps other items can be similarly repurposed as well. When I trip by a fancy hardware store, I spot the perfect carryall.

It's a carpenter's tool bag, made of canvas with a real leather bottom, big enough for a pair of shoes, a manuscript, and a change of scrubs. And it's only six dollars. A steal.

I buy the tool bag and stick my purse and scrubs into it, grab my suitcase, and head to the train.

It's been humid the past few days, and when I enter Samantha's apartment there's a closed-in smell, as if every odor has been trapped. I breathe deeply, partly due to relief at being back, and partly because this particular smell will always remind me of New York and Samantha. It's a mixture of old perfume and scented candles, cigarette smoke and something else I can't quite identify: a sort of comforting musk.

I put on the blue scrubs, make a cup of tea, and sit down at the typewriter. All summer I've been terrified about facing the blank page. But maybe because I went home and realized I have worse things to worry about—like not making it and ending up like Wendy—that I'm actually excited. I have hours and hours stretching before me in which to write. Tenacity, I remind myself. I'm going work until I finish this play. And I will not answer the phone. In an effort to make good on my promise, I even unplug it.

I write for four hours straight, until hunger forces me out in search of food. I wander dazedly into the deli, the characters still in my head, yapping away as I buy a can of soup, heat it up, and place it next to my typewriter so I can eat and work. I beetle on for quite a while, and when I finally feel finished for the day, I decide to visit my favorite street.

It's a tiny, brick-paved path called Commerce Street—one of those rare places in the West Village that you can never find if you're actually looking for it. You have to sneak up on it by using certain landmarks: the junk store on Hudson Street. The sex shop on Barrow. Somewhere near the pet store is a small gate. And there it is, just on the other side.

I stroll slowly down the sidewalk, wanting to memorize each detail. The tiny, charming town houses, the cherry trees, the little neighborhood bar where, I imagine, all the patrons know one another. I take several turns up and down the street, pausing in front of each house, picturing how it would feel to live there. As I gaze up at the tiny windows on the top floor of a red-brick carriage house, it dawns on me that I've changed. I used to worry that my dream of becoming a writer was just that—a dream. I had no idea how to do it, where to begin and how to continue. But lately, I'm beginning to feel that I *am* a writer. This is me. Writing and wandering the Village in my scrubs.

And tomorrow, if I skip class, I'll have another day like this one, all to myself. I'm suddenly overcome with joy. I run all the way back to the apartment, and when I spot my pile of plays on the table, I'm can't believe how happy I am.

I settle in to read, making notes with a pencil and underlining especially poignant bits of dialogue. I can do this. Who cares what my father thinks? For that matter, who cares what anyone thinks? Everything I need is in my head, and no one can take that away.

At eight o'clock, I fall into one of those rare, deep sleeps where your body is so exhausted, you wonder if you'll ever wake up. When I finally wrench myself out of bed, it's ten a.m.

I count the hours I slept—fourteen. I must have been really tired. So tired, I didn't even know how shattered I was. At first, I'm groggy from all the sleep, but when the grogginess dissipates, I feel terrific. I put on my scrubs from the day before, and without bothering to brush my teeth, go straight to the typewriter.

My powers of concentration are remarkable. I write without stopping, without noticing the time, until I type the words "THE END." Elated and a little woozy, I check the clock. It's just after four. If I hurry, I can get the play photocopied and into Viktor Greene's office by five.

I leap into the shower, my heart pounding in triumph. I slide into a clean pair of scrubs, grab my manuscript, and run out the door.

The copy place is on Sixth Avenue, just around the corner from the school. For once, it's my lucky day—there's no line. My play is forty pages long and copying is expensive, but I can't risk losing it. Fifteen minutes later, one copy of my play tucked neatly into a manila envelope, I gallop to The New School.

Viktor is in his office, slumped over his desk. At first I think he's asleep, and when he doesn't move, I wonder if he actually *is* dead. I knock on the door. No response. "Viktor?" I ask in alarm.

Slowly, he lifts his head, as if he has a cement block on the back of his neck. His eyes are puffy, the lower lids turned out, defiantly exposing their red-rimmed interior. His mustache is ragged as if rent by despairing fingers. He props up his cheeks with his hands. His mouth falls open. "Yes?"

Normally, I would ask what's wrong. But I don't know Viktor well enough, and I'm not sure I want to know anyway. I take a step closer, holding the manila envelope aloft. "I finished my play."

"Were you in class today?" he asks mournfully.

"No. I was writing. I wanted to get my play finished." I slide the envelope across his desk. "I thought maybe you could read it tonight."

"Sure." He stares at me as if he barely remembers who I am.

"So, uh, thanks, Mr. Greene." I turn to go, glancing back at him in concern. "I'll see you tomorrow, then?"

"Mmmm," he replies.

What the hell's the matter with him? I wonder, bounding down the stairs. I walk briskly for several blocks, buy a hot dog from a vendor, and ponder what to do next.

L'il. I haven't seen her for ages. Not properly, anyway. She's the one person who I can really talk to about my play. Who will actually understand. And if Peggy's there—so what? She's already kicked me out once. What can she do to me now?

I hike up Second Avenue, enjoying the noise, the sights, the people scurrying home like cockroaches. I could live here forever. Maybe even become a real New Yorker someday.

Seeing my old building on Forty-seventh Street brings back all kinds of memories—Peggy's nude pictures, her collection of bears, and those tiny little rooms with the awful camp beds—and I wonder how I managed to last even three days. But I didn't know better then. Didn't know what to expect and was willing to take anything.

I've come a long way.

I press impudently on the buzzer like I mean business. Eventually, a small voice answers. "Yes?" It's not L'il or Peggy, so I assume it's my replacement.

"Is L'il there?" I ask.

"Why?"

"It's Carrie Bradshaw," I say loudly.

Apparently L'il is home, because the buzzer goes off and the locks click open.

Upstairs, the door to Peggy's apartment widens a crack, just enough for someone to peek out while keeping the chain latched. "Is L'il here?" I ask into the crack.

"Why?" asks the voice again. Perhaps "why" is the only word she knows.

"I'm a friend of hers."

"Oh."

"Can I come in?"

"I guess so," the voice says nervously. The door creaks open, just enough for me to push through.

On the other side is a plain young woman with unfortunate hair and the remnants of teenage acne. "We're not supposed to have visitors," she whispers in fear.

"I know," I say dismissively. "I used to live here."

"You did?" The girl's eyes are as big as eggs.

I stride past her. "You can't let Peggy run your life." I yank open the door to the tiny bedrooms. "L'il?"

"What are you doing?" the girl bleats, right on my heels. "L'il isn't here."

"I'll leave her a note then." I fling open the door to L'il's bedroom and halt in confusion.

The room is empty. The camp bed has been stripped of its linens. Gone is the photograph of Sylvia Plath that L'il used to keep on her desk, along with her typewriter, ream of paper, and all her other belongings.

"Did she move?" I ask, perplexed. Why wouldn't she tell me?

The girl backs out of the room and sits on her own bed, pressing her lips together. "She went home."

"What?" This can't be true.

The girl nods. "On Sunday. Her father drove up and got her."

"Why?"

"How should I know?" the girl says. "Peggy was really pissed off, though. L'il only told her that morning."

My voice rises in alarm. "Is she coming back?"

The girl shrugs.

"Did she leave an address or anything?"

"Nope. Just said she had to go home is all."

"Yeah, well, thanks," I say, realizing I won't get anything more out of her.

I leave the apartment and walk blindly downtown, trying to make sense of L'il's departure. I rack my brain for everything she told me about herself and where she was from. Her real name is Elizabeth Reynolds Waters, so that's a start. But what town is she from specifically? All I know is that she's from North Carolina. And she and Capote knew each other before, because as L'il said once, "people from the South all know each other." If L'il left on Sunday, she must have reached home by now, even if she was driving.

I narrow my eyes, determined to find her.

CHAPTER TWENTY-SIX

Without knowing exactly where I'm going, I realize I'm on Capote's street. I recognize his building right away. His apartment is on the second floor, and the yellow old-lady curtains are clearly visible through the window.

I hesitate. If I ring his bell and he's home, no doubt he'll think I've come back for more. He might even presume that his kiss was so wonderful, I've fallen head over heels for him. Or maybe he'll be annoyed, assuming I've come to yell at him for his inappropriate behavior.

What the hell? I can't live my life worrying about what stupid Capote thinks. I press hard on his buzzer.

After a few seconds, the window flies open and Capote sticks his head out. "Who's there?"

"It's me." I wave.

"Oh. Carrie." He doesn't look particularly happy to see me. "What do you want?"

I open my arms in a gesture of exasperation. "Can I come up?"

"I've only got a minute."

"I've only got a minute too." Jeez. What a jerk.

He disappears for a moment, and reappears, jangling some keys in his hand. "The buzzer isn't working," he says, tossing the set down to me.

The buzzer is probably worn out from all his female guests, I think, as I trudge upstairs.

He's waiting in the entry in a ruffled white shirt and black tuxedo pants, fumbling with a shiny bow tie. "Where are you off to?" I ask, snickering at his getup.

"Where do you think?" He steps back so I can pass. If he has any memory of our kiss, he certainly isn't acting like it.

"I wasn't expecting to find you in a monkey suit. I never figured you for the type."

"Why's that?" he asks, somewhat offended.

"The right end goes under the left," I say, indicating his bow tie. "Why don't you use one of those clip-on things?"

As expected, my question rattles him. "It isn't proper. A gentleman never wears a clip-on bow tie."

"Right." I insolently run my finger over the pile of books on his coffee table as I make myself comfortable on the squishy couch. "Where are you headed?"

"To a gala." He frowns disapprovingly at my actions.

"For what?" I idly pick up one of the books and flip through it.

"Ethiopia. It's a very important cause."

"How big of you."

"They don't have any food, Carrie. They're starving."

"And you're going to a fancy dinner. For starving people. Why don't you just send them the food instead?"

That's it. Capote jerks on the ends of his bow tie, nearly choking himself. "Why are you here?"

I lean back against the cushions. "What's the name of the town L'il comes from?"

"Why?"

I roll my eyes and sigh. "I need to know. I want to get in touch with her. She left New York, in case you don't know."

"As a matter of fact, I do know. Which you would have known as well if you bothered to come to class today."

I sit up, eager for information. "What happened?"

"Viktor made an announcement that she'd left. To pursue other interests."

"Don't you find that strange?"

"Why?"

"Because L'il's only interest is writing. She'd never give up class."

"Maybe she had family issues."

"You're not even curious?"

"Look, Carrie," he snaps. "Right now my only concern is not being late. I've got to pick up Rainbow—"

"All I want is the name of L'il's hometown," I say, becoming officious.

"I'm not sure. It's either Montgomery or Macon."

"I thought you knew her," I say accusingly, although I suspect my disdain might actually be about Rainbow. I guess he's seeing her after all. I know I shouldn't care, but I do.

I rise. "Have fun at the gala," I add, with a dismissive smile.

Suddenly, I hate New York. No, scratch that. I don't *hate* New York. I only hate some of the people in it.

There are listings for three Waterses in Montgomery County and two in Macon. I start with Macon, and get L'il's aunt on the first try. She's nice as can be, and gives me L'il's number.

L'il is shocked to hear my voice, and not, I suspect, altogether pleased, although her lack of enthusiasm could be due to embarrassment at having abandoned New York. "I went by your apartment," I say, my voice filled with concern. "The girl there said you moved back home."

"I had to get away."

"Why? Because of Peggy? You could have moved in with me." No response. "You're not sick, are you?" I ask, my voice pitched with worry.

She sighs. "Not in the traditional sense, no."

"Meaning?"

"I don't want to talk about it," she whispers.

"But L'il," I insist. "What about writing? You can't just quit New York."

There's a pause. Then she says stiffly, "New York is not for me." I hear a muffled sob as if she's put her hand over the receiver. "I have to go, Carrie."

And suddenly, I put two and two together. I don't know why I didn't see it before. It was so obvious. I simply never imagined that anyone could be attracted to him.

I feel sick. "Is it Viktor?"

"No!" she cries.

"It *is* Viktor. Why didn't you tell me? What happened? Were you seeing him?"

"He broke my heart."

I'm stunned. I still can't believe L'il was having an affair with Viktor Greene and his ridiculous mustache. How could anyone even kiss the guy with that big bushy Waldo in the way? And on top of it, to have him break your heart?

"Oh, L'il. How awful. You can't let him force you out of class. Plenty of women have affairs with their professors. It's never a good idea. But sometimes the best thing to do is to pretend it didn't happen," I add in a rush, thinking briefly about Capote and how we're both behaving as if we never kissed.

"It's more than that, Carrie," she says ominously.

"Of course it is. I mean, I'm sure you thought you were in love with him. But really, L'il, he's not worth it. He's just some weird loser guy who happened to win a book award," I ramble on. "And six months from now when you've published more poems in *The New Yorker* and won awards yourself, you won't even remember him."

"Unfortunately, I will."

"Why?" I ask dumbly.

"I got pregnant," she says.

That shuts me up.

"Are you there?" she asks.

"With Viktor?" My voice trembles.

"Who else?" she hisses.

"Oh, L'il." I crumple in sympathy. "I'm sorry. So, so sorry."

"I got rid of it," she says harshly.

"Oh." I hesitate. "Maybe it's for the better."

"I'll never know, will I?"

"These things happen," I say, trying to soothe her.

"He made me get rid of it."

I squeeze my eyes shut, feeling her agony.

"He didn't even ask if I wanted it. There was no discussion. He just assumed. He assumed—" She breaks off, unable to continue.

"L'il," I whisper.

"I know what you're thinking. I'm only nineteen. I shouldn't have a child. And I probably would have . . . taken care of it. But I didn't have a choice."

"He forced you to have an abortion?"

"Pretty much. He made the appointment at the clinic. He took me there. Paid for it. And then he sat in the waiting room while I had it done."

"Oh my God, L'il. Why didn't you run out of there?"

"I didn't have the guts. I knew it was the right thing to do, but—"

"Did it hurt?" I ask.

"No," she says simply. "That was the weirdest thing. It didn't hurt and afterward, I felt fine. Like I was back to my old self. I was *relieved*. But then I started thinking. And I realized how terrible it was. Not the abortion necessarily, but the way he'd behaved. Like it was a foregone conclusion. I realized he couldn't have loved me at all. How can a man love you if he won't even consider having a baby with you?"

"I don't know, L'il—"

"It's black-and-white, Carrie," she says, her voice rising. "You cannot even pretend anymore. And even if I could, we'd always have this thing between us. Knowing that I was pregnant with his child and *he didn't want it*."

I shudder. "But maybe after a while . . . you could come back?" I ask carefully.

"Oh, Carrie." She sighs. "Don't you get it? I'm never coming back. I don't even want to *know* people like Viktor Greene. I wish I'd never come to New York in the first place." And with a painful cry, she hangs up.

I sit there twisting the phone cord in despair. Why L'il? She's not the type of person I'd imagine this happening to, but on the other hand, who is? There's a terrible finality about her actions that's frightening.

I put my head in my hands. Maybe L'il is right about New York. She came here to win and the city beat her. I'm terrified. If this could happen to L'il, it could happen to anyone. Including myself.

CHAPTER TWENTY-SEVEN

I sit tapping my feet in annoyance.

Ryan is at the front of the class, reading his short story. It's good. Really good—about one of his crazy late nights at a club where some girl with a shaved head tried to have sex with him. It's so good, I wish I'd written it myself. Unfortunately I can't give it my full attention. I'm still reeling from my conversation with L'il and the perfidy of Viktor Greene.

Although "perfidy" isn't a strong enough word. Heinous? Egregious? *Invidious?*

Sometimes there are no words to describe the treachery of men in relationships.

What is wrong with them? Why can't they be more like women? Someday I'm going to write a book called *World Without Men*. There would be no Viktor Greenes. Or Capote Duncans, either.

I try to focus on Ryan, but L'il's absence fills the room. I keep glancing over my shoulder, thinking she'll be there, but there's only an empty desk. Viktor has taken up residence in the back of the room, so I can't study him without boldly turning around in my seat. I did, however, do a little reconnaissance on my own before class.

I got to school twenty minutes early and headed straight for Viktor's office. He was standing by the window, watering one of those stupid hanging plants that are all the rage, the idea being that they will somehow provide extra oxygen in this nutrient-starved city.

"Yop?" he said, turning around.

Whatever I thought I was going to say got caught in my throat. I gaped, then smiled awkwardly.

Viktor's mustache was gone. Waldo had been thoroughly eradicated—much like, I couldn't help thinking, his unborn child.

I waited to see what he would do with his hands, now that Waldo was gone.

Sure enough, they went right to his upper lip, patting the skin in panic, like someone who's lost a limb and doesn't know it's gone until they try to use it.

"Errrrr," he said.

"I was wondering if you'd read my play," I asked, regaining my equilibrium.

"Mmmm?" Having concluded Waldo was, indeed, no more, his hands dropped limply to his sides.

"I finished it," I said, enjoying his discomfort. "I dropped it off yesterday, remember?"

"I haven't gotten to it yet."

"When will you get to it?" I demanded. "There's this man who's interested in doing a reading—"

"Sometime this weekend, I imagine." He nodded his head briefly in confirmation.

"Thanks." I skittled down the hallway, convinced, somehow, that he knew I was onto him. That he knew I knew what he'd done.

Capote's laughter brings me back to the present. It's like nails on a chalkboard, for all the wrong reasons. I actually like his laugh. It's one of those laughs that makes you want to say something funny so you can hear it all over again.

Ryan's story is apparently very amusing. Lucky him. Ryan is one of those guys whose talent will always outshine his flaws.

Viktor ambles to the front of the room. I stare at the bare patches of skin around his mouth and shudder.

Flowers. I need flowers for Samantha. And toilet paper. And maybe a banner. "Welcome Home." I wander through the flower district on Seventh Avenue, dodging puddles of water on which float wanton petals. I remember reading somewhere about the society ladies on the Upper East Side who send their assistants each morning to buy fresh flowers. I wish, briefly, that I could be that kind of person, concerned with the details of fresh flowers, but the effort feels overwhelming. Will Samantha send someone for flowers when she marries Charlie? He seems like the type who would expect it. And suddenly, the whole idea of flowers is so depressingly dull I'm tempted to abort my quest.

But Samantha will appreciate them. She's coming back tomorrow and they'll make her feel good. Who doesn't like flowers? But what kind? Roses? Doesn't seem right. I duck into the smallest shop, where I try to buy a lily. It's five dollars. "How much do you want to spend?" the salesgirl asks.

"Two dollars? Maybe three?"

"For that you'll get baby's breath. Try the deli down the street."

At the deli, I settle on a hideous bunch of multicolored flowers in unnatural hues of pink, purple, and green.

Back home, I put the flowers in a tall glass and place them next to Samantha's bed. The flowers may make Samantha happy, but I can't shake my own feeling of dread. I keep thinking about L'il and how Viktor Greene ruined her life.

At loose ends, I look doubtfully at the bed. Although not much has happened in it recently, besides the consumption of crackers and cheese, I should wash the sheets. The Laundromat's creepy, though. All kinds of crimes take place between the washers and dryers. Muggings and stolen clothes and fisticuffs over possession of the machines. Nevertheless, I dutifully strip the bed, stuffing the black sheets into a pillowcase that I sling over my shoulder.

The Laundromat is harshly lit but not crowded. I buy a package of soap from a vending machine and tear it open, the sharp particles of detergent making me sneeze.

I stuff the sheets into the washer and sit on top, staking my claim.

What is it about the Laundromat that's so depressing?

Is it the simple reality of literally exposing your dirty laundry to strangers as you shove it quickly in and out of the washer, hoping no one will notice your ragged under-pants and polyester sheets? Or is it a sign of defeat? Like you never managed to make it into a building with its own basement laundry room.

Maybe Wendy had a point about New York, after all. No matter what you think you *can* be, when you're forced to stop and look at where you actually are, it's pretty depressing.

Sometimes there's no escaping the truth.

Two hours later, when I'm hauling my clean laundry up the steps to the apartment, I discover Miranda on the land-ing, crying into a copy of the *New York Post*.

Oh no. Not again. What is it about the last two days? I put down my sack. "Marty?"

She nods once and lowers the newspaper in shame. On the floor next to her, the top of an open bottle of vodka juts from a small paper bag. "I couldn't help it. I had to," she says, explaining the alcohol.

"You don't have to apologize to *me*," I say, unlocking the door. "Bastard."

"I didn't know where else to go." She gets up and takes a brave step before her face crumples in pain. "Oh God. It hurts, Carrie. Why does it hurt so much?"

★ ★ ★

283

"I don't understand. I thought everything was great," I say, lighting a cigarette as I prepare to bring my best powers of relationship analysis to the situation.

"I thought we were having fun." Miranda chokes back tears. "I've never had fun with a guy before. And then, this morning when we got up, he was acting strange. He had this kind of sick smile on his face while he was shaving. I didn't want to say anything because I didn't want to be one of those girls who are always asking, 'What's wrong?' I was trying to do everything *right*, for once."

"I'm sure you were—"

Outside, there's a rumble of thunder.

She wipes her cheek. "Even though he wasn't really my type, I thought I was making progress. I told myself I was breaking the pattern."

"At least you tried," I say soothingly. "Especially since you don't even like guys. When I met you, you didn't want to have anything to do with them, remember? And it was cool. Because when you really think about it, guys are kind of a big waste of time."

Miranda sniffs. "Maybe you're right." But in the next second, a fresh round of tears clouds her eyes. "I used to be strong. But then I was taken in by . . ." She struggles to find the words. "I was betrayed by . . . my own beliefs. I guess I thought I was tougher than I am. I thought I could spot a creep a mile away."

A crack of lightning makes us both jump.

"Oh, sweetie." I sigh. "When a guy wants to get you in bed, he's always on his best behavior. On the other hand, he did want to be with you all the time. So he must have really been crazy about you."

"Or maybe he was using me for my apartment. Because my apartment is bigger than his. And I don't have any roommates. He had this one roommate, Tyler. Said he was always farting and calling everyone a 'fag.'"

"But it doesn't make sense. If he was using you for your apartment, why would he break up with you?"

"How should I know?" She pulls her knees to her chest. "Last night, when we were having sex, I should have known something was wrong. Because the sex was very . . . strange. Nice, but strange. He kept stroking my hair. And looking into my eyes with this sad expression. And then he said, 'I want you to know that I care about you, Miranda Hobbes. I really do.'"

"He used your full name like that? 'Miranda Hobbes'?"

"I thought it was romantic," she snivels. "But this morning, after he'd finished showering, he came out holding his razor and shaving cream and asked me if I had a shopping bag."

"What?"

"For his stuff."

"Ouch."

She nods dazedly. "I asked him why he wanted it. He said he realized it wasn't going to work out between us and we shouldn't waste each other's time."

My jaw drops. "Just like that?"

"He was so . . . clinical about it. Official. Like he was in court or something and I was being sentenced to jail. I didn't know what to do, so I gave him the damn shopping bag. And it was from Saks. One of those big red expensive ones, too."

I sit back on my heels. "Aw, sweetie. You can always get another shopping bag—"

"But I can't get another Marty," she wails. "It's me, Carrie. There's something wrong with me. I drive guys away."

"Now listen. This has nothing to do with you. There's something wrong with *him*. Maybe he was afraid you were going to dump him so he broke up with you first."

She lifts her head. "Carrie. I ran down the street after him. Yelling. When he saw me coming, he started running. Into the subway. Can you believe that?"

"Yes," I say. Given what happened to L'il, I'd believe just about anything right now.

She blows hard into a wad of toilet paper. "Maybe you're right. Maybe he does think I'm too good for him." And just as I'm beginning to hope I've gotten through to her, a stubborn, closed look comes over her face. "If I could just see him. Explain. Maybe we can get back together."

"No!" I yelp. "He's already run away once. Even if you do get back together, he'll do the same thing. It's his *pattern*."

She lowers the toilet paper and gives me a doubtful look. "How do you know?"

"Trust me."

"Maybe I can change him." She reaches for the phone, but I yank the cord before she can grab it.

"Miranda." I clutch the phone in my arms. "If you call

Marty, I will lose all respect for you."

She glares. "If you do not hand over that phone, I will have a very hard time considering you a friend."

"That stinks," I say, grudgingly passing her the phone. "Putting a guy before your friends."

"I'm not putting Marty before you. I'm trying to find out what happened."

"You *know* what happened."

"He owes me a proper explanation."

I give up. She picks up the phone and frowns into the receiver. She presses down on the hook a few times, and looks at me accusingly. "You did this on purpose. Your phone's out of order."

"Really?" I ask in surprise. I take the phone from her and try it myself. Nothing. Not even air. "I'm pretty sure I used it this morning."

"Maybe you didn't pay the bill."

"Maybe Samantha didn't pay the bill. She went to LA."

"Shhhh." Miranda holds up a finger as her eyes dart around the room. "What do you hear?"

"Nothing?"

"That's right. Nothing." She jumps up and starts flipping switches. "The air conditioner's off. And the lights aren't working."

We run to the window. The traffic on Seventh Avenue is in a snarl. Horns honk as several sirens go off at once. People are getting out of their cars, waving their arms and pointing at the traffic lights.

My eyes follow their gestures. The lights swaying over

Seventh Avenue are dark.

I look uptown. Smoke is billowing from somewhere near the river.

"What's happening?" I scream.

Miranda crosses her arms and gives me a tangled, triumphant smile. "It's a blackout," she declares.

CHAPTER TWENTY-EIGHT

"Okay. Let me get this straight," I say. "The lining from the uterus migrates to other parts of the body, and when you get your period, it bleeds?"

"And sometimes, you can't get pregnant. Or if you do, the fetus can actually develop outside the uterus," Miranda says, proudly displaying her knowledge.

"Like in your stomach?" I ask in horror.

She nods. "Or in your butt. My aunt had a friend who couldn't poop. Turns out there was a baby growing in her lower intestine."

"No!" I exclaim, and light another cigarette. I puff on it thoughtfully. The conversation is getting out of hand, but I'm enjoying the perversity. I figure it's a special day—a day that's outside of all other days and is therefore exempt from the normal rules.

The entire city is without power. The subways aren't

running and the streets are a mess. Our stairwell has been plunged into darkness. And there's a hurricane outside. Which means Samantha, Miranda, and I are stuck. For the next few hours, anyway.

Samantha arrived unexpectedly minutes after the blackout began. There was a lot of shouting in the stairwell, and people coming out of their apartments to compare notes. Someone said the ancient telephone building was struck by lightning, while another resident claimed the storm knocked down the phone lines and all the air conditioners caused a power outage. Either way, there are no lights and no phone service. Enormous black clouds rolled over the city, turning the sky an eerie grayish green. The wind picked up and the sky flashed with lightning.

"It's like Armageddon," Miranda declared. "Someone is trying to tell us something."

"Who?" Samantha asked with her usual sarcasm.

Miranda shrugged. "The Universe?"

"My uterus my Universe," Samantha said, and that's how the whole conversation began.

Turns out Samantha has endometriosis, which is why she's always in so much pain when she gets her period. But it wasn't until she got to LA that the pain became unbearable and she started throwing up, right in the middle of a photography shoot. When the photographer's assistant found her nearly passed out on the bathroom floor, they insisted on calling an ambulance. She had to have her insides scraped out, and then they sent her back to New York, to rest.

"I'm going to be scarred for life," Samantha moans now. She pulls down the top of her jeans to reveal two large Band-Aids on either side of her ridiculously flat stomach, and peels away the adhesive. Underneath is a large red welt with four stitches. "Look," she commands.

"That's awful," Miranda concurs, her eyes shining with strange admiration. I was worried that Miranda and Samantha would hate each other, but instead, Miranda appears to have accepted Samantha's position as top dog. She's not only impressed with Samantha's worldliness, but is doing her level best to get Samantha to like her. Which consists of agreeing with everything Samantha says.

Putting me in the position of being the disagreer. "I don't care about scars. I think they add character." I can never understand why women get so worked up about these tiny imperfections.

"Carrie," Miranda scolds, shaking her head in accordance with Samantha's distress.

"As long as Charlie never finds out," Samantha says, leaning back against the cushions.

"Why should he care?" I ask.

"Because I don't want him to know I'm not perfect, Sparrow. And if he calls, I need you to pretend I'm still in LA."

"Fine." It seems weird to me, but then again, the whole situation is weird, with the blackout and all. Perhaps it's even Shakespearean. Like in *As You Like It* when everyone takes on different personas.

"Sparrow?" Miranda asks, jokingly.

I give her a dirty look as Samantha starts talking about my sex life with Bernard. "You have to admit, it's odd," she says, propping her feet on the pillows.

"He must be gay," Miranda says from the floor.

"He's not gay. He was *married*." I get up and pace around in the flickering candlelight.

"All the more reason to be horny," Samantha laughs.

"No guy dates a girl for a whole month without trying to have sex with her," Miranda insists.

"We've had sex. We just haven't had intercourse."

"Honey, that ain't sex. That's what you do in sixth grade." Samantha.

"Have you even seen it?" Miranda asks, giggling.

"As a matter of fact, I have." I point my cigarette at her.

"It's not one of those bendy ones, is it?" Miranda asks as she and Samantha chortle.

"No, it's not. And I'm insulted," I say, in faux outrage.

"Candles. And sexy lingerie. That's what you need," Samantha coos.

"I've never understood sexy lingerie. I mean, what's the point? The guy's only going to take it off," I object.

Samantha flicks her eyes in Miranda's direction. "That's the trick. You don't take it off right away."

"You mean you run around his apartment in your underwear?" Me.

"You wear a fur coat. With sexy lingerie underneath."

"I can't afford a fur." Miranda.

"Then wear a trench coat. Do I have to teach you guys everything about sex?"

292

"Yes, please," I say.

"Especially since Carrie's still a virgin," Miranda screams.

"Honey, I knew that. I knew it the moment she walked in."

"Is it that obvious?" I ask.

"What I can't understand is why you're still one," Samantha says. "I got rid of mine when I was fourteen."

"How?" Miranda hiccups.

"The usual way. Boone's Farm Strawberry Hill and the back of a van."

"I did it on my parents' bed. They were away at a conference."

"That is sick," I say, pouring myself another drink.

"I know. I'm a very sick puppy," Miranda says.

When is this blackout going to end?

1:45 a.m.

"Babies! That's all it's about. Who ever knew the world would be all about babies?" Samantha shouts.

"Every time I see a baby, I swear, I want to throw up," Miranda says.

"I did throw up once." I nod eagerly. "I saw a filthy bib, and that was it."

"Why don't these people just get cats and a litter box?" Samantha asks.

2:15 a.m.

"I will never call a guy. Never ever." Samantha.

"What if you can't help it?" Me.

"You have to help it."

"It's all about low self-esteem." Miranda.

"You really should tell Charlie. About the procedure," I say, feeling wobbly.

"Why should I?" Samantha asks.

"Because it's what real people do."

"I didn't come to New York to be real."

"Didja come here to be fake?" I slur.

"I came here to be new," she says.

"I came here to be myself," Miranda adds. "I couldn't be, back home."

"Me neither." The room is spinning. "My mother died," I murmur, just before I pass out.

When I come to, light is streaming into the apartment.

I'm lying on the floor under the coffee table. Miranda is curled up on the couch, snoring, which immediately makes me wonder if this was secretly the reason Marty broke up with her. I try to sit up, but my head feels like it weighs a million pounds. "Ow," I say, putting it back down again.

Eventually I'm able to roll onto my stomach and crawl to the bathroom, where I take two aspirin and wash them down with the last of the bottled water. I stumble into Samantha's bedroom and crumple up on the floor.

"Carrie?" she says, awoken by my banging.

"Yer?"

"What happened last night?"

"Blackout."

"Damn."

"And endometriosis."

"Double damn."

"And Charlie."

"I didn't call him last night, did I?"

"Couldn't. Phones don't work."

"Are the lights still off?"

"Mmmm."

Pause.

"Did your mother really die?"

"Yep."

"I'm sorry."

"Me, too."

I hear her rustling around in those black silk sheets. She pats the side of the bed. "There's plenty of room here."

I heave myself onto the mattress and promptly fall into a greasy sleep.

CHAPTER TWENTY-NINE

"Hey, I found some food," Miranda exclaims. She places a box of Ritz crackers on the bed and we dive in.

"I think we should walk up to Charlie's." I brush my cracker crumbs off the sheet. "He's got the biggest apartment." And we've been stuck here for hours. I don't know how much longer I can last.

"No," Samantha says adamantly. "I'd rather starve then let him see me like this. My hair's dirty."

"Everyone's hair is dirty. Including Charlie's," I point out.

"Listen. What we talked about last night, we don't ever tell anyone, right?" Miranda says.

"I still can't believe Marty only has one testicle." I take another cracker. "That should have been a tip-off."

"I think it's a plus," Samantha says. "It made him work harder as a lover."

I feel around in the box for another cracker. It's empty. "We need supplies."

"I'm not moving." Samantha yawns luxuriously. "No power, no work. No Harry Mills trying to look up my skirt."

I sigh and change into my last clean pair of scrubs.

"Have you decided to become a doctor now?" Samantha asks.

"Where's your stethoscope?" Miranda hoots.

"They're very chic," I insist.

"Since when?"

"Since now." Hrmph. Apparently neither my sexual experiences nor my sartorial choices are much appreciated around here.

Miranda leans toward Samantha, and with an excited squeal demands, "Okay, what's the *worst* sex you've ever had?"

I throw up my hands. When I slip out of the apartment, the two of them are howling with laughter about something they've dubbed "The Pencil Problem."

I wander aimlessly around the Village, and when I spot the open door of the White Horse Tavern, I go inside.

In the dim light, I discover a few people sitting at the bar. My first reaction is one of relief that I've found someplace that's open. My second is dismay when I realize who's sitting there: Capote and Ryan.

I blink. It can't be. But it is. Capote's head is thrown back and he's laughing loudly. Ryan is hanging on to his bar stool. Clearly, they're both severely inebriated.

What the hell are they doing here? Capote's apartment is only a couple of blocks away, and it's possible he and Ryan got stuck at Capote's place when the power went out. But I'm surprised to see them, considering Capote's extensive alcohol collection. Judging from the looks of them, I guess they ran out.

I shake my head in disapproval, gearing up for the inevitable encounter. But secretly, I'm awfully glad to see them.

"Is this bar stool taken?" I ask, sliding in next to Ryan.

"Huh?" His eyes uncross as he stares at me in surprise. Then he falls upon me, embracing me in a bear hug. "Carrie Bradshaw!" He looks to Capote. "Speak of the devil. We were just talking about you."

"You were?"

"Weren't we?" Ryan asks, confused.

"I think that was about twelve hours ago," Capote says. He's soused, but not nearly as plastered as Ryan. Probably because he thinks it's "ungentlemanly" to appear drunk. "We've moved on from there."

"Hemingway?" Ryan asks.

"Dostoyevsky," Capote replies.

"I can never keep those damn Russians straight, can you?" Ryan asks me.

"Only when I'm sober," I quip.

"Are you sober? Oh no." Ryan takes a step backward and nearly lands in Capote's lap. He slaps his hand on the bar. "Can't be sober in a blackout. Not allowed. Barkeep, get this lady a drink!" he demands.

"Why are *you* here?" Capote asks.

"I'm foraging for supplies." I look at the two of them doubtfully.

"We were too." Ryan slaps his forehead. "And then something happened and we got trapped here. We tried to leave, but the cops kept accusing Capote of being a looter, so we were driven back to this lair." He breaks up with laughter, and suddenly, I do too. Apparently, we've got a serious case of cabin fever because we fall all over each other, holding our stomachs and pointing at Capote and laughing even harder. Capote shakes his head, as if he can't understand how he ended up with the two of us.

"Seriously, though," I hiccup. "I need supplies. My two girlfriends—"

"You're with women?" Ryan asks eagerly. "Well, let's go." He stumbles out of the bar with Capote and me running after him.

I'm not exactly sure how it happened, but an hour later, Capote, Ryan, and I are bumbling up the stairs to Samantha's apartment. Ryan is clutching the handrail while Capote encourages him forward. I look at the two of them and sigh. Samantha is going to kill me. Or not. Maybe nothing really matters after twenty-four hours without electricity.

In any case, I'm not returning empty-handed. Besides Ryan and Capote, I have a bottle of vodka and two six-packs of beer, which Capote managed to cadge from the bartender. Then I found a church basement where they were handing out jugs of water and ham-and-cheese sandwiches. Then Ryan decided to take a leak in an empty doorway. Then we got chased by a cop on a motorcycle, who yelled at us and told us to go home.

This, too, was extremely funny, although I suspect it shouldn't have been.

Inside the apartment, we discover Samantha bent over the coffee table, writing out a list. Miranda is next to her, battling several expressions, from consternation to admiration to out-and-out horror. Finally, admiration wins. "That's twenty-two," she exclaims. "And who's Ethan? I hate that name."

"He had orange hair. That's basically all I can remember."

Oh dear. It seems they've resorted to the vodka bottle as well.

"We're home," I call out.

"*We?*" Samantha's head snaps around.

"I brought my friend Ryan. And his friend Capote."

"Well," Samantha purrs, rising to her feet as she takes in my stray cats with approval. "Are you here to rescue us?"

"More like we're rescuing them," I say belligerently.

"Welcome." Miranda waves from the couch.

I look at her in despair, wondering what I've done. Maybe what they say about danger is true. It heightens the senses. And apparently makes everyone seem much more attractive than they are under normal circumstances.

Probably has something to do with the survival of the species. But if that's true, Mother Nature couldn't have chosen a more unreliable bunch.

I head into the kitchen with my sack of supplies and start unwrapping the sandwiches.

"I'll help you," Capote says.

"There's nothing to do," I say sharply, cutting the sandwiches in half to save the rest for later.

"You shouldn't be so rigid, you know?" Capote flips open a can of beer and pushes it toward me.

"I'm not. But someone needs to keep a level head."

"You worry too much. You always act like you're going to get into trouble."

I'm flabbergasted. "Me?"

"You get this sour, disapproving look on your face." He opens a can of beer for himself.

"And what about the arrogant, disapproving look on yours?"

"I'm not arrogant, Carrie."

"And I'm Marilyn Monroe."

"What do you have to worry about, anyway?" he asks. "Aren't you going to Brown in the fall?"

Brown. I'm paralyzed. Despite the blackout and our paltry supplies and the presence of Capote Duncan, it's the last place I think I'll ever want to be. The whole idea of college suddenly feels irrelevant. "Why?" I ask, defensively. "Are you trying to get rid of me?"

He shrugs and takes a sip of beer. "Nah. I'd probably miss you."

He goes back to join the others while I stand there in shock, holding the plate of sandwiches in my hands.

7:00 p.m.

Strip poker.

9:00 p.m.

More strip poker.

10:30 p.m.

Wearing Samantha's bra on my head.

2:00 a.m.

Have constructed tent from old blanket and chairs. Capote and I under tent.

Discussing Emma Bovary.

Discussing L'il and Viktor Greene.

Discussing Capote's views on women: "I want a woman who has the same goals as I do. Who wants to do something with her life."

I'm suddenly shy.

Capote and I lie down under the tent. It's nice but tense. What would it be like to do it with *him*, I wonder. I shouldn't even think about it though, not with Miranda and Samantha and Ryan out there, still playing cards.

I stare up at the blanket. "Why did you kiss me that night?" I whisper.

He reaches out, finds my hand, and curls his fingers around mine. We stay like that, silently holding hands for what feels like an eternity.

"I'm not a good boyfriend, Carrie," he says finally.

302

"I know." I untangle my hand from his. "We should try to get some sleep."

I close my eyes, knowing sleep is impossible. Not when every nerve ending is jumping with electricity, like my electrons are determined to communicate with Capote's across the barren space between us.

Too bad we can't use it to turn on the lights.

Then I must fall asleep, because the next thing I know, we're being woken by a terrific jangling, which turns out to be the phone.

I climb out of the tent as Samantha runs out of her bedroom with a sleeping mask on her head.

"What the—" Ryan sits up and bangs his head on the coffee table.

"*Could someone please answer that phone,*" Miranda shrieks.

Samantha makes a frantic slicing motion across her neck.

"If no one's going to answer it, I will," Ryan says, crawling toward the offending instrument.

"No!" Samantha and I shout at once.

I rip the receiver from Ryan's hand. "Hello?" I ask cautiously, expecting Charlie.

"Carrie?" asks a concerned male voice.

It's Bernard. The blackout's over.

PART THREE

Departures and Arrivals

CHAPTER THIRTY

My birthday's coming!

It's nearly here. I can't stop reminding everyone. My birthday! In less than two weeks, I'll be eighteen.

I'm one of those people who loves her birthday. I don't know why, but I do. I love the date: August 13. I was actually born on Friday the thirteenth, so even though it's bad luck for everyone else, it's good luck for me.

And this year, it's going to be huge. I'm turning eighteen, I'm going to lose my virginity, and I'm having my reading at Bobby's that night. I keep reminding Miranda that it's going to be a doubleheader: my first play and my first lay.

"Play and lay—get it?" I say, tickled by the rhyme. Miranda is, understandably, quite sick of my little joke, and every time I say it, she puts her hands over her ears and claims she wishes she'd never met me.

I've also become incredibly neurotic about my birth control pills. I keep looking into the little plastic container, checking to make sure I've taken the pill and haven't accidentally lost any. When I went to the clinic, I considered getting a diaphragm, too, but after the doctor showed it to me, I decided it was too complicated. I kept thinking about cutting two holes in the top and making it into a hat for a cat. I wonder if anyone's done that yet.

Naturally, the clinic reminded me of L'il. I still feel guilty about what happened to her. I sometimes wonder if I feel bad because it didn't happen to me, and I'm still in New York and have a play reading and a smart, successful boyfriend who hasn't ruined my life—yet. If it weren't for Viktor Greene, L'il would still be here, strolling the gritty streets in her Laura Ashley dresses and finding flowers in the asphalt. But then I wonder if it's *all* Viktor's fault. Perhaps L'il was right: New York simply isn't for her. And if Viktor hadn't driven her out, maybe something else would have.

Which reminds me of what Capote said to me during the blackout. About not having to worry because I was going to Brown in the fall. That makes me nervous as well, because with each passing day, I want to go to Brown less and less. I'd miss all my friends here. Besides, I already know what I want to do with my life. Why can't I just continue?

Plus, if I go to Brown, I won't, for instance, get free clothes.

A couple of days ago a little voice in the back of my head told me to look up that designer, Jinx, at her shop on Eighth Street. The store was empty when I walked in, so I

308

figured Jinx was in the back, polishing her brass knuckles. Sure enough, when she heard the sound of moving hangers, she emerged from behind a curtain, looked me up and down, and said, "Oh. You. From Bobby's."

"Yes," I said.

"Have you seen him?"

"Bobby? I'm doing a play reading in his space." I said it casually, like I was having play readings all the time.

"Bobby is weird," she said, twisting her mouth. "He is really one effed up mother-effer."

"Mmm," I agreed. "He certainly does seem a little . . . randy."

This cracked her up. "Harharhar. That's a good word for him. Randy. That's exactly what he is. Randy with no candy."

I wasn't exactly sure what she was talking about, but I went along with it.

In the light of day, Jinx looked less sinister and more, dare I say, normal. I could see she was one of those women who wore lots of makeup not because she was trying to frighten anyone, but because she had bad skin. And her hair was very dry, due to the black henna. And I imagined she didn't come from a very nice home and maybe had a father who was a drunk and a mother who yelled all the time. I knew Jinx had talent though, and I suddenly appreciated the efforts it must have taken her to get here.

"So you need something to wear. For Bobby's," she said.

"Yes." I hadn't actually gotten around to thinking about

what to wear to the reading, but once she said it, I realized it was all I should have been worrying about.

"I've got just the thing." She went into the back and came out holding a white vinyl jumpsuit with black piping along the sleeves. "I didn't have enough money for fabric, so I had to make it really small. If it fits, it's yours."

I wasn't expecting such generosity. Especially when I ended up walking out with an armload of clothes. Apparently I'm one of the few people in New York who is actually willing to wear a white vinyl jumpsuit or a plastic dress or red rubber pants.

It was like Cinderella and that damn slipper.

And just in time, too. I've gotten awfully sick of my ratty blue silk robe and my hostess dress and my surgical scrubs. It's like Samantha always says: If people keep seeing you in the same old outfits, they start to think you haven't any prospects.

Samantha, meanwhile, has gone back to chez Charlie. She says they're bickering about china patterns and crystal decanters and the pluses and minuses of a raw bar at their reception. She can't believe her life has been reduced to this, but I keep reminding her that come October, the wedding will be over and she won't have to worry about her life ever again. This caused her to make one of her notorious deals with me: She would help with the guest list for the play reading if I agreed to go shopping with her for a wedding dress.

That's the problem with weddings. They're contagious.

In fact, they're so contagious Donna LaDonna and her

mother are coming to New York to participate in the ritual. When Samantha mentioned they were coming, I realized I'd become so caught up in my New York life, I'd actually forgotten that Donna is Samantha's cousin.

The idea of seeing Donna again made me a little uneasy, but not as jumpy as giving Bernard my play.

Last night I screwed up my courage and finally presented Bernard with the manuscript. I literally delivered it to him on a silver platter. We were in his apartment and I found a silver platter that Margie had overlooked, and I tied a big red ribbon around it, and I served it to him while he was watching MTV. All the while, of course, thinking I should have been on that silver platter myself.

Now I wish I hadn't given it to him at all. The thought of Bernard reading my play and not liking it has made me frantic with worry. I've been pacing the apartment all morning, waiting for him to call, praying he will call before I have to meet Samantha and Donna LaDonna at Kleinfeld.

I haven't heard from Bernard, but I've had plenty of contact with Samantha. She keeps calling to remind me of the appointment. "It's at noon sharp. If we're not there on the dot of twelve, we lose the room."

"What are you? Cinderella? Will your taxi turn into a pumpkin as well?"

"Don't be funny, Carrie. This is my wedding."

And now it's almost time to meet Samantha, and Bernard still hasn't called to tell me whether he likes my play or not.

My whole life is hanging by one tulle thread.

The phone rings. Must be Bernard. Samantha has to have run out of dimes by now.

"Carrie?" Samantha practically shrieks into the phone. "Why are you still at home? You should be on your way to Kleinfeld."

"I'm just leaving." I glare at the phone, jump into my new jumpsuit, and careen down the stairs.

Kleinfeld is miles away, in Brooklyn. It takes about five subways to get there, and when I change trains, I give in to my trembling paranoia and call Bernard. He's not home. He's not at the theater. At the next station, I try him again. Where the hell is he? When I get off the train in Brooklyn, I rush right to a phone booth on the corner. The phone rings and rings. I hang up, destroyed. I'm sure Bernard is avoiding my calls on purpose. He must have read my play and hated it and he doesn't want to tell me.

I arrive at the temple of holy matrimony disheveled and disturbingly sweaty. Vinyl is not the thing to wear on a humid August day in New York, even if it is white.

Kleinfeld is nothing to look at from the outside, being one of those enormous soot-stained buildings with windows like sad, streaky eyes, but inside, it's another story. The decor is pink, plush, and hushed like the petals of a flower. Ageless saleswomen with put-on faces and soft demeanors glide through the waiting room. The Jones party has its own suite, complete with dressing room, raised platform, and 360-degree mirrors. It also contains a pitcher of water, a pot of tea, and a plate of cookies. And, thank heavens, a phone.

Samantha isn't there, though. Instead, I find a pretty, middle-aged woman sitting stiffly on a velvet settee, legs crossed demurely at the ankles, hair smoothed into a perfect helmet. This must be Charlie's mother, Glenn.

Seated next to her is another woman, who could be Glenn's polar opposite. She's in her midtwenties, dressed in a lumpy navy suit without a lick of makeup. She's not inherently unattractive, but given her messy hair and an expression that indicates she's used to making the best of things, I suspect she tries to deliberately make herself homely.

"I'm Glenn," the first woman says, holding out a long, bony hand with a discreet platinum watch clasped around her thin wrist. She must be left-handed, because left-handed people always wear their watches on their right wrist so everyone will know they're left-handed and, therefore, possibly more interesting and special. She indicates the young woman next to her. "This is my daughter, Erica."

Erica gives me a firm, no-nonsense handshake. There's something refreshing about her, like she knows how ridiculous her mother is and how this whole scene is kind of silly.

"Hi," I say, warmly, and take a seat on the edge of a small, decorative chair.

Samantha told me Glenn had a face-lift, so while Glenn smoothes her hair and Erica eats a cookie, I surreptitiously study Glenn's face, looking for signs of the surgery. On closer inspection, they're not hard to find. Glenn's mouth is stretched and tucked up like the grin of the Joker, although she's not smiling. Her eyebrows are dangerously close to her hairline. I'm peering at her so hard she can't help but sense my staring. She turns to me and, with a little flutter of her hand, says, "That's quite an interesting outfit you're wearing."

"Thank you," I say. "I got it for free."

"I should hope so."

I can't tell if she's being deliberately rude or if this is simply her usual demeanor. I take a cookie, and feel a little sad. I can't fathom why Samantha has insisted on my presence. Surely she isn't planning to include me on her journey into the future. I can't imagine where I would fit in.

Glenn shakes her arm and peers at her watch. "Where's Samantha?" she asks, with a quiet sigh of annoyance.

"Maybe she's caught in traffic," I suggest.

"It's terribly rude, being late for your own dress fitting," Glenn murmurs, in a low, warm voice intended to take the sting out of the insult. There's a knock on the door and I jump up to open it.

"Here she is," I chirp, expecting Samantha but finding Donna LaDonna and her mother, instead.

There's no sign of Samantha. Nevertheless, I'm so relieved not to be alone with Glenn and her daughter, I go too far. "Donna!" I shout.

Donna is all sexed up in a slouchy top with shoulder

pads and leggings. Her mother is wearing a sad imitation of Glenn's real Chanel suit. What will Glenn think of Donna and her mother? I can already tell she's none too impressed by me. And suddenly, I'm a tad embarrassed for Castlebury.

Donna, of course, doesn't notice. "Hi, Carrie," she says, like she just saw me yesterday.

She and her mother go to Glenn, who shakes hands nicely and pretends to be thrilled to meet them.

While Donna and her mother coo over the room, Glenn's suit, and the future wedding plans, I sit back and observe. I always thought Donna was one of the most sophisticated girls in our school, but seeing her in New York, on my turf, I wonder what I ever found so intriguing about her. Sure, she's pretty, but not as pretty as Samantha. And she's not the least bit stylish in that *Flashdance* getup. She's not even very interesting, babbling to me about how she and her mother got their nails done and bragging about how they shopped at Macy's. Jeez. Even I know only tourists shop at Macy's.

And then Donna blurts out her own very exciting news. She, too, is getting married. She holds out her hand, revealing a solitaire diamond chip.

I lean over to admire it, although you practically need a magnifying glass to see the damn thing. "Who's the lucky guy?"

She gives me a brief smile as if she's surprised I haven't heard. "Tommy."

"Tommy? Tommy *Brewster*?" The Tommy Brewster

who basically made my life hell merely because I had the bad luck to sit next to him in assembly for four years of high school? The big dumb jock who was Cynthia Viande's serious boyfriend?

The question is apparently written all over my face, because Donna immediately explains that Cynthia broke up with him. "She's going to BU and she didn't want to take Tommy with her. She actually thought she could do better," Donna smirks.

No kidding, I want to say.

"Tommy's going into the military. He's going to be a pilot," Donna adds boastfully. "He'll be traveling a lot and it'll be easier if we're married."

"Wow." Donna LaDonna engaged to Tommy Brewster? How could this happen? If I'd had to place bets in high school, I would have wagered that Donna LaDonna was the one who was on her way to bigger and better things. She was the last person I imagined would be the first to become a housewife.

Having dispatched this information, Donna veers the conversation onto the topic of babies.

"I was always a hands-on mom," Glenn says, nodding. "I breast-fed Charlie for nearly a year. Of course, it meant I could barely leave the apartment. But it was worth every minute. The scent of his little head . . ."

"The smell of his poopy diaper," Erica mutters under her breath. I give her a grateful look. She's been so quiet, I'd forgotten she was there.

"I think it's one of the reasons Charlie turned out so

well," Glenn continues, ignoring her daughter as she directs her comments to Donna. "I know breast-feeding isn't very popular, but I think it's terribly rewarding."

"I've heard it can make the kid smarter," Donna says.

I stare at the plate of cookies, wondering what Samantha would think of this discussion. Does she know Glenn is planning to turn her into a baby-making machine? The thought gives me the willies. What if what Miranda said about endometriosis is true, and Samantha can't get pregnant right away—or at all? And what if she does, and the baby is born in her intestine?

Where the hell is Samantha, anyway?

Boy, this is really making me uncomfortable. I've got to get out of here. "Can I use the phone?" I ask, and without waiting for permission, pick up the receiver and dial Bernard's number. He's still not there. I hang up, fuming, and decide to call him every thirty minutes until I reach him.

When I turn back to the room, the conversation has flagged. So much so that Donna actually asks how my summer is going.

Now it's my turn to brag.

"I'm having a play reading next week."

"Oh," Donna says, clearly unimpressed. "What's a play reading?"

"Well, I wrote this play, and my professor really loved it and then I met this guy, Bobby, who has a sort of performance space in his apartment, and I have a boyfriend who actually *is* a playwright—Bernard Singer, maybe you've heard of him—not that I'm not an actual writer but . . ." My voice gets smaller and smaller until it trails off into a painful little nothingness.

And where is Samantha in all this?

Glenn taps her watch impatiently.

"Oh, she'll show up," Mrs. LaDonna gushes. "We LaDonnas are always late," she says proudly, as if this is a plus. I look at her and shake my head. She's no help at all.

"I think your play sounds very exciting," Erica says, tactfully changing the subject.

"It is," I agree, praying Samantha will arrive at any moment. "It's kind of a big deal. Being my first play and all."

"I always told Erica she should become a writer," Glenn says, giving her daughter a disapproving look. "If you're a writer, you can stay at home with your children. If you actually decide to have children."

"Mother, please," Erica says, as if she's had to tolerate this discussion many times before.

"Instead Erica's decided to become a public defender!" Glenn exclaims grimly.

"A public defender," Mrs. LaDonna says, attempting to look impressed.

"What's that?" Donna asks, examining her manicure.

"It's a special kind of lawyer," I answer, wondering how Donna cannot know this.

"It's all about choice, Mother," Erica says firmly. "And I choose not to be chosen."

Glenn gives her a stiff little smile. She probably can't

move her muscles too much due to the face-lift. "It all sounds so terribly sad."

"But it isn't sad at all," Erica replies evenly. "It's freeing."

"I don't believe in choice," Glenn announces, addressing the room. "I believe in destiny. And the sooner you accept your destiny, the better. It seems to me you young girls waste a terrible amount of time trying to choose. And all you end up with is nothing."

Erica smiles. And turning to me, she explains, "Mother's been trying to marry Charlie off for years. She's pushed every debutante in the Blue Book in his direction, but of course, he never liked any of them. Charlie's not that dumb."

There's an audible gasp from Mrs. LaDonna as I peer around in shock. Donna and her mother look like they've had face-lifts as well. Their expressions are as frozen as Glenn's.

The phone rings and I automatically reach for it, wondering if it's Bernard, having somehow managed to track me down at Kleinfeld.

I'm such a dummy sometimes. It's Samantha.

"Where are you?" I whisper urgently. "Everyone's here. Glenn and Erica—"

"Carrie." She cuts me off. "I'm not going to be able to make it."

"What?"

"Something came up. A meeting I can't get out of. So if you wouldn't mind telling Glenn . . ."

Actually, I would mind. I'm suddenly tired of doing her

dirty work. "I think you should tell her yourself." I hand Glenn the phone.

While Glenn speaks to Samantha, a saleswoman peeks into the room, beaming with excitement, pulling an enormous rack of wedding dresses behind her. The atmosphere explodes as Donna and her mother rush toward the dresses, pawing and fondling the garments like they're sugary confections.

I've had enough. I dive into the rack of wedding dresses and fight my way through to the other side.

Weddings are like a train. Once you get on, you can't get off.

Sort of like the subway.

The train is stopped, again, somewhere in the dark catacombs between Forty-second and Fifty-ninth streets. It's been stuck for twenty minutes now, and the natives are getting restless.

Including myself. I yank open the door between the cars and step out onto the tiny platform, leaning over the edge in an attempt to discover the cause of the holdup. It's useless, of course. It always is. I can just make out the walls of the tunnel until they disappear into darkness.

The train lurches unexpectedly and I nearly tip off the platform. I grab the handle of the door just in time, reminding myself that I need to be more careful. It's hard to be careful, though, when you feel indestructible.

My heart does that jackhammer thing that happens whenever I get all anticipatory about the future.

Bernard read my play.

The minute I escaped from Kleinfeld, I ran to a phone booth and finally reached him. He said he was in the middle of casting. I could tell by his voice that he didn't want me to come by, but I kept insisting and finally he relented. He could probably tell by *my* voice that I was in one of those nothing-is-going-to-stop-me moods.

Not even the subway.

The train screeches to a halt just inside the platform at Fifty-ninth Street.

I bang though the cars until I reach the head compartment, then I do the dangerous thing again and leap from the train onto the concrete. I run up the escalator, zoom through Bloomingdale's, and race up to Sutton Place, sweating like a mad thing in the white vinyl.

I catch Bernard in front of his building, hailing a cab. I spring up behind him.

"You're late," he says, jangling his keys. "And now I'm late too."

"I'll ride with you to the theater. Then you can tell me how much you loved my play."

"It's not the best time, Carrie. My mind's not focused." He's being all business. I hate it when he's like this.

"I've been waiting all day," I plead. "I'm going crazy. You *have* to tell me what you thought."

I don't know why I'm in such a frenzy. Maybe it's because I just came from Kleinfeld. Maybe it's because Samantha didn't show up. Or maybe it's because I don't ever want to have to marry a man like Charlie and have a mother-in-law like Glenn. Which means I *have* to succeed at something else.

Bernard grimaces.

"Oh my God. You didn't like it." I can feel my knees buckling beneath me.

"Take it easy, kid," he says, hustling me into the cab.

I perch on the seat next to him like a bird about to take flight. I swear I see a look of pity cross his face, but it's immediately gone and I tell myself I must have imagined it.

He smiles and pats my leg. "It's good, Carrie. Really."

"Good? Or really good?"

He shifts in his seat. "Really good."

"Honestly? Do you mean it? You're not just humoring me?"

"I said it was really good, didn't I?"

"Say it again. *Please.*"

"It's really good." He smiles.

"Yippee!" I shout.

"Can I go to my casting now?" he asks, extracting the manuscript from his briefcase and holding it out to me.

I suddenly realize I've been clutching his arm in fear. "Cast away," I say gallantly. "Castaways. Ha-ha. Get it?"

"Sure, kiddo." He leans over to give me a quick kiss.

But I hold on to him. I put my hands around his face and kiss him hard. "That's for liking my play."

"I guess I'll have to like your plays more often," he jokes, getting out of the cab.

"Oh, you will," I say from the open window.

Bernard goes into the theater as I throw back my head

322

in relief. I wonder what I was so worked up about. And then it hits me: If Bernard didn't like my play, if he didn't like my writing, would I still be able to like *him*?

Luckily, that's one question I don't have to answer.

CHAPTER THIRTY-ONE

"And she has the nerve to tell Samantha I've got a big head."

"Well—" Miranda says cautiously.

"A big fat swollen head. Like a basketball," I say, leaning into the mirror to apply more lipstick. "And meanwhile, she's marrying this stupid jock—"

"Why do you care so much?" Miranda asks. "It's not like you have to see them again."

"I know. But couldn't they have been a little impressed? I'm doing so much more with my life than they ever will."

I'm talking, of course, about Donna LaDonna and her mother. After her no-show at Kleinfeld, Samantha took the LaDonnas to Benihana as a consolation prize. When I asked Samantha if Donna mentioned me, she said Donna told her I'd become completely full of myself and obnoxious. Which really pissed me off.

"Did Samantha find a dress?" Miranda asks, fluffing her hair.

"She never showed up. She had an important meeting she couldn't get out of. But that's not the point. What bugs me is that this girl, who thought she was such a big deal in high school—" I break off, wondering if I have become a monster. "You don't think I have a big head, do you?"

"Oh, Carrie. I don't know."

Which means yes. "Even if I do, I don't care," I insist, trying to justify my attitude. "Maybe I do have a bit of an ego. So what? Do you know how long it's taken me to even get an ego? And I'm still not sure it's fully developed. It's more of an 'egg' than an 'ego.'"

"Uh-huh." Miranda looks dubious.

"Besides, men have egos all the time and no one says they're full of themselves. And now that I have this tiny little bit of self-esteem, I don't intend to let it go."

"Good," she says. "Don't."

I march past her into the bedroom, where I snake my legs into a pair of fishnet stockings and slip the white plastic dress with the clear plastic cut-outs over my head. I pull on the bright blue Fiorucci boots and check my appearance in the full-length mirror.

"Who are these people again?" Miranda eyes me with a worried expression.

"Bernard's agent—Teensie Dyer. And her husband."

"Is that what you're supposed to wear to the Hamptons?"

"It's what *I* wear to the Hamptons."

True to his word, Bernard has actually come through

on his promise to introduce me to Teensie. In fact, he's gone above and beyond his call to duty and invited me to the Hamptons to stay with Teensie and her husband. It's only for Saturday night, but who cares? It's the Hamptons! All summer, I've been dying to go. Not just to find out why they're such a big deal, but to be able to say, "I went to the Hamptons," to people like Capote.

"Do you really think you should be wearing plastic?" Miranda asks. "What if they think you're wearing a garbage bag?"

"Then *they're* stupid."

Yep, I'm full of myself all right.

I toss a bathing suit, the Chinese robe, my new red rubber pants, and the hostess gown into my carpenter's bag. The bag reminds me of how Bernard said I needed a valise. Which leads me to wonder if Bernard is finally going to demand I have sex with him. I've been taking the pill, so I suppose there's no reason not to, but I'm pretty adamant about waiting for my eighteenth birthday. I want the event to be special and memorable, something I'll remember for the rest of my life.

Of course, the thought of finally doing it also makes me queasy.

Miranda must pick up on my mood, because she looks at me curiously. "Have you slept with him yet?"

"No."

"How can you go away with him and not sleep with him?"

"He respects me."

"No offense, but it sounds weird. Are you *sure* he's not gay?"

"Bernard is not gay!" I nearly shout.

I go out into the living room and pick up my play, wondering if I should bring it with me in case I have a chance to slip it to Teensie. But that might be too obvious. Instead, I have another idea.

"Hey," I say, holding up the manuscript. "*You* should read my play."

"Me?" Miranda asks, taken aback.

"Why not?"

"Didn't Bernard read it? I thought he liked it. He's the expert."

"But you're the audience. And you're smart. If you like it, it means other people will too."

"Oh, Carrie," she says, pulling at her lip. "I don't know anything about plays."

"Don't you *want* to read it?"

"I'm going to hear you read it on Thursday. At Bobby's."

"But I want *you* to read it, first."

"Why?" She looks hard at me, but then relents. Perhaps she can see how, underneath the bravado, I'm a nervous wreck. She holds out her hand for the manuscript. "If you really want me to—"

"I do," I say firmly. "You can read it this weekend and give it back to me on Monday. And sweetie? If you don't like it, can you please pretend you do?"

Bernard went out to the Hamptons on Friday, so I take the Jitney by myself.

I don't mind. From the sound of it, I kept picturing the

Jitney as some kind of old-fashioned cable car, but it turns out to be a regular bus.

It chugs along a crowded highway until eventually we turn off and start going through little beach towns. At first they're tacky, with bars and clam shacks and car dealerships, but then everything becomes more green and marshy, and when we cross a bridge and drive past a log cabin with totem poles on the front and a sign reading CIGARETTES $2 CARTON, the landscape changes completely. Old oaks and manicured hedges line the street, behind which I glimpse enormous shingled mansions.

The bus snakes into a picture-perfect town. Neatly painted white shops with green awnings populate the streets. There's a bookstore, a tobacconist, Lilly Pulitzer, a jewelry store, and an old-fashioned movie theater where the bus pulls over.

"Southampton," the driver announces. I pick up my carpenter's bag and get out.

Bernard is waiting for me, leaning against the hood of a small bronze Mercedes, his smooth bare feet pushed into Gucci loafers. Miranda was right: the plastic dress and Fiorucci boots that were perfect for the city feel out of place in this quaint little town. But Bernard doesn't care. He takes my bag, pausing for a kiss. His mouth is sublimely familiar. I love the way I can feel one of his incisors under his top lip.

"How was the trip?" he asks, smoothing my hair.

"Great," I say breathlessly, thinking about how much fun we're going to have.

He holds open the door and I slide onto the front seat. The car is old, from the 1960s, with a polished wooden steering wheel and shiny nickel dials. "This your car?" I ask, teasingly.

"It's Peter's."

"Peter?"

"Teensie's husband." He starts the engine, puts the car into gear, and pulls away from the curb with a jolt.

"Sorry," he laughs. "I'm a tad distracted. Don't take this the wrong way, but Teensie's insisted on giving you your own room."

"Why?" I frown in annoyance, but secretly, I'm relieved.

"She kept asking me how old you were. I told her it was none of her damn business, and that's when she got suspicious. You are over eighteen, aren't you?" he asks, half jokingly.

I sigh, as if the question is beyond ridiculous. "I told you. I'm a sophomore in college."

"Just checking, kitten," he says, giving me a wink. "And don't be afraid to stand up to Teensie, okay? She can be a bully, but she's got an enormous heart."

In other words, she's an absolute bitch.

We swing into a long gravel drive and park in front of a shingled house. It's not quite as large as I imagined, given the enormity of the houses I saw along the way, but it's still big. What was once a regular-sized house is attached to a soaring barnlike structure.

"Nice, huh?" Bernard says, gazing up at the house from behind the windshield. "I wrote my first play here."

"Really?" I ask, getting out of the car.

"Rewrote it, actually. I'd written the first draft during the day when I was working the night shift at the bottling plant."

"That's so romantic."

"It wasn't at the time. But in hindsight, yeah, it does sound romantic."

"With a touch of cliché?" I ask, razzing him.

"I went to Manhattan one night with my buddies," he continues, opening the trunk. "Stumbled across Teensie at a club. She insisted I send her my play, said she was an agent. I didn't even know what an agent was back then. But I sent her my play anyway, and the next thing I know, she opened her house to me for the summer. So I could write. Undisturbed."

"And were you?" I ask, trying to keep the apprehension out of my voice. "Undisturbed?"

He laughs. "When I was disturbed, it wasn't unpleasant."

Crap. Does that mean he slept with Teensie? And if he did, why didn't he tell me? He could have warned me, at least. I hope I won't discover any other unpleasant facts this weekend.

"Don't know where I'd be without Teensie," he says, slinging his arm across my shoulders.

We're almost at the house when Teensie herself appears, strolling briskly up a flagstone path. She's wearing tennis

330

whites, and while I can't speak for her heart, there's no mistaking the fact that her breasts are enormous. They strain against the cloth of her polo shirt like two boulders struggling to erupt from a volcano. "There you are!" she exclaims pleasantly, shielding her eyes from the sun.

She plants herself in front of me, and in a rush, says, "I'd shake hands but I'm sweaty. Peter's inside somewhere, but if you want a drink, ask Alice." She turns around and trots back to the courts, waggling her fingers in the air.

"She seems nice," I say, in an effort to like her. "And she has really big breasts," I add, wondering if Bernard has seen them in the flesh.

Bernard hoots. "They're fake."

"*Fake?*"

"Silicone."

So he has seen them. How else would he know all about them? "What else is plastic?"

"Her nose, of course. She likes to think of herself as Brenda. In *Goodbye, Columbus*. I always tell her she's more Mrs. Robinson than Miss Patimkin."

"What does her husband think?"

Bernard grins. "Pretty much whatever she tells him to, I imagine."

"I mean about the *silicone*."

"Oh," he says. "I don't know. He spends a lot of his time hopping."

"Like a bunny?"

"More like the White Rabbit. All he's missing is the pocket watch." Bernard opens the front door and calls out,

"Alice," like he owns the place.

Which, given his history with Teensie, I suppose he does.

We've entered the barn part of the house, which has been fashioned into a gigantic living room filled with couches and stuffed chairs. There's a stone fireplace and several doors that lead to unseen corridors. One of the doors flies open and out pops a small man with longish hair and what was likely once a girlishly pretty face. He's on his way to another door when he spots us and beetles over.

"Anyone seen my wife?" he inquires, in an English accent.

"She's playing tennis," I say.

"Ah, *right*." He smacks his forehead. "Very observant of you. Yes, very observant. That infernal game." He tumbles on without pause: "Well, make yourselves at home. You know the drill, Bernard, all very casual, *mi casa es su casa* and all that—we've got the president of Bolivia for dinner tonight, so I thought I might brush up on my *Español*."

"*Gracias*," I say.

"Oh, you speak Spanish," he exclaims. "Excellent. I'll tell Teensie to put you next to *el presidente* at dinner." And before I can demur, he scurries out of the room as Teensie herself reappears.

"Bernard, darling, will you be a gentleman and carry Cathy's suitcase to her room?"

"Cathy?" Bernard asks. He looks around. "Who's Cathy?"

Teensie's face twists in annoyance. "I thought you said her name was Cathy."

I shake my head. "It's Carrie. Carrie Bradshaw."

"Who can keep track?" she says helplessly, implying that Bernard has had such an endless parade of girlfriends, she can't keep their names straight.

She leads us up the stairs and down a short hallway in the original part of the house. "Bathroom here," she says, opening a door to reveal a powder-blue sink and narrow glassed-in shower. "And *Carrie's* in here." She opens another door to reveal a small room with a single bed, a patchwork quilt, and a shelf of trophies.

"My daughter's room," Teensie says smugly. "It's above the kitchen, but Chinita loves it because it's private."

"Where is your daughter?" I ask, wondering if Teensie has decided to kick her own daughter out of her room for the sake of propriety.

"Tennis camp. She's graduating from high school next year and we're hoping she'll get into Harvard. We're all so terribly proud of her."

Meaning this Chinita is practically my age.

"Where do *you* go to school?" Teensie asks.

"Brown." I glance at Bernard. "I'm a sophomore."

"How interesting," Teensie replies, in a tone that makes me wonder if she's seen through my lie. "I should put Chinita in touch with you. I'm sure she'd love to hear all about Brown. It's her *safety* school."

I ignore the insult and lob one of my own. "I'd love to, Mrs. Dyer."

"Call me Teensie," she says, with a flash of resentment. She turns to Bernard and, determined not to let me get the better of her, says, "Why don't we let your friend unpack."

A short while later, I'm sitting on the edge of the bed, wondering where the phone is and if I should call Samantha to ask for advice on how to deal with Teensie, when I remember Teensie on the floor of the Jessens' and smile. Who cares if she hates me? I'm in the Hamptons! I jump up, hang my clothes, and slip into a bikini. The room is a bit stuffy, so I open the window and take in the view. The bright green lawn ends at a manicured hedge, and beyond are miles of fields fuzzy with short leafy plants—potato fields, Bernard explained on the way over. I inhale the sweet, humid air, which means the ocean can't be far away.

Above the gentle sound of the surf, I hear voices. I lean out the window and discover Teensie and another woman seated at a metal table on a small patio, sipping what appear to be Bloody Marys. I can hear their conversation as clearly as if I were sitting across from them.

"She's barely older than Chinita," Teensie exclaims. "It's outrageous."

"How young *is* she?"

"Who knows? She looks like she's barely out of high school."

"Poor Bernard," says the second woman.

"It's just so pathetically textbook," Teensie adds.

"Well, after that horrible summer with Margie—didn't they get married here?"

"Yes." Teensie sighs. "You'd think he'd have the sense not to bring this young twit—"

I gasp, then quickly shut my mouth in the perverse desire not to miss a word.

"It's obviously subconscious," the second woman says. "He wants to make sure he'll never get hurt again. So he chooses someone young and wide-eyed, who worships him and will never leave him. He controls the relationship. As opposed to Margie."

"But how long can it possibly last?" Teensie moans. "What can they have in common? What do they talk about?"

"Maybe they don't. *Talk*," the second woman says.

"Doesn't this girl have parents? What kind of parent lets their daughter go away with a man who's clearly ten or fifteen years older?"

"It *is* the eighties," the second woman sighs, trying to be conciliatory. "The girls are different now. They're so bold."

Teensie gets up to go into the kitchen. I practically crawl out the window, hoping to hear the rest of their conversation, but I can't.

Numb with shame, I flop back on the bed. If what they said is true, it means I'm merely a pawn in Bernard's play. The one he's acting out in his real life to help him get over Margie.

Margie. Her name gives me the willies.

Why did I think I could compete with her for Bernard's affections? Apparently, I can't. Not according to Teensie.

I throw the pillow against the wall in rage. Why did I come here? Why would Bernard subject me to this? Teensie must be right. He *is* using me. He might not be aware of it, but it's no secret to everyone else.

There's only one way to save face. I have to leave. I'll

ask Bernard to drive me to the bus stop. I'll say good-bye and never see him again. And then, after I have my reading and I'm the toast of the town, he'll realize what a mistake he made.

I'm tossing clothes into my carpenter's bag, when I catch the sound of his voice. "Teensie?" he calls. I peer over the windowsill.

He's striding across the lawn, looking concerned and a bit peeved. "Teensie?" he calls again as Teensie appears on the patio.

"Yes, darling?"

"Have you seen Carrie?" he asks.

I detect a slight drop of disappointment in her shoulders. "No, I haven't."

"Where is she?" Bernard demands, looking around.

Teensie throws up her hands. "I'm not her keeper."

They both disappear into the house as I bite my lip in triumph. Teensie was wrong. Bernard does care about me. She knows it too, and it's driving her mad with jealousy.

Poor Bernard, I think. It's my duty to save him from the Teensies of the world.

I quickly pick up a book and arrange myself on the bed. Sure enough, a minute later Bernard knocks on my door.

"Come in!"

"Carrie?" He pushes open the door. "What are you doing? I've been waiting for you at the pool. We're having lunch."

I put down my book and smile. "I'm sorry. No one told me."

"Silly goose," he says, coming toward me and kissing the top of my head. He lies down next to me. "Love the bikini," he murmurs.

We fool around frantically until we hear Teensie calling our names. This cracks me up and causes Bernard to guffaw as well. And that's when I decide to break my own rule. I *will* have Bernard. Tonight. I'll sneak into his room and we'll finally do it. Right under Teensie's little bobbed nose.

CHAPTER THIRTY-TWO

At dinner, Teensie's husband, Peter, makes good on his threat and I'm seated next to the Bolivian president. He's a pockmarked thug of a man, with a heavy, self-important demeanor that frightens me. Knowing nothing about Bolivia or its politics, I'm determined not to say the wrong thing. I have a feeling if I do, I may possibly be eliminated.

Luckily, *el presidente*, as Peter keeps calling him, has absolutely no interest in me. We've barely unfolded our napkins and placed them on our laps when he takes one look at me, sums me up as being of no importance, and immediately turns to the woman on his left. At the other end of the table, Teensie has placed Bernard to her right. I'm too far away to hear their conversation, but Teensie, who is laughing and gesturing, appears to be keeping her little group engaged. Ever since the first guests began to arrive, Teensie's become a different person. There's no trace of the subtle, calculated nastiness she displayed this afternoon.

I take a bite of my fish, determined not to betray the fact that I'm becoming mortifyingly bored. The only thing that's keeping me going is the thought of Bernard, and how we can be together, later.

I idly wonder if Teensie's husband, Peter, knows about Teensie and Bernard. I take a sip of my wine and sigh quietly. I cut another piece of fish and stare at my fork, wondering if it's worth hazarding another mouthful. The fish is dry and plain, as if someone decided food should be a punishment instead of a pleasure.

"Don't like the fish?" Peter's voice comes from my left.

"Actually, I don't." I smile, relieved someone is talking to me.

"That bad, eh?" He pushes the fish to the side of his plate. "It's this newfangled diet my wife has going. No butter, no salt, no skin, no fat, and no spices. All part of a misguided attempt to live forever."

I giggle. "I'm not sure living forever is a good idea."

"Not sure?" Peter declares. "It's a bloody awful idea. How'd you get thrown in with this lot anyway?"

"I met Bernard, and—"

"I mean, what do you do in New York?"

"Oh. I'm a writer," I say simply. I sit up a little straighter, and add, "I'm studying at The New School, but I'm having my first play reading next week."

"Well done," he says, sounding impressed. "Have you talked to my wife?"

I look down at my plate. "I don't think your wife is interested in me or my writing." I glance across the table at Teensie. She's been drinking red wine, and her lips are a ghastly shade of purple. "On the other hand, I don't need your wife's good opinion in order to succeed."

That's the egg part of my ego rising to the surface.

"You're quite a confident young lady," Peter remarks. And then, as if to emphasize the fact that I've gone too far, he gives me one of those devastatingly polite smiles that could probably put the queen of England in her place.

I sit frozen in disgrace. Why couldn't I keep my mouth shut? Peter was only trying to be friendly, and now I've insulted his wife. In addition to committing the supposed sin of arrogance. It's acceptable in a man, but not in a woman. Or not in this crowd, anyway.

I tap Peter on the arm.

"Yes?" He turns. There's no sharpness in his tone, merely a deadening disinterest.

I'm about to ask him if I were a man, would I be judged so harshly, but his expression stops me. "Could you pass the salt?" I ask, adding quietly, "Please?"

I manage to make it through the rest of the dinner by pretending to be interested in a long story about golfing in Scotland, with which Peter regales our end of the table. When the plates are cleared, I hope Bernard and I can escape, but instead we're ushered onto the terrace for coffee and dessert. This is followed by chess in the living room. Bernard plays with Peter, while I perch on the edge of Bernard's chair, pretending to play dumb. The truth is, anyone who's halfway good at math can play chess, and after enduring several bad moves by Bernard, I begin quietly giving him advice. Bernard starts winning and a small crowd gathers to witness the spectacle.

Bernard gives me all the credit, and at last, I can see my esteem rising slightly in their eyes. Maybe I'm a contender after all.

"Where'd you learn to play chess?" he asks, fixing us another round of drinks from a wicker cart in the corner.

"I've always played. My father taught me."

Bernard regards me, bemused. "You've just made me realize I don't know a thing about you."

"That's because you forgot to ask," I say playfully, my equilibrium restored. I look around the room. "Don't any of these people ever go to bed?"

"Are you tired?"

"I was thinking—"

"Plenty of time for that later," he says, brushing the back of my hair with his lips.

"You two lovebirds." Teensie waves from the couch. "Come over here and join the discussion."

I sigh. Bernard may be willing to call it an evening, but Teensie is determined to keep us downstairs.

I endure another hour of political discussions. Finally, Peter's eyes close, and when he falls asleep in his chair, Teensie murmurs that perhaps we should all go to bed.

I give Bernard a meaningful look and scurry to my room. Now that the moment has arrived, I'm shaking with fear. My body trembles in anticipation. What will it be like? Will I scream? And what if there's blood?

I slip on my negligee and brush my hair a hundred times. When thirty minutes have passed and the house is quiet, I slip out, creep across the living room, and up the other set of stairs, which leads to Bernard's room. It's at the end of a long hall, located conveniently next to Teensie and Peter, but, like all the rooms in the new wing, it has its own en suite bathroom.

En suite. My, what a lot of things I've learned this weekend. I giggle as I turn the knob on Bernard's door.

He's in bed, reading. Under the soft light of the lamp, he looks sleek and mysterious, like something out of a Victorian novel. He puts his finger to his lips as he slides back the covers. I fall silently into his arms, close my eyes, and hope for the best.

He turns off the light and rearranges himself under the sheets. "Good night, kitten."

I sit up, perplexed. "Good night?"

I lean over and turn on the light.

He grabs my hand. "What are you doing?"

"You want to *sleep*?"

"Don't you?"

I pout. "I thought we could—"

He smiles. "Here?"

"Why not?"

He turns off the light. "It's rude."

I turn it back on. "Rude?"

"Teensie and Peter are in the next room." He turns off the light again.

"So?" I say in the dark.

"I don't want them to hear us. It might make them . . . uncomfortable."

I frown in the darkness, my arms crossed over my chest. "Don't you think it's time Teensie got over the fact that you've moved on? From her *and* Margie?"

"Oh, Carrie." He sighs.

"I'm serious. Teensie needs to accept that you're seeing other people now. That you're seeing me—"

"Yes, she does," he says softly. "But we don't need to rub it in her face."

"I think we do," I reply.

"Let's go to sleep. We'll figure it out in the morning."

This is my cue to flounce out of the room in anger. But I figure I've done enough flouncing for the evening. Instead, I lie silently, mulling over every scene, every conversation, fighting back tears and the gnawing realization that somehow, I haven't necessarily managed to come out on top this weekend, after all.

CHAPTER THIRTY-THREE

"I'm so glad you came to see me," Bobby proclaims as he opens the door. "This is a very nice surprise. Yes, a very nice surprise," he patters on, taking my arm.

I shift my bag from one side to the other. "It's really not a surprise, Bobby. I called you, remember?"

"Oh, but it's always a surprise to see a friend, don't you think? Especially when the friend is so attractive."

"Well," I say, frowning, wondering what this has to do with my play.

Bernard and I returned to the city late Sunday afternoon, hitching a ride with Teensie and Peter in the old Mercedes. Teensie drove, while Bernard and Peter talked about sports and I sat quietly, determined to be on my best behavior. Which wasn't difficult, as I didn't have much to say anyway. I kept wondering if Bernard and I stayed together, if this was what our life would be. Weekends with Teensie and Peter. I didn't think I could take it. I wanted Bernard, but not his friends.

I went back to Samantha's, vowing to get my life in order, which included calling Bobby and scheduling an appointment to discuss the reading. Unfortunately, Bobby doesn't seem to be taking it as seriously as I am.

"Let me show you around the space," he says now, with irritating insistence, especially as I saw the space when I was at his party. That night feels like ages ago, an uncomfortable reminder that while time is racing on, my own time may be running out.

The reading may be my last chance to establish a toehold in New York. A firm grip on the rock of Manhattan from which I cannot be removed.

"We'll set up chairs here." Bobby indicates the gallery space. "And we'll serve cocktails. Get the audience liquored up. Should we have white wine or vodka or both?"

"Oh, both," I murmur.

"And are you planning on having real actors? Or will it just be a reading?"

"I think maybe just a reading. For now," I say, envisioning the bright lights of Broadway. "I'm planning to read the whole play myself." After the class reading with Capote, it seemed easier not to get anyone else involved.

"Better that way, yes?" Bobby nods. His nodding—his unbridled enthusiasm—is starting to get to me. "We should have some champagne. To celebrate."

"It's barely noon," I object.

"Don't tell me you're one of those time Nazis," he

intones, urging me down a short hallway that leads to his living quarters. I follow him uncertainly, a warning bell chiming in my head. "Artists can't live like other people. Schedules and all that—kills the creativity, don't you think?" he asks.

"I guess so." I sigh, wishing I could escape. But Bobby's doing me an enormous favor, staging a reading of my play in his space. And with this thought I accept a glass of champagne.

"Let me show you around the rest of the place."

"Honestly, Bobby," I say in frustration. "You don't have to."

"I want to! I've cleared my whole afternoon for you."

"But why?"

"I thought we might want to get to know each other better."

Oh for goodness' sake. He can't possibly be trying to seduce me. It's too ridiculous. For one thing, he's shorter than I am. And he has jowls, meaning he must be over fifty years old. And he's gay. Isn't he?

"This is my bedroom," he says, with a flourish. The decor is minimalist and the room is spotless, so I imagine he has a maid to pick up after him.

He plunks himself on the edge of the neatly made bed and takes a sip of champagne, patting the spot next to him.

"Bobby," I say firmly. "I really should go." In demonstration of my intentions, I place my glass on the windowsill.

"Oh, don't put it there," he cries. "It will leave a ring."

I pick up the glass. "I'll put it back in the kitchen, then."

"But you can't go," he clucks. "We haven't finished talking about your play."

I roll my eyes, but I don't want to completely offend him. I figure I'll sit next to him for a moment and then leave.

I perch gingerly on the side of the bed, as far away from him as possible. "About the play—"

"Yes, about the play," he agrees. "What made you want to write it?"

"Well, I . . ." I fumble for the words but I take too long and Bobby becomes impatient.

"Hand me that photograph, will you?" And before I can protest, he's scooted next to me and is pointing at the picture with a manicured finger. "My wife," he says, followed by a giggle. "Or should I say my ex-wife?"

"You were married?" I ask as politely as possible, given those alarm bells are now clanging away like a bell tower.

"For two years. Annalise was her name. She's French, you see?"

"Uh-huh." I peer more closely at the image. Annalise is one of those beauties who looks absolutely insane, with a ridiculous pouty mouth and wild, scorching black eyes.

"You remind me of her." Bobby puts his hand on my leg.

I unceremoniously remove it. "I don't look a thing like her."

"Oh, but you do. To me," he murmurs. And then, in hideous slow motion, he purses his lips and pushes his face

347

toward mine for a kiss.

I quickly turn away and wrestle free from his grasping fingers. Ugh. What kind of man gets manicures anyway?

"Bobby!" I pick up my glass from the floor and start out of the room.

He follows me into the kitchen, wagging his tail like a chastened puppy. "Don't go," he pleads. "There's nearly a whole bottle of champagne left. You can't expect me to drink it myself. Besides, it doesn't keep."

The kitchen is tiny, and Bobby has stationed himself in the doorway, blocking my exit.

"I have a boyfriend," I say fiercely.

"He doesn't have to know."

I'm about to flee, when he changes his tack from sly to hurt. "Really, Carrie. It's going to be very hard to work together if I think you don't like me."

He has to be kidding. But maybe Samantha was right. Doing business with men is tricky. If I reject Bobby, is he going to cancel my play reading? I swallow and try to summon a smile. "I do like you, Bobby. But I have a boyfriend," I repeat, figuring the emphasis of this fact is probably my best tactic.

"Who?" he demands.

"Bernard Singer."

Bobby breaks into a glass-shattering peal. "Him?" He moves closer and tries to take my hand. "He's too old for you."

I shake my head in wonder.

The momentary lull gives Bobby another chance to

attack. He wraps his arms around my neck and attempts to mouth me again.

There's a kind of tussle, with me trying to maneuver around him and him trying to push me against the sink. Luckily, Bobby not only looks like a butter ball, but has the consistency of one as well. Besides, I'm more desperate. I duck under his outstretched arms and hightail it for the door.

"Carrie! Carrie," he cries, clapping his hands as he skitters down the hall after me.

I reach the door, and pause, breathless. I'm about to tell him what a scumball he is and how I don't appreciate being taken in under false pretenses—all the while seeing my future crumble before me—when I catch his pained expression.

"I'm sorry." He hangs his head like a child. "I hope—"

"Yes?" I ask, rearranging my hair.

"I hope this doesn't mean you hate me. We can still do your reading, yes?"

I do my best to look down my nose at him. "How can I trust you? After this."

"Oh, forget about it," he says, waving his hands in front of his face as though encased in a swarm of flies. "I didn't mean it. I'm too forward. Friends?" he asks sheepishly, holding out his hand.

I straighten my shoulders and take it. Quick as a wink, he's clutched my hand and is lifting it to his mouth.

I allow him to kiss it before I jerk it back.

"What about your play?" he pronounces. "You have to

allow me to read it before Thursday. Since you won't let me kiss you, I need to know what I'm getting into."

"I don't have it. I'll drop it off tomorrow," I say hastily. Miranda has it, but I'll get it from her later.

"And invite some of your friends to the reading. The pretty ones," he adds.

I shake my head and walk out the door. Some men never give up.

Nor some women. I fan myself in relief as I ride down the elevator. At least I still have my reading. I'll probably be fighting Bobby off all night, but it seems like a small price to pay for impending fame.

CHAPTER THIRTY-FOUR

"Who is this creep, exactly?" Samantha asks, tearing the top off a pink package of Sweet'N Low and pouring the powdered chemicals into her coffee.

"He's some kind of art dealer. He's the guy with the space. I went to the fashion show there?" I gather the tiny strips of pink paper from the middle of the table, fold them neatly, and wrap them in my napkin. I can't help it. Those damn leavings from fake sugar packages drive me crazy. Mostly because you can't go two feet without finding one.

"The space guy," Samantha says, musingly.

"Bobby. Do you know him?" I ask, thinking she must. She knows everyone.

We're at the Pink Tea Cup, this very famous restaurant in the West Village. It's pink all right, with twee wrought-iron chairs and ancient tablecloths printed with cabbage roses. They're open twenty-four hours, but they only serve breakfast, so if you time it right, you get to see Joey Ramone eating pancakes at five in the afternoon.

Samantha has left work early, claiming she's still in pain from the operation. But it can't be too bad, since she's managed to make it out of the apartment. "Is he short?" she asks.

"He had to stand on his tippy-toes when he tried to kiss me." The memory of Bobby's attempted assault causes a fresh round of irritation, and I pour way too much sugar into my cup.

"Bobby Nevil." She nods. "Everyone knows him. He's infamous."

"For jumping young girls?"

Samantha makes a face. "That would garner him no notoriety at all." She lifts her cup and tastes her coffee. "He tried to attack Michelangelo's *David*."

"The sculpture?" Oh, great. Just my luck. "He's a criminal?"

"More like an art revolutionary. He was trying to make a statement about art."

"Meaning what? Art sucks?"

"Who sucks?" Miranda demands, arriving at the table with her knapsack and a black Saks shopping bag slung over her shoulder. She grabs a handful of napkins from the dispenser and mops her brow. "It's ninety degrees out there." She waves at the waitress and asks for a glass of ice.

"Are we talking about sex again?" She looks at Samantha accusingly. "I hope I didn't come all the way down here for another conversation about Kegel exercises. Which I tried, by the way. They made me feel like a monkey."

"Monkeys do Kegel exercises?" I ask, surprised.

Samantha shakes her head. "You two are hopeless."

I sigh. I'd walked away from Bobby's thinking I could handle his underhanded behavior, but the more I thought about it, the more incensed I became. Was it wrong to assume that when I finally got a break, it would be based on my own merits, as opposed to the random horniness of some old coot? "Bobby tried to jump me," I inform Miranda.

"That little thing?" She's not impressed. "I thought he was gay."

"He's one of those guys no one wants on their team. Gay or straight," Samantha says.

"Is that an actual thing?" Miranda asks.

"They're called the lost boys of sexual orientation. Come on, guys," I say. "This is serious."

"There was a professor at my school," Miranda says. "Everyone knew if you slept with him he'd give you an A."

I glare at her. "Not helping."

"Well, come on, Carrie. This is nothing new. Every bar I've worked in has an unspoken rule that if you have sex with the manager, you'll get the best shifts," Samantha says. "And every office I've worked in—same thing. There's always some guy coming on to you. And most of them are married."

I groan. "And do you—?"

"Have sex with them? What do you think, Sparrow?" she asks sharply. "I don't *need* to have sex with some guy to get ahead. On the other hand, I'm not ashamed of anything

I've done. Shame is a useless emotion."

Miranda's face contorts into an expression that signi-fies she's about to say something inappropriate. "If that's true, why won't you tell Charlie about the endometriosis? If you're not ashamed, why can't you be honest?"

Samantha's lips curl into a patronizing smile. "My rela-tionship with Charlie is none of your business."

"Why do you talk about it all the time, then?" Miranda asks, refusing to back down.

I put my head in my hands, wondering why we're all so worked up. It must be the heat. It curdles the brain.

"So should I have my play reading at Bobby's or not?" I ask.

"Of course," Samantha says. "You can't let Bobby's stu-pid little pass make you question your talents. Then he'll have won."

Miranda has no choice but to agree. "Why should you let that squat little toad define who you are or what you can do?"

I know they're right, but for a moment, I feel defeated. By life and the never-ending struggle to make something of it. Why can't things just be easy?

"Did you read my play?" I ask Miranda.

She reddens. And in a voice that's too high, says, "I meant to. But I was so busy. I promise I'll read it tonight, okay?"

"Can't," I say sharply. "I need it back. I have to give it to Bobby first thing tomorrow."

"Don't get testy—"

"I'm not."

"It's right here," she says, opening her knapsack and riffling through it. She looks inside in confusion, then picks up the shopping bag and dumps the contents onto the table. "It must have gotten mixed up with my flyers."

"You took my play to Saks?" I ask, incredulous, as Miranda paws frantically through her papers.

"I was going to read it when things got slow. Here it is," she says in relief, holding up a few pages.

I quickly flip through them. "Where's the rest? This is only the first third."

"Has to be here," she mutters as I join her in going through each piece of paper one by one. "Oh my God." She sits back in her chair. "Carrie, I'm sorry. This guy got in my face yesterday. Grabbed a bunch of flyers and ran. The rest of your play must have been mixed up with them—"

I stop breathing. I have one of those terrible premonitions that my life is about to fall apart.

"You must have another copy," Samantha says soothingly.

"My professor has one."

"Well, then," Miranda chirps, as if everything's all right.

I grab my bag. "I've got to go," I squeak, just before my mouth goes completely dry.

Damn. Crap! And every other expletive I can think of.

If I don't have my play, I don't have anything. No reading, no life.

But surely Viktor has a copy. I specifically remember the day I gave it to him. And what kind of teacher throws out their students' work?

I run through the Village, barging through traffic and nearly knocking over several passersby on my route to The New School. I arrive heaving, take the stairs two at a time, and throw myself on Viktor's door.

It's locked.

I wheel around in a frenzy, trip down the stairs, and run all the way back to Samantha's place.

She's lying in bed with a pile of magazines. "Carrie? Can you believe what Miranda said to me? About Charlie? I thought it was very uncalled for—"

"Yeah," I say as I search the kitchen for the white pages.

"Did you find your play?"

"No!" I scream, flipping through the phone book.

I pat my heart, trying to get a grip. There it is: Viktor Greene. With an address in the Mews.

"Carrie?" Samantha asks, on my way back out. "Could you pick me up something to eat? Maybe Chinese? Or pizza. With pepperoni. And not too much cheese. Be sure to tell them no extra cheese—"

Argh!!!!!!

I haul myself back to the Mews, every muscle in my body screaming with pain from the exertion. I walk up and down the cobblestoned street twice before I find Viktor's place, tucked behind a portcullis and hidden by ivy. I bang on the door several times, and when I can't rouse him, plop down on the stoop.

Where the hell is he? Viktor's always around. He has no life, apart from the school and his occasional affair with one of his students. The bastard. I get up and kick the door, and when there's still no answer, I peek in the window.

The tiny carriage house is dark. I sniff the air, convinced I can catch a whiff of decay.

It's not surprising. Viktor is a pig.

Then I notice three days' worth of newspapers strewn next to the door. What if he's gone away? But where would he go? I snuffle around the window again, wondering if the smell is an indication that he's dead. Maybe he had a heart attack and, since he doesn't have any friends, no one's thought to look for him.

I bang on the window, which is totally useless. I look around for something to break it with, loosening a brick from the edge of the cobblestones. I raise it above my head, ready to attack.

"Looking for Viktor?" comes a voice from behind me.

I lower the brick and turn around.

The speaker is an elderly lady with a cat on a leash. She walks cautiously forward and bends down painstakingly to scoop up the papers. "Viktor's gone," she informs me. "I told him I'd save his newspapers. Lots of crooks around here."

I surreptitiously drop the brick. "When is he coming back?"

She squints. "Friday? His mother died, poor thing. He's gone to the Midwest to bury her."

"Friday?" I take a step and nearly trip on the brick. I grab a vine of ivy to steady myself.

"That's what he said. Friday." The old woman bobs her head.

The reality of my situation hits me like a truckload of cement. "That's too late!" I cry, as I let go of the vine and collapse to the ground in despair.

"Sparrow?" Samantha asks, coming into the living room. "What are you doing?"

"Huh?"

"You've been sitting there for over an hour with your mouth hanging open. It's not very attractive," she scolds. When I don't respond, she stands over me and knocks on my head. "Hello? Anyone home?"

I unhinge my eyes from a blank spot on the wall and swivel my head around to look at her.

She shakes a sheaf of newspaper pages in my face. "I thought we could have some fun. Work on my engagement announcement for *The New York Times*. You're a writer. This should be a snap for you."

"I'm not a writer. Not anymore," I respond dully.

"Don't be ridiculous. You've had one small setback." She settles in next to me with the pile of papers on her lap. "I've been collecting these since May. The wedding and engagement announcements in *The New York Times*. Also known as the 'women's sports pages.'"

"Who cares?" I lift my head.

"Everyone who's anyone in New York, Sparrow," she explains, as if talking to a child. "And it's especially important because the *Times* won't take just any old announcement. The man has to be Ivy League. And both parties need to come from the right sort of families. Old money is best, but new money will do. Or fame. If, for instance, the bride has a famous father, like an actor or a sculptor or a composer, she'll definitely get in."

"Why can't you just get married?" I rub my cheeks. My skin is cold, as if I've lost all circulation.

"Where's the fun in that?" Samantha asks. "Why get married in New York if you're going to be a nobody? You might as well have stayed home. A wedding in New York is all about taking your proper place in society. It's why we're getting married at the Century Club. If you get married there, it's a statement."

"Meaning?"

She pats my leg. "You belong, Sparrow."

"But what if you don't? Belong."

"For God's sake, Sparrow. You *act* like you do. What is wrong with you? Have you forgotten everything I've taught you?"

And before I can protest, she goes to the typewriter, rolls a piece of paper into the carriage, and points at the chair. "You write. I'll dictate."

My shoulders slump, but I follow her order and place my hands on the keys, more out of rote than of conscious action.

Samantha plucks a page from her pile and scans the announcements. "Here's a good one. 'Miss Barbara Halters from Newport, Rhode Island, known to her friends as Horsie . . .'"

If she's joking, it's completely lost on me. "I thought you were from Weehawken."

"Who wants to be from there? Put down 'Short Hills.' Short Hills is acceptable."

"But what if someone checks—"

"They *won't*. Can we please continue? Miss Samantha Jones—"

"What about 'Ms.'?"

"Okay. Ms. Samantha Jones, of Short Hills, New Jersey, attended . . ." She pauses. "What college is near Short Hills?"

"I don't know."

"Just say 'Princeton' then. It's close enough. Princeton," she continues, satisfied with her choice. "And I graduated with a degree in . . . English literature."

"No one's going to believe that," I protest, beginning to come to life. "I've never seen you read anything other than a self-help book."

"Okay. Skip the part about my degree. It doesn't matter anyway," she says with a wave. "The tricky part is my parents. We'll say my mother was a homemaker—that's neutral—and my father was an international businessman. That way I can explain why he was never around."

I take my hands off the keys and fold them in my lap. "I can't do this."

"Why not?"

"I can't lie to *The New York Times*."

"You're not the one who's lying. I am."

"Why do *you* have to lie?"

"Carrie," she says, becoming frustrated. "Everyone lies."

"No, they don't."

"You lie. Didn't you lie to Bernard about your age?"

"That's different. I'm not marrying Bernard."

She gives me a cold smile, as if she can't believe I'm challenging her. "Fine. I'll write it myself."

"Be my guest." I get up as she sits down in front of the typewriter.

She bangs away for several minutes while I watch. Finally, I can't take it anymore. "Why can't you tell the truth?"

"Because the truth isn't good enough."

"That's like saying you're not good enough."

She stops typing. She sits back and folds her arms. "I am good enough. I've never had any doubt in my mind—"

"Why don't you be yourself, then?"

"Why don't *you*?" She jumps up. "You're worried about *me*? Look at you. Sniveling around the apartment because you lost half your play. If you're such a great writer, why don't you write another one?"

"It doesn't work that way," I scream, my throat raw. "It took me a whole month to write that play. You don't just sit down and write a whole play in three days. You have to think about it. You have to—"

"Fine. If you want to give up, that's your problem." She starts toward her room, pauses, and spins around. "But if you want to act like a loser, don't you dare criticize me," she shouts, banging the door behind her.

I put my head in my hands. She's right. I'm sick of

myself and my failure. I might as well pack my bags and go home.

Like L'il. And all the millions of other young people who came to New York to make it and failed.

And suddenly, I'm furious. I run to Samantha's room and pound on the door.

"What?" she yells as I open it.

"Why don't *you* start over?" I shout, for no rational reason.

"Why don't you?"

"I will."

"Good."

I slam the door.

As if in a trance, I go to my typewriter and sit down. I rip out Samantha's phony announcement, crumple it into a ball, and throw it across the room. I roll a fresh piece of paper into the carriage. I look at my watch. I have seventy-four hours and twenty-three minutes until my reading on Thursday. And I'm going to make it. I'm going to write another play if it kills me.

My typewriter ribbon breaks on Thursday morning. I look around at the empty candy wrappers, the dried tea bags, and the greasy pizza crusts.

It's my birthday. I'm finally eighteen.

CHAPTER THIRTY-FIVE

My hands shake as I step into the shower.

The bottle of shampoo slips from my fingers, and I manage to catch it just before it breaks on the tiles. I take a deep breath, tilting my head back against the spray.

I did it. I actually did it.

But the water can't erase how I really feel: red-eyed, weak, and rattled.

I'll never know what would have happened if Miranda hadn't lost my play and I hadn't had to rewrite it. I don't know if it's good or bad. I don't know if I'll be celebrated or disdained. But I did it, I remind myself. I *tried*.

I get out of the shower and towel off. I peer into the mirror. My face looks drawn and hollow, as I've barely slept for three days. This is not how I was expecting to make my debut, but I'll take it. I don't have a choice.

I put on the red rubber pants, my Chinese robe, and

Samantha's old Fiorucci boots. Maybe someday I'll be like Samantha, able to afford my own shoes.

Samantha. She went back to work on Tuesday morning and I haven't heard from her since. Ditto for Miranda, who hasn't called either. Probably too scared I'll never forgive her.

But I will. And I hope Samantha can forgive me as well.

"Here you are," Bobby says gaily. "And right on time."

"If you only knew," I mumble.

"Excited?" He bounces on his toes.

"Nervous." I smile weakly. "Is it true you attacked *David*?"

He frowns. "Who told you that?"

I shrug.

"It's never a good idea to dwell on the past. Let's have some champagne."

I follow him to the kitchen, keeping my carpenter's bag between us so he can't try any of his funny business. If he does, I swear, I really will hit him this time.

I needn't have worried though, because the guests start arriving and Bobby scurries to the door to greet them.

I remain in the kitchen, sipping my champagne. The hell with it, I think, and drain the whole glass. I pour myself another.

Tonight's the night, I think grimly. My reading and Bernard.

I narrow my eyes. He'd better be prepared to do it this

time. Tonight he'd better not have any excuses.

I shake my head. What kind of attitude is that to take about losing your virginity? Not good.

I'm about to pour myself more champagne when I hear, "Carrie?" I nearly drop the bottle as I turn around and find Miranda.

"Please don't be mad," she implores.

My body sags in relief. Now that Miranda's here, maybe everything really will be okay.

After Miranda's arrival, I can't exactly describe the party because I'm everywhere at once: greeting guests at the door, worrying about when to set up the chairs, fending off Bobby, and trying to come up with something impressive to say to Charlie, who has shown up, unexpectedly, with Samantha.

If Samantha is mad at me from the other night, she's doing her best not to show it, complimenting me on my pants while holding on to Charlie's arm as if she owns him. He's a large man, almost handsome, and slightly gawky, as if he doesn't know what to do with his limbs. He immediately starts talking about baseball, and when some other people chime in, I slip away to find Bernard.

He's in the corner with Teensie. I can't believe he brought her after that disastrous weekend, but apparently, either he doesn't care or Teensie never bothered to give him an earful about me. Maybe because it's my night, Teensie is all smiles, at least on the surface.

"When Bernard told me about this event, I couldn't

believe it," she says, leaning forward to whisper loudly in my ear. "I said I simply had to see it for myself."

"Well, thank you," I reply modestly, smiling at Bernard. "I'm so glad you could make it."

Capote and Ryan wander over with Rainbow in tow. We talk about class and how Viktor disappeared and how we can hardly believe the summer is nearly over. There's more drinking and schmoozing, and I feel like a jewel, whirling in the center of all the attention, remembering my first night in New York with Samantha, and how far I've come since then.

"Hello, little one." It's Cholly Hammond in his usual seersucker uniform. "Have you met Winnie Dieke?" he asks, gesturing toward a young woman with a sharp face. "She's from the *New York Post*. If you're very nice to her, she might write about the event."

"Then I'll be very nice. Hello, Winnie," I say smoothly, holding out my hand.

By ten thirty, the party is packed. Bobby's space is a regular stop for revelers out on the town. It's got free booze, shirtless bartenders, and a hodgepodge of crazy characters to shake things up. Like the old lady on roller skates, and the homeless man named Norman, who sometimes lives in Bobby's closet. Or the Austrian count and the twins who claim to be du Ponts. The model who slept with everyone. The young socialite with the silver spoon around her neck. And in the middle of this great spinning carnival is little old me, standing on my tiptoes in an effort to be heard.

When another half hour passes, I remind Bobby that there is, indeed, entertainment, and Bobby tries to shuffle people into the seats. He stands on a chair, which collapses underneath him. Capote turns down the music as Bobby manages to right himself, and straddling two chairs instead of one, Bobby calls for everyone's attention.

"Tonight we have the world premiere of a play by this very charming young writer, Carrie Bradshaw. The name of the play is . . . uh . . . I don't really know but it doesn't matter—"

"*Ungrateful Bastards*," Miranda calls out the title.

"Yes, ungrateful bastards—the world is full of them," Bobby squawks. "And now, without further ado—"

I take a deep breath. My heart seems to have migrated to my stomach. There's a grudging round of applause as I take my place at the front of the room.

I remind myself that this is really no different from reading in front of the class, and I begin.

They say that people in stressful situations can lose their perception of time, and that's what happens to me. In fact, I seem to lose all my senses, because at first I have no awareness of sight or sound. Then I become conscious of a few chuckles from the front row, which consists of Bernard, Miranda, Samantha and Charlie, Rainbow, Capote, and Ryan. Then I notice people getting up and leaving their seats. Then I realize the laughter is not due to my play, but to something funny someone said in the back of the room. Then someone turns up the music.

I try to ignore it, but my face flames with heat and my

voice cracks. I'm dying up here. In the back of the room, people are dancing. I'm reduced to a mumble, a murmur, an afterthought.

Will this ever end?

Miraculously, it does. Bernard jumps to his feet, clapping. Miranda and Samantha yell their approval. But that's all. Not even Bobby is paying attention. He's by the bar, fawning over Teensie.

That's it? I think wildly. It's *over*? What was that? What just happened?

I thought there'd be cheering.

I thought there'd be applause.

I did all this work for nothing?

The truth begins to dawn on me, although "dawn" isn't the most accurate word. "Dawn" implies something pleasant. Hope. A better day. A new beginning. This is no beginning. This is an end. A disgrace. An embarrassment.

I suck.

Capote and my father and everyone else were right: I have no talent. I've been chasing a dream I made up in my head. And now it's over.

I'm shaking. What should I do? I look around the room, imagining the people turning to leaves, red and then brown and then crumbling to pieces onto the ground. How can I . . . what can I . . . ?

"I thought it was really good." Bernard moves toward me, his grin like the smile of the clown in a jack-in-the-box. "Quite refreshing."

"It was great," Miranda says, giving me a hug. "I don't

know how you stood up in front of all those people. I would have been so frightened."

I look to Samantha, who nods. "It was fun, Sparrow."

This is one of those situations where no one can help you. Your need is so great, it's like a black hole sucking the life out of everyone around you. I stumble forward, blindly.

"Let's get a drink," Bernard says, taking my hand.

"Yes, let's all have a drink," Samantha agrees. This is too much. Even Samantha, who's my biggest cheerleader, knows my play is a disaster.

I'm like Typhoid Mary. No one wants to be around me.

Bernard hurries to the bar, and, as if shedding a virus, deposits me next to Teensie, of all people, who is now talking to Capote.

I smile awkwardly.

"Well," Teensie says, with a dramatic sigh.

"You must have worked on it," Capote says. "Since class. I thought it was better than what you read in class."

"I had to completely rewrite it. In three days." And suddenly, I realize Capote was right. About what he said at the Jessens' dinner. Bobby *is* a joke. And a reading in his space wasn't the right way to get my work noticed. Why didn't I listen? The summer's over and the only thing I've managed to achieve is making a complete and utter fool of myself.

The blood drains from my face.

Capote must understand my distress, because he pats my shoulder and says, "It's good to take chances, remember?"

And as he wanders away, Teensie moves in for the kill. "I thought it was amusing. Very, very amusing," she purrs. "But look at *you*, dear. You're a mess. You look exhausted. And you're way too thin. I'm sure your parents must be very worried about you."

She pauses, and with a glittering smile asks, "Don't you think it's time to go *home*?"

CHAPTER THIRTY-SIX

I am trying to get drunk and not succeeding.

I'm a total failure. I can't even win at inebriation.

"Carrie," Bernard cautions.

"What?" I ask, lifting a purloined bottle of champagne to my lips. I snuck it out of the party in my carpenter's bag. I knew that bag would come in handy someday.

"You could hurt yourself." Bernard wrenches the bottle away from me. "The cab could stop short and you could knock out your teeth."

I pull the bottle back, clinging to it tightly. "It's my birthday."

"I know."

"Aren't you going to say happy birthday?"

"I have. Several times. Maybe you didn't hear me."

"Did you get me a present?"

"Yes. Now look," he says becoming stern. "Maybe I

should drop you at your apartment. There's no reason to do this tonight."

"But I want my present," I wail. "And it's my birthday. It has to be done on the day or it doesn't count."

"Technically, it's not your birthday anymore. It's after two."

"Technically my birthday didn't start until after two last night. So it still counts."

"It's going to be okay, kiddo." He pats my leg.

"You didn't like it, did you?" I take another swig and look out the open window, feeling the stinky summer air whooshing across my face.

"Like what?" he asks.

Jeez. What does he think I'm talking about? Is he really that thick? Is everyone this thick and I just never noticed before? "My *play*. You said you liked it but you didn't."

"You said you rewrote it."

"Only because I had to. If Miranda—"

"Come on, kiddo," he says, reassuringly. "These things happen."

"To me. Only to me. Not to you or anyone else."

It seems Bernard has had enough of my histrionics. He folds his arms.

His gesture scares some sense into me. I can't lose him, too. Not tonight. "Please," I say. "Let's not fight."

"I didn't know we *were* fighting."

"We're not." I put down the bottle and cling to him like a limpet.

"Awwww, kiddo." He strokes my cheek. "I know you

had a rough night. But that's the way it is when you put something out there."

"Really?" I sniff.

"It's all about rewriting. You'll rework the play, and it'll be great. You'll see."

"I hate rewriting," I grumble. "Why can't the world come out right the first time?"

"What would be the fun in that?"

"Oh, Bernard." I sigh. "I love you."

"Yeah, I love you, too, kitten."

"Honest? At two in the morning? On Madison Avenue? You love me?"

He smiles.

"What's my present?" I coo.

"If I told you, it wouldn't be a present, now, would it?"

"I'm giving you a present," I slur.

"You don't have to give me a present."

"Oh, but I do," I say cryptically. Even if my play was a disaster, losing my virginity could salvage it.

"Here!" Bernard says, triumphantly, handing me a perfectly wrapped box in shiny black paper complete with a big black bow.

"Oh my God." I sink to my knees on the carpet in his living room. "Is it really what I think it is?"

"I hope so," he says nervously.

"I already love it." I look at him with shining eyes.

"You don't know what it is yet."

"Oh, but I do," I cry out in excitement, tearing away

the paper and fingering the raised white lettering on the box. CHANEL.

Bernard looks slightly uncomfortable with my over-whelming demonstrance. "Teensie thought you'd like it."

"Teensie? You asked Teensie what to get me? I thought she hated me."

"She said you needed something nice."

"Oh, Bernard." I lift the cover from the box and gently open the tissue paper. And there it is: my first Chanel handbag.

I lift it out and cradle it in my arms.

"Do you like it?" he asks.

"I love it," I say solemnly. I hold it for a few seconds more, savoring the soft leather. With sweet reluctance, I slip it back into its cotton pouch and carefully replace it in the box.

"Don't you want to use it?" Bernard asks, perplexed by my actions.

"I want to save it."

"Why?" he says.

"Because I always want it to be . . . *perfect*." Because nothing ever is. "Thank you, Bernard." I wonder if I'm going to cry.

"Hey, puddy tat. It's only a purse."

"I know, but—" I get up and curl next to him on the couch, stroking the back of his neck.

"Eager little beaver, aren't you?" He kisses me and I kiss him back and as we're starting to get into it, he takes my hand and leads me to the bedroom.

This is it. And suddenly, I'm not so sure I'm ready.

I remind myself that this should not be a big deal. We've done everything but. We've spent the entire night together a dozen times. But knowing what's to come makes it feel different. Even kissing is awkward. Like we barely know each other.

"I need a drink," I say.

"Haven't you had enough?" Bernard looks worried.

"No—I mean a drink of water," I lie. I grab one of his shirts to cover myself and race into the kitchen. There's a bottle of vodka on the counter. I close my eyes, brace myself, and take a gulp. I quickly rinse my mouth with water.

"Okay. I'm ready," I announce, standing in the doorway.

I feel all jumbly again. I'm trying to be sexy, but I don't know how. Everything feels so false and artificial, including myself. Maybe you have to learn how to be sexy in the bedroom. Or maybe it's something you have to be born with. Like Samantha. Sexiness comes naturally to her. With me, it would be easier to be a plumber right now.

"Come here," Bernard laughs, patting the bed. "And don't get any ideas about stealing that shirt. Margie used to take my shirts."

"Margie?"

"Let's not talk about her, okay?"

We start making out again, but now it feels like Margie is in the room. I try to banish her, telling myself that Bernard is mine now. But it only makes me feel more diminished in comparison. Maybe after we get it over with, it'll be better. "Let's just do it, okay?" I say.

He raises his head. "Don't you like this?"

"No. I love it. But I just want to do it."

"I can't just—"

"Bernard. *Please.*"

Miranda was right. This is terrible. Why didn't I get this over with a long time ago? At least I'd know what to expect.

"Okay," he murmurs. He lies on top of me. He wriggles around a bit. Then he wriggles some more.

"Has it happened?" I'm confused. Boy, Miranda wasn't kidding. It really is nothing.

"No. I—" He breaks off. "Look. I'm going to need you to help me a little."

Help him? What is he talking about? No one told me "help" was part of the program.

Why can't he just do it?

And there we are, naked. Naked in our skins. But naked mostly in our emotions. I wasn't prepared for *this*. The raw, unfortunate intimacy.

"Could you just—?" he asks.

"Sure," I say.

I do my best, but it isn't enough. Then he tries. Then it seems he's finally ready. He gets on top of me. Okay, let's go, buddy, I think. He makes a few thrusting motions. He puts his hand down there to help himself.

"Is it supposed to be like this?" I ask.

"What do you think?" he says.

"I don't know."

"What do you mean, you don't know?"

"I've never done it before."

"What!" He draws back in shock.

"Don't be mad at me," I plead, clinging to his leg as he leaps off the bed. "I never met the right guy before. There has to be a first time for everyone, right?"

"Not with me." He darts around the room, snatching up my things.

"What are you doing?"

"You need to get dressed."

"Why?"

He pulls at his hair. "Carrie, you cannot stay here. We cannot do this. I'm not that guy."

"Why *not*?" I ask, my obstinance turning to panic.

"Because I'm not." He stops, takes a breath, gets ahold of himself. "I'm an adult. And you're a kid—"

"I'm not a kid. I'm eighteen."

"I thought you were a sophomore in college." More horror.

"Oops," I say, trying to make a joke of it.

His jaw drops. "Are you insane?"

"No, I don't think so. I mean, the last time I checked I seemed to be fairly normal—" Then I lose it. "It's me, isn't it? You don't want me. That's why you couldn't do it. You couldn't get it up. Because—" As soon as the words are out of my mouth, I realize this is just about the worst thing you can say to a guy. Ever. Because I can promise you, he's none too happy about it himself.

"I can't do this," he wails, more to himself than to me. "I cannot do this. What am I doing? What's happened to my life?"

I try to remember everything I've read about impotence. "Maybe I *can* help you," I falter. "Maybe we can work on it—"

"I don't want to have to work on my sex life," he roars. "Don't you get it? I don't want to have to work on my marriage. I don't want to have to work on my relationships. I want them to just happen, without effort. And if you weren't such an asshole all the time, maybe you'd understand."

What? For a moment, I'm too stung to react. Then I draw back in hurt and indignation. I'm an asshole? Can women even be assholes? I must really be terrible if a man calls me an asshole.

I shut my mouth. I pick up my pants from where he's dropped them on the bed.

"Carrie," he says.

"What?"

"It's probably best if you go."

"No kidding."

"And we . . . probably shouldn't see each other anymore."

"Right."

"I still want you to have the purse," he says, trying to make nice.

"I don't want it." This, however, is very much a lie. I do want it. Badly. I want to get something out of this debacle of a birthday.

"Take it, please," he says.

"Give it to Teensie. She's just like you." I want to slap him. It's like one of those dreams where you try to hit a guy and keep missing.

"Don't be a jerk," he says. We're dressed and at the door. "Take it, for Christ's sake. You know you want it."

"That's just gross, Bernard."

"Here." He tries to shove the bag into my hands but I yank open the door, hit the elevator button, and cross my arms.

Bernard rides down in the lift with me. "Carrie," he says, trying not to make a scene in front of the elevator man.

"No." I shake my head.

He follows me outside and raises his hand to hail a cab. Why is it that whenever you don't want a taxi, there's one right there? Because half of me is still hoping this isn't actually happening, and a miracle will occur and everything will go back to normal. But then Bernard is giving the driver my address and ten dollars to get me home.

I get into the backseat, fuming.

"Here," he says, offering me the bag again.

"I told you. I don't want it," I scream.

And as the cab pulls away from the curb, he yanks open the door and tosses it inside.

The bag lands at my feet. For a moment, I think about throwing it out the window. But I don't. Because now I'm crying hysterically. Great, heaving sobs that feel like they're going to rip me apart.

"Hey," the taxi driver says. "Are you cryin'? You're cryin' in my cab? You want sumpin to cry about, lady, I'll give you sumpin. How about them Yankees then? How about that goddamned baseball strike?"

Huh?

The cab pulls up in front of Samantha's building. I stare at it helplessly, unable to move for my tears.

"Hey, lady," the driver growls. "You gonna get out? I don't have all night."

I wipe my eyes as I make one of those rash and ill-advised decisions everyone tells you not to. "Take me to Greenwich Street."

"But—"

"*Greenwich Street.*"

I get out at the phone booth on the corner. My fingers are trembling as I search for a dime and drop it into the slot. The phone rings several times. A sleepy voice says, "Yeah?"

"Capote?"

"Yeah?" He yawns.

"It's me. Carrie Bradshaw."

"Yeah, Carrie. I know your last name."

"Can I come up?"

"It's four in the morning."

"Please?"

"*All right.*" The light goes on in his window. His shadow moves back and forth, back and forth. The window opens and he throws down the keys.

I catch them neatly in the palm of my hand.

CHAPTER THIRTY-SEVEN

I open one eye and close it. Open it again. Where the hell am I? This must be one of those bad dreams when you think you're awake but you're still actually asleep.

I don't feel asleep, though.

Besides, I'm naked. And it kind of hurts down there.

But that's because . . . I smile. It happened. I am officially no longer a virgin.

I'm in Capote Duncan's apartment. I'm in his bed. The bed with the plaid sheets his mother bought him. And the two foam pillows (why are guys so chintzy about pillows?), and the scratchy army blanket that belonged to his grandfather. Who got it from his father, who fought in the Civil War. Capote is very sentimental. I can hear Patsy Cline still crooning softly on the stereo. "I Fall to Pieces." From now on, every time I hear that song, I'll think of Capote and the night we spent together. The night he kindly took my virginity.

I guess I'm lucky, because it was pretty much the way I'd always hoped it would be. And while we were doing it, I honestly felt like I was in love with him. He kept telling me how beautiful I was. And how I shouldn't be afraid. And how happy he was to be with me. And how he'd wanted to be with me from the beginning, but he thought I couldn't stand him. And then, when I started dating Bernard, how he figured he'd lost his chance. And when I actually managed to write a play, he decided I'd think he wasn't "good enough." Because he hadn't managed to write much of anything.

Yow. Guys can be so insecure.

Naturally, I told him he'd gotten me all wrong, although it is true—which I didn't tell him—that I didn't find him terribly attractive at the beginning.

Now, of course, I think he's the most gorgeous creature on earth.

I peek at him. He's still asleep, lying on his back, his face so peaceful and relaxed, I actually think I can detect a slight smile on his lips. Without his glasses, he looks shockingly vulnerable. Last night, after we kissed for a bit and he did the sexy librarian thing and took off his specs, we stared and stared into each other's eyes. I felt like I could see his entire history in his pupils.

I could know everything about him in a way I'd never known anyone before.

It was a little eerie, but also kind of profound.

I guess that's what I found most surprising about sex: the

knowing. How you can understand a person completely and vice versa.

I lean over the edge of the bed, searching for my Skivvies. I want to get out while Capote's still asleep. A deal's a deal, and I said I'd leave first thing in the morning.

I raise myself slowly, sliding carefully off the bed so as not to jiggle the mattress. The mattress itself is about a hundred years old, left here by the original owners. I wonder how many people have had sex on this bed. I hope a lot. And I hope it was as good for them as it was for me.

I find my clothes splayed around the couch. The Chanel bag is by the door, where I dropped it when Capote grabbed my face and backed me up against the wall, kissing me like crazy. I practically tore his clothes off.

But I'm never going to see him again, so it doesn't matter. And now I have to face the future: Brown.

Maybe, after four years of college, I'll try again. I'll storm the gates of the Emerald City, and this time, I'll succeed.

But for now, I'm too tired. Who knew eighteen could be so exhausting?

I sigh and wriggle my feet into my shoes. I had a good run. Sure, I messed up a few times, but I managed to survive.

I tiptoe back to the bedroom for one last look at Capote. "Good-bye, lover," I murmur quietly.

His mouth pops open and he wakes, pounding his pillow in confusion. He sits up and squints at me. "Huh?"

"Sorry," I whisper, picking up my watch. "I was just—"
I indicate the door.

"Why?" He rubs his eyes. "Didn't you like it?"

"I loved it. But—"

"Why are you leaving then?"

I shrug.

He feels for his glasses and puts them on, blinking behind the thick lenses. "Aren't you going to at least allow me the pleasure of giving you breakfast? A gentleman never lets a lady leave without feeding her, first."

I laugh. "I'm perfectly capable of feeding myself. Besides, you make me sound like a bird."

"A bird? More like a tiger," he chuckles. "C'mere." He opens his arms. I crawl across the bed and fall into them.

He strokes my hair. He's warm and snuggly and smells a little. Of man, I suppose. The scent is strangely familiar. Like toast.

He pulls back his head and smiles. "Did anyone ever tell you how pretty you look in the morning?"

At about two in the afternoon, we manage to make it to the Pink Tea Cup for breakfast. I wear one of Capote's shirts over my rubber pants and we eat pancakes and bacon with real maple syrup and drink about a gallon of coffee and smoke cigarettes and talk shyly and eagerly about nothing. "Hey," he says, when the check comes. "Want to go to the zoo?"

"The zoo?"

"I hear they have a new polar bear."

And suddenly, I do want to go to the zoo with Capote. In my two months in New York, I haven't done one touristy thing. I haven't been to the Empire State Building. Or the Statue of Liberty. Or Wollman Rink or the Metropolitan Museum or even the Public Library.

I've been sorely remiss. I can't leave New York without going on the Circle Line.

"I need to do one thing first," I say.

I get up and head to the restroom. There's a pay phone on the wall outside the door.

Miranda picks up after the first ring. "Hello?" she asks urgently, as if she's expecting bad news. She always answers the phone like that. It's one of the things I love about her.

"I did it!" I squeal triumphantly.

"Carrie? Is that you? Oh my God. What happened? How was it? Did it hurt? How was Bernard?"

"I didn't do it with Bernard."

"What?" She gasps. "Who *did* you do it with? You can't go out there and pick up some random stranger. Oh no, Carrie. You didn't. You didn't pick up some guy at a bar—"

"I did it with Capote," I say proudly.

"That guy?" I can hear her jaw drop. "I thought you hated him."

I glance back at Capote. He casually tosses a few bills onto the table. "Not anymore."

"But what about Bernard?" she demands. "I thought you said Bernard was The One."

Capote stands up. "Change of plans," I say quickly. "He

couldn't do it. I had to abort the mission and find another rocket."

"Carrie, that's disgusting. Did Samantha tell you to say that? You sound just like her. Oh my God. This is insane. What are you going to do now?"

"Visit the polar bear," I say, laughing. I gently hang up before she can ask any more questions.

Have I ever been in love? Really in love? And why is it that with each new guy I think I'm more in love with him than the last? I think briefly of Sebastian and smile. What on earth was I doing with him? Or Bernard? I lean over the wall to get a better view of the polar bear. Poor Bernard. He turned out to be even more messed up than I am.

"What are you laughing about?" Capote asks, wrapping his arms around me from behind. We haven't been able to take our hands off each other, leaning into each other on the subway, walking arm in arm as we strolled up Fifth Avenue, and kissing at the entrance to the zoo. My body has turned to butter. I can't believe I wasted the whole summer pursuing Bernard instead of Capote.

But maybe Capote wouldn't like me so much if I hadn't.

"I'm always laughing," I say.

"Why?" he asks sweetly.

"Because life is funny."

At the zoo, we buy hot dogs and polar bear baseball caps. We run down Fifth Avenue, past the old man who sells pencils in front of Saks, which reminds me of the first time I met Miranda. We join a line of tourists inside the Empire State Building and ride the elevator to the top. We look through viewfinders and make out until we're breathless. We take a taxi back to Capote's.

We have sex again, and don't stop until we both realize we're starving. We go to Chinatown and eat Peking duck, which I've never had before, and we wander through SoHo and laugh about how Teensie took a pill at Barry Jessen's opening and all the other crazy things that have happened to us during the summer. It's pretty late by now—after midnight—so I figure I'll spend one more night with him and go home in the morning.

But when morning comes, we still can't manage to tear ourselves apart. We go back to my place and make love on Samantha's bed. I change my clothes, stick my toothbrush and a change of underwear into my carpenter's bag, and we head out to be tourists again. We do the Circle Line and the Statue of Liberty, climbing all the way to the top and laughing about how small it is once you finally get up to the crown, then we go back to Capote's.

We eat hamburgers at the Corner Bistro and pizza at John's. I have my first orgasm.

The hours pass in a fuzzy, dreamlike way, mingled with a thread of despair. This can't last forever. Capote starts a job at a publishing company after Labor Day. And I have to go to Brown.

"Are you sure?" he murmurs.

"I don't have a choice. I was hoping something would happen with my play and I'd be able to convince my father to let me go to NYU instead."

"Why don't you tell him you changed your mind?"

"I'd need a pretty big excuse."

"Like you met a guy you're crazy about and want to be with him?"

"He'd have a heart attack. I wasn't raised to base my decisions on a guy."

"He sounds like a tough old nut."

"Nah. You'd like him. He's a genius. Like you." Three days with Capote have taught me that what I thought was Capote's arrogance was simply due to his deep knowledge of literature. Like me, he has a searing belief that books are sacred. They might not be to other people, but when you have a passion, you hold on to it. You defend it. You don't pretend it isn't important at the risk of offending others.

And suddenly it's Wednesday morning. Our last class is today. I'm so weak with sadness I can barely lift my arm to brush my teeth. I'm dreading facing the class. But like so much in life, it turns out I needn't have worried.

No one really cares.

Ryan and Rainbow are chatting outside the building when Capote and I arrive together. I drop Capote's hand, thinking it's not a good idea for people to know about us, but Capote has no such compunction. He takes back my hand and drapes my arm over his shoulder.

"Ho, ho, are you guys an item now?" Ryan asks.

"I don't know." I look to Capote for confirmation.

He answers by kissing me on the mouth.

"Gross," Rainbow declares.

"I was wondering how long it would take for you two to get together," Ryan says.

"There's a new club opening on the Bowery," Rainbow remarks.

"And a reading at Cholly Hammond's," Ryan says. "I've heard he throws a great party."

"Anyone want to go to Elaine's next week?" Capote asks.

And on and on they go, with no mention of the fact that I won't be around. Or of my play. They've probably forgotten it by now anyway.

Or, like me, they're too embarrassed to mention it.

When in doubt, there's always plan C: If something really horrible happens, ignore it.

I follow the group inside, trudging my feet. What was it all for, anyway? I made friends with people I'll probably never see again, dated a man who turned out to be a dud, found a love that can't be sustained, and spent all summer writing a play that no one will ever see. As my father would say, I didn't use my time "constructively."

CHAPTER THIRTY-EIGHT

"What's going to happen with you and Capote?" Miranda demands. "Do you actually think you're going to have a long-distance relationship? Sounds like a case of the deliberate subconscious—"

"If it's deliberate, how can it be subconscious?"

"You know what I mean. You choose the end of the summer to fall in love with this guy because secretly, *you don't want it to last.*"

I fold the white vinyl jumpsuit and press it into my suitcase. "I don't think my subconscious is capable of being that conniving."

"Oh, but it is," Miranda says. "Your subconscious can make you do all kinds of things. For instance, why are you still wearing his shirt?"

I glance down at the light blue shirt I took from him after our first night. "I forgot I was wearing it."

"You see?" Miranda says victoriously. "That's why it's so important to have analysis."

"How do you explain Marty, then?"

"Subconscious again." She flicks her shoulders in dismissal. "I finally realized he wasn't for me. Even though my conscious was trying to break the pattern, my unconscious knew it wouldn't work. Plus, I couldn't go to the bathroom the whole time I was with him."

"Sounds like your intestines were the problem and not your subconscious." I yank open a drawer and remove three pairs of socks. Which I haven't seen since I put them there two months ago. Socks! What was I thinking? I throw them into the suitcase as well.

"Let's face it, Carrie," Miranda sighs. "It's *all* hopeless."

Men, or the fact that I have to leave New York? "Isn't that what they call wish fulfillment?"

"I'm a realist. Just because you had sex once doesn't mean you have to fall in love," she mutters. "And I never thought you and Samantha would turn out to be those dopey types who moon over their wedding dresses and the smell of their man's shirt."

"First of all, Samantha didn't even show up for her wedding dress. And secondly—" I break off. "Do you think you'll visit me in Providence?"

"Why would I want to go there? What do they have in Providence that we don't have in New York?"

"Me?" I ask mournfully.

"You can visit me anytime," Miranda says firmly. "You can sleep on the couch if you don't mind the springs."

"You know me. I don't mind anything."

"Oh, Carrie," she says sadly.

"I know."

"Got anything to eat in this place? I'm starving," she asks.

"Maybe some peanut butter crackers left over from the blackout."

Miranda goes into the kitchen and returns with the last of the blackout food. "Remember that night?" she asks, tearing open the package.

"How can I forget?" If only I'd known then what I do now. I could have started seeing Capote. We could have been together for two weeks by now.

"What's Samantha going to do with this place anyway? Now that you're leaving and she's getting married?"

"Dunno. Probably find someone like me to rent it."

"Well, it's a shame," Miranda says. I'm not sure if she's referring to my leaving, or the fact that Samantha wants to hang on to her apartment when she has somewhere much better to live. She munches thoughtfully on a cracker while I continue to pack. "Hey," she says finally. "Did I tell you about this course I'm going to take? Patriarchial Rituals in Contemporary Life."

"Sounds interesting," I say, without much enthusiasm.

"Yeah. We study weddings and stuff like that. Did you know that everything leading up to the wedding—the showers and the registering and picking the ugly bridesmaid dresses—was solely designed to give women something to do back in the days when they didn't have careers? And also to brainwash them into thinking that they had to get married too?"

"Actually, I didn't. But it makes sense."

"What are you going to do? At Brown?" Miranda asks.

"Dunno. Study to be a scientist, I guess."

"I thought you were going to become some big writer."

"Look how that turned out."

"The play wasn't that bad," Miranda says, brushing crumbs from her lips. "Have you noticed that ever since you lost your virginity, you've been acting like someone died?"

"When my career died, I died along with it."

"Bullshit," Miranda declares.

"Why don't you try standing in front of a room full of people while they laugh at you?"

"Why don't you stop acting like you're the biggest thing since sliced bread?"

I gasp.

"Fine," Miranda says. "If you can't take constructive criticism—"

"Me? What about you? Half the time your 'realism' is just another word for bitterness—"

"At least I'm not a Pollyanna."

"No, because that would imply that something good might happen—"

"I don't know why you think everything should be handed to you."

"You're just jealous," I snap.

"Of Capote Duncan?" Her eyes narrow. "That's beneath even you, Carrie Bradshaw."

The phone rings.

"You'd better get it," Miranda says tightly. "It's probably *him*. About to declare his undying *love*." She goes into the bathroom and slams the door.

I take a breath. "Hello?"

"Where the hell have you been?" Samantha shrieks.

This is very unlike her. I hold the phone away from my ear. "Were you worried? You're going to be so proud of me. I lost my virginity."

"Well, good for you," she says briskly, which is not the reaction I was expecting. "I'd love to celebrate, but unfortunately, I've got a crisis of my own on my hands. I need you to get over to Charlie's place immediately."

"But—"

"Just come, okay? Don't ask questions. And bring Miranda. I need all the help I can get. And could you pick up a box of garbage bags on the way? Make sure they're the big ones. The kind those pathetic people in the suburbs use for leaves."

"Enjoy it," Samantha says, gesturing to her face as she opens the door to Charlie's apartment. "This is the only time you're ever going to see me cry."

"Is that a promise?" Miranda says tartly. We're still a bit edgy from our almost-fight. If it weren't for Samantha's crisis call, we'd probably be at each other's throats.

"Look," Samantha says, dabbing her eye and holding out her finger for inspection. "That is an actual tear."

"Could have fooled me," I say.

Miranda looks around in awe. "Wow. This place is *nice*."

"Check out the view," Samantha says. "It's the last time you'll see it, too. I'm leaving."

"*What?*"

"That's right," she says, strolling to the sunken living room. There's a stunning vista of Central Park. You can practically see right into the duck pond. "The wedding's off," she declares. "Charlie and I are *over*."

I look at Miranda and roll my eyes. "Surely, this too shall pass," I murmur, heading to the window for a better view.

"Carrie, I'm serious," Samantha says. She goes to a glass tray on wheels, picks up a crystal decanter, and pours herself a healthy dose of whiskey. "And I have you to thank for it." She slugs back her drink and turns on us. "Actually, I have both of you to thank."

"Me?" Miranda asks. "I've hardly even met the guy."

"But you're the one who told me to tell him."

"Tell him what?" Miranda says, mystified.

"About my condition."

"Which is?"

"You know. The thing," Samantha hisses. "The lining . . ."

"Endometriosis?" I ask.

Samantha holds up her hands. "I don't want to hear that word. Ever again."

"Endometriosis is hardly a 'condition,'" Miranda remarks.

"Try telling that to Charlie's mother."

"Oh boy." I realize I could use a drink too. And a cigarette.

"I don't get it." Miranda goes to the Plexiglas case that contains Charlie's collection of sports memorabilia. She leans closer. "Is that a real baseball?"

"What do you think? And yes, that really is Joe DiMaggio's signature," Samantha snaps.

"I thought you were picking out China patterns," Miranda says, as Samantha gives her a look and disappears down the hallway.

"Hey, I just figured something out. You know how Samantha always says Charlie wanted to be a baseball player and his mother wouldn't let him?" I ask. "Maybe Charlie secretly thinks he's Joe DiMaggio and Samantha is Marilyn Monroe."

"That's right. And remember how Joe DiMaggio always resented Marilyn's sexuality and tried to turn her into a housewife? It's practically textbook."

Samantha returns with a pile of clothes in her arms, which she dumps onto the Ultrasuede couch as she glares at me. "And you're as much to blame as Miranda. You were the one who told me to be a little more real."

"I didn't mean it though. I never thought—"

"Well, here's what real gets you in New York." She runs back to the bedroom and returns with another pile, which she drops at our feet. Then she grabs the box of garbage bags, rips one open, and begins frantically shoving clothes into the bag. "This is what it gets you," she repeats, her voice rising. "A kick in the teeth and fifty cents for the subway."

"Whoa. Are you serious?" I ask.

She pauses for a moment and thrusts out her arm. "See this?" She indicates a large gold Rolex encrusted with diamonds.

"Is that real too?" Miranda gasps.

"Hold on," I caution. "Why would someone who's breaking up with you give you a giant Rolex?"

"You could probably buy a small country with that," Miranda adds.

Samantha rocks back on her heels. "Apparently, it's a tradition. When you break off an engagement, you give your ex-fiancée a watch."

"You should get engaged more often."

In a fury, Samantha rips off the watch and throws it against the Plexiglas case, where it bounces off harmlessly. Some things are simply indestructible. "How did this happen to me? I had it all figured out. I had New York by the balls. Everything was working. I was so good at being someone else."

If only we could all put our hearts in a Plexiglas case, I think, as I kneel down next to her. "You weren't so good about showing up at Kleinfeld," I say gently.

"That was an exception. One slipup. And I made up for it by telling Glenn I'd be happy to use her decorator to redo the apartment. Even if it meant living with chintz. What's wrong with a few flowers here and there? I can do roses if

397

I have to—" And suddenly, she bursts into tears. Only this time, they're real.

"Don't you get it?" she sobs. "I've been rejected. For having faulty fallopian tubes."

In the annals of dating, being rejected for your fallopian tubes has got to be right up there with—well, you name it, I suppose. But maybe dating in New York really is like what Samantha always says: everything counts, even the things you can't see.

And what you *can* see is usually bad enough.

I mentally count the number of garbage bags strewn around Charlie's apartment. Fourteen. I had to run out and get another box. Two years in a relationship and you can really accumulate a lot of stuff.

"Baggage," Samantha says, kicking one of the bags out of the way. "All baggage."

"Hey!" I exclaim. "There are Gucci shoes in that one."

"Halston, Gucci, Fiorucci? Who cares?" She throws up her hands. "What's the difference when your entire life has been ripped away?"

"You'll find someone else," Miranda says nonchalantly. "You always do."

"But not someone who will marry me. Everyone knows the only reason a man in Manhattan ever says 'I do' is because he wants children."

"But you don't know that you can't have children," Miranda points out. "The doctor said—"

"Who cares what he said? It's always going to be the same old story."

"You don't know that," I insist. I grab a bag and pull it toward the door. "And do you really want to spend the rest of your life pretending to be someone you're not?" I take a breath and gesture at the Plexiglas furnishings. "Surrounded by *plastic*?"

"All men are jerks. But you knew that." Miranda retrieves the watch from under the coffee table. "I guess that's the last of it," she says, holding out the Rolex. "Don't want to leave this behind."

Samantha carefully weighs the watch in the palm of her hand. Her face scrunches in agony. She takes a deep breath. "Actually, I do."

She places the watch on the table as Miranda and I look at each other in bewilderment.

"Where's the bag with the Gucci shoes?" she orders.

"There?" I ask, wondering what's come over her.

She rips open the bag and dumps out two pairs of loafers. "And the Chanel suit. Where's that?"

"I think it's in here," Miranda says cautiously, pushing a bag into the center of the room.

"What are you doing?" I ask anxiously, as Samantha extracts the Chanel suit and places it on the table next to the watch.

"What do you think I'm doing?"

"I have no idea." I look to Miranda for help, but she's as mystified as I am.

Samantha finds a tennis dress, and holds it up, laughing. "Did I tell you Charlie wanted me to take tennis lessons? So I could play with Glenn. In Southampton. As if I would actually enjoy hitting balls with that mummy. She's sixty-five years old and she says she's fifty. Like anyone's going to believe *that*."

"Well—" I sneak another glance at Miranda, who shakes her head, stupefied.

"Do you want this, Sparrow?" Samantha tosses me the tennis dress.

"Sure," I say hesitantly.

I'm wondering what to do with it, when Samantha suddenly changes her mind and rips it out of my hands. "On second thought, *no*," she shouts, hurling the dress onto the pile. "Don't take it. Don't make the same mistake I did."

She continues on in this vein, tearing through the bags and removing every item of clothing from her life with Charlie. The pile gets bigger and bigger, while Miranda and I watch in concern. I bite my lip. "Are you really going to leave all this stuff?"

"What do you think, Sparrow?" she says. She pauses and takes a deep breath, hands on her hips. She tilts her head, and gives me a fierce smile.

"It's baggage. And even if I'm not the most real person in the world, I'll tell you one thing about Samantha Jones. She can't be bought. At *any* price."

"Remember when I first moved here and you made me pour that carton of milk down the drain because you said the smell made you sick?" I ask, rearranging myself on the futon. It's two a.m. and we're finally back at Samantha's apartment. All the packing and unpacking has me beat.

"Did she really do that?" Miranda asks.

"Oh yeah." I nod.

"Adults shouldn't drink milk anyway." Samantha exhales as she throws back her head in relief. "Thank God that's over. If these fallopian tubes could talk—"

"Luckily, they can't." I get up and go into the bedroom. I look at my own meager belongings, and with a sigh, open my suitcase.

"Sparrow?" Samantha calls. "What are you doing?"

"Packing," I say loudly. "I'm leaving tomorrow, remember?" I stand in the doorway. "And after this summer, I really don't think I'm a sparrow anymore. Haven't I graduated by now?"

"You have indeed," Samantha agrees. "I now declare you a pigeon. The official bird of New York City."

"The *only* bird in New York City," Miranda giggles. "Hey, it's better than being a rat. Did you know that in China, rats are good luck?"

"I love the Chinese." Samantha smiles. "Did you know they invented pornography?"

CHAPTER THIRTY-NINE

"Stanford White," Capote says. "He designed the original Pennsylvania Station. It was one of the most beautiful buildings in the world. But in 1963 some idiot sold the air rights and they tore it down to put up this monstrosity."

"That is so sad," I murmur, riding down the escalator behind him. "I wonder if it smelled as bad then as it does now."

"What?" he asks loudly, over the hubbub.

"Nothing."

"I always wish I could have lived in New York at the turn of the century," he says.

"I'm glad I was able to live here at all."

"Yeah. I don't think I'd ever be able to leave New York," he adds, his words causing another jolt of despair.

All morning we've been saying the wrong things to each other, when we've managed to say anything at all.

402

I've been studiously trying to bring up the future, while Capote keeps studiously avoiding it.

Hence the history lesson about Penn Station.

"Listen," I begin.

"Look at the time," he says quickly, nodding at the clock. "You don't want to miss your train."

If I didn't know better, I'd think he was trying to get rid of me.

"That was fun, wasn't it?" I venture, shuffling in line to buy my ticket.

"Yeah. It was great." For a moment he yields, and I see the little boy in him.

"You could come and visit me in Providence—"

"Sure," he says. I can tell by the way his eyes dart to the side that it's never going to happen, though. He'll have found another girl by then. But if I weren't leaving, maybe I could have been The One.

He has to find her someday, right?

I purchase my ticket. Capote picks up my suitcase as I buy copies of *The New York Times* and the *Post*. I won't be doing that for a while, I think sourly. We find the escalator to my gate. As we descend, I'm filled with a blinding emptiness. This is it, I think. The End.

"All aboard," the conductor shouts.

I place one foot on the step and pause. If only Capote would rush forward, grab my arm, and pull me back to him. If only there was a sudden blackout. If only something would happen—anything—to prevent me from getting on that train.

I look back over my shoulder and find Capote in the crowd.

He waves.

The trip to Hartford is three hours. For the first hour, I'm a puddle of misery. I can't believe I've left New York. I can't believe I've left Capote. What if I never see him again?

It isn't right. It's not the way it's *supposed* to be. Capote should have declared his undying love.

"Should," I suddenly recall myself saying to Samantha and Miranda, "is the worst word in the English language. People always think things 'should' be a certain way, and when they're not, they're disappointed."

"What happened to you?" Samantha asked. "You had sex and now you know everything?"

"I not only had sex, I had an orgasm," I said proudly.

"Oh, honey, welcome to the club," Samantha exclaimed. And then she turned to Miranda. "Don't worry. Someday you'll have one too."

"How do you know I haven't?" Miranda shrieked.

I close my eyes and lean my head back against the seat. Maybe it's okay about Capote. Just because something doesn't last forever, it doesn't mean it wasn't meaningful while it did last. It doesn't mean it wasn't important.

And what's more important than your first guy? Hey, I could have done a lot worse.

And suddenly, I feel free.

I shuffle through my newspapers and open the *New*

York Post. And that's when I spot my name.

I frown. It can't be. Why is my name in Page Six? Then I look at the title of the piece: "Disaster and Plaster."

I drop the paper like I've been bitten.

When the train pulls into New Haven for a twenty-minute layover, I race out of my compartment and run to the nearest phone booth. I catch Samantha in her office, and shaking and spluttering manage to ask if she's seen the *Post.*

"Yes, Carrie, I did. And I thought it was terrific."

"What?" I scream.

"Calm down. You can't take these things so personally. There's no such thing as bad publicity."

"They said my reading was the worst thing they've seen since their high school Christmas pageant."

"Who cares?" she purrs. "They're probably jealous. You got a mention for your first play in New York City. Aren't you excited?"

"I'm *mortified.*"

"That's too bad. Because Cholly Hammond called. He's been trying to get in touch with you for days. He wants you to call him immediately."

"Why?"

"Oh, Sparrow," she sighs. "How should I know? But he said it was important. I've got to go. I've got Harry Mills in my office—" And she hangs up.

I stare at the phone. Cholly Hammond? What can he want?

I count out more change. Normally, the cost of making a long-distance call from a pay phone would be a problem, but I happen to be kind of flush right now. In the spirit of Samantha, I sold my brand-new, never used Chanel bag to the nice man at the vintage shop for two hundred and fifty dollars. I knew the money wasn't near what it was worth, but I wouldn't need the bag at Brown. And besides, I was kind of happy to get rid of it.

Baggage.

I drop several quarters into the slot. The phone is answered by a bright young thing.

"Is Cholly there?" I ask, giving my name.

Cholly immediately gets on the line.

"Little one!" he exclaims, like I'm his long-lost friend.

"Cholly!" I reply.

"I saw your mention in the *Post* and found it very intriguing," he enthuses. "Especially as I've been thinking about you for weeks. Ever since I sat next to you at Barry Jessen's opening."

My heart sinks. Here we go again. Another old geezer who wants to get into my pants.

"I kept musing about our oh-so-amusing conversation. Pun intended."

"Is that so?" I ask, trying to recall what I might have said that could be so memorable.

"And since I'm always on the lookout for something new, I thought, wouldn't it be interesting to try to get some younger readers to *The New Review*? And who better to capture them than a young woman herself? In a sort of column, if you will. New York through the eyes of an ingenue."

"I don't know how good it would be. Given how badly my play went over."

"Goodness gracious," he exclaims. "But that's the whole point. If it *had* been a swimming success, I wouldn't be calling you. Because the whole idea behind this enterprise is that Carrie Bradshaw never wins."

"Excuse me?" I gasp.

"Carrie never wins. That's the fun of it, don't you see? It's what keeps her going."

"But what about love? Does she ever win at love?"

"Especially not at love."

I hesitate. "That sounds like a curse, Cholly."

He laughs loud and long. "You know what they say: One man's curse is another man's opportunity. So what do you say? Can we meet in my office this afternoon at three?"

"In New York?"

"Where else?" he says.

Whoo-hooo, I think, swaying through the first-class cabin on the train headed back to the city. The seats are enormous and covered in red velvet and there's a paper napkin on each headrest. There's even a special compartment where you can stash your suitcase. It's a heck of a lot nicer than coach.

"Always go first-class." I hear Samantha's voice in my head.

407

"But only if you can pay for it yourself," Miranda counters.

Well, I am paying for it myself. Via Bernard and his lovely gift. But what the hell? I deserve it.

Maybe I'm not a failure after all.

I don't know how long I'll stay in New York, or what my father will do when I tell him. But I'll worry about that later. For the moment, all I care about is one simple fact: I'm going back.

I teeter up the aisle, looking for a place to sit and someone decent to sit next to. I pass a balding man, and a lady who's knitting. Then I spot a pretty girl with a luxurious mane of hair, flipping through a copy of *Brides* magazine.

Brides. She's got to be kidding. I take the seat next to her.

"Oh hi!" she says eagerly, moving her bag. I smile. She's just as sweet as I thought she'd be, given that gorgeous hair.

"I'm so glad to get you as a seatmate," she whispers intimately, looking around. "The last time I took the train to New York, this creepy guy sat right next to me. He actually tried to put his hand on my leg. Can you believe it? I had to move my seat three times."

"That's terrible," I say.

"I know." She nods, wide-eyed.

I smile. "Getting married?" I ask, indicating her magazine.

She blushes. "Not exactly. I mean, not yet. But I hope to be engaged in a couple of years. My boyfriend works in New York. On Wall Street." She ducks her head prettily.

"My name's Charlotte, by the way."

"Carrie," I say, holding out my hand.

"What about you? Do you have a boyfriend?"

I burst out laughing.

"What's so funny?" she says, confused. "They say Paris is romantic, but I think New York is romantic too. And the men—"

I laugh even harder.

"Well, really," she says primly. "If you're going to laugh the whole way to New York . . . I don't see what's so funny about going to New York to find love."

I howl.

"Well?" she demands.

I wipe away my tears. I sit back and cross my arms. "Do you really want to know about love in New York?"

"Yes, I do." Her tone is curious and a little bit cautious.

The train toots its horn as I lean forward in my seat.

"Sweetie," I say, with a smile. "Have I got a story for *you*."